CONFLICT OF II

CONFLICT OF INTEREST

Book One in the Taking Chances series

KATIE BACHAND

MINNEAPOLIS, MN

ISBN **978-1-7334326-0-3**

FIRST EDITION

Cover Illustration and Design by:
Lance Buckley
Print | Publishing | Branding | Design

Author Image by: Studio Twelve:52

Conflict of Interest is a fiction novel. Names, characters, places, incidents
and plot lines are used fictitiously and are a result of the author's
imagination. Thus meaning, any resemblance to persons alive or
deceased, buildings, establishments, locals, or events is coincidental.

For Dad, Mom, and Nate

For Mark and Winslow

For my Friends

Books by Katie Bachand

Taking Chances Series:
Becoming Us (Prequel)
Conflict of Interest (#1)
In the Business of Love (#2)
A Business Affair (#3)
Betting on Us (#4)

Standalones:

Christmas Novels:
Postmark Christmas
Waiting on Christmas
A Borrowed Christmas Love Story _(coming Nov 2022)_
The Worst Christmas Wife _(coming Dec 2022)_

Before you get started take a quick minute to join Katie's Newsletter.

Head to Katie's website at www.katiebachandauthor.com and join her newsletter for fun content, great deals, free books, and more.

Enjoy!

Conflict of Interest

PROLOGUE

Grace Thomas, of Thomas and Jane, LLC – now the only Thomas – walked out into the night to escape the feeling of death that wrapped her father's funeral like a stale fog. Inside the funeral home, the extreme sadness consumed her, the conversation leaving her with a feeling of despair. She was desperate to escape as people mingled, shared memories, and shook their heads in disbelief that such a wonderful man could have died so young. Now, as she walked through the darkness, she felt numb.

The street lights guided her way on the walk she'd taken thousands of times. Outside of their old brick building, Grace stared up at the office. Her fingertips scraped lightly on the rough red divots as she moved toward the door. They'd taken this walk many times together. Father and daughter. Laughing, talking, planning. Or, simply walking in silence. She longed to hear his voice, to see his face – but not the face she'd seen tonight, lifeless and unmoving. She wanted to see the one that was vibrant and comforting. Sturdy and confident. The one that emanated only love.

Grace closed her eyes when she reached the door emblazoned with their company name. The last time she walked through this door, it was together. That was three weeks ago when her father hadn't been weak or withdrawn. Now he was gone, and she was the weary one. Grace wondered, how could she feel all-consuming exhaustion, and a heart that ached so badly she thought it might rip out, and still be living herself.

Grace pulled the door open and started up the stairs. This building was their place. Together.

She'd learned everything she knew from her father, and he had been eager to teach her. Her eyes welled and stung as they moistened the dry, aching feeling. But no tears fell. He wouldn't want her to cry anymore, and she would do what he wanted because she was his girl. Daddy's girl. Her brother William always joked that she was her dad's favorite. She would only laugh because she knew it was true. William also knew and felt their dad's unconditional love and the pride their father had in him, so it wasn't hard to poke fun in her direction. There was just something between them: father and daughter. There was a spark, life, excitement, and wonder. Constant comfort and security. They shared everything.

With each step she took, she thought of her mom. Her amazing mom. Only moments ago, at the funeral, she had taken hug after hug of warmth and generosity from family and friends with such strength. Grace wondered how she was able to hold herself together so well.

William, she supposed, helped. Her brother offered a warm and comforting hand on their mother's shoulder as she exchanged tender thank yous and tried not to get weepy with every new guest.

William had caught Grace staring at that moment and offered a tilted-head smile and a quick wink. It was like him, always the fixer, always willing to put himself last. The feelings he must have had, yet been unwilling to show, for the sake of their mom, and her. Grace had shrugged back at him. Her *what do we do now* shrug. An *I'm never going to make it* shrug. At that moment, William would have gone to her. She saw it in his eyes, asking if she needed him. Yes. *Yes* was the answer she'd wanted to give but wouldn't dream of pulling him away from their mom. So she'd shook her head and mouthed *thank you* and added an *I love you*. William had mouthed the words back, and she smiled at how easy it had always been for him to say those words when he meant them.

As if they were answering a prayer, she then had been swaddled up, arms surrounding her from all directions.

Now, she wrapped her arms around herself to mimic the feeling she'd had when the tight pull of her three best friends had cocooned her. She had closed her eyes and let herself feel safe, even if just for a moment. It was the last time she'd cried, being held by the friends that had been with her through everything. The arms around her tightened as her breath hitched.

"I don't know what I'm going to do." Here in the office, alone, she whispered the same words she'd said through quiet gasps of air. And her friends' words from the funeral filled the silence in her mind.

"Right now, you don't have to do anything," Rachel had said as she'd stroked her back, trying to comfort.

"Yes, no words right now. Let us hold you and love you. Do not think," Aimeé's French accent had soothed.

Casey had said nothing. She wouldn't have been able to find the words. Being tender wasn't her. Neither was seeing the bright side. She'd been through her own share of heartbreak. But she was there and would be any time Grace needed her, for anything. There was never a moment or time when Casey wouldn't come through. Casey knew what alone felt like. It's why, Grace imagined, she'd never let one of her friends have that feeling.

Casey had gripped her hand and covered the other girls' arms as they'd stood in their circle, holding their embrace.

Grace opened her eyes. Reality reminded her all of those memories were real. Her dad had still suffered, was still forced to leave them.

From the reception area, her eyes scanned the door of her favorite office, her dad's. Raymond Thomas, President. The plaque was the only object that stated his title, and he'd only kept it because it was a gift from the first client he'd secured. Nostalgia won out with Raymond every time.

Grace walked slowly along the thick shelves of the library wall, touching trinkets and looking at pictures of the great man she – they – had lost. She stopped at a photograph of her mom and dad. Both of their eyes closed in laughter; her mom doubled over, and her dad leaning backward. Each was encircling an arm around the other. It wasn't a picture you'd expect anybody to keep. It wasn't flattering – you could barely see their faces – but it was perfect. They were perfect. Their love was perfect.

Guilt wasn't a feeling she was used to, but she felt it now. She felt it because in that instant she wished she would have found a love like that. Wished her father could have met the person that would make her laugh, or laugh with her, like that.

It was a selfish notion, especially now. She pushed the thought away, along with the guilt. She needed to move forward. She had other people, and this business, to take care of.

She moved to the leather chair that ruled the office, regally hovering behind the desk, and sat. She swiveled back and forth and finally paused and looked out the window into the night. This was her place, she thought. She felt safe here. She felt her dad here. And she made a promise.

"Dad, it hasn't been more than a week. I already miss you more than I can bear. But I promise you I'll still try and make you so proud. I know I won't have to, but I'll take care of mom and Will. And here," she spun and looked toward the opening that gave her a view of the whole office, "I'll work so hard to make Thomas and Jane every bit the company you envisioned. People will remember what you built. I'll make sure of it. No matter the cost."

—

The girls had watched Grace leave the funeral and knew they needed to let her go, at least for tonight. Grace had endured a very public loss; she didn't need a public grieving. They'd all received too much attention from the guests as they'd shared their embrace. When Lydia Thomas took notice of the commotion the four friends were causing, she'd covered her mouth in a brief moment of happiness and appreciation.

Lydia apologized to the next guest in line, excused herself, and walked toward the huddle. She needed to see the girls. Her girls. Rachel and Casey had made the Thomas house their own growing up. And later, when they had moved on to college, Aimeé was taken in by the inseparable trio of Casey, Rachel, and Grace. It was hard to imagine now that she hadn't been there all along. When Lydia got close enough, the three girls blanketed her as they had Grace only moments before.

She was a mother to them all. Lydia remembered the day Grace had sat Raymond and her down at the kitchen table, telling them they needed another room because Casey and Rachel needed a pretty bedroom to sleep in when they came over. Raymond had reminded Grace her friends didn't live there, and he reminded Lydia they weren't her children. But he had seen their hopeful faces, ran it by William (who'd always had a crush on Rachel anyway) and when he said, "Yeah, whatever," Raymond couldn't help but smile and agree. Anything for his girl, or more appropriately, girls.

"Oh, my girls," Lydia sighed gratefully. "I love you all so much. Thank you for coming."

"We wouldn't – couldn't – be anywhere else," Rachel spoke for the group. "What can we do? Anything at all. Please let us help you."

"You can help me," Lydia said.

The girls unwrapped their arms from one another and stared, eager to do whatever they could.

"Anything," Casey and Aimeé confirmed simultaneously. Rachel looked on hopefully, relieved that any one of them could offer something to help.

"Watch out for her. Be there for her like you've always been. As hard as this is for us," Lydia motioned to herself and William, "it will be harder for her. He was everything to her. He was her steady guide and her listening ear. Everything she sees in herself that is good, she believes came from him. Most of it did. She'll feel lost for a little while, but I'm hoping the three of you can help make her way back just a little easier."

"Of course," Rachel confirmed. "We already have a plan and a rotation. We've already decided for the first couple weeks she only gets one night alone, never two in a row. Otherwise, one or all of us will be there. The move will help keep her mind occupied." Rachel became wistful for just a moment. "I'm happy he was able to see Grace's new home before..." She couldn't say it. On her exhale, William, who had trailed his mother when she joined the girls, reached forward to brush the stray tear away, and she let him. Today she would allow him to show her the affection she'd cut off years before.

Lydia watched her son's tenderness toward Rachel and thought, another time, another place.

She continued. "You know she will throw herself into work. Please, do anything you can to make her live. She's dreamed her whole life about having a family like the one she had growing up. Though hers will be her own, I'm afraid she'll stop looking for it and spend every waking hour at that office building. Raymond did that. Which I'll never regret, but I'd be lying if I said I didn't have just a little wish we would have had him home a bit more. Because, well, you just never know."

"And," Lydia drew their attention back as their eyes had followed her own to the casket, "I, well...Raymond gave me this to give to Grace."

They all looked down. The envelope was sealed and had the company logo on it.

"It just seems so silly to worry about work right now. It seems so," Lydia searched for the word, "insignificant. I don't want the last thing Grace reads from her dad be about work."

"Perhaps waiting is best," Aimeé offered, knowing from experience financial matters were the last thing somebody wanted to deal with when there was a death in the family.

7

Lydia held the envelope close to her heart. "Then, we'll wait. Maybe not for the right time, but a better time."

CHAPTER 1

"Did you hear the rumors?" Abbi asked.

Grace looked at her beautiful aunt and current CFO of Thomas and Jane LLC, Abigail Jane, and saw more confidence and poise in the woman than she'd seen in an entire boardroom of men.

"That Wallace is on the hunt?" Grace asked as Abbi sat in the guest chair of her dad's old office, "Yes, I heard."

"And?"

"*Over my dead body* was the first thing I thought." She smiled and turned away from the window and leaned her long frame against the pane. "Then I thought about all the people out there," she nodded toward the team of amazing employees they'd earned, groomed, and grown to love over the years. "And I don't know. I made a promise I wouldn't change what was important about this company, and that's these people. If Wallace takes us over, sure, it would be a nice payday – but what happens after that?"

Abbi turned, following Grace's gaze, and looked down the long bank of beautiful wooden desks. She nodded.

"I agree, it should never be about the money. Do you realize the number of shares they would have to buy? The amount of money? I'd be lying if I didn't say, at my age, it seems appealing to-"

"If you say retire I'm going to greet you as *old aunt Abbi* for the rest of my life."

It wasn't a feeling of disappointment, but she was certainly surprised her aunt would ever want to leave. In her mind, she had always thought of Abbi as her other half, the Jane to her Thomas. She grew up admiring Abbi as she watched her hold her own in what was usually a room full of powerful men.

Grace looked at her aunt, a dark-complexioned, black-haired beauty. The polar opposite of Abbi's brother, Raymond. Grace had gotten her blonde hair and light complexion from her dad. For the first time, though, she noticed the overworked lines that shadowed below her beloved aunt's eyes.

"Abbi, you know what this means to me. To us." She turned and looked out.

"I know. It could be a busy couple of weeks." Abbi tried to remember it was business – yes, at the end of the day, it was business. But for this precious, ambitious, girl – woman – she had the blessing of calling her niece, she knew it reached far beyond personal. "I don't think we'll have much of a choice, should they decide on a takeover."

"We do have a choice. We have options. We can force options." Grace's head turned at the comment, and her body followed to face Abbi straight on. "Giving in would be taking the easy way out. Wallace will take this place and slowly dismantle everything we've worked for."

Grace paused for a moment to gather her usually organized thoughts and held up both hands to stop Abbi from commenting.

"We – you, dad, mom, everybody out there – we've put in too many hours, too many tears. Too many relationships were built here not to try. Who knows if they will still have their jobs on day two?"

Abbi watched, bemused, as Grace moved to the window once more and gestured toward the bank of desks. This beautiful girl, who, if the Wallace deal happened, wouldn't have to work another day in her life, was standing here worried about everybody but herself.

It was time to be the aunt.

Abbi met Grace at the window and watched Fall begin to settle over a Minneapolis scene. In a month or two it would be covered in snow. The leaves on the trees lining the city sidewalk had already begun to turn their September yellows. She draped an arm around Grace's shoulder as she tried her best to comfort.

"It's only a rumor, for now. But rumors usually start for a reason. Take your two weeks off, rest, try not to think about this, and we'll deal with whatever we need to when you get back. There is a lot that will need to happen if, well, it happens. Even then, after the due diligence process, Wallace could decide it's not worth it. Until then, we keep working," she said firmly.

Grace laid her head on Abbi's shoulder, closed her tired, aching eyes, and silently prayed that no matter the outcome, she would make her dad proud.

CHAPTER 2

"One triple hazelnut latte with cinnamon, for one very depressed face."

Grace looked at Aimeé and offered the most pathetic smile she could muster.

With a wink, Aimeé set the latte down and turned back to the bar. Over her shoulder, she said, "Closing in ten. Then we can get down to details. Casey and Rachel are on their way. We have important things to discuss."

Important things to discuss? Her livelihood was important. But damn if she didn't love them and feel a little curious.

As the espresso machine hissed and blender whirred, she watched Aimeé effortlessly move behind the coffee bar, laughing in conversation with her loyal patrons. All of whom Aimeé knew by name. Grace had seen more than one customer flush at the way their name sang out in the sweet French accent Aimeé had brought with her when she moved to the United States. Aimeé arrived at the tender age of eighteen and brought some coffee and pastry heaven with her. Why and how Aimeé decided on Minnesota, Grace still didn't know – and it wasn't for lack of trying – but she couldn't be happier this is where her dear friend had landed.

Laughter filled the front of the shop. She could only assume one of the loyal patrons was offering a marriage proposal as payment for a black coffee and a butter scone – as many often did.

"For tomorrow's breakfast." Grace heard the hoarse voice as she watched an old man lift a folded paper bag and travel cup.

Grace was skeptical the treat would make it until morning. If only he were sixty years younger, he might have a shot with her black-haired, beautiful French friend.

Never before had she seen a more stunning person. Aimeé's black wavy bob perfectly framed her delicate features. Almost-black eyes and brows added dangerous allure and insane sex appeal to her appearance. One look at Aimeé and you'd guess runway model, not pastry chef.

The chime of the bell sitting on top of the coffee shop door pulled her away from her thoughts. Grace felt the cold gust of wind that accompanied her two friends through the doorway. Completely wrapped up in each other's words, Casey and Rachel continued their enthusiastic conversation, ignoring the stares that followed them on their path to the table.

"I'm serious. This is a horrible idea." Casey unwrapped her scarf, her eyes intense on Rachel.

"You brought up the idea. And it is not a very bad idea. It's simply a little..." Rachel looked up to ponder the correct choice of words and brightened as she found a fit: "A little nudge."

"A nudge?"

"A nudge." Rachel confirmed.

"Grace doesn't need a nudge; besides, I changed my mind. And she has bigger things on her plate right now." The two stood facing each other after they had disrobed their fall layers and heaved their bags onto the backs of their chairs.

Rachel folded her arms across her chest. She stated her rebuttal as if it were gospel, "There is never too much on your plate when it comes to the matters of the heart."

Silence fell between the two in the middle of the emptying shop, as they contemplated the end of their conversation.

"We'll see." It was all that Casey – the ever-worrying, cynical, and even she admitted, glass-half-empty type – could muster.

Grace, still sitting mutely, having witnessed the intense exchange, moved her eyes from one to the other and back again.

"Hi," she said pointedly.

Both turned their stares in her direction, having been so caught up in their discussion that they were surprised to see she was present.

"I don't mean to be nosey, but I thought I overheard my name in there?" Amusement filled Grace's green eyes as her two friends sat side by side across from her without saying a word. How was she lucky enough to find these fantastic, slightly chaotic, dazzling friends?

When neither of them spoke, Grace tried once more. "I'm curious as to what's so good that you two are choosing to be up at ten on a school night? Spill."

Rachel smiled, and Casey raised her hand. Without missing a beat, in the middle of her closing duties, Aimeé called on her from behind the bar like a teacher calls on an eager student. "Yes, Casey?"

"I think we might need a bottle of wine."

"One bottle of wine, coming up. Be over in five. Any preference?" Aimeé inquired to the group as she ushered out the last of her crowd into the night and locked up the front entrance.

"The alcoholic kind," Rachel put in, with a wry smile pasted on her face.

"Why don't you start with the company stuff? Did you hear the rumor today? Wallace Corporation is on the hunt for its next takeover. Does the coffee wonder woman back there know? I'm assuming you've been here since you left the office today?" Casey said, always the one getting down to business.

Grace was too tired to ask how Casey knew the company was being sought after by the much larger firm. Maybe she bugged the office, or hacked into the security cameras. Grace didn't want to know because it would just mean extra work. Sometimes Casey, a brilliant technologist, knew just a little too much about everything.

"Thomas and Jane is a brilliant, sophisticated, and beloved company. Therefore, it is very appealing to larger, poopy-er, corporate-y-er companies. Companies like Wallace, for example." Grace said with just a tiny trace of bitterness, as she took a sip of her latte.

"Your sophisticated word choice astounds me. No wonder people can relate to you, you can really dumb it down." Casey grinned as Grace narrowed her eyes in disapproval. So maybe the description was less than elegant? It was what might happen – would probably happen – she corrected herself.

"Want me to screw up some of the paperwork?" Casey offered, wiggling her eyebrows up and down. "Find some dirty gossip on Wallace? Maybe plant an email or five? Couple people pay a fine, go to jail, you get to keep the company, happy ever after." She waved her hand as if to say, *no big deal.*

Grace laughed in spite of herself. "Case, I love you. I would love to utilize your hacking skills, but I would also like *you* not to go to prison.

"Prison? What kind of a hack do you think I am? I'm better than that. And you might want to tell your security team to check their firewalls. And maybe the single sign-on he set up. That should do it, though."

"I should send you to prison myself. No more snooping." Grace pointed at Casey, who shrugged innocently.

Huffing out a breath, Grace resigned, thankful for wine and somebody to talk to. "It's just a bummer is all."

As Aimeé sashayed over, she presented the wine to the table, the cork already removed. Four glasses and a second bottle peeking out from under Aimeé's arm followed. Grace eyed the red juice and thought, this night was either going to be really   good,   or   really   bad.

CHAPTER 3

Swallowing nearly half of her second glass of wine she paused, mostly for effect.

"No. Absolutely not."

Grace looked from one to the other, pausing at last on Rachel – she would cave.

"You." She pointed at Rachel. An accusing finger lifted from her glass and held from across the table. She would figure out whose idea this was.

"It is done." Aimeé waved her hand away as if it was all said and done.

"What is done?"

"What our dear Aimeé means is, we might have already scheduled the date. You're meeting tomorrow for drinks. Then if the drinks are good, you go to dinner." Rachel quickly followed with, "And who doesn't like a free drink? If it were me, I would go just knowing it was free. What?" Rachel turned her palms upward innocently as her friends groaned. She wasn't ashamed. "Teacher here."

Rachel added, "Before you can say anything, we know he's a good guy. I have it on competent authority – Casey – that he's a gentleman and treats all people with respect. Including, but not limited to, opening doors, walking along the street on the outside, helping coats off and on, pulling out chairs, and last but definitely not least, paying for meals." She and Aimeé clinked their glasses together.

"And just how might you know that?"

Aimeé drank, feigning innocence, and Rachel stared at Casey.

"He was on a dating site a couple of years back. Not mine," Casey tried not to sound offended, "but it was easy enough to get ahold of some information."

"You haven't dated since the fall festival date disaster. We decided to give you a little break, but it's time to get back out there."

Grace groaned and covered her eyes with her hand. Rachel was referring to the last date she'd been on. He'd taken grunge to a level that bordered on just plain dirty. She tried to be kind, which he misread, and by hour two, he was professing his love-at-first-sight feelings. More than his smell made it uncomfortable.

At her recall, Grace reiterated, "No. But I would like you to explain. Why me, why now?" She couldn't figure out why her well-intentioned friends would think this was a good time for her to begin dating again.

"Honey, the fall festival date disaster was over a year ago." Rachel said.

"And," Aimeé joined the barrage, "we made a promise to your mom."

"About what?" Grace was surprised. What did her mom have to do with this?

"To look after you. To make sure you still looked for love. For as long as we can remember, you've always wanted a family. It doesn't just happen without some effort. It was what your mom asked of us when your dad passed away."

"You are cold and ruthless. Pick on this one or this one?" Grace sloshed her drink in Rachel's direction first, then Aimeé's.

"Rachel can't, that's why I brought the second bottle of wine."

"Then, why not you?" Grace pressed.

"I'm promiscuous and French. I take lovers, not husbands."

Unfortunately for Grace, everybody seemed satisfied with that response. And Casey? Well, Casey didn't need to explain. Casey didn't believe in relationships. She called herself a realist. After she had witnessed her parents tear each other apart with no regard for her, and often using her as a pawn, she didn't believe in eternal bliss. And she often reminded whoever was willing to listen, that almost fifty percent of married people would agree, because if they weren't going through a divorce already, they would be.

Nodding to herself, Grace gave her friends an answer, "Look, I'm busy with work, and truth-be-told – dating is exhausting. I'm still a romantic, I still love the idea of being in love, holding hands, building a life with somebody..." she drifted off, trying to push away those images she so desperately wanted to be her reality, and continued, "But if it's not meant to be, it's not meant to be. I don't want to force it. Especially with everything that's going on at work right now."

Casey lifted her glass to toast her friend's unsettling viewpoint on dating and love, "I'll cheers to that." Their glasses clinked, filling the silence until Casey edged in for one final shot: "Right after you meet for drinks tomorrow."

"Hypocrite," Grace said

"I accept." Casey smiled at a victory she knew she'd won.

Knowing there wouldn't be a way to get out of this date with her stubborn friends leading the charge, Grace's head fell, defeated, and she agreed. "Fine. But only one. And when this one doesn't work, there can be no more snooping, no more logging into other people's online dating accounts, and definitely no more dates without my knowing." Her finger pointed at each girl in turn as she spoke.

The girls sipped in triumph, not doing much to hide their smiles behind their quickly emptying wine glasses. Rachel shuffled around in her bag then slid a five across the table to Casey.

"What?" Rachel asked defensively, seeing Grace's narrowed eyes. "I never thought you'd agree to it."

"And you, what's your explanation?" Grace demanded, looking to Casey.

"I knew we were catching you in a moment of weakness. And knew Aimeé would bring out the big guns and mention your mom," Casey said matter-of-factly.

Grace rolled her eyes.

"I can't talk about this anymore. I'm going to leave it at this and only say it once. If this ends badly, I mean like, serial killer badly, I'm coming back to haunt all of you for the rest of your – what I'll make terrible – lives." She looked directly at

Aimeé. "And worse, ensure you have terrible sex for the rest of your lives."

"Terrible sex, huh?" Rachel asked. "You're a real ball-buster."

"I'm going to need another glass. Hey," Grace said, gesturing toward Rachel, "start explaining why Rachel can't date."

The hesitation was brief, but it was enough. Grace and Aimeé traded glances with each other after seeing Casey's eyes. Her expression said she wasn't quite sure if she was supposed to talk about Rachel's love life. Meaning there was one. The realization came to the two of them before Casey could get a word out.

"You're seeing somebody?" Grace all but cheered while throwing her hands in the air. "This is exciting! What's his name? What does he do? Is he cute?"

Rachel shrugged and tried for nonchalance, "His name is Richard. He-"

"His name is Richard?" Grace didn't let her go any further.

Anybody else would have been offended, but Rachel just laughed because she tended to agree that Richard was a pretty unfortunate name.

"It's a minor setback for what seems to be a generally good guy. I'm going to tell you his last name, but you have to hold back your comments until I have finished. Okay?"

"Okay." Aimeé agreed for the group knowing she would be able to compose herself. The others, probably not.

"His name is Richard Dick."

Snorts came from Grace and Casey as they painfully tried to stifle their laughs. Aimeé wasn't as lucky. The wine she sipped spewed over the table and sent cabernet droplets flying. Uncontrollable laughter had the girls holding their sides and wiping tears out of their eyes.

Rachel waited while her friends composed themselves. She rolled her own eyes and tried to hide the humor she shared. Out of duty, she felt like she couldn't fully participate. She should defend Richard a little.

"In an effort to keep the floor, I will not be saying his name anymore. He is an engineer. He's cute in kind of a nerdy way but has a solid foundation. I do not love him yet, but I'm not completely counting it out at this point. I like to believe love does not have to be at first sight, so maybe it will happen over the course of our relationship when we are both ready. He's a maybe." She took a breath but saw more questions coming, so hurried on, "We've only gone out twice. Once was for coffee and the next was for dinner. So far, he's getting pretty good at conversation, and I think come date number three he won't just awkwardly stare at me when we aren't saying anything. I would say as far as dating and attraction go we are moving in the right direction. I would like him to make it to date number five before I let you all meet him because I would like to fully see how I feel about him at that time without having you yahoos influencing my decision. Now, you may speak."

The floor was open. Rachel must have covered a lot of ground with her opening statement, as silence was now filling their close-knit space. After what seemed like minutes of blinking at each other, Casey pulled the crumpled five bucks out of her bag and slapped it in front of Aimeé who gleefully picked it up and put it in her apron. Rachel stared at Aimeé, eyes jokingly narrowed.

Aimeé shook her head slightly, "What? I told Casey you weren't in love with him."

Grace jumped in. "See how it feels? Come on over to my side of the fence." She topped off their glasses and clicked hers to the one sitting in front of Rachel.

CHAPTER 4

The walk home offered cold and much needed fresh air. A few leaves fell and swirled, swished, and crackled as they scraped the ground before getting swept up into another gust of wind. Grace lifted her head to breathe in the Fall weather that was settling in. The street lights glowed in bright halos on the sidewalk, guiding her three-block walk home. Not a lot of people understood why she didn't drive much or why she chose to live within walking distance to work, but at this time of night when the streets were quiet and the night was hers alone, it made perfect sense.

The hours, sweat, and tears spent at work over the years might have been grueling, but it afforded her the old brownstone. With a little love and a couple of big checks, it had become her sanctuary. The price was steep, even for its rundown condition, but the moment she saw the three-story skinny brick building, she knew it had to be hers. It reminded her of old New York. Rustic, romantic, and utterly charming.

The fresh air had all but eliminated her three-glass buzz. Okay, maybe four. But she only had one more day; then she was officially on vacation. As she walked up the steps to her massive wooden door, the sobriety set in and she could not believe she'd given in to her friends to go out with a stranger. She was losing her strict don't-let-people-push-her-around attitude she'd worked hard to build over her years in the corporate world. There was a time to cave a little and a time to hold firm – tonight was a night she should have held firm.

The lock clicked as the key turned and let her in. She flicked the entry light on and what seemed like a million little crystals danced across her walls. Her shoes clacked to the floor and her bag made a dull thud as she set it on the black and white tile of the foyer. The fireplace sparked to life with a flip of a switch, and warmth filled the room.

She sat to enjoy it, even if getting up early tomorrow would be terrible. It would be hard seeing as she wasn't as young as she used to be. The thought of her younger self had her smiling. The one who'd had dreams of buying a place like this. The one who'd had fantasies about one day sharing it with a husband. They would host friends and family for drinks, dinners, and holidays. They would share stories and laugh together, cheer during big games, or gossip about the latest at work. The bedrooms on the third floor would be just enough for their family of four. One master suite big enough for a bassinet, and two little rooms that would transform from nursery to hideaway as their babies grew into teenagers.

It wasn't a feeling of sadness or longing as she slid into her leather armchair. She just thought she'd be there by now; that she'd have those things. She thought her dad would be there for it. She would give everything to watch her husband and her father shake hands. To have known a blessing for marriage had been asked. Then, to have her father watch her become a mother. The fantastic way she would feel seeing the pride in his eyes as he sat with his grandchildren.

"I guess sometimes it just doesn't go according to plan," Grace said to herself as she stood to turn out the fire and the lights. And that, she thought accusingly to herself, is why your irritating friends have set you up on a blind date, and you drunkenly   agreed.

CHAPTER 5

The slit where she had left the window open allowed the crisp morning air to gently push and pull the sheer curtains that hung in her bedroom. Cocooning the plush comforter around her body, Grace burrowed in and reveled in the feeling.

Grace cherished the quiet morning. She was thankful for the safety and comfort of her room, the protection of the house, for peace and silence. It was routine for her to naturally wake up ten minutes before her alarm sounded at five.

There was something about the dark. Only the glow of streetlights and stars, the moon if it was in the right position, hanging like a ceiling light framed by her beautiful, thickly-trimmed window.

These mornings always reminded her of her dad, Mr. Raymond Thomas, of Thomas and Jane LLC. The mornings were his time as well. "We have to beat the birds to their wakeup, Gracie," he would whisper after tip-toeing into her room to coax her out of bed. It was their time — Dad and daughter against the world.

The tradition didn't stop when she'd gone off to college or even when she'd moved out. It was always the same: up before five, have coffee and prep for the day. They didn't have to race into work to be the first ones there – they always crossed paths at the Bistro beneath the building at five-forty-five.

With their fresh brews in hand, they would take the steps to the top floor and work with only their desk lamps lighting the still-dim office. Then Maggie Sheffield, who had become the company's first administrative assistant would come in and turn on the floor lights to welcome in the rest of the staff as they shuffled in for a long day's work.

She longed for one more moment with her dad. One more hug, one more coffee, one more wink across the hall of their office from his desk to hers. He was her support system, her confidant, her hero. All she had left of him was the company. She couldn't allow for it to be lost. It's not what he wanted. And she wasn't ready to hand it over.

Still wrapped in her comforter, Grace moved her hands to her face with a moan, in a rare but seemingly necessary moment of worry. The what-in-the-world was she going to do moment. The company was bigger than her. It was business. It wasn't supposed to be personal, but for her, it was overwhelmingly personal.

No, she thought, she would fight. Fight for the company, fight for her dad who wasn't here to do it himself. For her mom, too. She was just as much a part of Thomas and Jane. Just as dedicated. Maybe not at the office, but making sure the rest of their lives were running just as smoothly.

If Grace thought it was terrible when she lost her father, she couldn't imagine what it was like for her mother to lose her husband. The two of them were inseparable. They had chosen each other and never wavered in their decision. They were the perfect balance of compromise and stubborn. Both would give selflessly, and yet only on rare occasions did either one of them feel as though they were making a sacrifice. If Raymond Thomas was working late to make their lives and luxurious goals a reality, Lydia would make sure he, and all who were working late with him, had a home-cooked meal. And maybe a little doggie bag to bring home to their families. The thought made Grace smile. What a partnership, she thought.

It would be wonderful to have that kind of love. If it was even half as magnificent as her parents' love, she would take it.

"Crap."

Speaking of love. Grace rolled her eyes as the mutter came out, and the realization hit her. The date was tonight.

Maybe love could wait. At the thought of having to put herself together after a long day of work to meet a stranger, the idea of love suddenly seemed irritating. Besides, wouldn't love just happen when the timing was right?

She leaned toward the nightstand and stretched for her phone, tapping the buttons with a hint of bitterness. She found the group message right at the top.

"Just because I'm going doesn't mean I'm going to be nice or like it. In fact, I might be the worst version of myself to spite you all." She spoke the words under her breath as she typed and hit send on the text.

Immediately the responses flooded in.

"He'll love you."

"Hard to get. Very nice."

And from Casey, a string of pictures. She didn't know what they meant, but she had to assume the worst.

"Gross."

Grace rolled her eyes and finally flung the covers off and shimmied on the wool robe waiting for her at the foot of the bed. Without much thought, she began to pick out her wardrobe for the day. Something sleek and professional that she could transition to an evening date with a quick shoe change. A black pencil skirt with a sheer black blouse. Tiny little pearl buttons fit the shirt tight around her neck. Maybe she would tie her hair back in a long and low, thick blonde pony, and add a big wavy curl. Mom's pearl earrings for a finishing touch. Yes, that will do just fine.

Thirty minutes later, nearly to the second – if Grace was anything, she was efficient – she was out the door. The air felt good when she stepped out into the morning. All the running around inside had left her walking out with her arms stretched wide, letting the fresh air flow around her. She might not care about her appearance tonight, but pit-stains were a little much.

She inhaled and knew this would be a busy day. She would be preparing for a lovely two-week stay-cation, and doing that wasn't easy.

Glowing street lamps lit her way to the most precious view of her morning: The Bistro coffee shop, conveniently located on the street level of her office building. She could see Aimeé swiftly moving in and out of the kitchen with massive trays that seemed to dwarf the thin French woman beneath them. She could only assume they were delicious, flaky croissants or puffy chocolate beignets. The fragrant scent of sweet dough lured even the nuttiest of health nuts through the not so subtle white, French wooden doors, where they would be swallowed up by the only smell that could be better than a bakery: rich and savory coffee grounds made from the best decadent brown beans.

"It really is like walking into heaven. I'll never get over it. Every single time, it's heaven." Grace shrugged before unbuttoning a fitted gray toggle coat that reached just past her skirt.

"Oui, oui! Food is not just the key to a man's heart, sweet Gracie, but also the sensual way into a woman's."

Finally admitting it to herself and to the two elderly men who came in for their morning jolt, Grace smiled and said, "Yes. It's true. I am in love with you, and you have sensualized my entire being with your chocolate beignets. I'll take two, and a nonfat latte when you have the time. No rush." Grace added as she made her way around the room that had transformed overnight into an autumnal haven of orange, red, and yellow flowers in tall, fat vases. Cinnamon scented pinecones were scattered throughout. Cleverly placed in coffee mug displays and resting in glass bowls on random tables. Amber candles adorned every table, nook, and cranny, allowing for dimmed overhead lights and an ambiance so immensely warm it made you want to live right there in the shop.

"Did you even go home last night?" she inquired loud enough for her voice to reach the back kitchen while bending down to take in the sweet cinnamon scent of a candle.

"Nope! She was here the whole night. Moving around like a mad-woman at three when I walked in."

Jumping at the startle of the unexpected voice, Grace grabbed her heart, "Holy Jesus. Shit. Jimmy. Hi."

"Good morning to you too. I've been waiting to have that effect on you since I was sixteen. Two years later and I have it." Jimmy beamed as he tied the black apron around his waist and logged in to the cash register.

Jimmy was Aimeé's favorite staff member. The rest of the kitchen and the customers loved him, too. He was dedicated and needed just a bit more sleep than Aimeé, which was probably around three to four hours a night. He didn't have baking aspirations, seeing as he was going to school for business, but he had a love and an obsessive appreciation for great food. That and his charm, won Aimeé over when she'd been hiring two years earlier.

Grace laughed, "If only I were twelve years younger," wistfully looking skyward for effect, "Jenna and I could battle it out for you – and bless her heart, she'd win because your girlfriend is the sweetest, most beautiful girl I've ever met."

Jimmy blushed and nodded, "She doesn't know it yet, but this job is going to get her the biggest diamond ring money can buy come graduation. Only four years away. Three, if Aimeé back there keeps letting me work the early shift to fit in an extra class or two in the afternoon."

"Seriously. Do either of you sleep?" Grace said in disbelief.

As he made his way back to the kitchen to help his fearless baking leader, Jimmy's matter of fact "Nope!" repeated its way to Grace's ears. All she could do was smile at the pair.

The table – their table – was placed perfectly in the corner of the Bistro for an idyllic window-scape view of the entire city block. She flipped open her laptop to get a head start on emails and caught a glimpse of Christopher Finnegan outside the window, standing on the sidewalk.

Chris was Grace's grade school friend and a serious goofball. He drove the teachers crazy and his classmates into hysterics. He usually got in a little too much trouble in school but had ended up a Minneapolis city cop, and one of the best. She tried to catch his attention.

What was he looking at? His eyes were fixed, no – fixated – she thought, on the lovely, Aimeé Beaulieu. As if on cue, Aimeé leaned back in a stunning bout of laughter.

Well, isn't that something? Grace thought, bemused. She wrapped her knuckles against the window to get his attention. Chris smiled, and the action warmed the outside world by at least ten degrees.

As he jogged across the intersection, she couldn't help but wonder how long he'd been pining over Aimeé. Had it been a recent interest, or years and she hadn't taken the time to notice? He came in here almost every day, and they crossed paths regularly at casual parties or walking the streets downtown.

When he walked in the door, Grace saw his first look was most definitely not in her direction. He offered a quick, shy nod of the head and a boyish wave to Aimeé. This was adorable Grace thought, as she chuckled to herself. She watched as Aimeé brightened and offered a much more confident wave in return. It nearly stopped Chris dead in his tracks.

"Chris! Hi, how are you?" Grace hoped to bring him back with some friendly conversation.

He staggered but seemed to pull himself together nicely and turned toward her window table.

"Grace, I'm great. How are you doing? How is your mom?"

The bear hug engulfed and delighted her. It reminded her of William and the familiar, smothering hugs he would give her.

"You know, she's been pretty good. She is keeping busy. Still making food for the masses upstairs at the office when she can. It's weird. You know? Not normal seeing her show up to places by herself. Or walk into the office and not have Dad there to greet her. She probably doesn't feel it, but now when I see her standing alone, my heart breaks for her. And I have no idea what to do or how to make it better."

Realizing she'd said more than intended, she quickly apologized. "Sorry, I didn't intend to pour that out. But she is good – we are good."

"Don't be sorry at all. Your dad was the best." His genuine tone was a comfort, more than she'd expected.

"So..." The pause was deliberate. She continued, "What has you out and about on the early shift this morning? Most people usually come inside to take in the smells, the coffee, and the pretty sights." Her voice was sly hoping she'd get a reaction out of him.

Grace stared expectantly. Not even a blink. Men, she thought. No gossip, just: "Oh, one of the guys just had a baby, and he's trying to get up at night so his wife can sleep a bit more. I don't mind the early shift. It's kind of nice being up before the world. I never used to be one for mornings, but the older I get, the less sleep I need. It's unreal. Everything mom and dad used to tell me would happen, is happening. It's funny how things change."

The older we get. The words echoed in Grace's mind. Wasn't that the truth. And, the older Christopher seemed to be a continuous improvement. His vibrant personality could have gotten him anywhere in life he'd have wanted to go. What she hadn't realized before today was his transformation into a seriously attractive man. The slightly rounded cheeks from grade school had all but disappeared. There wasn't a little belly hanging over his uniform as there had been his jeans and gym shorts. His shaggy hair was professionally trimmed, and the day-old stubble on his chin had him looking as handsome as ever.

"You know what I mean?" Chris brought her back to reality.

"More than ever." Her full agreement was in every word.

CHAPTER 6

Like they had for years, the office lights came on behind her, and she knew her time alone had come to an end. The chaos of another workday was about to begin. She'd listen to strategy, make decisions while wondering if they were the right ones, she'd analyze reports and emails from top to bottom, and take more than one look at their bottom line.

The smell of coffee found its way to her desk. She stood, stretched her neck, and grabbed her mug for a fresh cup. Maggie always started a new pot upon her entry to the office.

Her dad's old corner office – now Grace's – and her old corner office sandwiched Abbi's on the far end of the building. Maggie's desk sat like a guard in front of the three rooms. She acted like one too. If guards gave out candy, extended an ear to listen to, offered a shoulder to cry on, and had the ability to keep the three of them – or the two of them now – and the entire company on schedule. Maggie was like Yoda or Mary Poppins. If either of them had been administrative assistants.

"That's not a terrible view to start my day," Grace joked as she walked up behind Maggie. The smile on her face grew as she watched Maggie's bottom half shift back and forth like a pendulum on her swivel chair as she reached for something under her desk. The muffled laugh that came from the trenches offered a slight shake to Maggie's rear movements.

The plump bum disappeared and a round face with a light-colored cap of hair appeared as Maggie spun around. Grace couldn't tell when the hair had gone from blonde to subtle gray, but the color was so similar that maybe it had always been that way. Perhaps the face under the hair was the only thing that actually changed. The face had rounded out over the years, wrinkles crackled the edges of her eyes, and the smile got bigger. She could easily have doubled for Mrs. Claus, in the looks department and baking skills.

"Well look at you today!" The exclaim came as a bit of a surprise when their eyes finally met. "You just don't know what a knockout you are." Maggie made a spinning motion with her pointer finger as silent instruction to make a turn so she could get a full view of Grace's outfit.

"Do you have a meeting today? Special occasion? Oh, I know." Maggie's hands rested on the sides of her hips and smiled knowingly.

"What do you know?" Grace asked, her tone dubious as she rounded out her twirl.

"Well, for one, you're not wearing your typical blouse, skinny trousers, and loafer combo today – and I do love a good patent leather – reminds me of the good 'ol days. Anyway, this is much more play to your usual business."

Maggie stepped around her fortress to get a better look and agreed with herself, "Yes, I think there is a little more going on here. The black is pretty and shows off your curves and your enviable legs. I'm allowed to say that because I'm old enough to be your grandmother. If I were a betting woman, I'd say that extra curl in your ponytail has a pair of matching heels in your bag."

Amused, Grace wondered, How does she do that?

"Who is the guy, what does he look like, and where are you going?" Maggie asked the matter-of-fact questions as she made her way back to the perch on the other side of the desk. Seven o'clock on the dot. It's like she knew she had exactly two minutes of conversation before she needed to retreat and flick on the computer to begin the day precisely on the zeros before continuing her inquisition. Unreal.

It was impossible to be discouraged while talking to Maggie, so she let it spill: "The girls did this to me. They set me up on a blind date. I would show you a picture, but I can't, because – well – blind. Do you know what kind of people want to go on blind dates?" She continued to answer her question, "The ones that think you might not talk to them if you knew what they looked like. I agree that everybody is attractive in their own way, but Mags, come on. These girls are killing me. I'll be trapped. I'll have to find an excuse to turn down dinner after drinks. Then find a way to nicely tell him after the fact that I'm not interested. Then I'll be on to, what is it, date number at-least-ten with nothing to show for it?"

Maggie just smiled at her with compassion. "Honey, you've got to keep getting out there. He may be attractive, or he may not be, but he might be wonderful. I believe that's the very essence of a blind date. You're stunning, but that's not the most beautiful thing about you. And no, you're not shallow, and being attracted to a person is very important, but don't count him out before you even get a glimpse of this guy. He could be very handsome. The good news is if he's not, you can always try and fix that. A little haircut here, a new shirt there, and ta-da! A handsome man! That's what I had to do with my Fred down there. Personalities don't usually change, but looks…" Her head nodded to the front of the building where Fred Sheffield had his desk. More than 30 years of marriage to each other and they still goofed around like school kids.

"I hope you know it's impossible to find a guy like Fred out there in the world." Grace joked, but Fred was indeed a great man.

"Don't I know it. He's one of a kind, but he's my one of a kind. You'll find your one of a kind, and when you do, you'll know. Something about him will make you smile without trying. You'll catch yourself in one of those smiling moments, and it will hit you. You'll be head over heels and in trouble. The good news is, whoever it is, he'll get one look at you and be in love. So, you'll have your pick of the litter. Choose wisely. Now run and get your refill and I'll have your agenda by the time you get back so you can have a kick-butt day before heading out for your date. And," she added, "you start your vacation next week. Drop off any files you need me to take care of while you're gone and don't worry about a thing."

She did have files that needed to be taken care during her vacation, but dang it, did she leave them at home? Grace's eyes looked to the ceiling, trying to remember where she'd been working on them. It wasn't like her to forget. This date was throwing her off.

"I do, but I think they are still on my desk at home. I'll run there tonight and have them on your desk by Monday morning." Before Maggie could tell her not to inconvenience herself, Grace argued, "I have to run home anyway and give myself a little touch-up, so it's no trouble at all."

"You're a sly girl, letting me think it's a good idea for you to run home." There was teasing in her voice. "But thank you." Maggie leaned in and lowered her voice just a bit even though the office was vacant. "Have you heard the rumors?" She was undoubtedly referring to the Wallace acquisition.

"I will not agree that any such rumors exist," Grace said coyly. "But, if such rumors were true, I would say that as of yet, we have not heard of any actions taken."

Maggie's excitement wasn't for the takeover of the company, and Grace knew that. Maggie liked the challenge of keeping up with the demands of a fast-moving company and all that entailed. Wallace would be a lucky man if he saw in Maggie all she was worth. Less an administrative assistant, more the wheels that kept the company rolling. Maggie would see right through him if he was anything less than honest. Grace supposed she liked the thought of that, as long as Maggie got to keep her job and keep ruling the world from her post guarding the executive offices.

Coffee was just the refuel she needed. An extra jolt of morning happiness. She sighed as she leaned against the counter in the kitchenette, savoring the feel of the warm mug in her hands. Everybody had a comfort food, and this was hers. It made her pity those who didn't drink it. To live a life without even the smell of coffee was no life at all.

Her dad used to say that to Aimeé nearly every week, first when she came over to the Thomas home during their college breaks, then when she'd opened her Bistro. Aimeé loved him a little more for it. They agreed on nearly everything, but their love of coffee is what bonded them straight away.

Grace found her dad's thoughts and voice in her head so much these days. It was a comfort and a sorrow. To know he was still there, but knowing she couldn't have him back.

"Aren't you a vision." The words jolted Grace back to the present. "I would say if Raymond could see you now, he'd be hooting and hollering. But then again, he knows how beautiful you are." Abbi's wistful voice filled the kitchenette, and it comforted Grace knowing she wasn't the only one who missed her dad.

"I heard from a little bee you were down here and looking pretty today." Grace watched Abbi's eyebrows flutter up and down.

"Good news really does travel fast," Grace responded dryly. "Did this bee also tell you he's probably hideous? And no, since you asked," Grace felt herself pour on the pity party, "I can't show you what he looks like. Because, my friends are terrible."

"Absolutely, and I was sent here to reinforce that it is not always about beauty, my dear," Abbi put on her best Maggie voice, "it's the beauty inside of him that will make you fall in love. That, and he better darn well make you laugh. That's just my two cents though." Abbi grew silent as she filled her cup from the thermos, fragrant steam rising from the carafe. She looked at Grace when she was finished. "You know, I have a good feeling about tonight. I don't know what it is, but I think something wonderful is going to come your way. Maybe it's the Fall chill in the air or knowing that the holidays are right around the corner. I get a little spring in my step come Fall."

Abbi drew Grace in and steered her back to their offices. With a quick, warm squeeze of her arm, they made their way back to Maggie to take their daily orders.

"One for you, and one for you." Maggie handed each of them their schedules. Grace eyed her own and wondered if everybody realized it was this woman who really ran the company.

"Abigail, don't forget about your ten o'clock with Gear North. It's nothing formal, as they are stopping in to meet with Matt to renew their account contract, but I booked you for fifteen minutes at the start of it to shake hands and kiss babies."

Directing her attention to Grace, "As for you, if you thought you had outgrown paperwork, I'm sorry, you have not. I went through end-of-month financials to try and ease the pain and made notes where I thought attention needed to be paid. The stack, and I mean *stack*, has been moved to the corner of your desk. Neither of you has lunch scheduled today, so I'm assuming..."

Her words trailed off while both of the women shuffled through the papers in the files and analyzed their busy days without looking up.

Brusquely Maggie said, "I'll order in," and with that, Abbi and Grace were off in separate directions, one to the right and one to the left of the desk. Both stopped just before walking through their office doors and turned, saying almost in unison, "Thank you, Maggie."

Grace lingered for a moment longer to add in a slightly quieter tone, "For everything."

CHAPTER 7

Why did she always do this to herself? She was the model of efficiency and order at work. Then she always tried to do one more thing before she left, and all the efficiency and order of her personal life flew out the window. It left her flying down the stairs, and now she would probably be late. She supposed it would give the nerves less time to shimmy in.

She raced passed the Bistro when she reached the ground floor, pausing briefly for a knock on the window and a hurried wave for her friend, a daily custom. Without stopping her task at the counter, Aimeé blew a kiss toward the window and kept her hands flying around the espresso machine, quickly filling orders with the grace of a well-trained ballerina.

Her phone buzzed to life as she was rounding the corner. Without missing a step, she clicked the Bluetooth button on the side of her earpiece and gave a breathless, "Hello."

"You're heavy-breathing! Please tell me you met your date early, you skipped drinks and dinner, and went straight for a sexy romp session."

Rachel's giggle on the other end was contagious, but abruptly stopped and her tone switched to immediate concern as she said, "Oh my god, please tell me that you don't answer the phone during a sexy romp session."

This time a rueful laugh escaped Grace's lips as she scurried up the street toward the brownstone.

"Unfortunately, this is far from sexy romp," she huffed as she absently thought to herself, holy crap, Thomas, you're out of shape. "I had to-" another heavy breath heaved in and out, stopping her words, and it was so pathetic she gave a choked snort of laughter in spite of herself, "—to work late—so much frickin' paperwork. Okay, seriously, can we all start going to those kickboxing classes again? Or, maybe start our morning or after work jogs? This is painful."

Rachel ignored every word, "Shoot. I had high hopes for sexy romp. I should have known better. I'm not like that either. But how amazing would it have been if that's what you'd been doing?"

The idea hung in the air long enough for Grace to realize it had been a year since she'd been on her last date. And with that realization, it had been even longer since she did anything *sexy* with anybody. Seriously depressing. She wasn't promiscuous, but was a good romantic make-out session – that may lead to just a little more – too much to ask?

"About this working out thing – I'm in. I need to firm up before Christmas. I will not let the holiday food win – not this year. I'll call the girls," Rachel took the initiative before Grace had the chance, knowing Grace was usually the one to get everybody together. "You have more important things to do, like prep for your date. Do you know where you're going? What are you wearing? Are you going to try and knock him dead?"

Grace flew up the stone steps at an impressive rate. Especially while on the phone. She ran into the door with a painful whack of her knee because she couldn't quite get the key turned quickly enough, but barely noticed the pain – she was on a mission. All of her bags and jacket were strewn on the bench near the front door as she sprinted upstairs to start the pre-date fuss. It was a ritual. All women fussed, and she was no different.

"Yeah, the plan is set. I have his number, and that's all, graciously provided by my invasive friends." The accusatory tone of her voice teasingly exaggerated. "We are meeting at Parlour for a cocktail, then if all goes according to plan, moving up a block for dinner at Bar La Grassa. If shit hits the fan, at least I know I'll get a hell of a homemade pasta out of the deal. I'm trying to hurry so I can drop some paperwork off at the office before I get there. He – whoever he is – will be awaiting a text from me at seven sharp. I should probably show up fashionably late, so I plan to hang out at the Bistro, then walk over."

Grace paused when she got into the bathroom to analyze her next move. She listed off her tasks in her head. Makeup touch-up, swap out the heels – she'd been calculating all day if the black pumps she threw in her bag were the right choice, and came to the conclusion that they were not – and lastly, be sure to pick up the paperwork to drop off for Maggie so she can get working on it Monday morning.

Grace analyzed her face in the mirror, and tipped her head back and forth, letting the light hit each angle. Yeah, she thought, not too bad after a long day of work. She threw a fresh layer of concealer around her green eyes, a streak of eyeliner, and a bit of blush on her angled cheekbones. Then the job was done.

"I like it." Rachel, now on speaker, echoed throughout the bathroom while Grace touched up. "What are you wearing? Your body is the envy of every woman on earth, so please tell me you're showing it off."

"That might be a stretch," Grace said as she glanced at her body in the mirror. She had always been on the thin side but could see the stress and grief of her father passing had skimmed off an extra five pounds or so over the last twelve months. "I decided to go with the black pencil skirt. I think you were with me at Nordstrom when I got it. Black blouse. Suede heels."

The encouraging "Oh yeah!" that came from the phone was all the approval she needed.

"The hair is up for this round," Grace eyed the full outfit with the newly appointed heels in her grandmothers' old wardrobe mirror. "I am going for sleek and sexy."

Even though she liked to believe she didn't care about this mystery date that she had protested vehemently, the nerves she thought she'd avoid were slinking in. She hated first dates – figuring out what to talk about, the awkward silences, trying to listen and retain everything they are saying while trying to think of the next thing to say. Why in the world do people do this to themselves? She thought, shaking her head.

"Stop worrying." Rachel's affirming words bleated out of the speaker. "You're gorgeous, and you'll have him breathless at first glance. If he's not talking, it's because he can't."

"What if-"

"If it doesn't go anywhere?" Rachel knew her so well. She didn't have to hear the rest of Grace's sentence. "Then it just…doesn't. You'll move on to the next one with nothing but a free drink and dinner invested."

She grabbed the phone off the counter and took one last look at her appearance in the mirror. Her makeup looked perfect. Her outfit was effortless but dripping with elegance. At the bottom of the stairs, she took a couple of final deep breaths. Some to prep for the speed walk to the Bistro and a quick run up to the office. Then a couple more to ease the nerves.

"Rach, thank you," she told her friend. "And tell the girls to do their own recon next time." A smile crept to the corner of her lips, and she heard the smile and sheepishness in Rachel's voice.

"I offered to make the pre-date pump-up-the-confidence call. Besides, Casey is working, or whatever she does on that computer of hers, and Aimeé decided she needed to sleep today. She said she saw you run by while she brewed up her last cup of the day. We have a plan to gossip about you later on and speculate about how your date is going. It's going to be great. We'll let you know how the night played out in our minds. Text if you need to escape and one of us will be there. I'll let you know if I get the girls to agree to a morning workout tomorrow," she added, "Love you!"

"Love you, too."

Jacket, black bag, and keys. She picked each up from where she'd dropped them and was out the door. She shrugged her arms into her jacket and was down the steps of her brownstone. She got halfway down the block when irritation hit her – she forgot the papers for Maggie.

She had to go back. Grace spun around. Her turn was quick and gave her just enough time to let out a squeal before slamming into a man. A very solid man.

"Crap." The grunted word that escaped her was barely audible. She'd lost her breath, or the collision scared it out of her.

As Grace tried to get her bearings, the man lightly gripped her shoulders to steady her.

"Oh my gosh, I am so sorry." She was flustered, and felt for the poor man she'd nearly steamrolled.

When she looked up, she noted he was indeed a solid man. He was a remarkably handsome solid man.

She stammered as she tried her best to regain balance. "I, shoot, are you okay? Wow, you're...wow."

Wow, you're wow? For goodness sakes, she thought. Pull yourself together.

He was tall. Grace felt herself staring but didn't seem to care. His face was long and lean with sharp features. The thick, coffee-colored hair, was trimmed neatly in a crew cut. It fit his polished look. The dim city sidewalk light made his eyes take on the same espresso hue. They were framed by heavy eyebrows, adding to the intensity of his features.

Then he smiled. Her heart skipped a beat, and her nerves took on a new nervous flutter.

"I think I might manage." He said.

As he smiled, his face had brightened and changed every chiseled angle into a boyish grin. "How are you faring? Everything intact? In a bit of a hurry?"

His head dipped low to get a better angle as he gazed at her face.

A quick burn of blush heated her cheeks as she moved a stray wisp of hair behind her ear self-consciously. She was going to be late, she thought, as Grace suddenly remembered why she had been turning around so abruptly in the first place, leading to this encounter.

"Yes. I'm sorry, I'm in a hurry." Though you'd never know it at the rate you're lingering, she thought, and tried her best for a smile. "Ah, paperwork – forgot it. And I'm fine. I hope you are too. Again, I'm so sorry." She forced her body to turn toward the stairs, "I have to run and grab something, my paperwork." Crap, she already said that. "Then, run. A date." As if she needed to say that? She groaned inwardly. Why was she being so awkward?

Her eyes stayed on his as she walked up the stone steps. At the door, she paused and broke her gaze away long enough to grab the handle, but turned back to see him still standing there. She smiled once more, this time more amused at him staring back with that damn grin.

"I'm sorry," she burst out with a laugh, "Do I know you from somewhere?"

He shook his head as he pushed his hands into his pockets and shrugged. "Nope, I don't think so." Then he nodded a bit to himself, then to her, "But I think I'd like to." His body rocked from heel to toe, whether from bashfulness or playfulness, she couldn't tell.

The shiver of excitement in her belly was probably from the adrenaline. Yes, adrenaline. Now get moving, she thought, dismissing the feeling at once.

"I'm sorry. I really do have to run," Grace stammered as she slid the key in the door, and looked back, giving one last smile.

She stepped inside and closed the door.

CHAPTER 8

It took a minute to get settled down once she made it inside. Her heart was still pounding. Was it the brisk walk and her out-of-shape lungs? Or had she been holding her breath that whole time? Grace let out a gasp.

Wow, she thought again, he was so unbelievably gorgeous. She should leave it alone. But, what could it hurt just to ask him his name? She heaved herself off the door and quickly opened it.

"Hey, I," she started to ask his name, and he was gone. She looked out onto the empty street below.

The hint of disappointment she felt surprised her but didn't make it less apparent. She closed the door and walked to her home office, sliding the pile of work into her arms. She leafed through it once to make sure it was all there and found the ripped piece of paper her date's phone number was on, tucked into the pages. She rolled her eyes at forgetting it. She put it on top of the file, closed it, and shoved it in her bag. Here we go, she thought, and was out the door once more.

"I'm Luke."

She startled at the sight of him. Just like that, he was there again, right outside her door. All she could do was smile, and a sense of relief washed over every inch of her.

She stopped and stared for the second time.

"I don't think I was quite ready for our earlier encounter." His hands slapped together as he imitated their introduction, and she laughed.

"You probably know this, but you're beautiful. I got about a foot around the block and realized I'd be an idiot to walk away without asking you for a drink. My dad has this saying, something about when you see something you want you should go for it." He paused. "That sounds too aggressive, but you get the idea, maybe?" He cleared his throat nervously.

Her laugh was quick. She appreciated that he seemed to be having just as hard a time as she was.

"I have a full-time job, I live in my own condo not too far away, I eat anything within reason, and I like a good whiskey to end my day. I have to try and be a little smooth right now without getting too creepy, but maybe I've already lost that battle?" he said with a small, almost imperceptible shrug.

His shrug seemed to her an offering.

When she said nothing, waiting for him to continue, he nodded and rubbed his hand on his chin, then chuckled to himself and continued.

"I'm going to step to the side in case you want to start running away. Your date, he's a lucky guy. But, sorry," Luke went on. He couldn't help himself, "I have to be obnoxious for a little bit longer. What if you did join me for a drink? No strings attached. Then you can meet your date. Besides, I might think you're terrible."

He watched her try and stifle the bit of laughter that trickled out, but when he heard the sweet, light sound, it burned in his gut in the best way.

"A drink?" She questioned.

"One drink." He tried not to sound too hopeful.

Grace couldn't curb the sincere curl of her lips. It crept across her face as she shrugged. An action to mimic his. Grace tried her best at flirting, and to think of something to say that would shield her intrigue. But with the spark of attraction wreaking havoc on her brain, all that came out was, "Okay."

CHAPTER 9

There was not even a slim chance he was succeeding in playing this cool. Did he just fist pump? Luke could feel his dorky, wide grin, and when he exclaimed, "Okay!" it didn't improve the situation. Oh my God, he thought.

Typically, Luke didn't have to worry about being corny – because he wasn't. He liked to think he was skilled in the area of women, but right now, it was mortifying. What in the hell came over him? She was pretty, sure – okay stunning – but he'd seen his fair share of stunning women. He'd taken his fair share to his bed. She should be no different. Besides, he knew who she was.

Luke should have been ready for this. He should have let the night play out how he'd intended. It would have given him time to regroup.

Okay. He tried to focus. He had obligations. Business obligations. If his father taught him anything, it was to follow through. Be on time and follow through, his father's voice echoed in his mind. He'd have to find a way to make this work, seeing as once he saw her, he had found it necessary to throw all of his plans out the window. Besides, his father tended to be a little strict and believed less in fate than in hard work and dedication. Luke believed the same but thought luck and chance played a more significant role than none at all − or at least he liked to think so. Besides, how often do you run into Grace Thomas?

He waffled and decided that was a bad example. His research told him he could run into Grace at any time. He knew where she worked and that she lived on this street. He knew she was diligent and followed through. He had it on multiple people's word that she didn't back down easily, and she always put her clients first. He knew she had the lowest employee turnover rate he'd ever seen. She was efficient, and she was smart. What he didn't expect, though, was for her to knock him off his feet. He'd have to work on that.

He took her in again. He wondered, was it the glow of the streetlamp that made her eyes that vivid green? He stared as wisps of softly curled hair fluttered in front of her face. It was all he could do to stop himself from brushing them behind her ear, to tuck them away for safekeeping. How long was her hair? He'd seen pictures, but until now he hadn't wanted to see it down and untamed.

If her personality was even half as beautiful as the face he was staring at, he'd be crazy not to fall in love with her. Then again, that might not be the best idea either. It was a slight conflict of interest. But really, what's the worst that could happen?

Luke removed his hand from his pocket and held it out. "I can't remember everything I rambled earlier, but to be fair, I was trying to get you to not sprint in the other direction. You move pretty quickly." His eyebrow peaked humorously, and the hint of a smile played on his lips.

"I'm Luke." he said again, making the introduction official with his outstretched hand.

"Hello, Luke."

Hearing her voice say his name was like walking into heaven. Her smile kicked his heart rate up a notch. He bet that smile had won her more battles in her lifetime than she'd care to admit.

Their hands met, and he felt it. Electricity. A delicate shock, a feminine jolt. He wanted to lift her hand to his mouth and kiss it, but that would be weird. He nearly shook his head to rattle the thought loose.

"Nice to meet you. My name is Grace."

Of course, he thought. He'd read it a million times, but hearing her say it was something else entirely.

Luke turned his body to stand side-by-side.

As they walked down the lamp-lit street, he mused at the situation. He had known the meeting would happen, but he couldn't quite believe the chain of events. It was interesting.

Everything he'd read about Grace Thomas had led him to believe she wouldn't have agreed. She was conservative; she played by the rules. Every clip or piece of information he had found on the internet seemed to attribute her success to her work ethic – doing vast amounts of research and paying excruciating attention to detail. She'd surprised him. Twice now. The first, he mused, when her body had launched into his only a few lucky moments earlier, and a second time when she agreed to drinks. Things could – and probably would – get a little more complicated, but it was going to be a hell of a lot more fun.

He glanced at the beautiful woman walking next to him
and   grinned.

CHAPTER 10

The atmosphere at Parlour was effortlessly cool.

Grace waited by the lounge door while Luke wandered through a mixture of plump vests and boots, and sleek jackets and heels. Girlfriends at tables for happy hour and co-workers enjoying an after-work beverage of choice. The dim lighting gave everybody sultry shadows across their faces and amplified their beauty. The room was decorated carefully in a style that was both eclectic and rustic. High heel shoes didn't click on the hard-wood floor. They clapped a manly beat with each step.

From across the room, Luke waved his hand up over a sea of bodies and caught her eye. His hand motioned toward his body.

The way he had come in, searched for a table, done the work to find them a seat in the masses, so she didn't have to weave through the crowd, struck her has gentlemanly. And, she realized, she was already giving points to the cute guy. Luke, she silently corrected herself.

"This place." She stopped to relish in the chic, cave-like ambiance as he helped her out of her jacket. "It's great. I can't believe I haven't been here before. This place screams Casey," she said, still taking it in.

He started to nod, then tilted his head curiously.

"Casey?"

"Sorry, my best friend. One of them. She's a tech whiz and could probably make your life miserable. Be warned." Grace was half-joking.

"Very good to know. But it's good, right? My buddy, Mave – Travis – loves coming here after work. It's lounge-y, a little bit sophisticated, a little old-fashioned. I love their drinks – here's the list. If you don't like one of these, they'll make you anything you want. I can almost guarantee it will be the best drink you ever have."

"The best?" Grace raised her perfectly arched eyebrow, doubtfully.

"Yes. Because of the beards," Luke said matter-of-factly.

"Did you just say, 'beards?'"

"Absolutely. It's proven that any drink made by a man, or a woman, with a lumberjack-hipster beard, is better." He grinned.

"Is that right?" Her laugh was full and sincere. She composed herself as the waiter approached their table and asked, "Are you ready?"

"Ready when you are." Luke nodded in her direction.

"I'll have a lemon drop, please."

"I'll do a whiskey on the rocks. And can we get a couple of cherries if you can sneak them out?" Luke spoke with the casualness of a frequent customer.

The waiter and his beard walked away and they sat. She liked the way he leaned his body into the table toward her.

"Here we are," he said. "I can't believe you agreed to drinks," he blurted out.

"I can't believe you asked me for drinks," she responded honestly, still slightly amused at this evening's events.

"Why is it that if a man is in a bar and asks to buy a woman a drink, it's okay. But, when a man sees or gets run into on the street by a beautiful woman, it's kind of..." Luke moved his hand in a so-so motion to imply it might make him creepy.

"That's an interesting question. Why is it that some women are eager to find a relationship, but when set up on a blind date, they do everything they can to get out of it?" Grace found herself feeling comfortable boldly sharing with this person she'd only just met. Seeing as he already knew she'd ditched her date to share drinks with him, maybe it wasn't too much.

"Also, an interesting question," Luke repeated her words. "It looks like tonight's chain of events played in my favor. Am I allowed to start testing you yet?"

"I thought – as the woman – that was my job?" Grace countered flirtatiously.

"Oh, sorry, right. You go ahead." He smiled. He liked her banter.

"Why, thank you. Let's go with the most important." Grace thought back to the sidewalk when she'd been taken by his captivating, and undeniably cute speech, "You mentioned a job. I believe you even used it to sell me on drinks. Now I'm curious as to what it is you do?"

"That's the most important?" Luke joked, "What about married with children?"

"Are you married?" Grace exclaimed, trying to sound surprised, but feeling she knew the answer was no. She hoped this would give him just a little embarrassment to see how he handled it, as she had noticed a couple of the close tables now looking their direction.

When his eyes caught on, his laugh was deep.

"Nicely done," he admitted. "Okay, no kids here, no marriages. And yes, I confirm I have a job."

He wondered how far he could go on that subject. Good news tends to travel fast within the industry, and Minneapolis was a small town as far as he was concerned.

"I am an accountant," Luke began. "I work with my dad and my best friend. I feel like I hit the employment jackpot. It's awesome. Am I allowed to ask the same?"

"Very interesting." Grace leaned in and rested on her elbows. "I work for my dad's company. It was my dream to run the business one day. I love it, and I love him." Her voice only shook a little as she mentioned her dad.

"You like working closely with your dad? All the time?" Luke asked.

"Yes." Grace didn't want to lose the fun in their conversation, but she felt herself open up a bit. "It's funny. When you're in it – the work I mean – with family, you don't realize how great it is. It's easy to take it for granted, is what I mean. Anyway, enough there. Way too serious." She shook her head and gave a tiny chuckle, placing her hands in her lap.

They quieted only long enough for the waiter to place two expertly crafted cocktails and a cup of cherries in front of them.

"Never too serious," Luke broke the silence, lifting his glass. "To cherishing time together." And, he noted, there was the first glimpse of the business woman he'd heard the good things about.

She clinked her dainty glass to his, "To cherishing time together."

They both sipped and looked around. She realized the date she had ditched was probably here already. Or, depending on the time, had been here and left.

"Do you know," Grace pulled his attention back in and tried to be inconspicuous, "*this* is where I was supposed to meet my date?"

"Here?" Luke looked around at the bustling lounge, noting the rising volume.

"*Here.*"

"And you have no idea who he is?" he asked.

"None at all." Grace said. She didn't feel as worried as she was letting on. In fact, she felt a huge sense of relief. She didn't have to try and put on a show, or be polite, or try to impress like she would have to on the blind date. Luke was very handsome, sure, but this encounter was so unexpected, she figured any expectations could be thrown out the window.

Grace watched Luke glance around the room and his eyes came back to rest on her.

"Do you regret it?"

She paused long enough to see his confidence to waver before answering, "Not yet."

"Would ordering food make you regret it?" There was teasing in his voice.

"Food sounds good. It might even make me like it a little more. What are your suggestions?" She skimmed the menu.

"The burger, hands down. Share the fries."

"I can't argue with either of those things," she admitted.

"You impress me." His voice startled him. He didn't mean share his surprised thoughts.

"I didn't know I was supposed to. How so?" Grace said with a smile.

"Ditching dates, eating hamburgers."

Even he had to laugh at his poor attempt at recovery. It wasn't his intention to be careful. But the longer they sat together, the more he found himself less interested in revealing who he was. And even less in gathering information about her work. He was, though, beginning to feel very interested in her love life.

"You said your friends set you up on the date. Why?" He asked, tapping the menu absently on the table.

"We're going to need another drink to get through that," she said, showing the defeat she'd faced date after date.

"That   could   be   arranged."

CHAPTER 11

It only took two drinks before she felt a buzz, but it didn't change her view as she glanced around the room.

It was sexy, Grace thought. Everything cast in a black shadow. Light from the slit-windows had faded with the sun, and glowing, amber candles, only offered the shadow of faces. She wondered if it was vain to hope the shadows added to her appeal. It had only taken two drinks and two hours with Luke to have her wondering what it would be like to see him again.

She also wondered if a stranger walked by, would they know the two of them just met? She hoped it looked as natural and as comfortable as it felt.

"Favorite sports team – go. Wait, do you like sports? You're a woman – I mean, a very attractive woman – but a woman nonetheless..." Shit, he thought. Wordlessly begging her to realize he was joking and not a sexist jerk.

He did his best to cover the sheepish grin that spread across his face as he trailed off.

"I see what you did there. Disguising insult by sliding me a compliment. I've used that at work. I'm onto you." She pointed a drink stick knowingly in his direction.

"That could have gone so badly if you hadn't realized I was joking," he said, running a hand through his hair as he laughed. "And my mom and all of my girl cousins would probably kick my ass for saying that."

"I think I like them. And it's a wonder you're single. Hey!" she said suddenly, encouraged by the two lemon drops that had gone down a little too smoothly. "Why *are* you single?"

"Can I get either of you another round?" A voice cut through their conversation as the waiter strode up to the table.

Before she gave the waiter her full attention, she said to Luke, "Don't think I'm going to forget where we left off."

The exchanged look was easy, humorous, and a bit hopeful. Grace was surprised she wanted to stay. Dinner, drinks, and a sexy atmosphere wasn't her typical Friday night. And Grace, for the first time in a long time, hoped the guy wanted to stay, too.

"Why don't you give us another minute? Thanks." Luke asked the waiter.

Luke grabbed her attention once again. "I would love another drink, but I also love the idea of not spending my Saturday hungover," he added with playful, wide-eyes that watched her chuckle. "At my old age, hedging eerily close to my mid-thirties for those that might be interested."

"Hedging?" Grace cut him off, suppressing a smile as she spun the ice around in her empty glass.

"Exactly. I might be close, but I'm not there yet. Anyway, I'll be lucky if I make it after these two," Luke finished.

The pang of disappointment hit her when she least expected it. Of course, it was ridiculous to assume the possibility of this – whatever this was – going beyond tonight. Sadly, as the night went on, she found herself hoping – no, wanting – to see him again. And unfortunately, she understood all too well the effect of a third drink.

"I agree," she replied after a slight pause. "And without committing the ultimate woman-crime and admitting my age," she went on, "I know the hangover to which you are referring."

So, she would let him off the hook.

"Thank you, for this," Grace said, suddenly serious. "I can't remember the last time I enjoyed drinks with a handsome, seemingly put-together man. It wasn't the night I was expecting, but I'm glad it happened. I hope we cross paths again."

Shit, Luke thought, regretting his decision to turn down a third drink. He didn't want the hangover but he didn't want her to leave either. He was having a great time. Was she using this to dodge him? Was she dodging? She was dodging.

That's not how he was supposed to get close to her. His luck couldn't run out now, he thought, his concern growing. Running into Grace like this, her agreeing to drinks, their easy conversation. Her laugh. Her smile. The way her hands held the curved glass drink and the way she ever-so-slightly closed her eyes to sip and enjoy. Okay, he thought, trying to get a handle on the situation, you're getting carried away.

Focus. He'd gotten off track. But, he thought, he needed to keep this going for a little bit. He needed to gauge how hard the next couple of months would be. He had a plan, after all. And if he was going to convince his dad to change things up, he was going to need her.

No, he couldn't let her dodge.

"Let me walk you back?" He offered the words as a question. "I dragged you over here. It's the least I can do."

"If you don't mind a detour, I think that'd be nice," Grace said, as she guided herself out of the low booth, and grabbed her wool coat off the hook next to their table.

Outside, the brisk weather didn't keep the rest of the city indoors. The sidewalks carried people in and out of the restaurants, lounges, and hotels on Washington Avenue. Side streets were busy with apartment and condo residents, some with furry pets in tow. It was lively and spontaneous, not unlike their night together.

Grace liked the movement, the bustle, the city life. The street lamps and crossing signals were shining on a group of young friends, a family pushing a stroller, the two lovers who walked in front of Grace and Luke, swinging their held-hands playfully. She noted how comfortable they were, inspired by their happiness. That longing deep inside her heart flared up once more.

"They fit," Luke said, gesturing to the couple.

Grace wondered for a moment if she'd been thinking out loud.

"Sorry?"

"Their hands," Luke said, again, "they fit."

She liked how he lowered his voice not to be heard by the pair. It was silly, but it felt intimate.

"It's cute, isn't it?" She tried to play it cool. When was the last time she tried to do anything cool?

"Cute?" Luke said. His shocked impression gained a laugh, "Your outright ignorance surrounding the subject of hand-holding astounds me."

"Oh yeah?" she asked, genuinely intrigued at where he would go with this.

The couple turned back at them, and the girl smiled and nodded in their direction. Luke and Grace looked at each other like they'd been caught and tried to stifle their giggles from bubbling up while offering casual waves.

"Yes," he whispered, "but I'd be lying if I told you I wasn't disappointed. As a female, you should know these things. This is your territory. You know, romance."

"You should probably help me out then. It would be terrible to have to look like an amateur on my next date," Grace said, feigning seriousness.

"Right. I should. Well, once, a very wise, very old – it was my mom–" Grace gave a snort of laughter at his admission "-told me the hand can predict the fate of two lovers, even before they know they are lovers. Now, they have to be interested, and their intentions have to be pure," he went on as if reciting old folklore.

"Pure?" She hoped her skepticism would egg him on.

"As I said, it's a mom story. I'm lucky she used the word 'pure' instead of 'celibate.'"

"Ha! No truer words have ever been spoken. I wonder what you were doing to deserve such wisdom?" Grace said, fully amused.

"Don't jump ahead. Intentions must be pure. But," Luke took a chance and took her hand, intertwining their fingers for display, "when two people link hands, their futures together can be predicted. It must be comfortable. It has to feel natural. It can't be forced – that's not the way relationships work." He winked and continued, "Roles have to be accepted and appreciated."

"Lost me again. Roles?"

"Absolutely," he lifted their hands, "See, I've taken the bottom, and you've taken the top."

"Bottom and top..." she repeated in a teasing tone.

"Grace, I'd never. Mind straight to the gutter." Luke's shock was fabricated, but it paid off.

"So sorry, please continue," Grace said, laughing.

"Thank you. Besides, the part indicating sexual compatibility comes last. You can't lead off with that. Anyway, there's a supporting hand and a trusting hand. This is very important because often how you choose the hand position at the beginning is how they will forever be held. So, if you're a top, you should never take the bottom and vice versa. It's initial commitment."

He continued. "If we," his spare hand waved a finger between the two of them, "were both interested parties, our hands would be telling us I would like to support you, and you would trust me to do that. You also sneak your thumb inside of mine. That's a rare quality. You're willing to let me keep you safe."

At the sweetness of his insight, she intentionally held his hand a little tighter. "Very interesting. All from a simple hand-hold. But I have to admit, now I'm curious."

"About the sex, right?"

Her head leaned as if to say, well, yeah. Naturally.

"Right." He took a breath.

"It's first base."

"It's, wait, first base?" Grace said incredulously.

"First base." He confirmed.

"You're kidding?"

"Nope." He shook his head.

"You're telling me your mom said holding hands was getting to first base?"

He swung their hands playfully, mimicking the couple ahead of them.

"Okay, maybe I added that part myself."

"You almost had me." Grace felt herself grinning.

"Had you? This is prophecy."

"Whom can I ask prompted your mother's prophecy?"

Luke wistfully sighed, "Gemma Kramer. The love of my life."

Jealousy wasn't her forte, but she'd be lying to herself if she said a quick flash of it didn't make a swift run through her. It stayed only until her curiosity could take over. It was easy to imagine Luke in a high school romance – that's what she imagined prompted Mom's advice. If he was anything then like he was now, he was probably the school heartthrob, charming girls while leaning casually on lockers. The thought made her smile. As much as she didn't know this man, she realized she wanted to.

"Second grade."

His recollection cut into her thoughts.

"I was a toothpick with big teeth. I was eight. Gemma was seven. Her red curls in two of those twined things." Luke's hand demonstrated by twirling his fingers down from his head. "Green eyes, like yours. So many freckles, she glowed. I held her hand on the last day of school that year. Anyway, she screamed and said my hand was sticky and that I was gross. I was devastated. Naturally."

"Oh, you poor thing." Grace grinned at the thought of eight-year-old Luke.

"When I got home, Mom sat me down and laid the prophecy on me. Alas, Gemma and I were never meant to be." Luke smiled and looked deeply into Grace's eyes. Wishing this moment would last. It was the best feeling of intense. Not serious, but searching.

"I'm very sorry to hear that. Heartbreak is never fun, especially at such an impressionable young age. But, I do have to say, Gemma missed her chance. I happen to think your hand is not very sticky at all. Or not enough to make a fuss. Dare I say, if forced, I would even hold it again. But," she didn't give him time to respond, "this is where I have to stop."

They were outside the Bistro. It was rare to see it dark and lifeless, but in a few hours, the scents of butter, chocolate, and espresso would seep out to the street and wake the block. The smells would lure her out of the brownstone even as she enjoyed her time away from the office. It was equal parts delicious and ritual. Then she'd return as the winter months and end-of-the-year tasks set in, but the morning ritual would remain.

When you lived and breathed the accounting world, the term 'calendar year' was nothing to mess with. Especially when your clients depended on you, and you them. She'd have a day or two off around Thanksgiving, and then Christmas Eve and Day. But that was it. So she took her "winter break" early. In these coming weeks, she'd miss everybody upstairs, of course, but not enough to prevent her from enjoying herself while she was out.

The building was old and beautiful. Grace looked at the transformed paper mill that sat on top of what was now Aimeé's Bistro.

Many of the old brick warehouses downtown had been purchased. In contrast to the other's, theirs had been only slightly renovated with a more modern façade. Thomas and Jane LLC, had been in the one-hundred-year-old building for sixty years, but not much had changed. Her grandpa, who had purchased the old mill, didn't have the money to update it. When her dad had taken over, there was too much nostalgia to change anything, even though they could have built an entirely new building. She loved it even more for its industrial appearance.

Grace stole a glance at Luke, who was at her side, staring up at the same building.

"I would like to know what you're thinking," Luke said. He realized his desire to see into her mind was as much for business as it was pleasure.

"Love," Grace said after a slight pause.

"It's only been a couple of hours but, I get it," Luke dead-panned.

"Wait, you – no! Good Lord."

When she saw his smirk, she nudged him with her elbow playfully.

"No, no, it's okay. I won't make you explain yourself. Many have fallen to my charm. I'm awesome. I get it."

"I'll give you cute," she said, not wanting to deny that the attraction had grown in their short evening together and his charm was much to blame. "But love?" Grace pointed to the building. "This is my true love."

"A building. I suppose there are weirder things." He scratched his head and motioned to the building.

An act, she thought, to get her laughing. He was good at entertaining. She thought back to Maggie's advice on the importance of laughter in a relationship. Grace dismissed it just as quickly. Relationship? She thought, don't get ahead of yourself.

"Well, I guess the only way to get you to change that is to ask you out properly."

"Was that an invitation?" She turned to face him.

"I wouldn't mind being seen with you in public. Say, around noon tomorrow. I could find a dark corner table somewhere," Luke said casually.

"Your charm is slipping," she warned, trying not to smile.

"How long do I have?"

"To charm me or make me fall out of love with the building?" Grace loved their banter.

"Both."

"Two weeks." She didn't always have free time, but wouldn't mind spending a bit of what she did have getting to know this handsome, and, if she admitted it, charming man.

"It's less time than I'd like to have, but I'll take it."

"Noon tomorrow?" Grace confirmed.

"Let's meet right here." Luke pointed to exactly where they stood now.

"It's a deal."

"It's a date," he corrected, and lingered a bit longer pondering how he could suavely say goodbye without making an outright fool of himself.

CHAPTER 12

Grace felt giddy. A man had never made her feel giddy. She'd seen it in the rom-coms Rachel made them pile in the basement to watch on repeat during high school. But she'd never felt this type of excitement – this type of longing.

With her heels in hand, Grace took the stairs up to the office two at a time. She felt light and on top of the world. She swirled through the door onto their floor, floating on air until she rammed into the corner of Maggie's desk after what she thought would be a graceful spin. The papers flew everywhere.

"Oh, come on," she muttered to herself while rubbing her thigh. The abrupt stop had Grace suddenly aware of her panting. The two-drink buzz must be wearing off. She knelt, and one after the other, she piled the papers back into their folders, and let her mind drift to Luke.

He was handsome and light-hearted. Completely unexpected. Her side and cheeks hurt from laughing and smiling too much during their date. Could she call it a date? And, she thought, once more feeling the giddiness sparkling inside, he wanted to see her again.

"At noon tomorrow, right here." She murmured his words dreamily as she sat back, resting on her heels.

Grace looked down and picked up the now-worn and wrinkled piece of paper she'd forgotten she'd put in the folder. A man's number. The man she'd stood up. She shook her head. She couldn't believe she stood somebody up. It wasn't like her to break a plan. But there was something about Luke that made her take that chance.

The silence of the office shattered with the shrill ring of her cell phone. Grace rested one hand on her heart as she answered, hoping to slow its pace.

"Holy crap, hello."

"Holiest of craps to you, too." Aimeé's voice played at her ears. She sounded tired, but the familiar voice was still music to her ears.

"Sorry." Grace laughed to herself at Aimeé's effortless and clever way of speaking. "I was dropping paperwork off at the office, and it's a ghost town up here. The phone scared me half to death. How are you? Did you finally get some sleep? You've been going at that Bistro nonstop." They had their concerns about Aimeé and her working habit. But who was she to speak on it?

"I did, and the sleep felt wonderful. But I don't care about me at the moment. I want to know why you're not still on your date?"

Was Aimeé whispering?

"Are you whispering? Where are you?" Grace lowered her voice to mimic Aimeé's and rolled her eyes.

"Just, one…" Aimeé's voice trailed off as the sound of shuffling swished through the phone. "There." Her voice was back.

"You're with a man. Oh my God, who is he?" Grace exclaimed, still in her whisper.

"You do not know him," Aimeé said airily.

"Of course I don't. I never do. It doesn't stop me from wanting the details." Grace pressed.

The scattered papers were just about piled. She set the phone down and put Aimeé on speaker to heave the stack onto Maggie's desk.

"You first. I'll tell you mine if you tell me yours," Aimeé teased.

Grace smiled at Aimeé's use of her second language, and the reaction she was about to get.

"I stood him up." Grace couldn't help but feel a little proud of herself for being unpredictable for once.

"You what?" Aimeé's surprised voice filled the quiet office. "It's not like you to do this. What happened? You looked so sexy today. You were ready."

Every woman should get to hear a French-accented voice tell them they look sexy every day. It did wonders for the ego, Grace noted.

"I did look sexy today," Grace agreed. "So sexy that the handsome man I ran into on the sidewalk – and I mean literally ran into – persuaded me to join him for drinks. And I did! Can you believe it?"

"I-no. I cannot." Aimeé was shocked at this out-of-character sequence of events.

"Believe it. He is the most attractive man I've ever seen. I am seeing him again tomorrow as a matter of fact." Grace's heart did a little flip as she said it.

Grace grabbed the phone, turned and gave one last look to the office, and headed for the elevator. Realizing she'd drop

Aimeé's call if stepped into the metal box, she looked from the elevator to the stairs once more and sighed. Looks like it's round two. She ambled back down the stairway and gave Aimeé the details along the way.

"I don't know what to say," Aimeé said when Grace finished her story.

"To which part?"

"The entire thing. I'm going to need time to process. Did you call the blind guy?"

Grace laughed, "No, I didn't call the blind date. I wouldn't know what to say. 'I met a charming man on the street, sorry buddy?'" Even for a stranger, that seemed a bit too brutally honest. Like, I'm not meeting you because I found somebody that I find more exciting than your blind date. No way.

"You've been hit on by charming men before. Many of them. Why this one?"

"I don't know. I'm drawn to him. He seems," Grace looked up as she searched for the words to describe how he made her feel, "familiar. Funny. Did I mention he was handsome?"

"And you didn't sleep with him?" Aimeé said searching.

"No, not all of us have your stamina. Or tilted moral compass."

"This is true. Then, you *must* see him again. The others will be jealous I was the first to learn of – what's his name?"

"Luke. Isn't that sweet?" Grace could hear the swoon in her voice as she let the feeling of being swept off her feet fall over her.

"Interesting," came Aimeé's response after a pause.

Grace was too distracted to notice Aimeé's uncharacteristic pause at hearing Luke's name. She rambled on.

"Aim, I'm walking out." Grace heaved the door open at the bottom of the staircase with a loud squeak. "I'll see you tomorrow morning?"

"The whole gang."

"Have fun with...whoever you're with. Love you."

"Love you, too."

A kiss smooched through the phone, and Grace was left alone for the rest of the walk home. She felt her smile reach her eyes, and as it did, she added a little skip to her step.

CHAPTER 13

Grace exhaled and a white cloud puffed in front of her. It was freezing. *She* was freezing. The day before it had been sixty-five and sunny, and today, it felt like a long winter was about to set in.

Aimeé and Rachel looked the part, stretching before the run in their leggings, jackets, and running shoes, along with mittens and headbands that seemed to be keeping them warm.

Grace looked down at her layers of running clothes from Target and realized she was numb from the fingertips inward. I love you, Target, but I must get better gear, she admitted sadly and made a mental note to add running clothes to her shopping list.

Nobody seemed overly concerned that Casey hadn't arrived yet. Case had never been one for working out. Her Mountain Dew desk diet seemed to keep her at a comfortable size, never tipping the scale too far at either end. How did she do that? Some people have all the luck. And the rest of us run, Grace thought wryly as she joined her friends.

"I can't handle it. I'm freezing," Grace greeted Aimeé and Rachel. "If Casey isn't here in five minutes, I'm taking off. And if you want to hear about last night, you're either going to have to keep up or wait until coffee." She couldn't help the flutter in her chest and didn't mind wondering if Luke was thinking about her, too. She hoped he was. Now that was a strange and thrilling feeling.

"With a daydream face like that, I should have just stayed home. I knew this was a bad idea," A teasing voice walked up from behind.

All three looked up to see Casey in at least two pairs of oversized sweatpants and what appeared to be two undershirts, a sweatshirt, and a puffy jacket – each layer a different color. A full stocking cap was hiding nearly all of her red hair, and on her hands were gigantic yellow mittens that looked fit for a trip to Antarctica.

Grace couldn't help but laugh at the sight. "Are you actually running in that? Or were you planning to sit on the park bench next to that guy?" The three moved their gaze to a statue of a man sitting on the bench, smiling at people as they strolled by. He might have been there twenty minutes or all night, and neither scenario seemed to bother him.

"Hardy har-har," Casey responded sourly. The sarcastic, comical look on her face, made it harder for the other girls to stifle their enjoyment.

Rachel was the first one up from their stretching position, jumping up and down to loosen up for the run. "One time around and we'll see how we are doing? How does that sound?"

"Is it too late for just coffee instead?" Casey gave it one last shot.

Grace had to admit she wanted to give in to Casey's plea, but her stubbornness won out. It won out every time. She'd committed to this and it had been her idea.

"Why is working out always such a great idea the night before we do it?" Grace asked. "Last night I imagined the four of us, visions of perfect form and condition with nothing but the wind on our faces and our calories melting away. Now it's morning and it's the worst idea I've ever had."

Grace thought back to the morning when her alarm sounded an obsessive beep and she wanted to throw it across the room. Her bed turned into a luxury-resort-style king, her sheets cool to the touch, yet she was splendidly warm. Her fluffy down blankets and pillows made it impossible to get up, tempting her in every possible way to sleep in and savor.

"It's still a great idea. Run, then coffee," Aimeé said firmly to Grace then eyed Casey. "You came for the date update, I assume?" She started for the path at their usual warm-up walking pace, giving the rest of them no choice but to follow her like defeated toddlers following an insistent mother. "Grace, start from the beginning."

.

CHAPTER 14

Lake Harriet was the picture of perfection in Autumn. Bright oranges, yellows, and reds burst from the trees as the morning sun streaked through the leaves. Extravagant homes towered and lined the boulevard circling Harriet. Styles varied; old Victorians stood regally next to modern lines, and southern plantation-style homes were the perfect contrast to Italian-style villas. Everything was enchanting, amplified by gold autumn hue.

Their surroundings and Grace's timeline of last night's events left them satisfied as they turned into the curve marking mile number three. Except for Casey, who simply cocked her brow waiting for a response from Grace.

"I've never seen this guy before. I would know it if I had," Grace insisted, leaning out in breathy response to look at Casey, three runners over, "He's cute. Memorably cute. No, he's handsome. But when he smiles, so cute. I have definitely never met him."

Casey still didn't like it. "In any case, I still think there is something wrong with a person when they ask a stranger to drinks on the side of the road. I should do some digging."

"No way." Rachel wasn't having it. "You can't. No background checks, no internet history searches, no email bugs, nothing. Besides you need approval and Grace doesn't! That's the rule."

The rule had been put in place when Aimeé had begun a steamy affair with a local news anchor. It wasn't an 'affair' until Casey had done some digging and to Aimeé's misfortune found some dirt. He'd been married with four children. It was probably for the best in the long run – all but Aimeé agreed to that. Aimeé accepted this man loved his family. She was only in it for, well, everything but love. So, the rule had been created. Casey, going forward, would need permission from that point on to do any digging, spying, or otherwise.

"It wouldn't have been weird if we had already been at the lounge and he'd offered me a drink," Grace pointed out. "Or, if we'd met in the Bistro and he had made small talk. Or, passed each other in the hall at work or in a store while shopping. The only part of this that makes it seem strange is, aside from a smile while passing on the street, people tend to ignore each other. We happened to collide, and by we, I mean *I* ran right into him. I've seen weirder stuff than that happen. More awkward, too. Just think of how weird a blind date is," Grace finished, satisfied with her logic.

"Yeah, in a movie," Casey argued. "This is real life."

"I think it was flattering," Grace protested. She knew her friend loved her dearly, but why was Casey trying to rain on her parade?

Not one to usually accept defeat, Casey seemed to take the answer for now with rolled eyes and a sigh, possibly feeling too tired to talk and run simultaneously.

The friends continued on their jog, huffing and puffing. Now all of them sweating in their layers. And none of them willing to comment they still had another curve of the lake to run before they could decide to leave.

Rachel still wanted more details, so she pressed on. The spontaneity wasn't like Grace. If a guy was able to charm her from sidewalk to drinks, she had to know more.

"I need more details. This is amazing." Rachel gathered her thoughts, "Okay, so we know you went for drinks, and he was pretty much perfect, but how did you end the night? What about your blind date guy? Did you make plans to reschedule? Or how did you tell him you wouldn't make it?"

Feeling as though she could – and wanted to – talk about her night forever, she happily obliged Rachel's string of questions.

"I just...didn't go." Her face radiated guilt, and with a bit of shame, she watched her three friends turn to look in her direction.

"Like, at all?" Casey and Rachel piped up in unison.

"At all."

Grace saw their disapproving looks and heard the surprised silence.

"Okay, here it is. I don't know a lot about Luke," Grace shrugged, "but what I know so far is worth giving him a chance. And I think he felt the same way. I also know that for the first time in a long time, I had fun with a man. I felt comfortable and liked being the center of his attention the whole time. In the middle of getting drinks, I realized I liked him. By the time dinner came, I wanted him to like me. And by the end of the night, I knew I wanted to see him again. I am excited for lunch today. In a nervous, 'I'm going to mess up my entire closet trying to find what to wear' sort of way."

"Oh," Rachel said gently, understanding exactly what Grace was saying.

Casey nodded and agreed the best she knew how for the sake of her friend's apparent happiness, but couldn't help herself: "Are you going to tell us what we really want to know?" She slowed to a walk and added, "Some things can't be discussed while running."

They all slowed and moved to the right. Another group of runners passed them talking happily, without any difficulty breathing.

"I hate them," Casey muttered, glancing at the group of avid runners. "Now, tell me – us. Did you?"

"I'm assuming you're asking if we ended up in the same house, in the same bed?"

"Is there any other thing worth telling? Really?" Casey asked, showing the obviousness in her question.

"Of course," Rachel exclaimed, giving Casey a playful punch on the shoulder. She had to defend romance.

"There was no love-making or otherwise. But, our hands fit. It's prophecy." Grace said, her cheeks flushing at the memory of their hands intertwined.

"Prophecy?" It was Aimeé's turn to question.

"Yes." Grace's dreamy response had the women grinning at their love-struck friend.

"And no version of this story has you back at the Brownie?" Rachel pressed, using her beloved term for Grace's brownstone.

"Not a single one. And there isn't another scenario you could offer me that could make it a better night. It was perfect."

Casey stood by her comment. "I still think a naughty, sweaty, romp outshines anything you throw at it."

"I wouldn't sleep with a guy on the first date. Call me old fashioned. Or...not European," Grace said, with a joking sideways glance at Aimeé

"But you've-" Casey began.

"No." Grace pointed a finger, "No, we do not talk about that."

Aimeé and Rachel exchanged smirks as they recalled Grace's twenty-third birthday. Who could blame them, or her? It was her golden birthday, and they had been in France. If you couldn't one-night-stand in France, where could you?

Grace patiently accepted the bout of laughter that escaped from the girls. She tried her best to focus on how Luke had left her the night before. A night she remembered in vivid detail unlike the France episode, which she recalled in a blurry, champagne-tinged haze.

"It was perfect." Grace regained their attention and refocused them on her evening with Luke. "After we left Parlour, we got to the office. I told him about you, Aimeé, when we passed the Bistro, and how it's yours and how much we love it and you. I told him about Casey and Rachel when he asked who *the girls* were, telling him about our morning run. Then I had to run the papers up to Maggie's desk, so that's where we said goodnight."

"Typical guy," Casey muttered. "Can't close."

"I'm not finished." The coy smile on Grace's face stopped the girls' forward progress, and they stared in impatient expectancy.

"I panicked and held out my hand to shake his," Grace hid her face with her gloved hand in humiliation as she recalled the memory, "and told him how unreal it was to run into him – literally – and have such a great night. I told him I was thankful I did. He took my hand, and instead of shaking it, he pulled me toward him and leaned in and just kind of lingered. It was the best feeling of anticipation. I would have let him kiss me, for the record; but all he did – and all he needed to do to make it just perfect – was lean in and press his lips softly on my cheek. It was the sweetest, most caring, gentlemanly thing that's ever happened to me. I could have stayed there forever. He whispered, 'thank you' into my ear and then backed away. I was speechless." Grace couldn't keep the smile off her face, or the tingle that heated the side of her face where he'd let his lips linger when she replayed the memory of that moment.

"When I could speak, as he was walking away, I tried to be cool – but all I could get out was, 'what for?' He turned, walking backward for a couple of steps, gave me his incredible smile. Then he did this little shrug with his hands in his pockets, and he said, 'For two weeks.'"

"Two weeks?" Rachel said, confused.

"My vacation. It's the perfect time for me to date. He said he's going to try and make me fall for him. He just might do it. Might have done it already."

"Yes!"

Their attention turned to Casey. She looked so happy she could cry, and they realized it was not due to Grace's recounting of last night's events. They had reached the end of their run.

"We're done." She added to Grace, "I mean, that's exciting, too. But let's finish this with coffee. I'll get a table. See you there."

"Well, that settles it. Off to the Bistro," Aimeé said as they watched Casey, who was already at her car, stripping off her puffy layers. She threw her jacket inside, then removed the outer shell of clothing, and piled herself inside with the remaining clothes that proved too difficult to take off.

The other three stared for a minute before Rachel cut in.

"You know, she would have done ten more laps had there been sex in that story."

"Why do you think I didn't bring up my night?" Aimeé said with a casual wink and sauntered away.

"She really is promiscuous," Rachel said with a grin and a shake of her head, playing at disapproval.

"Yes," Grace sighed, "but it looks so good on her."

CHAPTER 15

The shot Luke took felt like a bullet. It was too fast and too early. The foam ball slapped the side of his face. He felt the distortion as if it happened in slow motion.

"Too soon," he groaned. He felt groggy. It was only eight in the morning, for shit's sake. And where did they get a foam ball?

"I will kick you out, and you will have to grow up and learn to live on your own like a real boy," he threatened.

Against his better judgment, and because he couldn't help himself, Luke picked the ball off the step where it had landed and whipped it back as hard as he could. It connected with the back of Mave's head like a fastball to a catcher's mitt. Under his breath, but loud enough for Mave to hear, he mumbled, "Don't start a game you can't win."

Luke walked behind the couch where his life-long friend, Travis Mavens, was sitting. He heard the grunt from the impact and a chuckle that matched the up and down bobbing of Mave's shoulders.

The sound of CNN on TV, Mave wrinkling newspaper pages, and the clap of Luke opening and closing the cupboards in search of breakfast didn't drown out his thoughts of Grace. She had slipped in and out of his mind since he left her the night before. But mostly in. She was stunning. She had stunned him, he admitted to himself.

He wondered if she knew how gorgeous she was? She must have some idea the way she'd made herself up, sleek and undeniably sexy. Luke liked knowing it had been intended for him. Of course, she didn't know that. Grace's intention was for her blind date.

What a lunatic he was last night. He ran a hand through his hair as he recalled the night's events. He'd prepped for their encounter for a week, and still the sleek and sexy made him feel like a blubbering fool. Real smooth, he thought, as he joined Mave in the living room.

Luke took a seat on the armchair that forced him to turn his head to see the TV. *His* TV. How was it that Travis Mavens had moved in, taken over the guest bedroom, the kitchen, and his beloved couch that had a crease on the middle cushion that was supposed to be his. His ass had made that indent. When he slumped with his feet up on the coffee table, the angle to the TV was perfect. Yet here he was, watching his best friend, for as long as he could remember, slowly take over everything that was his.

A rough time, Mave had said a year earlier when he came knocking on the door after what seemed to be a pretty shitty breakup. Mave had come home after a work trip to find the locks had been changed. *For safety,* Kat had said after the fact. How was she to know how he would react to the news of no longer being with her? His furniture – well, most of it – and his things had been moved into a storage locker in his name that he could access any time that was convenient for him, she had innocently explained. And don't worry, it's on your credit card, so they shouldn't give you any hassle. Kat had said it as if she were doing Mave a favor. What was Luke supposed to do, let his best friend be homeless?

He couldn't do that. Wouldn't do that. But, had he known the condo – the very nice condo if he did say so himself – would slowly transform into more of bachelor pad than a home, he might have written up a contract. A big contract. One with a lot of pages and a lot of rules.

So here they were. Might as well settle in. Luke slouched in his new spot and wiggled his butt to start the dent-making process over again. He set the box of Captain Crunch on his lap and let his eyes scroll through the news ticker at the bottom of the screen. Why anybody ever thought they were too old for Captain Crunch was beyond him. Breakfast of champions. He wondered what Grace would think? If the night before was any indication, she'd laugh beautifully and dig her hand into the box. She'd be standing in the kitchen wearing only his shirt from the night before, or casually sitting on the counter drinking a glass of orange juice. Maybe the Crunch would be a morning snack while he made some eggs and bacon. Sipping on coffee from that Bistro place her friend owned. He would run and get them a couple of coffees as she relaxed here waiting for him. Her hair would be messed from bed and a night full of – okay, get ahold of yourself, Luke thought.

"Hey." The shit-eating grin on Mave's face meant he didn't need to reply. "Welcome back."

"She stood me up," Luke blurted out as if the night hadn't gone according to plan. That ought to get him, the know-it-all. Even though he couldn't gather himself enough for the straight-faced, woe-is-me, look he was going for. It did happen to be the best date stand-up of his life, he thought to himself. Not that there were many. The events the night had handed him far outweighed any blind date, or scheduled date, he'd ever gone on a million to one.

Without lifting the remote, Luke poked at the mute button with his pointer and slowly moved his full attention away from CNN's latest.

Mave waved his hands in front of himself, offering Luke the floor, urging him to go on.

"There's nothing to say really. She stood me up. Didn't even get a text." He did his best to portray a man in agony and continued, "It hurts, Mave, it hurts really bad."

"No shit," Mave said in disbelief. "Stood up. Who would have thought in a million years you, Mr. Hotshot himself?"

He's eating this up, Luke thought.

"So, you didn't get any of the goods? So much for precious recon." Mave shook his head. "I told you it was a bad idea anyway."

"You think everything is a bad idea."

"Allison Pullman," Mave offered, with a pointed expression.

"Great idea for the first ten hours. Then, minor residual damage."

"She lit your car on fire."

"Nothing that couldn't be replaced," Luke retorted.

"Bad idea. What'd you do? You didn't get home until eleven-thirty."

"You'll never believe who I ran into on my way. Literally," his hands smacked together in front of his face, "ran into. Crashed into is probably more appropriate. We survived."

"You've got to be kidding me," Mave said dryly. He had a feeling he already knew who his luckier-than-shit friend ran into.

"I kid you not. The blonde bombshell herself. A one, Grace Thomas. Before you know it, I'm asking her for drinks. I wasn't particularly cool about it. At one point, I begged. I got a little creepy. Probably not my best moment." He recalled their accidental meeting. "She said yes, by some miracle. Drinks were awesome. She was awesome. The end of the night was awesome."

Mave rolled his eyes. "I get it. It was awesome." He dragged the word out. "It is seriously irritating, dude. The luck you have with women."

"You can't hit home runs if you don't play the game," Luke said simply.

"In your case, they've been more like grand slams. And that's not how that saying goes."

"Should be though, the saying. In fact, you should be playing."

"Can't strike out if you don't play the game," Mave shot back.

"I see what you did there." Luke pointed to Mave, talking through another mouthful of cereal. "Anyway, I think it's time for me to stall for a bit."

"Wrong game. Anyway, why? She break your heart already?"

"Nope, I'm currently not interested in anybody else."

"That *is* interesting. And here I thought it was just a business reconnaissance mission. An 'intellectual business investigation' meeting." Mave threw his love-struck friends' words from the previous week back at him.

"Something about her. It does make it a little more complicated, but God, she's amazing. I have two weeks to get her to fall in love with me."

"Did you just say 'love?'"

"Yeah." He nodded, wondering if Mave hadn't heard a single word he'd said.

"Two weeks?" Mave said incredulously.

"Yeah." Okay, he was listening. "She's on vacation from work for two weeks. Talk about good timing, right?" Luke didn't wait for Mave to respond. "That's going to be the easy part. Or the hard part, I guess. Keep her away from work, but make her fall in love in two weeks." Luke was more or less talking himself through the scenario he found himself in.

"I'm trying hard to keep up," Mave sighed.

"You can't rush love, Mave."

"Can't rush love," Mave spoke to himself and tried to process what he was hearing. "You, my friend, have never been in love."

"Not true. Gemma Kramer. And," he held up his finger, "Grace Thomas."

"Let me try and put this together. You left last night intending to go on a blind date for 'business,' that I managed to get you, with Grace Thomas. You ran into the same Grace Thomas on the way, then made yourself a creepy fool."

Luke bobbed his head but didn't interrupt.

"You offered – no – begged her for drinks rather than wait to see her on the scheduled blind date. She agreed, you went out. And now you love her?" Mave said dubiously.

"Yeah, but when you say it like that I should have let her go after the collision and then we could have had one of those movie moment things at Parlour where we separate on the street then see each other from across the room and think, *no, it couldn't be, but – it is.* Would have been so smooth and a great story." Dammit, Luke thought. He hadn't been quick enough on his feet. Oh well.

"Great story?"

"To tell people, our kids, you know? 'Our story.'" His fingers made quotes. "Grace doesn't know it yet, but I'm going to marry her."

"A better story than you attempting to date her to get inside information because your dad's company is buying her company and essentially making her company disappear?" Mave was nothing if not blunt.

"Hmm." Luke popped a couple more Crunch Berries in his mouth and spoke through the mush, "I suppose that wouldn't have been bad either."

Mave's laugh came loud and heavy.

"You don't think a couple of those details might actually make her not love you? Toss me one of those." Mave motioned toward the Berries box.

Luke looked at Mave, to his hand, and back again. He wound up and threw two Berries, a dead-on shot to Mave's face. Without flinching, Mave closed his eyes, took the punishment. He picked them up from where they'd landed on his lap, and popped them into his mouth.

105

"Throw like a girl," Mave said through his own chewed mess.

"No, that's why I need her to love me. Meeting her for lunch today."

"You think a dinky thing like love is going to save you? Lunch today?"

"Mm-hmm." Luke could feel his excitement rising as he thought about what the day would bring.

"I hate to tell you this, my friend, but relationships do not work. My parents and I are living proof. And don't sell your condo, whatever you do." Mave warned.

"Yeah, about that, sorry, Mave. She's the one." Pushing himself up off the couch, Luke dropped the Crunch Berry box next to Mave, "I have to go buy her a coffee."

"I thought you were meeting for lunch?"

"I only have two weeks. Then she's going to know, you know? Have to charm her early."

"Do you even know she's there? *You know*, where coffee is?" Mave copied Luke's words out of sarcasm and to show a little bit of his frustration with trying to navigate the conversation.

"Nope," Luke said casually over his shoulder as he walked   away.

CHAPTER 16

The girls talked, laughed, and made fun of one another as they met once again after parking and finishing their walk to the Bistro. The sharp sunlight was a welcome guide as it gradually warmed the brisk morning away.

Maybe it was the exercise-induced endorphins kicking in, but Grace couldn't help but smile at everything surrounding her. Two full weeks of bliss ahead of her. No schedules, meetings, deadlines. It would be month-end when she got back and they'd head full-steam into October.

That's what Grace loved about accounting – the work never ceased. But with it came demanding hours, and grueling, long days. Month-end was a time for reaching out to clients, closing their books, and starting it all over again for another month. The lifeline, successes, and failures would come together on paper reports and tell a story with the results.

But for these precious two weeks, she'd let her structured life take a vacation.

Grace smiled and thought about her dad's – no, she corrected – her company. It told its own story, and it was a very successful one.

It wasn't surprising, the rumors of Wallace wanting to buy. Thomas and Jane LLC, was appealing to anybody who had enough money. If she were to go along with the acquisition, they might lose some of their smaller clients who liked the personal interaction, true. But for the most part, Wallace would attract more companies that hadn't been willing to take a risk on her currently small-to-medium-sized operation. She just wanted to be a part of it all, and sometimes, more often than not, that wasn't the case. Companies came, bought, and conquered. Then they ousted the current leadership. That would include her. She'd have to find a way to change their minds.

Her view on the subject today was far different than the day before. She was less angry and not intimidated. She was confident and ready. She was going to fight for her company and her people. But at the end of the day, she'd do what needed to be done.

She made a mental note to refresh her knowledge surrounding the art of buying and selling. Sadly, she'd done little to no research on it yet. And frankly, anything she did know about acquisitions, she'd learned over a decade ago in school.

Maybe she could ask Tracy? She didn't particularly like William's girlfriend, but she did seem smart and knew a lot about business dealings. Or, at the very least, tried hard to make people think she did. Grace thought back to Thanksgiving the year before, and Tracy's somewhat annoying insistence on talking about businesses and buyouts and her role – her crucial role – in all of them.

What was her brother thinking with that one? Please be just a phase. Let it only be about long legs and boobs. Because, for Tracy, life seemed to be only about status and money, and Grace knew that's not how she and her brother had been raised.

The girls passed the windows that lined the front of the Bistro, and Grace caught a glimpse of their reflection. She might be biased, but only a bit. She and her friends made an impressive sight. Each one of them individually striking.

Rachel had long wavy hair that was startlingly dark. It accentuated her massive, almond-shaped, blue eyes and the heavy, thick part, framed her baby-doll face. Her petite frame gave her maybe an inch or two over five feet. Rachel said it gave her the perfect excuse to wear sky-high heels. Grace wasn't quite sure how, as a teacher, Rachel managed to stand in heels all day long, but she supposed when you tipped the scales at only one-ten you could wear whatever kind of shoe you wanted.

The swish of Casey's layered sweat pants and jackets pulled her attention away. With the mountain of clothes, you couldn't tell – well, even on an average day you couldn't tell due to sweatshirts and clothing that didn't necessarily accentuate the body – but Casey had deadly curves. The only one of them seemingly blessed with the boob gene. Her curves started on top, veered inward somewhere around her waist, then jutted out again to account for the hips and the butt that were still in the right place. Gravity had been kind to her. The dimples on Casey's flawless face were only outshined by round cheeks that sat high on her face. When she wore her red hair twisted into a bun that sat on the top of her head, as she usually did with her straight hair, Casey drew the attention of every room she entered.

There wasn't anything that could describe Aimeé. As far as Grace was concerned, extraordinary wasn't good enough. When she moved around in the Bistro, you could watch her for hours without taking your eyes away. She knew full well what Christopher saw in her. The trouble was everybody else saw the same thing. They saw her wavy crop of black hair, usually pinned back, and as the day went on, wisps of curl that had lost their way would fall to her face. She would force them away with her always light-pink manicured fingers that were usually covered in flour. She dressed the part of a French woman. Effortlessly cool and casual chic. She made simple ankle jeans and black and white striped t-shirts look like a magazine spread.

When she grinned at the thought, she tried to sneak a glance in Aimeé's direction and was caught. Aimeé offered a black-eyed wink and a natural smile from lips that, even for today's run, were painted in red.

The bell chimed on the top of the door as Aimeé held it open so they could single-file to their table. It was the perfect spot. Two walls of windows merged at the corner where they sat and had most of their gossip sessions. From there they could catch the sunlight, the streetlamps, the people who passed by, and on a day like today, relish the heat from the fireplace that pillared from floor to ceiling in the middle of the room.

The table was empty in a noisy crowd, which meant Aimeé had called and had Jimmy hold it for them as soon as it was vacated.

"Grace!"

Jimmy's voice yelled from across the room to get her attention. She paused before sitting to see him excitedly wave her over. Jimmy's girlfriend was joining him today, she noted, the young beachy-blonde seated at the counter bar with what looked like schoolwork scattered before her. Grace did not miss those days one bit.

"Morning, Jenna." She rested a hand on Jenna's shoulder, waiting for Jimmy who seemed eager to speak. The energy wasn't out of character for the boy, but his insistence usually didn't come on this strong.

"You are never going to believe this." Jimmy's game show host-like enthusiasm did have her a little excited for whatever he was about to present.

"Look!" he held up a to-go cup of coffee from the shop like it was an Olympic gold medal.

Her blank stare traveled from Jimmy to Jenna, to a random person who was also witnessing Jimmy's exclamations. Jimmy gave them an exasperated why aren't you excited and playing my game look and turned toward the cup to inspect it. "Oh," he said, registering the confusion at the cup's misaligned angle. He turned the cup slightly to show the writing on the side.

Writing that looked like chicken scratch that some five-year-old wrote with his non-dominant hand.

She squinted toward the cup and realized what the buzz was all about. She barely made out the words Grace and lunch and Luke. Her heart surged. Luke had scrawled a message just for her.

Her arm shot across the counter, making Jimmy jump backward far enough to bump the display shelf behind him. She snatched the cup so her eager eyes could re-inspect every word.

Like a bobblehead, her eyes moved from the cup to Jimmy to the cup and back again. Surprise and excitement streamed through her.

To reassure, or perhaps live vicariously through Grace, Jenna felt the need to cut in. "I was here when he came in earlier. I love Jimmy, of course," she glanced sweetly in Jimmy's direction, "but that is one good-looking human being, Grace. We read it. You're meeting him at Smack Shack, right? You're going. You need to go."

"I'm not ashamed to say that I might have a man-crush," Jimmy hastily agreed. "I've already decided I want to be him. He's so," Jimmy searched for the words and came up with, "cool."

"Interesting," was all she could muster, before walking back to her table, barely able to register their words.

The girls watched her move like a lion stalking prey. They had witnessed a wordless chain of events. When she reached the table, she gently placed the cup in the middle for everybody to see. It was looked over and examined as if they'd found an ancient artifact. It was twisted around in light circles with only two fingers as if they'd break it if they handled the cup too roughly.

"I should like him, right?" Emotions inside of her churned to get out, but she held her noncommittal facade. She couldn't look to Casey for this one. She needed optimism and an open mind. Aimeé was her girl. Rachel would be on her side too, but Aimeé wasn't afraid of the consequences as a result of a potentially wrong decision. Grace walked around the table and squeezed her chair between Aimeé and Rachel.

"Right?" she repeated. It was a question, but more out of her want for her best friends' reassurance. She needed to be told this wasn't stupid or ridiculous. She grabbed the arm closest to her. She needed an answer. A best friend, one of them – any of them – to say this was worth a shot.

"He took the time to seek you out right away," Aimeé began, ticking off the facts like a bulleted list. "He wants to have a daytime meal with you, which generally forces conversation, and I think we can all agree has zero sexual expectations – for now. He knew he would see you at noon but sought you out before then. A smart man bringing it here – even if you hadn't shown up before your lunch date, the chances word would get back to you were high. I think it's quite clever and lovely," she concluded.

"Okay, here's the deal. I'd be lying if I said I wasn't eager, or, a bit enthusiastic even. We connected." She didn't need to explain herself, but she realized it was more for her peace of mind than for her friends. "But I like him. And oh my God, I want him to like me." Her chest rose with a heavy sigh and fell again.

Then Rachel – perfect Rachel – came through.

"What if he's just like you? A beautiful, normal, hard-working person that happened to crash into the right person at the right time? I don't think men typically ask women to lunch or buy them coffee if they aren't at least interested in learning more."

Rachel was right. Grace had watched her brother William try hard enough to get Rachel to reciprocate his feelings all these years, and his intentions were good, from what she could see at least. Too bad he messed that one up. She wouldn't miss her chance, she thought.

Grace got up and grabbed the cup. She rounded the table, giving each of her friends a kiss on the cheek, and walked out the door into the chilly air.

CHAPTER 17

Holy. Crap. Grace tried to push them down, but the nerves fluttered from the pit of her stomach to the ends of her fingertips. The walk over to Smack Shack – where the "if you get this, let's meet here for lunch" coffee note suggested – went way too fast. And though it never bothered her before, today there were not enough windows lining the street to give her a good look at herself. She only wanted to confirm if she'd made the right choice in outfit, hair, or shoes.

One measly storefront window a block away was her last chance. She turned, angled, to get one last look. Who cared if the strangers who stared as they passed by thought she was a little vain? This was important, dammit.

The oatmeal-colored turtleneck sweater, along with the washed look of the dark, tight, skinny jeans, seemed pretty but not too overdone. Her black suede booties gave a little peek of her bare ankle and lifted her in height about two inches. Hopefully, they lifted her buns a bit too.

She shifted her bag to her other hand. She had to admit; it was a fabulous bag. The distressed black leather clutch was just a little too big to carry in hand, and she loved that she had an excuse to tuck it under her arm to rest at her side. She tousled her hair for a bit of volume and thought the long waves were laying rather nicely today. She might do after all.

"Here we go," she said to herself after smacking her lips together to smudge around the pale pink lip cream and walked the final stretch of cobblestone.

Grace gripped the door and yanked it open, with more force than she anticipated having to use, and walked inside. She roamed, slowly eyeing the room, and searched for Luke.

CHAPTER 18

The restaurant was crowded and full of life. People gathered inside and out. It smelled of salty lemon and garlic. She didn't see him right away, and Luke was glad for it. It allowed him to watch her search, watch her move, watch her smile at the people who walked by her and couldn't help but follow with their eyes. Her body and the way she maneuvered was casual, he decided, but everything about her said classy.

Luke noticed she was careful not to move too fast, each step was slow, methodical. The movements accentuated her lean legs in jeans that must have been tailor-made for her body.

He watched her shift the clutch she had nestled under her arm. She pressed it against her chest and crossed her arms over it to make room for a waiter with a buttery tray of crab legs to steam by. Her body twirled to follow and inhale the delectable scent. The satisfied smile she gave as she closed her eyes, truly relishing the aroma, tangled a knot in the pit of his stomach.

Luke was still staring when she found him. Their eyes locked, and his instincts had him shoving away from the table to stand and greet her. *A gentleman stands.* His grandmother's words were ingrained in his mind. As his chair scratched the floor, his mind drifted and new thoughts took over. He found himself wishing he was the man she'd always meet for lunch – or dinner – for the rest of their lives.

They stood for a minute face-to-face over the table, and they smiled.

"Hi," she said, shrugging, thinking, *here we are.*

"You look beautiful," he replied. It came out more stunned than he'd intended.

He slid around the table to pull out her chair. When he got closer, he saw her cheeks warm to pink with the compliment.

"Thank you. You do, too. I'm happy you wrote." Her eyes glinted playfully, showing off their emerald color. "And that you suggested Smack Shack, it's one of my favorites."

"I'm glad you got the coffee." Luke said, visibly relieved.

"It was just what I needed this morning. And very cute. You've already gained unanimous approval from the girls. It's an impressive thing you did."

He laughed. "Impressive since you got it. Less impressive would have been you sitting too many blocks away, wondering if I stood you up."

"I'm glad it worked out." Grace lifted a sexy eyebrow. "You were the talk of the town at the Bistro this morning. A lot of impressed and jealous ladies up there."

"Oh, good, I was going for jealous. Hoping to impress the masses. Did Jimmy let you know it took me three-and-a-half paper cups to get it right?" Luke asked.

"He didn't mention the half. Must be guy code," Grace teased.

"He's a good man."

"So." Grace began, wanting to settle her curious mind. She needed to ask. "We are here due to an unlikely encounter last night, and an extremely cute, unexpected coffee note. I'm thinking you might be interested in me?"

"You might be onto something," he said flirtatiously, but confirmed her inquisition. He was definitely interested.

The waitress interrupted the conversation by asking for drink orders. Why did the simple act of watching Grace, and wondering what she was going to order, seem exciting? Luke questioned. It was a damn drink order.

Without looking at a menu, Grace looked at the pretty waitress and ordered whatever white wine she recommended with the lobster.

"Sir?"

The stare from the waitress went unnoticed as he gazed at Grace, and she patiently waited for his order.

"Let's make it a bottle. We'll share."

"Sounds good." The waitress seemed genuinely pleased to get to choose for the two, and exclaimed, "I'll be right back."

"Okay, where were we?" Seriously, if he could kick himself under the table, he would. *Where were we?* Was he eighty-five years old?

"We were analyzing." Grace didn't seem to fault him for his phrase of choice. "Or I was. As a female, I'm entitled to wonder what you're thinking, and you're supposed to drive me crazy wondering if you like me or not."

"I knew the coffee was against the rules."

"Very much so. I didn't get enough time to pine for you or wonder about your signals this morning," Grace said, her banter apparent.

"Well," he defended himself, "I only have two weeks."

"True. So, what do we do now?"

"We ask and answer all of the questions you should never ask on a first, second, or third date. Are you up for the challenge?" Luke leaned back in his chair and took a sip of water as he watched Grace's delighted eyes grow wide and nod with the challenge.

"Absolutely, get the hard stuff out of the way. It's not easy casually bringing up wanting thirteen kids," Grace said. Her face serious and exaggerated.

He nearly choked on the water he had sipped and felt relief when Grace laughed at her joke.

The scary part of that little exchange, the part that had him choking, was the realization that if she wanted to have thirteen kids, he would somehow find a way to make it happen. And a nanny, or two. Luke didn't say as much since she probably already thought he was nuts; he might as well keep as much crazy to himself as he could. Besides, it was going to be hard enough keeping her interested in him once she found out who he was.

He wondered, if he told her now, would she get up and leave? Or, would she sit and have a conversation? Either way the dynamic would change, and that's something he wasn't willing to shift. At this point it was too risky, he decided. A nagging feeling of guilt tugged at his conscience, but he pushed it aside.

Grace's instincts had her hand resting on his to make sure he was okay after his choking fit with the water.

"I'm sorry, I had to," she said, still laughing. "I promise I don't want thirteen kids. I think three would be a nice number, but I'm not against rounding up or down. Have you ever thought of kids?"

He swore he was listening, but all he could feel was her touch tingling on his hand. It seemed so simple, but he had to trap her hand on his for a moment longer, so he turned his hand so their palms would face, and he rested his thumb on her fingers. She didn't pull away, and she didn't flinch – she just sat calmly letting her question linger in the air between them and waited for him to respond.

"I didn't think being an only child was too hard. Made it easier for everybody, especially Grandma, to spoil me. But I wouldn't have minded a roommate. Yeah, I would say starting with one or two and seeing where the count ended up wouldn't be a bad thing. I'd be up for being outnumbered if that's what my wife wanted."

"Wife, then babies? In that order?"

"Marriage isn't for everybody, but it's for me – and the women who'd probably have my hide if it wasn't in that order." He lifted his glass in a silent toast to his mom and grandma and watched the amusement light up her face. He needed to keep the game going.

"What's your favorite thing to do when you're not at work?" he asked. He suddenly felt the urgent need to know everything about this beautiful woman. He needed to know what she liked to do, what kept her interest, what sparked her joy.

"Oh, let's see." She leaned her body closer to the table to rest her elbows. The movement hiked up her shoulders but brought her closer to him, so they both hovered over the table in an intimate huddle. "I love to wander the city. But I also love being in my home. There is this huge window in the room where I keep my desk. It's not really an office, but I love the space because the window faces the street, and there is a fireplace kind of adjacent to the window."

She pulled her hand away but only to bring her hands together to form a V and demonstrate where the window and fireplace sat in her house. "I sit in a huge, squishy, chair and flip through a magazine, read, or just sit. The light from outside and the warmth from the fireplace are perfect."

"Okay. Let's see," Grace continued, stopping her daydream. "I know you're employed."

He waited for the waitress to fill their glasses and was thankful they'd covered that ground the night before.

"Ah, the subtle insurance. Validate employment." He said, raising his eyebrows knowingly.

She laughed, and he felt himself relax.

"That's the thing, though. I've thought about it," she said, "we are both accountants." The words were matter-of-fact. Grace lifted her water and rinsed the nervous dry out of her throat. "It'll never work," Grace said as she shook her head slowly and her face became serious.

"Sorry?" Panic filled his chest as he tried not to let it reach his face. Had she known who he was all along?

"Accounting. Finance. It'll never work. We, combined, are far too boring. We work all the time, never take vacations at the beginning or end of months, which leaves too little time in the middle of the month. Then there're the stereotypes – we are math nerds, penny-pinchers, and when it gets right down to it, not fun at all. We are doomed."

He was relieved to hear the playful way she spoke. He recovered slightly. "You're not giving us enough credit. You were kind of fun last night, and I'll spring for date number two.

You're on your own for three, though." His head gave a single nod in her direction to imply he wasn't joking, but his smile disputed his words.

"Kind of fun?" Her hand covered her heart, pretending to take offense.

It was his turn to laugh. He had tried to anticipate every scenario that could have played out over the past two days. The idea that he'd try and learn more about Thomas and Jane by meeting her on an allegedly "blind" date seemed far away. He'd wanted to learn more about their willingness to sell. He would introduce himself as the youngest Wallace and, though she might be reserved at first, he would make calculated strides toward learning what it would take to make both sides of the business deal come out unscathed. It might not have been the most conventional way to meet, but when Mave had said he had a way to make it happen, he couldn't resist.

His ideal scenario? They'd meet, have a drink, discuss the business plan over dinner. Then somewhere in the middle, they'd both be happy it wasn't an actual date, and they'd move forward, completely aware of the other party's intentions. Then they'd walk away.

The least ideal scenario? She'd hear his name upon his introduction, turn, and immediately walk out the door.

What he didn't expect was to run into her on the sidewalk just outside her home. He also didn't expect her to be attractive, or at least so attractive he'd throw out his plans, ask her out, and convince her not to go on a blind date with, well, himself. He hadn't expected her laugh to send fireworks straight to his gut. He wasn't ready for any of that. And now, here they were. Sharing lunch, flirting, learning. He wasn't prepared for her to know the truth. And he definitely wasn't willing to let her get away.

"I find myself wanting to know what you're thinking," she said when he didn't immediately respond, noticing that he'd become lost in thought.

"I often wonder the same thing about myself," he said. Might as well go for it, he thought. It was an opening. "I wonder how you'd feel about dinner tonight and lunch tomorrow?"

"We aren't finished eating lunch today," she said, genuinely surprised but flattered. "If I didn't know any better, I'd think you were trying to court me."

"Do people still use that word?"

"People who read old, lusty, romance novels do."

"Then yes," He had to answer quickly as not to let the image of lusty romance fill his head. "I would like to court you."

They'd found time to order midst their casual flirting and conversation. Lobster roll – Connecticut Style – the warm butter, lemon, and chives on a steamy, warm bun, called to her. It called to him, too, after her description seduced him.

The buttery lumps spilled out of the buns and onto their plates. Juices ran down their arms. The wine was shared, and the bottle emptied. It probably wasn't the cleanest way to spend lunch, but it was more fun than she'd had on a date in…ever.

He had a quick way about him. He wasn't cocky, but he could have been. He was confident. He wasn't forceful but seemed to know what he wanted. He was decisive.

"When was your last relationship?" she asked casually, taking a moment to wipe off the trickle of butter at the edge of her slender wrist.

Luke tried for stupefied, but his deer-in-headlights look was more funny than nervous. He set his roll down and wiped his hands and mouth, held up a finger, then sipped his wine, placing his napkin back on his lap.

"This," he swallowed, "is more embarrassing than I remember it feeling. It never seems as weird when I get grief from my buddies."

"It can't be that bad."

"It's strange for this stage of my life," he admitted.

"This stage?" She laughed. "All mid-thirty of you?" Grace was more concerned than she thought she'd be. How many women could he have been with? And would it matter if he was the man she'd been hoping for?

"Thirty-four, and now it's worse because I can't lie about my age. Typically, I can avoid the subject because there hasn't been a serious enough woman to know."

"Now, I'm intrigued." Grace leaned in.

"Okay, here goes." Luke took a breath, "I've never been in a relationship."

He paused, unmoving, and waited for her reaction.

"You?" she started. Does he mean?

No, she thought. Really?

"Like, ever? But you've..." Oh, how do you ask this? she wondered, "You've – you know?"

Grace was practically begging him to read her mind. All she could do was clap her hands in front of her face to aid in her explanation.

When Luke realized what she was asking, a roar of laughter burst out.

"Yes, yes. I've done-" he pointed to her clapped hands, "-that. And I like to think a little more delicately," he said pointedly. And she laughed.

"I feel like I have to explain." He cleared his throat and gave a rueful smile.

"This is already the best date I've ever been on." She took a large swig of wine, amused.

"Funny," he said at her cute tone. "Here it is. I've dated, but I've never felt like it was worth my time. Wait," he stopped himself, and her from speaking up. "Not in the way you might think. What I mean is, I never thought it was fair to somebody else if I wasn't willing to give them enough of my time. They'd be investing theirs in me, so it's only right I'd be willing to spend my time on them. Until you and I had drinks last night, I'd never felt like I wanted to see somebody the next day, or for the next date, until I ran into you."

"Hmm," was all she offered. She suppressed a smile. A feeling of warmth spread through her in response to Luke's candid words.

"Hmm good, or hmm bad?" he asked nervously. Maybe we should have gotten two bottles he thought absently, as he drained the last of the wine from his glass.

"Good hmm," she said. In a way, she understood what he meant. For most of her dating life, she'd been there. The man would be investing his time, and she wouldn't want to reciprocate whole-heartedly.

"When was the last time you broke a guy's heart? I assume that's what normally happens," he asked, and her heart fluttered.

"Heartbreak? I can't be certain. But my last date? About a year ago now. It was at a fall festival, and let's just say it was a disaster. And we, the girls, are not allowed to talk about it. I'd quit dating cold turkey, until yesterday when I was supposed to go on the date you saved me from."

"The poor world of men who missed you for a year. I'm happy to get to brag about nailing you," he said, and half a second later, realized his choice of words, was mortified. "Down! Nailing you down. I'm usually much smoother than this."

"I find it flattering." Grace eased his embarrassment, "It makes me feel like you're telling the truth. Can't fake your fumbles.

"So, no relationships," she continued. "I assume that includes divorces, or any secret lives I should know about?"

"No divorces – Grandma would kill me. I guess the only other thing I should mention is I'm a super-secret agent, but that's about it. I should note here that I always try to make it home for dinner."

"This all sounds promising." She hid her smile behind her glass.

"I'm, upon current analysis, surprisingly ordinary. I'm just a guy, standing in front of a girl."

The laughter snorted out as her hand covered her mouth attempting to keep the wine in. "Did you just quote *Notting Hill?*"

"That's embarrassing. I should have calculated the odds that you would have seen that."

"Thanks to Rachel, I've seen it at least one hundred times. Don't feel bad. I find Hugh Grant looks good on you."

"Thank you. Then I probably don't have to remind you, Hugh gets the girl in the end."

"Then I guess I'll have to agree to dinner." Grace said, hoping her outward appearance was cooler than the dorky girl who was cheering on the inside.

She loved this. Their banter, their conversation, their ability to enjoy each other's company. It made her heart feel light and hopeful.

"You surprise me," Luke said aloud what he'd been thinking for the past twenty-four hours as he watched her move a long curl behind her ear and lean in.

"You had expectations?" she said softly, taking in those dark eyes.

"No," he caught himself. "Just looking forward to dinner."

CHAPTER 19

"Well?"

"She's perfect." Luke walked in, looking around.

"Doesn't exist!" Mave yelled from wherever he was in the condo when he heard the door close.

"On my life, she's perfect. Like," shock set in and it had Luke pausing, holding his keys over the island, frozen, "like, holy shit perfect."

"I'm assuming she got your coffee. And your lunch went well?" Mave asked while walking down the stairs with his laptop open keying something as he took the steps slowly, one by one.

"Mave! Watch out!" Luke yelled jokingly, knowing nothing was on the stairs in front of his friend.

Mave stumbled two steps down after the yell. His heel skimmed off the level he missed. Luke watched Mave grab his chest with his laptop-free hand and lean against the wall, attempting to prevent a heart attack. Eyeing the steps, he quickly realized there wasn't anything in his path, and the pounding heart was due to the lack-luster humor of his soon to be dead friend.

With zero playfulness, he turned to face Luke. "I'm going to fucking kill you."

He made the rest of the way down and perched his laptop on the kitchen island and hopped up next to it. Interested in hearing about the details of the date, he forgot about the steps.

"Honestly, she's stunning. Sexy, long hair. Sexy, long legs. Sexy and beautiful face."

"Does she also speak? Or is she more of a sexy, mute type?" Mave rolled his eyes.

"Sexy personality. And she speaks. And she laughs. And I'm still going to marry her. It wouldn't be a struggle to spend the rest of my life with Grace."

"Ah, Grace." Mave swiped the bag of Cheetos Luke had found. "You're even on a first-name basis. Impressive. Before you know it, you'll be living together, and she'll be changing the locks." He had tried to say it as a joke, but the bitterness crept in.

So, Mave was still bothered. Luke thought maybe after a couple of months he would have gotten over the breakup, but the sting must be sticking around.

"When you meet Grace, you'll know what I mean." Curious about the status of the ex-girlfriend, he thought it appropriate to pry since the subject had come up. "You talked to Kat since the lockout?" he said casually, toying with a pen that was sitting on the island.

Mave drew his eyes away from the conversation and tossed the Cheeto bag back in Luke's direction. He began to get up and walk away, offering little. "We sent a text or two after everything settled down." And back up the stairs he went.

A few moments of silence followed before Mave's voice trailed down the stairs. "Don't forget our meeting on Monday moved to seven. The morning, seven, not the evening one."

Fuck.

"Yeah, got it." Walking over, Luke leaned over the railing and yelled, "You're still working on those numbers, right?" More silence.

"Hey," Luke yelled up the stairs again.

"I heard you," Mave called back testily.

"Oh, I almost forgot, I need you to leave tonight. Grace is coming over for dinner."

"Dude, I hate you."

Luke huffed out a laugh at Mave's response. He knew Mave usually headed to his mom and step-dads' house for dinner unless he made other plans, which would have had him out of the house anyway. It saved him from feeling like a complete ass.

He lingered over the railing for a second and thought about Monday. Morning meetings were the worst. With only two more weeks of crunching the preliminary numbers his dad was going to be on edge. Luke knew his dad would need more than a simple forecast presentation for his idea to take hold – he needed to basically promise the future. And that would take a lot more work.

Looks like he'd be channeling Grace a bit with her early rising. Maybe he could leave her another note on a latte as he passed by the Bistro? He wondered if two times was too much, too close together? He thought on it a minute and decided he didn't care.

The slightly altered new mission couldn't leave any room for Grace to be anything but head over heels for him. It seemed he needed to even the playing field in the feelings department. Seeing as she had wholly enchanted him. He needed her to fall for him – and fall hard.

CHAPTER 20

The Bistro was alive with the scent of savory, flaky, pastries, French cheeses, crusty baguettes, and buttery crab bisque. Aimeé took it all in, breathing deep and closing her eyes to savor the moment.

She did this. Herself. All of it on her own. She didn't require her family's assistance and better yet, didn't have to go back – which would have been the case if she'd failed.

The happy chime of patrons coming and going reminded her she didn't have to linger on the bad what-ifs – or the burden of her family – and she definitely wouldn't let it ruin her mood.

"Where are you right now?" Casey asked, snapping Aimeé back to reality.

"Lost in the blissful scent of Bistro," Aimeé said, gracefully turning her attention back to her work.

"Your sex appeal is irritating," Casey said dryly while watching Aimeé dance a hand toward her face, wafting the smells.

"And yours, my friend – for as sexy as you are – is nonexistent."

"Don't I know it. You wouldn't want to share a bottle of wine and some of those ham and cheese croissants, would you? If you can pull yourself away from your desk? And why is your desk so clean?" Casey said with friendly annoyance as she swiped a finger along the edge, not finding a hint of dust.

Casey's desk probably didn't have dust either. But that's because there were too many papers, pens, notepads, stray cords, and Mountain Dew bottles strewn about for dust to settle.

Aimeé's desk sat in the back of the kitchen and looked more like an antique vanity than a desk. It had detailed, intricate legs and rounded corners. The one piece of France she had brought with her.

"That sounds wonderful." Aimeé stood. "Let me go see about a table. Ours might not be available. Try one of those chestnut éclairs. Something in the weather told me they'd be perfect for Fall." Aimeé's hand waved behind her in a motion that seemed eloquent and utterly European.

"I'll try one!" Rachel sang as she entered the kitchen and their conversation. "And you two," she pointed from Casey to Aimeé, "have explaining to do."

Rachel walked between the two and took a sample of the éclair, groaning at the light and creamy flavors.

"She has it." Aimeé mused to Casey as they watched Rachel eat.

"What do I have?" Rachel mumbled, her mouth full of pastry.

"Sex appeal," Casey answered for Aimeé. "It's irritating."

Rachel smacked her lips together and blew a kiss, then followed up with a perky, "Don't I know it. Do you ever have those days where everything feels good? Your hair curls just right, your jeans don't feel too tight, and – I don't know, I guess that's it – but it feels good." She smiled brightly at her friends.

"No."

"Yes." With her agreement, Aimeé walked away from the two to look for a table. They watched her walk out, and Rachel did a little bounce as she handed Casey an éclair and took a second for herself. Then she turned to Casey for her interrogation.

"I know you know more than you're telling me about Grace's date. I want to know who, how, and why."

Casey's eyes melted with the flavors in her mouth.

"Oh my God, this is to die for," Casey agreed.

"Right. I don't know how she does it."

"Lots of butter," Aimeé confirmed when she walked back in. "We have our choice of table – in or out?"

"Out." The girls said in unison, and they filed out on the right side of the heavy, two-way French door.

"Great. Our order is already in, and wine is heading to the table," Aimeé said as the girls stood with their bodies facing each other and heads leaning slightly back, their eyes closed in pastry heaven.

"I love you," Casey confessed without looking up.

"I know. Now let's get Rachel drunk, so she goes easier on you. She's the happy-drunk type. And Rachel," Aimeé added as Rachel reached for a third éclair before making it out of the kitchen, "if you leave some for the kitchen staff I'll make you a box to take home."

"I love you, too," Rachel said through a mouthful of sweet dough.

The wine was waiting for them at the table with vibrant green salads on simple black plates.

"I don't know how we survived without this place," Rachel admired as she took out her phone and snapped a picture. She picked up the red blend and smiled as she swirled it in front of her face. "My favorite. You are trying to butter me up. Not gonna work. You owe me an explanation. You two shared an *oh shit* moment yesterday when Grace said his name was Luke. Now spill and tell me about this not so mysterious date."

"Oh, my God." Casey slunk down in her chair and hid behind a dessert menu, ignoring Rachel.

"Amazingly enough, I can still see you." Rachel smiled.

"Yes," Casey whispered, "but he can't."

Both of the girls turned to see an extremely attractive man with rust-red hair walking in their direction.

"Case, who is he?" Rachel asked, "He is ca-ute."

"He is obnoxious. And, obnoxiously attractive. Don't make eye contact."

A minute passed in silence.

"Is he gone? He's not terrible, but he drills his stupid blue eyes into me and makes stupid jokes and tries to hit-"

"Well, at least I'm not terrible." The baritone voice cut off Casey's words.

Casey peeked over the menu and slowly slid it away from her face, thankful she didn't finish her sentence.

"How long have you been here? How long has he been here?" Casey was mortified. This was as much their fault as his.

"Apparently," he began, taking the lead, and grinning at the staring duo sitting next to Casey, "I'm obnoxious."

"That long?" Casey rolled her eyes and hissed to Rachel and Aimeé, "You two are no help."

"How may we help you, sir?" Aimeé batted her black eyelashes and offered a hand.

"No." Casey swatted Aimeé's hand away. "You will not sex-appeal him."

"Aimeé, Rachel, this is Travis Mavens. Travis, this is Aimeé and Rachel. And you're interrupting our wine."

"I think he's okay to stay for a bit. Travis, would you like to join us?" Rachel asked, taking all the pleasure she could in Casey's rare moment of discomfort.

"He can't," Casey said, more of a plea than a statement.

"I'd love to." He slid up a chair, ignoring Casey.

"They're having dinner tonight," Travis continued, speaking mostly to Casey, but kept the other two in the conversation.

"Of course they are." Casey rolled her eyes and took a sip of her wine.

"What do you mean, 'of course?'" said Aimeé, confused. She looked from Travis to Casey and back. "He's talking about Grace, right? We know she's going out with Luke, why 'of course?'"

"Yes." Casey agreed they were in-fact talking about Grace.

"Just, yes." Aimeé made a flat line with her hand for emphasis, slightly irritated with the minimal bit of information. "Can you start from the beginning? Apparently, there are fascinating details that even I do not know."

"Sure," Travis agreed.

"Not you." Casey pointed an accusatory finger at Travis, then sighed and turned to Rachel first, then Aimeé.

"Travis hired me at Wallace as their technology consultant," she began. "I would have refused, but they offered me too much money for the simple job. Sorry, it's true," she added, addressing Travis' squinting eyes. "So, I agreed. After spending some time around the office, I noticed Luke. And I kept thinking he might find Grace appealing, and vice versa. I put some of their attributes into my matchme.com algorithm, and from what I saw, it seemed like a great fit. They appeared to be ninety-six percent compatible. So-"

"Wait. You *wrote* the algorithm to the matchme.com questionnaire?" Travis said incredulously, feeling a bit uncomfortable knowing he'd filled out the same questionnaire and had a profile on the site. He'd matched with Kat, his ex, two years earlier.

"She wrote the whole company." Aimeé nonchalantly confirmed, to move the story along, and Rachel simply nodded as if this was common knowledge.

"You *created* matchme.com?" Travis was still staring, trying to wrap his mind around this.

"Yes," Casey said clearly, nodding her head with a look that said *did you not just hear what she said?*

"Anyway," Casey went on, "I might have briefly mentioned something about Grace while at their office, and before too long Travis asked me to set the two of them up. Aimeé thought it was a good idea."

"It was a man and a woman together. Drinking. Of course, Aimeé thought it was a good idea. I would have told you it was a good idea, too, if you'd have asked me." Rachel said defensively, folding her arms to pout in disapproval.

"No, you wouldn't have," Aimeé said flatly.

"Yes, I would," Rachel insisted. "It's the one thing we promised her mom we would do. Why wouldn't I?"

Rachel couldn't help but feel a little confused – and hurt – they left her out of the loop. Why did her friends think she wouldn't want to keep her promise to Mrs. Thomas?

Travis watched their conversation fly across the table, swinging his eyes from Rachel, to Aimeé, and back.

"I can't tell you," Aimeé said, leaning back and crossing her long legs.

"You're kidding." Rachel said.

"Can I tell them?" Casey asked Travis, wondering if talking about Wallace's intent to purchase Thomas and Jane was common knowledge.

"It's probably not a good id-"

"They'll be fine," Casey reassured him, waving her hand. She decided to answer her own question, cutting him off. She turned to face Rachel, who weeks earlier had innocently agreed to the setup without knowing *who* they were setting Grace up with. "Aaron Wallace is the one trying and acquire Thomas and Jane. Luke is his son."

"Say that one more time." Rachel said, knowing she must have heard that wrong.

"How do you know that?" Travis eyed Casey, asking about the purchase, not the familial relationship. Now it was his turn to be surprised.

"Extra security, extra privacy. Huge data pulls. Other things." Casey decided she'd quit while ahead. "Besides, it's the Aaron Wallace track record. Acquire small, very competitive competitors. You've got it down to a science. The best model I've seen.

"Do you see what I did there?" Casey asked Rachel and Aimeé, "I gave him a compliment so it would take longer for him to come up with an angry response because his brain thinks it should be a good one."

"I'm right here," Travis said, reminding her he was still at the table. But, he admitted to himself, he was having a difficult time coming up with any response, much less an angry one.

"Let me get this straight." Rachel rubbed her temple and set down her wine glass with a dainty clink. "You willingly set up Grace with the man who is going to ultimately force her out of a job? I thought this was just some date. I was excited yesterday. Now she'll think I was in on it."

"Jesus." Was all Travis could say.

"Brilliant." Aimeé was much more impressed. "I definitely would have still agreed to that."

"You sound like Luke." Travis grinned.

"Drama sex is better than regular sex."

"Not so much like Luke on that one, but I'm sure he'd find it hard to disagree," Travis said with a laugh.

"You were right," Rachel said after a quiet pause. "I definitely would have disagreed."

CHAPTER 21

The wardrobe in Grace's vast walk-through closet was meticulously organized. Blouses, sweaters, jeans, skirts, dresses, and shoes. Grace's hand skimmed the sleeves of her shirts as she walked, wondering what she should wear. Dinner at his place. After an over-three-hour lunch.

She'd indulged in a long afternoon nap, waking to the Fall sun streaming through her window. She made herself an afternoon coffee and started the process of getting ready. It wasn't hard for her to admit she liked the fuss, the detail, that went into the process. She loved the amount of preparing and caring that went into a date – not necessarily the date itself, until now. Sure, she didn't have a great dating track record, but it didn't mean she didn't try and knock 'em dead by making herself up for the occasion.

Casual, definitely, but not too much, she mused as she studied the clothes that hung patiently and dutifully in front of her. Jeans, dark and skinny. A low-cut black sweater that cinched and cropped at her waist. Then, she moved to the end of the closet and stared at the wall of shoes. She picked out a pair of gold heels, as they'd go perfectly with her slightly oversized hoop earrings.

Now for the real challenge. Grace placed her clothes on the bed and walked to her dresser. How much of her clothing was she willing to let him see?

Grace opened the top drawer and sifted through the delicate fabric inside. She smiled when she held up the cream-colored lace with just a hint of gold thread sparkling through. It didn't matter if he saw them or not, she thought. She loved them, and they made her feel sexy. Like she had her own little secret. At the end of the night maybe she'd share it with him, or maybe not.

Satisfied with her appearance, she made her way down from her room, coffee in one hand, fabulous gold heels looped in the other. Grace replaced the coffee with an unopened bottle of red. What they'd eat for dinner was a mystery, but she'd waited a long summer of fresh, crisp whites, to savor a bold red with the cooler weather.

She gathered her bag and, wine bottle in hand, she happily stepped out into the crisp air and warm sun.

The walk was her favorite part of living downtown. She could think, stare, and wonder about people's lives as they made their own way. Except, she thought as she looked down at her buzzing bag, when it was interrupted by her ringing phone. She eyed the caller ID and smiled tenderly.

"Hi, Mom."

"Hi, Gracie, what are you up to? I was calling to see if you'd want to come over for dinner and an old movie? Maybe stay the night?" The sound of her mother's voice was like warm caramel hugging her soul.

A night in with Mom, curled up on the couch with popcorn and blankets, probably watching Tom Hanks and Meg Ryan navigate love in the cutest way, then drifting off or retiring to her childhood bed.

"That sounds like my kind of night, but," She dragged it out just a bit. "I am actually on my way to a date."

"With a man?" Her mom squealed, her excitement was evident.

"Yes, with a man." Grace beamed, laughing with the sound of her mom's giggles through the phone.

"You call your girls nights 'dates' all the time, so I had to make sure I was excited for the right reasons." Lydia Thomas gained control of herself and got serious, "Well?"

Grace knew the *well* all too well. Her mom, always the romantic, wanted the details.

"What if I asked for a rain check? Tomorrow night I can come over and give you all the details?" Maybe not *all* the details, she thought, as she felt her confidence and lace while walking down the street.

"I think that sounds wonderful. Now, is he nice? Some things just can't wait, and moms need to know," Mrs. Thomas pressed, but Grace could hear the smile in her voice.

Grace sighed. "He's so nice, mom. So nice and funny. You'll enjoy that his grandma is his favorite person."

"Oh, I do like that."

The silence was brief but long enough for Grace to notice the street lamps come to life.

"Okay, tell me. Is he cute?" Lydia asked.

She knew it was coming. Her whole life, her mom would ask how dates went, and she'd lead off with how cute, or how handsome – or not – a man was. Her mom would tell her that it was not the most important thing about a man. So, they'd go over all of the personal details, then end up back to how cute he was and laugh that excited laugh only a crush and the belief in love could bring.

"He is. Oh, God, Mom. He is unbelievably handsome. He's tall and lean. He has this long jaw, but then he smiles, and these dimples show and his eyes light up. I would have remembered his face, the whole thing, if I'd never seen him again," Grace gushed.

"Just like your father. I remember that feeling. I'm so happy for you, Gracie. I'll let you go, but remember."

"Be safe." She finished the words for her mom.

"That's my girl. Okay, I'll see you tomorrow, then."

"See you. And love you, Mom."

"Love   you,   too."

CHAPTER 22

This is why he didn't cook. This is why restaurants existed.

How did people do this? The house had been cleaned, groceries purchased, candles lit – and he was exhausted. Then, rather than a nap, he had to start cooking – and it's damn good he did – because the prep had taken the rest of the afternoon. Luke kissed any chance of relaxation goodbye after his attempt at picking up his bedroom. It didn't help that he kept imagining Grace in it with him. He wasn't necessarily planning on them ending up there, but he'd be lying to himself – and mother nature – if he claimed he hadn't imagined what it would be like having Grace beneath him at least one hundred times since they met.

Now here he was with his sleeves rolled up, sweating his ass off in the kitchen, trying to make something called coq au vin. Why would he think that was remotely possible? And why, he asked himself, did he decided to make this? Because Mave was an asshole.

"Make coq au vin," Luke mumbled to himself, "*It'll impress the girl,* he said. *She'll be head over heels before dessert,* he said. What a dick."

At least he had the sense to buy some of those awesome crème brûlées from the Bistro for dessert. So, he was confident in precisely one thing they would eat that night.

He'd drenched the chicken in wine, chopped the vegetables, cooked the bacon, seared the chicken, sautéed the onion and garlic, and loaded it all into a giant pot his mom had gotten him years ago. It might have been the first time using it, but the smells coming from it were pretty damn good if he said so himself.

Luke eyed the recipe and what seemed to be step number thirty-five and cursed Julia Child for her existence. It might not be appropriate to drink before your date arrived but, desperate times. Grace would arrive in about twenty minutes, he assessed, as he snagged the left-over wine that hadn't been used on the chicken and started pouring his glass. Quick and effective.

The living and dining rooms were the cleanest, and if he admitted it, the prettiest it had ever been. At the Bistro, Aimeé had given him some simple, attainable, advice: flowers and candles on the table. He'd done a little extra and added some little – what did they call them? Votives – to the coffee table and mantle, too. The piney, musky, fireside scent he'd picked out for the candles didn't seem too girlie – it was even a bit manly, he thought.

The knock on the door came too early. Luke's stomach flipped, a mixture of nervousness and anticipation. Well, he thought as he took a sip, he was as ready as he was ever going to be. A deep breath and he swung open the door.

"Wow." It was all his brain could process. She was unreal.

"Wow, yourself," came her sultry response.

"I just...would it be too forward if I-" Luke hesitated for only a moment before he stepped toward her. With his free hand he cupped side of her face and touched his lips to hers. Her fragrance filled him. Her lips were soft. The combination nearly killed him.

It was simple and sweet, but Grace felt every part of her body heat in response. When Luke pulled his head away ever so slightly, he grinned, and her knees felt weak.

"Hello," he said.

"Hello," she replied softly. And with that, she knew she was his. She was falling for him in a way she never knew was possible. She had never experienced this kind of attraction before – and was becoming certain she never would with another man again.

Luke didn't take the bottle from her hand. Instead, he held out his hand for her free one. Their fingers laced as they had the night they met, and he led her through the door.

The clean, dark lines of the condo were all man. Gray walls wrapped around an open kitchen, dining, and living room. Grace had noted on the elevator that she was brought to the top floor. She just hadn't realized she'd be on the entire top floor. Windows surrounded her and, for reasons other than sleeping with Luke, she wanted to relish this room in the morning as the sun came up. She could imagine the pink and orange rays reflecting and bouncing off the Minneapolis skyline.

As her gaze traveled from corner to corner, she saw the candles glowing around the room. A vase was overflowing with a mixture of white flowers and big leafy greens. It was precious.

And romantic. It was, she mused, something she would have done. It was beautiful.

"It's perfect in here. I love every detail. And that smell." Grace turned and started for the kitchen. "It is heavenly. What is that?"

Maybe he wouldn't kill Mave after all, he thought, noting the impressed tone of her voice as she peered into the oven.

"It's called coq au vin. And not at all spelled like it sounds. Google made me feel slightly inferior when it suggested the correct spelling."

"Who cares how it's spelled," she said as she wandered farther into the kitchen. "With a smell like that, it can be spelled however it wants. You made this?"

"I did. But I feel I should confess, not a whole lot normally happens in this kitchen aside from takeout, reheats, and frozen pizza."

"I had you for a takeout kind of guy," Grace said, curving the edge of her lip up ever so wryly. "I should warn you, I tend to try and use my kitchen as much as I can. Usually, for new recipes – not all of them work out," she admitted, recalling some of her failed experiments. "But I like moving around after work in my own space. I love my home, and I love being in it. It's my comfort. And, I don't feel bad about pouring a nice glass of wine while I'm at it."

He could imagine her there. Casually moving about. Long hair tied back. Relaxed. Dicing, stirring, sipping. She always seemed casual, or at ease, when he imagined her. Did she say 'warn me' as in…

"Warn me?" Luke asked as he handed her a glass of wine from the bottle she'd set on the island. "As in, you're warning me, so I know what I'm getting myself into? As in, you might be interested?"

The smart way he spoke amused her, and she wondered if there would come a time when he would stop trying to charm her. There was only one way to find out.

"As in, you are very interesting to me," she demurred, her eyes sparkling.

"Interesting enough to continue to date me?"

"I think I would like to date you," Grace confirmed, nodding agreement to herself as much as Luke, sipping her wine.

"Do you dance?"

Grace eyed him curiously, one eyebrow raised. "Is it a dating prerequisite?"

"No." He moved to her, set her wine on the counter, and pulled her in. "I just needed an excuse to get close to you."

There was no music, but she didn't need any. Luke swayed, and she followed.

Grace leaned back to look at him when he pulled her hand in to gently press his lips to it. The hand resting on her lower back was sending goosebumps up and down the length of her body. She'd never wish a man to be indecent or too forward, but at this moment she longed for him to make a move. She wanted his hand to inch its way up and down. Lust was taking her over. She wanted him to feel what she was feeling. How was he able to be this close and not want?

Grace moved her body into his, her curves pressing against him.

The swaying movements slowed, and his eyes darkened as they looked into hers.

"Grace." His voice was throaty and low.

"Luke."

"I'm not going to be able to keep my gentlemanly control if we keep at this."

"It was your idea." She pressed closer yet and felt his control waning, her need pulsing inside.

"I haven't had a bad idea yet," he whispered, his breath on her neck.

He let her hand go only to surround her entirely with his arms. When their lips met, their bodies were already melted together. She so willing to give and he willing to take.

Her lips tasted like wine as he slowly savored them. He fought to move slowly as she gently nibbled his lip. The groan came from his growing need for her, and his hands followed. They roamed her back and teasingly down her body. He wanted more. He wanted all of her. If they didn't stop now, he'd lose all of his control. And most of his dignity.

Grace's heart raced, and the ache deep within her throbbed as she felt his hand slide toward her crease just below her bottom. Dangerously close to the center of the ache.

Her sultry moan yearned for him.

At the sexy sound, control was lost, and his dignity be damned. Luke paused for just a moment to look at her to see any sign of hesitation in her eyes. All he saw was the most beautiful woman he'd ever seen. She was staring back at him, radiating confidence mixed with desire. Her grin, a sensual victory she'd won. It was all the confirmation he needed.

His lips crashed into hers, devouring, taking. When she parted, his tongue sought.

Desire matched desire. His arms tightened around her, engulfing her in his need, driving her hunger and yearning to places she'd never known. She wanted him, needed him to give her release.

Grace's hand hunted for the buttons of his shirt as she rushed to remove the barrier.

As she worked, his lips found her neck and feasted on the delicate angles that led to her chest. Where the deep-v of her sweater blocked his way to the crease, he slid his hands beneath it, grazing her soft skin as he lifted it from her slim, silky body.

Luke stared. Had to take her in. She was a vision. The light pale of her skin matching the lace that covered the small, supple rounds of her breasts.

She let him stare as she removed his shirt, one arm after the other. Her hands were warm with desire as she loosened the button and zipper of his jeans and slid them down. He couldn't touch, not yet. Watching her body move and sway had him entranced as she removed her own jeans and let them fall to the floor.

The air was thick between them, and he parted it with a step to her. His hands rounded the curves of her body, drew the lines from her breasts to her hips. Then soft kisses replaced the trail of heat from his hands as they moved. When her body felt the need to arch, she leaned her head back and yearned for him to be inside of her. She parted her legs and braced against the island, her vivid eyes and racing heart pleading for him to enter.

When Luke's body straightened his face leveled with hers, he caressed and held the delicate edges of her face and brought his forehead to hers, he breathlessly whispered to her, "Let me take you upstairs."

Grace's fingertips grazed his chest and down his torso until they found the edge of his briefs. Two fingers played beneath the band, skimming too close for any control. She slid the briefs down, and he bound to freedom. Her warm hands skimmed, feeling the bumps they left in their wake as they maneuvered around, pulling him closer. They teased and tantalized, ignoring his words and the offering of a more comfortable setting. When she found him in her hands, she leaned in, so his most sensitive part grazed the texture of the cream lace. Her head tilted up, and she whispered in return.

"Luke, I want you now." Confidence and hunger strained her soft voice.

It was a fierce craving he'd never known; never knew could exist. Luke was hypnotized by her movements, bewitched by her voice, and straining for control with every move she made.

"Grace," was all he said as he lifted her to the counter. Her hands dove into his hair and pulled him into a frenzied kiss. Her fire filled his hands, and the damp he felt as his hand slid between her outmatched his restraint. He couldn't wait a moment longer. Luke slid the soft, cream-colored lace aside and filled her in a hard, demanding thrust.

Their moans of pleasure encouraged and reassured the heavy, quickening pace. There would be a time for slow, fragile love-making, but it wasn't now. The yearning was simply too much.

"Faster." Grace begged, needing more.

Luke obeyed and their bodies collided in miraculous pleasure. The rhythm and pace excruciating; the sensations, unimaginable.

His eyes fought to watch her, but the ecstasy coursing through his veins clouded his vision in a lust-filled haze. The insurmountable gratification was nearly too much as he plummeted into the deepest part of her.

Grace felt her need building and building. He filled her until she required release. At her peak, she let go – and the explosion of pleasure ripped through her.

The wet sensation engulfed him, and he came gloriously. Relief flooded his body in sweet liberation.

"Wow," Grace said when she could finally speak again, mimicking the words she'd heard when he met her at the door.

"Right back at you."

CHAPTER 23

The table was set, more wine was poured, and a new hunger took them over.

Luke's button-down shirt draped loosely from Grace's slender body. Sweatpants had replaced his jeans, and his blue undershirt was his new top. They'd accomplished what their original attire had set out to achieve; now it was time for comfort and enjoyment.

They ate their starters in silence. They exchanged flirty smiles over bites of salad and sips of wine, playfully eyeing each other, gleaming; languishing in the wake of their passion.

Luke offered more drink with a gesture to the bottle that sat between them, and Grace responded with an eyebrow raise and a slow nod.

He'd miscalculated her again, he mused as he filled her glass. He had anticipated straight-laced and stuffy. Buttoned-up and serious. What he'd gotten was willing and spontaneous. And, as he'd just experienced, unexpected and undeniably sexy.

It wasn't surprising to him that he was captivated by Grace or that he wanted to know more about her – everything about her. He realized he wanted to understand why she loved her job so much, and why she was so successful at it, but not because of his initial intentions.

He wanted to know more in the same way a couple shared stories of their day over dinner; how it would come up in casual conversation due to two lives that had intermingled and become invested and interested.

Not just the business details, Luke realized. He wanted everything. He wanted to know and see Grace and her cool, casual, and comfortable in a different environment. He wanted to see her leading a boardroom discussion, talking a group of leaders through a round of strategic planning, or meeting with a client. He would bet everything he owned that he'd find it pretty damn sexy. Okay, stop now, he ordered himself. He'd get the chance to see her in action soon enough. And they'd cross that bridge when they got there.

Grace paused as she noticed Luke stop and stare. Her head leaned slightly to the left, questioning, but not willing to break the silence.

Yeah, he was a goner.

"How about the main course?" Luke asked as he lifted the top off the pot and thick, savory steam billowed out. "If we eat, you'll have a harder time catching me in my next daydream. Guys aren't supposed to do that because we are macho," he said, displaying seriousness.

Grace inhaled a laugh and let her eyes feast on the culinary brilliance. "You can be whatever you want if you cook like this."

"We haven't tasted it yet." Luke was still wary of the outcome of his culinary attempt.

"There is no way that doesn't taste good," Grace said, pointing at the steaming, fragrant food.

"You're good at pumping the ego. Is that how you operate things at work?"

"You assume I operate things?" Grace questioned, setting her glass down and smiling.

"Just a hunch." He shrugged, dished their plates, and reminded himself to be careful. He now had more to lose than just a good business deal. "Tell me about it, the job. You light up when you talk about it. That's not an accountant's normal reaction to work."

"Are you telling me you don't love your job?" she teased.

"You're telling me that you do?" His response was quick.

"Oh, my God. Hold on." Grace reveled in the sensations of her first bite. "I can't respond. This is so good. Just," she held up a finger, "whatever you want me to say, imagine that I said it and respond accordingly. This is nirvana."

"I can't tell you what I'm imagining, because the food moans you're making are sending my brain to round two of our kitchen scene."

"This is worth round two, and probably three," she said, taking another bite.

He was definitely going to owe Mave. And why the hell was he thinking about Mave with an intoxicating half-dressed woman in his kitchen?

"Okay," Grace said when she had regrouped. "I think I can manage conversation now. But don't be surprised if it's in one to two-word sentences to start."

"That's good, I'm in a bit of recovery mode myself." Luke worked his mind and wandering eyes away from the island that would never be the same. "How about start with where you work?"

Shit. He nearly flinched at his stupid question. Her natural response would be to ask him the same – a topic he was not ready to delve into just yet.

"I work at Thomas and Jane LLC. It's a private accounting firm in the city."

His next question came out almost before she had finished. "I've heard of it. What do you do there?"

"I'm the CEO and acting president."

"I knew you'd have to be impressive. Anything less wouldn't have suited you." He would have said it for conversation, for charm, before he knew her, he thought. But now he realized he meant it.

"I think I got it from my dad." Grace continued, the pride gleaming in her eyes.

"Tell me what he's like."

"Oh, he," she started, folding her hands in her lap, "I don't think I told you last night. He passed away last October."

Luke saw that the hurt was indeed still fresh. But he noted her dignity in being strong. He found himself respecting the man he wished he knew. He had wondered how she was handling it. The word had gotten around in their small accounting world that Raymond Thomas had passed away. He was known just as admirably by his competitors as he had been by his friends.

"No," he said. "I'm sorry, I just assumed. I shouldn't have."

Her smile was faint but genuine. She circled her glass of wine on its end and watched the red liquid swirl in the curved glass.

"He was," her shoulders lifted and fell in a sigh, "everything. Not just to me. I mean to everyone. He was a dad, a husband, a friend, one of the guys. He was," she paused thoughtfully, "all of the roles a person could be, and he was the best at them all."

She stopped to take a sip, then continued. "He worked so hard during the day, and late nights too, I suppose. When I went to work for him – with him – it was like getting to work with your idol. He was my hero. You always knew where you stood with him." Her lips curved upward, and her eyes misted. "If he loved you, you knew it. I never once had to question his love. It was always there. It was my comfort and my safety net."

"He sounds like the best." Luke felt for her – wanted to reach out to her. He could see how genuine her love and admiration for her father had been.

"He was. And now that you've got me crying on a date," Grace said with a small chuckle, sniffing and quickly blotting the corners of her eyes. "I'd like you to tell me about you so I can recover and attempt to save my mascara. It's supposed to impress you, not smudge around my face and scare you away." She cleared her throat, changing the subject back to him. "So why accounting?" she asked, trying to shift the conversation off of herself so she could regain composure.

"Isn't it obvious? The ladies."

It made her laugh, and she appreciated him for it.

"Naturally," she bantered while wiping an eye with the back of her hand.

"I guess a little of the dad thing, like you. But I thought my dad was James Bond, wearing fancy suits every day. There was no way he dressed like that to go to a boring desk job. He would leave in the morning and come home acting like he'd conquered the world. And to him, I guess he was. He lives for his job."

Luke paused to take a bite of his own dinner and was pleasantly surprised. He had to say, he nailed it. Take that, Julia Child, he thought triumphantly.

"I started saying to my mom, 'I'm gonna 'countant,' and she'd laugh, and now I know what she was laughing at – knowing full-well what I was signing up for. Luckily, when I realized I wasn't going to team up with Halle Barry to save the world, I ended up liking the challenge of balancing, audits, financial reports, and forecasting. You can see a business unfold in the numbers. It became a fun game. I was good at it. And if I hadn't been, Dad wouldn't have given me a job there, even the unpaid intern role he made me start in."

He realized as he spoke that he loved it, too. Even on the terrible days. He raised his glass to Grace. It might have been cheesy, but he couldn't help it.

"To doing what we love with the ones we love."

The gesture and the sentiment was sweet. Grace clinked her glass to Luke's and echoed him. "What we love with whom we love."

"Speaking of what and whom," Luke asked as he sipped. "What are your thoughts on dessert and a movie?"

"I have many thoughts on those topics, most of them good."

"Most? It's dessert and a movie. Are we going to have our first fight?" he said playfully.

"Only if you don't have an extra pair of sweatpants I can borrow."

"I often watch movies in the nude." He made the suggestion seriously.

"Nice try."

"It was worth a shot for round two."

He made his way up the stairs to dig out some sweatpants for her, as she started to clear the dishes. He was thankful she didn't see him stop in his tracks at her next comment.

"We might have time round two."

Grace chuckled to herself as she heard him pause and make a slight trip up the next step. He might be able to melt her heart, but she wasn't above making him a little hot in return.

CHAPTER 24

Two mornings after their coq au vin date, Grace woke to the Fall sun warming her childhood room through the window. The feeling of fresh, morning sheets and the warmth of the bed surrounded her.

She laid there and reminisced about what had to have been one of the best weekends of her life. Three dates. Not counting an amazing, lounge-y, and incredibly sexy breakfast in bed. Then, a night with the best mom a girl could ask for, and ended with a sweet goodnight message from Luke. If he intended to have her falling asleep thinking about him, he had succeeded.

Thoughts of their night together replayed in her mind. She went over every detail, every fragment. All of them made her grin. Even the heartfelt way he'd asked about her dad. He made her laugh. Her mom always said laughter is what gets two people through the bad times, makes the normal times great, and the best times magical. Of course, she was right. And because of it, she felt herself falling fast. She'd be lying if she said her mind didn't drift in his direction more often than not.

Grace rolled to her phone that was charging on the nightstand where she'd left it, and where it had sat throughout high school and college. She'd had a giant brick of a phone that her parents made her wait until 11th grade to get. Grace remembered how cool she felt, and even more so when her parents let her upgrade to a flip phone as a graduation present. Grace shook her head now as she looked at the latest model that she, and what seemed like the rest of the world, needed to survive. When she saw Luke had beat her to a morning wake-up message, her heart skipped a beat.

"Because my mind seems to slip to you first thing in the morning, I thought I'd be the first to say good morning and happy vacation Monday. Also, waking up next to you is better than waking up not next to you. Now imagining you in bed. Must get up to take a cold shower." Grace read the text aloud and laughed. She found she was always smiling and laughing when it came to Luke. Grace couldn't believe she'd finally found a man that gave her a feeling of constant joy. She prayed he never wanted to stop.

"Good morning, to you, too," she tapped out on the screen. "Was just thinking it would be nice to have you in bed with me. Was also thinking," she spoke as her fingers flew, "I wonder if Luke likes pizza?"

The light knock on her door reminded her where she was. Grace let the hint of nostalgia at the sound rush over her.

"Hi, Mom. Come in."

Lydia Thomas was a beautiful woman. Her once-blonde hair, which had been the same golden shade that Grace's was now, had slowly become white. Her frame was long and lean, leaving no doubt Grace was her mother's daughter. Eyes green and steady. Though, Grace thought, more playful in her later years. It seemed the worry had left them. They had found a bright and carefree glint that had been missing.

Grace wondered when that had happened? When had her mom transitioned from widowed mother to a beaming, and quite attractive, woman again? It flooded her with relief and added to her already good day.

"What is this smiling face for?" Lydia asked as she sat on the side of the bed.

"You're a knockout, Mom."

Lydia laughed and ignored her faint blush.

"I assumed it was due to the new handsome gentleman you've been swooning after." Lydia appreciated the attention but didn't care for it. So, she'd shifted the conversation.

"Swooning? And yes, that might be part of it." Grace sighed happily.

"It's swooning because this Luke of yours is making you giddy and it seems you may be on the verge of emotional involvement." Lydia's eyebrows raised, her emerald eyes gleamed knowingly.

"Emotional involvement," Grace repeated her mom's words. "Dating sounds cuter."

"Dating it is. Have any plans this morning?"

"I thought I'd share a cup of coffee with you. Maybe we could convince Aimeé to mix us up a latte and a good breakfast at the Bistro. Something Fall-y. Would you want to come?"

"It sounds wonderful, but I think I might walk to the club and circle the gym a couple times. Then pretend I'm somewhere tropical while sitting in the sauna."

"Now that – the sauna part," Grace said to be clear, "sounds wonderful."

"You could join me," Lydia offered.

"Not that wonderful."

The two laughed, and Lydia swept a hand across Grace's cheek as she had since she was young.

"My girl. You make my world go 'round."

"Love you, Mom."

"Love you, too, sweetie. See you downstairs.

CHAPTER 25

Randy Flamingo was the scum of the earth. Unfortunately, he was a fucking smart scum of the earth. At least as far as Luke was concerned.

Fucking Flamingo.

Luke walked into the office at what was at least a quarter before seven, yet here was Randy, buttering up Luke's dad. He was probably telling him to bend over so he could kiss his ass, Luke thought, annoyed just at the sight of his smarmy coworker.

Luke heard Mave walk up behind him and stop to stand next to him. The two peered at Aaron Wallace's office from where they stood alone. All other offices and the mass of cubicles behind them were empty at the early Monday morning hour.

Their heads peeked out over one of the cubicle walls closest to the massive corner office, looking like they were participating in a game of whack-a-mole. Sure, the spying was pathetic, but Luke needed time to build up his anger.

Luke's dad was certainly not a dumb man. Aaron Wallace just had a particular and calculated way of doing things

– not unlike Grace, he thought, letting his mind dally before snapping his attention back to the task at hand. Luke knew if his dad was listening to Randy blow rainbow hearts up his ass, there had to be a reason.

The two spies watched Randy and Wallace shake hands, right before his dad held his stomach in a belly laugh. The act made Luke grin, but only because watching his dad hold his slightly too big belly as he laughed too hard always made his dad seem like a real person again.

At work, he was "Mr.," or "sir," or "Aaron" to those who had been working at the company long enough, or who Aaron respected enough to request it from. Luke's humor-filled eyes shifted to Randy, and all joy was lost. Disgust came over him. If his eyes could have rolled any farther, they would have been facing the cubes behind him.

"Fucking Flamingo," Mave muttered.

"Fucking Flamingo," Luke agreed, echoing his earlier thoughts and Mave's agreeable words.

Both of the men came out from hiding and began walking down the aisle of cubes, straightening their jackets and suit pants on the way, smoothing any lingering wrinkles. Mave stopped to drop his things off in his office before they continued on.

When they got to the door, his dad told them to come in before Mave even had a chance to knock. The boys filed in and stood at attention, Luke giving Randy a glowering look that he tried to cover with a tight smile.

"How's it going this morning, gentlemen? Let's sit down." Aaron gestured to the chairs that faced his broad Cherrywood desk as he took a seat in his high-backed leather office chair. He greeted his son and Mave nearly the same way every day. He said time and again that 'gentleman' was an essential term that allowed one man to greet another with courtesy and consideration.

"Not bad. You both look chummy this morning," Luke said, gesturing from Randy to Wallace. "Good news?" He tried to mask the irritation in his voice.

Randy spoke before Aaron could muster a methodical thought, blurting, "We are so ready we could begin the Thomas and Jane takeover process tomorrow. There is no way we won't profit immensely from this, long term. We need to stay the course and not ruffle any feathers. Stay the course." Randy added for emphasis, each word stated as if it was its own sentence. His hand irritatingly punctuated his words like karate chops.

Randy was a short, round man, who at one point probably didn't look bad. Somewhere along the line, he had let himself go, and time had not been kind. Time had actually slapped him in the face. A pathetic attempt at a comb-over tried to cover the glistening scalp on top of his head. He always missed shaving a patch of hair just below his nose which must have itched because at least ten times a minute Randy would fervently run his pointer finger back and forth beneath it, often resulting in a sneeze. Not just any sneeze either. An explosion. It usually caused new employees to look up, stunned, from their desks, wondering who was capable of that sound and questioning if they'd possibly get infected. And it left tenured employees just feeling bad for those who were within spitting distance.

Apparently, Randy had thought there was long enough pause. He repeated himself. "Stay the course. We've prepped the final numbers for the stock purchase, and we are ready to file the thirty-day acquisition."

"That's what I wanted to talk to you about." This was Luke's opening. "I know we typically don't deviate from the plan, but Mave – Travis," he corrected – it was damn hard having your best friend work beside you in business, "is working on forecast reports that currently show a huge benefit to a friendly acquisition, rather than a full wipeout. A wipeout takes time, people, and resources. As in huge dollars. We've seen those dollars."

He had to emphasis the cost. If his dad was anything, he was a penny-pincher and wouldn't allow for one morsel to go out that didn't have to. Strategy. It was how his dad became successful. Only spend what you make, but spend big on the biggest returns.

"Let's see what you've found, Travis," Aaron said, looking Mave's direction.

Mave sprang to action, "It's not quite finished yet, but when it is, I think you'll be impressed." He was moving to a chalkboard.

A chalkboard. Luke appreciated nostalgia, but a chalkboard? He'd never get over it. Probably because it was sitting right next to an enormous touchscreen TV that was meant to be interactive, display state-of-the-art presentations, and take the world over one meeting at a time. Instead, it played CNN or occasionally *The Price is Right.* Aaron did have a fun side.

"It's just not the same with old Bobby gone," Aaron would say. He and Bob Barker were on a first-name basis. Half the employees were too young to even know Bob Barker was the long-time game-show host.

Mave made it as far as picking up a broken piece of chalk before he was halted by Aaron's decisive, crisp tone.

"There isn't a point in showing me something that isn't complete. We have a well-oiled process that has worked time and again, and I promise you just showing me a concept won't do. If you want me to take what you're presenting seriously, finish it up, and have a more than impressive meeting with me when you're ready. I don't want to drag this out."

Mave quietly set the chalk down, pretending he'd never picked it up in the first place. Luke watched as Mave backpedaled to the chair next to his own and lowered himself.

"Yes, sir." They said in unison. It seemed all they could say.

It wasn't wrong or right. It was true: Wallace had perfected the takeover process, and to introduce an entirely different plan at this stage in the game was rocking the boat. They needed to come up with a complete business plan to convince Aaron that the friendly acquisition would be much more efficient than a hostile takeover. More efficient, and if he was right, extremely profitable in the long run.

The idea, purchase Thomas and Jane LLC and let it operate independently with the existing leadership. The only change would be funding for rapid growth.

This was going to be a busy damn week, Luke thought, after mentally walking through everything they'd need to have prepared by the end of the it. Visions of dates with Grace, Thursday night football with the guys, and fourteen-hour days at the office were already wiping him out and it wasn't even seven-thirty.

Hopefully, Grace got his message that he'd be a little late for dinner. What was better than pizza, beer, and the woman you loved? *You loved.*

Luke paused at the ease of his thought, wondering where it came from. He should probably keep that one to himself for a little while. Besides, if all things went according to plan — barring she didn't think he was crazier than usual after he asked — they'd have a fantastic weekend together.

He walked out of the office with Mave. "Ready for this helluva week?"

"Late nights and takeout at the office, throw a little football on the TV." Mave held out his fist toward Luke and added, "Except for pizza night, I know. You're spoiled already."

Luke pounded the fist with his own. "Don't I know it."

CHAPTER 26

Grace slid into the chair across from Casey in the Bistro. Casey was firing her fingers across her laptop keys and didn't stop typing when she looked up and grunted.

"Ugh, you have it, too."

"Did you just ugh?"

"Yes, I ugh'd."

"What for? And what do I have?" Grace chuckled, confused.

"One and the same. You have sex appeal."

"As a matter of fact," Grace leaned in and whispered. "It's because I've been sexed."

The keys fell silent, and Casey gave a sly smile. She slowly repeated the words.

"You've been sexed."

"I've been sexed," Grace confirmed, keeping her volume low.

"You've been sexed!" Casey exclaimed loud enough to reach across the room and get a cheer from Aimeé who was behind the espresso bar.

"Oh, my God. And now, I'm mortified." Grace covered her face as some of the surrounding tables cheered along in laugher and others smiled politely and pretended they didn't hear. She hoped, seeing as most were older, they didn't.

"I want to know everything." Casey ignored Grace's embarrassment.

Jimmy walked up to the table with a steaming white mug and plate full of thick, flakey, pastries. He sat them in front of Grace with a way-to-go shoulder-nudge.

"I'm going to kill you," Grace said across the table.

"Don't shoot the messenger," Jimmy said as he looked from Casey to Grace. "Proud of you, Grace."

They watched Jimmy saunter off, Grace wide-eyed and Casey smug.

"An eleven-year-old is proud of me," Grace said dully.

"He's a twenty-year-old college student in a relationship. He's getting laid more than this entire room combined." Casey paused briefly before adding, "If you don't include Aimeé."

"You have a point. He's certified to be proud of me. That's depressing. But this," Grace inhaled the latte, "is not. What is this?"

"I had one, too. You'll never be the same."

"It's a molasses and candied ginger latte." Aimeé slid into the chair next to Grace. "It's sophisticated and Fall." Her hand motioned out the window.

"It's to die for." Grace sipped and relished the full sweet, smoky, and just a bit bitter, flavor hitting her taste buds.

"Your Luke thinks so as well," Aimeé said with a grin.

Grace's eyes went soft with adoration. "He came here?"

"He did. Asked if you'd been in. He must know you're an early-riser, seeing as it was close to six when he came," Aimeé said, propping her chin on a fist.

The sigh wasn't exaggerated. "I'm swooning." Grace decided on her mom's word, after all.

"As you should be. I'm fond of him."

"Hold on there, sister, I ran into him first."

Aimeé laughed at Grace's fictive jealousy. "I'm fond of him because he is causing you to swoon – and contributing to business. He seems equally as fond of you."

"Isn't he amazing," Grace said. A statement, not a question. She couldn't deny she felt a bit spoiled by his initial wooing and attention. "I'm sure after time it will fade a little, but oh, it's so nice to be a little sought after."

"Did you say, 'after time?' As in, you're making a run at this?" Aimeé prodded.

Grace didn't need to pause, but she did. She leaned back, absently tracing the sides of her mug with her fingers, and thought about the cute guy she'd run into. The thoughtful man who'd bought her a coffee. The funnyman who had her laughing through a three-hour lunch date. The sexy man that nearly had her begging in the kitchen and, well, other places. The caring and sentimental man who'd asked about her dad. And the same man who couldn't entirely slip from her mind.

"Yes," she said finally. "For the first time in – oh my gosh – years, I want a man. I constantly want to see him. I always want to know where he is, what he's doing, what he's thinking. Even when we are together, I want more. His voice, his touch. Even if it's just sitting close to him on the couch, I want him to take my hand. It's insane." Now that she said it out loud, she knew she sounded a bit over-the-top, but continued on, "I can see myself with him. More than that, I want to see myself with him. I want to be with him."

Aimeé smiled over her own latte and thought, that's good because you're going to need all the want in the world to get through what he has in store for you. But she couldn't deny the happiness she held for her dear friend. It might get a bit messy on the business end, but she was excited. She had a good feeling.

"I'm sure," Grace continued, "eventually something about him will bug me. Maybe he'll leave his razor out on the counter or his socks on the floor. But even then, right now, at this moment, I want that."

"Oh, no doubt there will be disappointment," Casey said knowingly and received a kick from Aimeé along with a look of disapproval. "I mean, you know, eventually." Casey rubbed her shin.

"Disappointment is a strong word." Grace defended Luke. "I honestly don't believe that could happen. Not knowing what I know so far." She thought of his beautiful dark eyes, how they crinkled at the edges when he smiled at her that night after their collision in the street.

Casey simply raised her eyebrows and took a sip of coffee. She might be a pessimist, but she'd seen first-hand the fallout and disappointment her parents had caused for each other. That and she was starting to rethink this matchmaking idea. Grace was well on her way to falling in love, and Luke, from what Travis Mavens had mentioned, was already there.

Shit, Casey thought.

CHAPTER 27

The cool rain and wind splatted and whooshed on the windows. It seemed to try with all its might to break inside. Grace stood on the other side, in the warmth and quiet, next to the fire. The scent of salty pizza dough, parmesan, garlic, and fresh basil wafted throughout the house.

Luke, as it turned out, loved pizza and whatever kind of red, white, amber, or brown drink it came served with. He was a human – a living, breathing human – after all. Grace grinned at the texted response she'd received to her pizza-preferences question earlier that day and unfolded her arms to take a sip of her own red-colored drink.

A car service pulled up, framed by her window, and she looked out. Luke was laughing, head back, in the passenger seat of the car. Luke talked with the driver, or exchanged good-byes, she couldn't tell, then they shook hands, and he was running toward her door.

Grace started to head for the door when Luke saw her through the window and stopped. She mirrored his pause on the other side of the glass. In the middle of the rain, he stood, staring at her.

Luke lifted a dripping hand, waved, and sent her the most handsome, drenched grin she'd ever seen. He mouthed *hello,* and she felt her hand cover her heart in an instinctive reaction to it skipping a beat.

Then and there, for all of the unknown reasons, and the too little time they'd spent together, Grace fell in love. He defied her logic, her reason, and the countless other failed attempts at love.

—

"This is the best night of my life."

Luke murmured the words as he looked out the same window he'd been standing outside of just hours earlier. She was a picture of perfection in her loose checkered flannel, slightly baggy jeans, and hair tied back. As he had stood on the curb, he could see the lines of her face, the shadow of angled cheekbones, even through the haze of rain.

"The best?" Grace walked to him from the kitchen. "I'd like to do a quick run-through of your history of 'bests' to believe that."

She stood next to him and looked out.

"The best," he emphasized. "And it wouldn't take long. Nothing compares to the way I feel when I'm around you. There's never been anybody I've felt this way about."

Luke couldn't believe how comfortable he felt being open with her – not that he could help the words that seemed to spew from his mouth when he was around her. Grace had that effect on him. He needed – and wanted – to explain to her how she made him feel.

Luke turned to face her.

"What are you doing this weekend?" he asked, taking her free hand in his.

"I can't say I have any plans." She had figured she'd sleep in, maybe do another torturous-but-necessary three-mile run with the girls – followed, of course, by the reward of coffee – but nothing was set in stone.

"What would you say if I asked you to come away with me this weekend?" Luke asked, looking into her eyes.

The tilt of her head showed intrigue and a trace of mischief.

"I'd say Casey has me watching too many crime shows to wonder if this is the part where you kill me and 'nobody saw it coming.'" She said the last part with her rabbit-eared fingers making quotation marks.

Luke barely kept the beer he'd just sipped in his mouth. A snort, rather than liquid, came out, and he supposed in the long run that was better.

"I really didn't see that coming," he said, laughing and wiping his mouth with the back of his hand. "Of all the practice attempts I made asking you to come with me, I have to say, not one of your responses came close to that."

"That is surprisingly comforting." She liked being unpredictable, being able to surprise him. And knowing she wouldn't find her way to the local news wasn't bad either.

"And I guess, unless you think my grandma will bore you to death, you're probably safe."

"You're taking me on a romantic getaway...to your grandma's house?" Grace said, laughing skeptically, but touched by the fact that he clearly loved his family. That kind of close-knit family was exactly what she was searching for in life.

He thought about it.

"Though I didn't mention the romance, now that you say it like that, yes. Absolutely. Romantic getaway to Grandma's."

"Then I'm in." Grace grinned.

"You're in!" Luke clutched her face with both hands and kissed her.

He didn't have long enough to appreciate his next thought, the happy realization that he could kiss her anytime he wanted, before the warmth seeped in and desire started to take over.

Luke held the kiss while he danced her to the mantle, where he set down his drink and took hers to do the same. Her willingness for him to gently move her across the room was intoxicating. She'd let him take the lead, but he knew who was really in charge.

With her hands now free, they ran through his hair, pulling him closer as they maneuvered and finessed their way across his back.

His own hands found the delicate skin beneath her shirt and circled around her narrow middle. He lifted her ever so slightly, forcing their bodies to align, sensitive parts rubbing, the sensation of pressure touching in all the right, longing places.

Grace leaned into his ear and whispered, "Follow me."

When she tried to part, Luke held her close and lifted her up, her legs wrapped around his body, her yearning at the opening, causing a low, lusty moan. He walked to the stairs and headed up.

Their lips came together in a long and excruciatingly slow, passionate caress. At the top of the stairs, he turned and looked at the next flight.

"Okay, now I'll follow you."

Grace's head fell back as he set her down. With a breathy laugh, she said, "Since you might be a bit tired, let me help you with my clothes. Grace turned and slowly undressed as she walked up the flight.

He watched, amazed, as clothing dropped to the stairs with each new step, draping the discarded garments over the railing.

"Are you coming?" she asked with a suggestive smile.

"Probably too soon," he said, his words matter-of-fact.

Her throaty, seductive, chuckle turned to a shriek when he darted after her, taking the steps two at a time. He caught her as they reached the bedroom door and he lifted her around him once more to walk through.

This time, it wasn't gentle. Their bodies collided with a force that had Grace wishing he was inside her, hammering, pummeling. The frantic race to discard his clothes only increased the desire, the need, their craving for one another.

Grace bent and slid his jeans and briefs to the floor in one fluid motion. On her way back to standing, her hand encircled him as her mouth sought his.

"Grace," he groaned, thick and foggy with blinding need. She was driving him over the edge.

She pushed away and walked to the bed. When she gracefully sat, he knew all fight for control was lost as he watched her lithe body lay back and open. Ready for him to come to her.

Luke walked to her, leaned to kiss her, and trailed desperate kisses down her neck. He paused only to take her breast with his mouth and tease her nipple with his warm tongue. Luke moved down, agonizingly, slowly, taking care to appreciate every silky inch of her soft skin. His kisses left the sensation of warm wet, followed by a damp chill on the inside of her tender thigh, but he didn't stop there.

Grace sighed shakily as the fire inside burned and her body prepared to erupt.

He laid a lazy trail down her legs to her ankles and lifted her feet gently as he climbed onto the bed. He paused only for a moment, her hands covered his, as he held her legs high, and drove into her. Then he drove them both over the exhilarating edge.

———

It wasn't an obnoxious snore, it was a low, hearty grumble. Though, she smiled, at this point she probably would have thought a loud, booming snarl would have been cute, too.

Grace peeled the covers back and gently slid out of bed, trying her best not to wake Luke. She made it to the bathroom before she turned at the sound of his rustling in bed and smacked her elbow on the door frame.

"Shit," she whispered, trying to hold in a squeal while holding her elbow.

"What time is it?" Luke's groggy voice questioned from behind her.

"Sorry, it's just before five. Sleep, it's early."

Grace turned, shook her elbow out, and returned to her mission of finding sweatpants and a sweatshirt to cover up. She paused in front of the intricate floor-length mirror. It leaned heavily on and almost covered the entire back wall of her bathroom. It was way too much, and a little too over the top for the space, but it was just right.

Grace looked at herself. She felt tender in all the right places. They had crashed, stroked, caressed, and plummeted together. Her body felt the beautiful ache lingering. She'd never felt it before, but now she understood what women meant when they said *he made me feel beautiful*. It wasn't necessarily what *he* had done, but rather what she'd allowed to happen. She'd let herself let go. Let him ravage. Let him love. And it was glorious and powerful combination.

A shadow walked up behind her as she admired herself. She felt Luke's arm fold around her, enveloping her from behind.

Grace leaned her head back, letting her naked body sink into his as his rough hands slid adoringly, lightly, over her breasts. And over her hips, torturously close to her moistening center. She felt him hard, pressing against her back. She closed her eyes at the sensation and prayed she would always feel this way.

"I thought I said sleep," she teased, her breath faint and quickening.

"I thought I saw the most beautiful woman in the doorway," Luke said as he kissed her neck and the side of her cheek. He nestled in and slowly began to sway.

As they moved, one arm held her as the other wandered. Stroking, searching. The rough fingertips tantalized her, lightly scraping as they moved. They lingered as they found their way back to her supple mounds and made a leisurely path down her torso. From behind, Luke found her mouth when her head turned to his. They kissed, their movements like a boozy dance, drunk with seduction. His roaming hand found her most sensitive spot, still aching from their night together, and drove her deliriously to another pleasurable release.

CHAPTER 28

Luke wandered down to the kitchen while Grace finished showering. Something about lingering in the heat and steam, he remembered her saying. He would have caught all the words, but she had a way of causing a bit of distraction.

The fridge seemed as good a place to start as any. When he opened it, his hungry eyes screamed jackpot as the leftover pizza sat perfectly in its wonderful little bag. It's official, he thought. He was in heaven.

He threw a slice in his mouth and held it there while he zipped up the bag. He chewed as he continued his search for breakfast. There was a cupboard filled with more spices than he would ever know what to do with. Another with rice, beans, sauces and marinades, and spilling out of a basket at the bottom were potatoes and onions. Luke closed the cupboard door and before opening the next, took a second to admire her taste. He wasn't one to usually notice, but it looked good, rich.

The kitchen wasn't white like you see in so many other places or all of those TV shows his mom watched. The cabinets were dark, stained espresso, with matching dark hardware. The light fixtures were a mixture of the same stained wood and iron.

It wouldn't have seemed like a woman's home, or what he envisioned when he thought about it, but there were touches of the woman he was in love with. A cream-colored vase sat in the middle of the island with fresh flowers spilling out. He'd have to buy her flowers on his way home one day.

Home. Huh, that was a strange notion, he thought.

Thick, heavy, wooden frames surrounded pictures – or prints, he supposed – of foliage. He silently congratulated himself on his accurate description.

Luke noticed a single frame sitting on the bar table under a kitchen window. On his way to check it out, he snuck a look into the last cupboard and whispered, "I love you," knowing Grace was still upstairs. He reached down and pulled out the box of Peanut Butter Crunch and hugged it. Luke one-armed the Crunch and pulled a chair over to the side table and sat. Deciding against reaching his hand inside like the bachelor version of himself had done millions of times, he popped up, found a bowl, and sat again. He held the bowl close as he threw the Captain Crunch in his mouth a couple at a time.

"You," he said, "must be Raymond Thomas." Luke looked at the photograph of a well-built man standing over a grill, smiling at the camera.

"I'm Luke, it's nice to meet you." He slanted an eye at the man in the picture. "I'm sorry for what you saw, and most likely heard last night. Had I known you were watching, well, you're right, I wouldn't have stopped. We'll just leave it at sorry. Also, I would have put clothes on when I ran down to get a bottle of water."

"Anyway," Luke went on, crunching. "I'd like to ask permission to date your daughter. I should tell you, I'm not taking this lightly. As I see it, the way things are going now-" he paused as he threw another handful in, "-seeing as I'm pretty much a goner when it comes to your daughter, I'll most likely want to ask her to marry me before too long. I'm getting up there in marriage years. All but one of my friends got married before the age of twenty-nine." He went on with his one-sided conversation. "You're an accountant? Sorry, I knew that. Me, too. My dad said-"

"Luke," Grace spoke from the steps. "Who are you talking to?"

She appeared from the staircase, and he felt like – and probably looked like – a deer in headlights and stopped mid-crunch.

"Ah." He motioned his head toward the picture and slowly finished his mouthful.

"You're talking to my dad?"

He didn't feel completely crazy the way she'd asked, but it was something close.

"Yes," he admitted, "I took a gamble in my assumption it was him, so we sat down and talked for a bit. I mean, I mostly did the talking."

"And what exactly were you talking about?" Her smile was gradual as she walked over to him.

"I thought it appropriate that I ask if I could date his daughter."

"Did he give his approval?"

"Absolutely. Though he did request that I wear pants during our next water break."

Grace flung her arms around him, and they stood for a long moment, just holding each other. Her tight hug pulled at his heart, and he knew from that moment on, he was hers. Then she shoved her hand right into the box of Captain Crunch, and he couldn't believe just how perfect she was.

CHAPTER 29

The girls stretched out across Grace's bed as she packed like they had countless times before. Rachel fluttered her feet back and forth off the edge of the bed. Casey rested her head on Rachel's back. And Aimeé sat against the headboard, her feet propped on Casey.

"This is so romantic. I love him. Do you love him yet?" Rachel asked in her wistful, romantic way.

"How could anybody love somebody in a week?" Casey asked, reasonably.

"Hopefully everybody on your dating site, seeing as it's one of your meal-tickets." Grace retorted as she poked her head around the closet opening.

"She evaded," Rachel perked up. "You evaded," she directed at Grace.

"She evaded," Aimeé and Casey agreed.

"I didn't evade. What do you think?" Grace walked out with two flannel shirts, two sweaters, and a sweatshirt.

"I love them, but isn't it only two days?" Rachel asked, staring at the pile of clothing in Grace's hands.

"Three, if you count today," Grace said, defending her selections.

"Do you love him?" Aimeé asked again, not willing to let the topic slip.

Grace walked into the bedroom from the closet and sat on the edge of the bed.

"If I don't, the way I'm feeling will land me there fast. He's everything I – no – I couldn't even imagine somebody as great as Luke," she corrected herself. "Yet, here he is giving me his time and attention. It's something as close to love as I think one could get without being all the way there."

"And a trip to Grandma's," Casey quipped, and the girls laughed.

"It's funny, but even *that* I love. I'm close with my family, too. We have the same interests." Grace folded a flannel shirt and set it on the bed.

"You're both accountants, working to maintain your fathers' legacies," Casey added, treading lightly, seeing if Grace had any indication of just how their two companies fit together.

"We are," Grace agreed absently. "But honestly, work is the furthest thing from my mind right now. I can't believe I'm saying this, but I like Luke more than I love my job."

Aimeé's head rose, and Casey lifted hers. "You're kidding."

"Not at all," Grace said. It was as simple as that, she thought.

"That's interesting," Casey said, curiously.

"It's wonderful." Aimeé jumped in, cutting Casey off before she could take away from the moment. "What will you do? While you're there," she added. "Is there an agenda?"

"I have no idea." Grace simply liked the idea of being with Luke. Wherever, doing whatever, it didn't matter.

"That's very not like you." Rachel bounced a little on the bed. "I can't wait to hear about it."

The doorbell rang, and they sprang into action.

"He's early!"

Grace threw her clothes into the overnight bag that already held her essentials, while the three other women raced down the stairs like a herd of elephants.

"No. It's okay. You all go down. I don't need any help." Grace said sarcastically to the empty room and hauled the bag to the stairs. Maybe it was a lot for two – no, three days. But she'd be ready for anything.

Grace made it to the bottom of the staircase and laughed as she came upon Luke answering her friends' onslaught of questions. She shot him an apologetic grin, and he shrugged casually as if to say, no big deal.

"Will you guys lock up for me?"

"Lock up?" Casey scoffed. "I'm staying."

Grace pointed a finger at her. "Don't drink all of my coffee."

"You clean a girl out once."

"Every time." Grace pulled Casey in for a hug. "Every single time. But I love you anyway."

"You, too. Be safe. Take care of her," Casey added to Luke.

Luke grinned and watched Grace hug the other two, wondering if they realized she'd be back again on Sunday night. They waved from the steps like parents would for a kid going away to camp. He definitely wouldn't mind having these

191

women around. They were fun. And they all had something in common. They all loved Grace.

Rachel, Aimeé, and Casey watched until they were out of sight.

"I'm a schmuck," Casey admitted, finally pulling her hand down from the wave.

"Don't be so sure," Rachel defended her.

"I agree. I like him. I like them," Aimeé agreed agreeably.

"It's going to get ugly." Casey turned to walk inside her home for the weekend.

"Casey has the nicest two houses – *two* – out of all of us. Why does she stay here? Maybe I can stay at one of her places?" Rachel examined jokingly.

"She's closer to family here."

Rachel nodded, understanding Aimeé was talking about them.

"Let's stay, too." Rachel said as she leaned her head on Aimeé's shoulder.

"Let's."

CHAPTER 30

The road sign that marked ten miles to Little Falls zoomed past them, and at that moment, Luke reached over and intertwined his fingers with hers. He gave her hand a little squeeze, and their hands rested on her lap the rest of the way.

Grace wanted to keep her eyes open to take in the golden hue of Fall that only happened in this sweet spot of September. But she took a brief second to close her eyes and appreciate how happy she was at this very moment. She let the quiet beat of the music fill her head. The whirling speed of the tires sending a slow vibration through her. The feeling of Luke's hand warming hers. When Grace opened her eyes, she admitted she'd never felt better, or happier.

It was a little before five o'clock when they pulled into a long driveway that led the way to a picturesque two-story home. When she took in the white wrap-around porch and the wooden rockers sitting out front, she couldn't contain her excited giggle. She looked over at Luke, beaming, and got out of the car, leaving him inside with whatever he was about to say to her. She had the sudden urge to be in this home, to look around, to wander.

Beyond the porch sat a white house with faded black shutters and old charm. The front door that matched the shutters swung open as Grace gaped at the beauty she saw. The green landscape and colorful trees seemed to go on for miles.

A woman with a nest of white hair appeared in the doorway with her hands on her hips, one hand holding a dishrag. She was tall and lean, and Grace immediately saw the resemblance between the two. Luke gestured and motioned with a nod of his head to come over. He took her hand and together they walked toward the elegant woman, who at the moment was wrapped in oversized bib overalls that no doubt had been her late husband's. They draped over her thermal long-sleeve shirt and rolled near her ankles. It made perfect sense. From the silver clasps all the way down to her red rubber rain boots. She was a vision.

Grace had never been happier to have decided on wearing the chambray shirt and Sorel ankle snow boots. The two of them kind of matched.

"Bring this blonde beauty up here so I can get a closer look at her!" the woman yelled from the porch.

Luke led her up the stairs and handed her off while making the introduction, "Grandma Edna, this is Grace. Grace, this is Grandma Edna. She's old and crotchety, but she's the best looking – best baking – lady around town. It's why they let her stay," he said with a grin.

Edna took both of Grace's hands and held them out wide to take her all in. Getting a good look, she supposed. That didn't stop Luke from bear-hugging his grandmother off of the ground. Edna and Grace's hands stayed clasped, and they rose and fell with the lift of Luke's hug.

"Put me down you big lug, I need to take in this beauty you've brought to visit me."

Edna was lowered much gentler than she was hoisted. Once down, she resumed her analysis.

"So, this is beautiful Grace?" The regal smile Edna donned reminded Grace of old-Hollywood glamour. Something you'd see in a black and white film.

"Yes, I think she'll do just fine." Edna added a wink.

It was a mannerism Grace had seen Luke offer more than once, and had her grinning at their similarity.

"Now, let's get you inside and changed before the big game." Edna cheered her fists into the air.

"The big game?" Her curiosity followed Edna into the house.

"Oh yes, the season has started for our high school boys' football team. I haven't missed a home game in nearly thirty years. I just love it. Let me take you to your room so you can settle in and get changed. I hope you don't mind, but I took the liberty of getting you a little something with school spirit. We'll be matching."

Edna opened the door to a quaint bedroom just up the squeaky stairs. The room had lemon-colored walls adorned with framed prints of dainty flowers. A small white writing desk sat beneath a window that was wrapped with flower-patterned curtains. A cream quilt draped the double bed and was adorned with daisies that were stitched in light yellow.

"I'll leave you for a bit, and don't worry about wearing the clothes if they aren't quite your style. It's just a little keepsake." Edna squeezed her hand and added, "Come down whenever you're ready. We'll have a quick meal. Nothing too big. We need to save room for some game-food. And Grace, he doesn't do things he isn't sure about, so I hope you can understand why I am so happy to have you here and to be the first to meet you."

With that, she was out the door and down the stairs whistling a peppy tune Grace couldn't quite place.

Grace sat on the end of the bed and picked up the purple gift bag. The sparkling tissue paper was removed with care, revealing a purple crewneck sweatshirt with an iron-on print of Little Falls Football. Beneath the soft fleece were two more gifts: a white stocking hat and matching gloves with the same print as the sweatshirt, sewn in the same purple.

The crewneck took her back to the memories of high school when she, Rachel, and Casey would get ready for football games. They'd put on makeup and braid their hair beneath matching stocking caps. She hugged the sweatshirt, inhaling the nostalgia, and had never been more excited to have that Friday night football feeling again.

Grace was still smiling to herself when she heard the creak in the floor and turned to find Luke leaning against the doorframe.

"Are you going to be okay in here?" He was genuinely concerned.

"Of course, this is perfect. I love it in here," Grace said honestly, looking around at the quaint room.

"I know we hadn't talked about the sleeping arrangements, but being bound in matrimony is a must for same-bedroom sleeping around here." He moved toward her and raised her off the bed to face him. "I'll spend the night wishing I was next to you."

"Do you practice lines like that?" She asked, smiling at the cuteness of his words.

The sensation from the soft kiss placed in the tender nape of her neck seeped into her, igniting every sensual, sensitive feeling. A mixture of moisture and heat burned into her. She had no choice but to close the eyes that had blurred from the simple touch. Luke's hand cupped the back of her neck when her response had her leaning back, exposing more of her neck.

"You just kind of do that to me."

Luke accepted her offering forging a trail of kisses, tracing a path to her parted lips. The destination was soft and tender. Their noses brushed as they kept their faces close, breathing each other in, feeling the closeness between them. His hand moved lightly from her neck down her back, working its way to her hip, pulling her into him. Their breathing was thick and wanting, growing hoarse as their bodies pressed against each other.

His kisses continued their path to the opposite side of her neck, and when they stopped, his staggered whisper struggled out, "You fascinate and captivate me. I didn't mean to start this here," he placed one more kiss on the edge of her ear, and she felt his smile form into her cheek, "but I'm not sorry for this feeling."

This time it was her turn to return the favor. Her hands skimmed his chest slowly with their heads still side by side. When her hands stopped just below his pockets, she angled her head to press long, slow kisses of her own on the chiseled edge of his jawline. She gently forced her body deeper into his and knew he felt just as much when an uncontrolled grumble escaped him.

"I'm not sorry either." The warm breath filled his ear, and she knew it was just about too much for him to handle, so she backed away before they could go any further.

"I think we can maybe make it through the rest of the weekend." She grinned and looked up at Luke.

"So, this is what torture feels like." He grunted and was only   kind   of   kidding.

CHAPTER 31

"That was the best game!"

Grace's excitement was genuine as she all but skipped into the house, doing a little twirl. The smell of popcorn from the concessions, the bleachers full of students chanting and cheering on their young men heading into battle, the chill in the air that bordered on freezing. She forgot how much she loved bundling up and seeing her breath as she joined in the cheers. She hadn't remembered how cold it actually was at the games because they were always penned in one section of the bleachers, without an inch to move, shoulder to shoulder, from end to end. One giant mass of team spirit keeping each other warm.

She had kept her hands warm in her gloves by pressing both hands firmly around the hot chocolate and warm apple cider. Luke and Edna had sandwiched her body, scooting close, so each had a spot on the folded blanket used to soften the metal underneath them and keep the cold out.

She felt her nose and cheeks turn rosy red but remembered how warm it had felt when Luke had wrapped an arm around her shoulder for a brief moment to pull her to him and place a kiss on the apple of her cheek, and another tenderly on her forehead, where he lingered for just a moment. The gesture was simple, but the sincerity of it made her feel like nothing she'd felt before. Warm, satisfied, safe. The moment had lasted long enough to not be ruined by the reprimand Edna shouted at the ref for a bad call. The voice that flew out of the old woman was impressive, to say the least.

Edna's voice, much calmer now, brought her back, "Well, I think this old hag has had enough excitement for one night. The older you get, the longer the beauty sleep should be, in my opinion."

She felt Edna's spindly arms wrap tightly around her body. How could someone so small give off so much strength, so much love?

"Goodnight, Edna. Thank you so much for everything, and for letting me stay with you this weekend." She did her best to hug back with all sincere appreciation she could muster.

"Grace, you are now welcome here any time you feel like making the trip. With or without the baggage." Edna's head motioned toward Luke as she spoke.

One final squeeze and Edna made her way to Luke and hugged him with the same force. She whispered something in his ear that was just loud enough for Grace to overhear: "If there were ever a perfect woman for you, this is her. Hold her tight and never let her go. Remember, when you finally realize the future you want, you want it to start as soon as possible. Our time here with the people we love is too short. Embrace her."

Luke's eyes looked over his grandmother's head and into Grace's, and for a moment, they simply stared. She didn't want him to know she had heard but did her best to look back at him with all the care she could. She was in love.

"Goodnight, Grandma."

Luke was squeezed one final time, and Edna was up the stairs for the beauty sleep that had proven very effective.

Then Luke listed her options.

"You can either," Luke began, the drill sergeant tone comically adding to the edge in his voice, "choose to join my grandmother in beauty sleep that you clearly do not need being as beautiful as ever, or you can change into PJ's and join me downstairs for a late-night movie, and we could possibly sneak a late-night beverage. The choice is yours."

She pretended to ponder her options, but she knew her choice. Hold tight and never let go. Edna's words still lingered in her ears. She hemmed and hawed her way over to him before saying, "Well, I'm not sure about the company, but I sure could go for a nice glass of wine, or whatever my bartender happens to be serving."

As if he didn't hear a word of her questioning the company he offered her, he perked up and said, "Great! I'll meet you down there."

CHAPTER 32

The basement reminded Grace of a time before her family had prospered. It brought back happy memories of holidays at her own grandmothers' house before everything had been updated.

Dark, heady, ash-stained wood panels lined the walls. Thick, plush, brown carpet laid beneath her feet. Grace felt like she was thrust back in time to the early eighties.

She supposed for its time, the bar on the back wall was a luxury. And as her eyes scanned she noted all of the fixtures and knobs were still shiny, yellow gold. Peach wallpaper lined the small bathroom and matching orange-pink towels were draped gracefully on a long three-tiered rack.

It was wonderful and pristine. It looked as if Edna had cleaned and cared for the space as she would've her own children whom she wanted to grow into beautiful, well-maintained individuals.

It struck Grace as charming. Beauty in old style and tradition – not unlike Edna – Grace thought.

"Here's my theory on all of this 'you and me' business, are you ready?" Luke asked while pouring bourbon over ice to finish off his Old Fashioned. Effectively pulling Grace from her admiration.

Grace laughed and tucked her feet beneath her, resting on the back of the couch. From this vantage point, she could easily enjoy her wine and enjoy the view of the handsome man who was now tossing a bag of microwave popcorn around in his hands like a hot-potato as he tried not to get burned. It was precious.

"Ready." She acknowledged his question and watched him plop the piping-hot bag on the counter. "As long as it's not some crazy thing like, you traveled back in time just to run into me at this exact moment. I heard one of those theories on a tipsy night in college. It didn't work then either." Grace added the last bit for playful effect.

She watched him pause and give her a chiseled-face blank stare, and his jaw hit the floor.

"How did you know?" Luke said, his bewildered act perfected. "If I can't give you *that* explanation, I'm going to have to lie. There'll be no coming back from that."

He didn't anticipate the flare of guilt that sparked when he mentioned telling a lie. But, he wasn't really lying, was he? Just simply omitting the truth, that's all.

"Maybe," she grinned her way through the words, "try for a close second, and we'll see how far from the truth it is?"

"Oh, yeah, good idea." He returned his attention to the buttery popcorn and continued, "So, as I was saying, you and me. I think two people meet – and just stick with me on this –" He eyed her tentatively until she nodded. "Two people meet when they are exactly ready to find the person they are supposed to be with for the rest of their lives."

"It's an interesting theory," she said, taking a sip of wine to hide her eager smile.

"I'm not done." Luke tossed a piece of popcorn in his mouth and went on. "It's a time when two people are willing to let feelings take over and put in the work to make it work. Then, fate steps in and they just *run into each other.*" Luke winked, as she touched her nose and pointed back to him.

Luke balanced his drink and some bowls on a tray to join her on the couch and continued. "I've thought about it a lot. There isn't a scenario I've been able to play out in my mind that wouldn't have had me wanting to know you.

"Had I met you anywhere else, under any other circumstances, I would still have tried." Luke paused and reached out to run a finger down her cheek.

"So, while you were going on with your life, and I was going on with mine, we ran into it." Luke finished by popping a couple more pieces of popcorn into his mouth, he mumbled with a grin, "Literally."

His theory didn't seem to be completely ridiculous. In fact, she thought, maybe fate had stepped in.

Grace reached for her own handful of popcorn and turned to face him. She contemplated and let his speech linger before giving him the satisfaction of an explanation well done. She even bobbled her head back and forth as if she were on the fence about what she'd heard. Without the ability to hold it long, her contemplative face fell apart, and the drained look on his face fell with it.

"You might be onto something," she conceded.

She slid down on the cushion next to Luke, and he welcomed her with a lift of his arm, letting her nestle in. They seemed to fit together in every way. Their personalities, their bodies, their interest in one another.

"Can I ask you something?" she said, brushing the hair away from her face, shifting her head slightly to look up toward him.

"You can ask me anything, or tell me anything, always."

It was an easy phrase. Luke seemed so trusting and sure. She wondered if this was how he would always be? Would he always give her his full attention? Constantly impress her? Would he stick with her through family, work, and other things life would throw at them? Like her current situation with the rumored acquisition? Would he give advice? It would be nice to have somebody supporting her, and something told her he would.

"It's more of an opinion, actually."

Luke looked down, knowing. It would have come up eventually, so he would answer as honestly as possible. He kissed the top of her head. "Fire away."

"I have this problem at work. It's actually a big problem, or, maybe not a problem at all. Problem is the wrong word. But for the first time ever, I feel like I don't really have control." She rested her head again and looked forward. "I told you about my grandpa and my dad, how they started our company?"

Grace felt Luke nod his head intently, and heard, "I do remember, yes."

"My aunt and I are running it beautifully," she continued. "We love everybody we work with and their families. I should warn you," she cut herself off, "I'll have to kill you if you tell anybody about this. And I'm not fit for jail."

He couldn't hide the humor and let out a chuckle while he assured, "I think we are both safe." For now, he thought.

Depending on how the next couple of minutes play out, he might not be.

"We are a successful company, and I'm not ashamed to say that. We've worked hard and didn't cut corners. We put a huge emphasis on making our employees and our clients number one. It has – it still – pays off."

When Grace looked up again, Luke nodded, showing he was following along. It wasn't unlike how his own dad had done things. Aaron Wallace just happened to pursue growth as well.

"We might lose it. Rumors." Grace added when she noticed Luke's interest peak with a slight raise and crinkle in his forehead lines. "It's the one piece of my dad I have left, and what's more, it's who I became. Everything I am I put into this company. I'm afraid if I lose it, I'll lose a part of myself too. I've never even hinted at the notion of doing – of being – someone else."

Silence filled the space between them.

Without speaking, Luke pulled her tighter to him. She felt his strength or what felt like him trying to protect her, holding her close.

The truth, he thought. Because the truth always won out. Or maybe, he guessed, honesty was more appropriate. As much as he could give without risking his family's business, and without losing her. He couldn't lose her. Not now.

His head rested on the side of hers. She could feel his warm breath gently brushing her ear.

"I would say," he paused wondering if he would regret the advice he was about to give, "anything that means that much to you is worth fighting for. Do what you can, try as hard as you can, and I'll be here for you. And because sometimes what happens in business is out of our control, if in the end it doesn't go your way, you'll know you did everything you could.

"I'm not going to tell you it's not personal. I know how the saying goes and whether or not we tell ourselves it is or isn't personal, it always is. And if that's the case, it seems when you give everything you have, moving on seems to be a bit easier."

Grace closed her eyes and replayed Luke's words. He was right.

"Okay."

"Okay?"

"Yes, okay. You're right." Grace agreed. It's what she knew was right, in her heart. But something about hearing it from Luke, a man she so quickly trusted and respected, made it true.

Luke tugged the back of her long ponytail and agreed, "Yeah, well, I usually am. You know, right."

Her laugh filled the room, and her heart, as she gave him an elbow to the ribs.

He wondered if it wasn't the last elbow – or fist, or any other extremity that could injure him – she'd give as time crept closer to her knowing the whole truth.

"Don't you know if this is going to work out, *I* always have to be right?" she joked.

"Of course, of course. As long as you agree with me, honey, you'll always be right."

Luke's arms engulfed her and bound her in a hug so tight that rather than fight, she gave in and took it. There was a place and time for fighting, she realized. This was a time to let him   win.

CHAPTER 33

A long drawling creak of the old wooden floor barely woke her from a deep sleep. Grace could feel the comfort of sleepy darkness still surrounding her, and it felt glorious. She turned over and found a new, untouched, cool spot of sheets, and nuzzled in. She smiled and peeked over the fluffy mound of blankets to glance at the clock. Just before five o'clock. For the first time in a long time, she decided to stay and embrace sleep and comfort.

The feeling of peace stopped abruptly when she felt his presence. Grace closed her eyes tightly, but he was there, waking her from her precious deep sleep. She bordered on the edge of no return when she'd be too awake to fall back asleep. She opened one eye and saw the sharp slope of Luke's nose, the rest of him hidden by the side of the bed. Even through her squint, she could see the excitement in his eyes.

"Did you know you're beautiful even when your hair is a mess, and your mouth is wide open while you sleep?" he whispered from his perch.

She held the smile back as she whispered, "Do you think I'll still be beautiful after I'm forced to kill the perpetrator waking me from my beauty sleep?" Her lip slipped up into a half-smile at one end.

He found her hand and slid it toward the edge of the bed where his lips were waiting.

"I didn't want to have to wake you this early, but we won't have any other time to get it done."

"We are getting something done today? Does it require clothes?" Her mind slipped to sensuality as the moisture from his kisses traced her palm to the tender underside of her wrist. She let herself fall into her need for him.

When Luke dropped her hand, it fell limp on the bed, and she was snapped back to reality. Before she had a chance to register his movements, he was up and drawing her curtains. The sudden shift in reality had her sitting up, confused.

"Hold on." The slight irritation of being turned on and left wanting, dangled in her voice. "We are actually doing something, right now? Like, an activity?" *One that isn't sexual*, she added sarcastically to herself.

An image of what Luke would have been like as an excited child flashed through her mind. Then he was at her bedside again handing her clothes. Where did these come from? She wondered.

The jeans were recognizable, but the pale blue puffer jacket and matching hat and gloves looked to be the same age as she was. What in the world was going on? Did he lose his mind?

There was a difference, Grace decided, between being up at five in the morning and being happy about it at home, and what she was experiencing now. The difference? At home, she didn't actually have to participate in anything other than coffee. And it definitely didn't involve the freezing outdoors which is where a person goes with the blue abomination she was holding.

October mornings were for hot drinks, robes, slippers, a fireplace, and anything warm, really. A gentle, slow, wakeup. This? Not this.

She looked at Luke, whose butt was already passing the bedroom exit heading down the stairs for what must be other exciting things.

He's lucky he has a good butt, she thought, her irritation ebbing, and on the verge of slipping away. Very lucky he was so cute. Very, very, lucky he had been incredible to her thus far.

Her thoughts were enough to get her out of bed. She slid on the jeans and the thickest clothes she brought that she could shove under the puffy coat. Then the scintillating scent of coffee and the gurgling noise that spewed from the pot drifted up to her. Grace inhaled as she braided her hair in a long rope to fit under the stocking cap, and couldn't wait for her first sip.

As Grace rounded the corner at the bottom of the stairs, she found Luke filling two travel mugs with coffee.

"What, I have to ask, is the grand adventure we must take at this godforsaken hour?"

The overly dramatic tone wasn't lost on Luke as he smiled and continued to pour.

"We, my beautiful Grace, are going to not take a grand adventure per se, but a grand tour." His hands shot up in the air, encouraging her to join in his excitement.

The excitement wasn't entirely shared yet, but she was almost over wanting to crawl back into bed. And she had to admit, Luke's fervor was starting to rub off.

"There's this tour of Little Falls. I found it on the Google."

211

Amusement lit her face as she mouthed *the Google*.

He was amazing. Hilarious. All she received in return from her silent repetition was an excited, exaggerated nod as he rambled on.

"It's a walking tour. We just click the tour links on the website. We can drink our coffees and listen. Can you believe it? Listen to the history of each site through our very own earbuds. Did you know that the Little Falls Library was funded by Carnegie himself?"

This side of him reaffirmed her love for this man. She could vaguely imagine him with their children, how he'd be on holidays and special occasions, or even a simple morning breakfast with the family on the weekends. He was it.

Warmth and light cascaded through her. And everything inside of her beamed at the feeling. Fireworks exploded in the pit of her stomach, and all she could do was wrap herself in her arms and try to contain the overpowering feeling.

"It is truly unbelievable," she said softly, answering him and the emotional sensation that swept through her.

He would realize she was in love with him in due time, but for now, Grace would cherish her special-kept secret.

"Well, my fearless leader, let's start our journey, shall we? And you said 'Carnegie' right? Like the guy with the hall in New York?"

"The one and only." Luke handed her one of the to-go mugs and ushered her out the door as quickly as he possibly could.

It wasn't until they had visited and listened to the historian's tale of a historic school and convent, two mansions, and two hotels before she realized it wasn't even six yet. As she stared at an old Sands' Café she realized she didn't know *why* they had to do this so early. She waited until the recording of this location had played in entirety before she spoke.

"Can I ask you a question that has been haunting me since I was graciously awakened?"

Luke nodded.

"*Why* is it that we are taking this," she tried to find a non-offending word, "surprisingly lovely tour at this hour of the day?" Her smile didn't face him while he answered.

"Easy." Luke said, as if it was common knowledge.

"Grandma has weekend breakfast ready by eight. We definitely don't want to be late for breakfast."

Definitely, she thought as he took her hand without further explanation. They moved on and stopped in front of the Falls Theater then stood in silence as they hit play on the next recording.

CHAPTER 34

They were late for breakfast. And now, Grace understood. It was less about punctuality and more about self-indulgence.

The smell of salty bacon and sweet, caramelly, cinnamon rolls lured them up the driveway. Her feet ached from the walk in borrowed boots, but she wasn't above running toward the heavenly scents.

They made their way to the front door and took stock of the new cars in the driveway that hadn't been there before. New, meaning new to the driveway – not to the world. A rusty bronco was the first to pull in, and it now sat trapped by an old gray Buick and a shiny, light blue, Lincoln Continental. The clientele was not of their decade or any of the recent decades before that. Grace grinned at the car analysis and didn't hold back her amusement.

Laughter and scratchy voices that only the wonder of age could create bellowed through the halls. Dishes clanked and silverware clinked. The clatter led them to the porch where a sprawling dining table sat. Floor to ceiling windows with thin, white, wooden frames were the walls that boxed them in. There were no shades or panels to block the light. Just simple drapes hanging loosely at their sides like flowing summer dresses. The floor was wooden to match the rest of the old house with a shaggy, soft rug nearly the size of the room sitting under the farmhouse table.

Steaming food and a mixture of orange and red flowers were scattered in the middle of the table. Sitting around the food were eight white and gray heads gossiping like they were seventeen.

"Don't be late is right," she joked behind her to where Luke had trailed, smiling as he took in the view.

"Don't be late is right," Luke confirmed as he caught up and ushered her closer to the table.

Their movement caught the eye of a four-foot-five frail woman, Marvel Shovel. Hair, so gray it looked blue, sat bound in a bun on the top of her head. Marvel could talk all day and every day about nothing at all but was usually the life of the party and the first one to bring you up if you were down. Marvel was the first to give a hoot and holler about the two handsome young people who had just walked in.

"Well, oh my goodness, what a sight these two are!" Her exclaim matched the speed at which she rocketed out of her chair to get a closer look. Her speed walk looked like she'd had a lot of practice circling malls.

"Aren't you the most beautiful blonde-haired girl, I mean woman," she corrected, "in the whole world. Darling," she looked skyward to peer at Grace in admiration, "you are every bit of your name. In fact, you remind me a little of Grace Kelly. So elegant and pretty. We knew our Luke Aaron here was smart, but we didn't give him nearly enough credit for snagging you as we should have. You're the talk of the town. We've heard a lot about you, and so far, all good."

They left Luke in the dust as Marvel linked her arm with Grace's and walked her to the end of the bench where she was sitting.

"I tend to forget a little too much these days. I can't remember what it is that you do?"

They both scooted in, and Grace smiled at the new, wrinkled faces at the table.

"I'm an accountant. I work for my dad's company. I started there during college. Actually, before then, but that was mostly to see all of the people who worked there. And to eat the desk candy." Grace added, not ashamed of admitting her young indulgence.

"My kind of girl." A raspy, unsmiling tone interjected.

Rodney looked like a grumpy old man with a squished, square face. Glasses sat on the edge of his nose and looked as though they were going to fall into the scrambled eggs piled high on his plate. His smile came and went so quickly it was hard not to stare or to second guess that he'd actually done it at all.

She did a double-take just to be sure the noise had come from him. When the silence grew, Marvel piped-in once more.

"Edna, where are your manners? We need to do introductions!"

Edna rolled her eyes and rested her chin on her fist to let Marvel take the lead, not willing to exert the energy to remind Marvel that often when she was around, there wasn't a lot of open airtime.

Marvel went around the table one by one, "Across from you is Sarah Barthel, she lives just down the road here, the first house when you pull into town. Next to her is Harold Barthel, Sarah's husband of fifty years this year."

Marvel paused just long enough to let Grace add congratulations before quickly moving on.

"Next to Harold is Rodney, the town grump, but we are willing to let him come have Saturday breakfast with us. We have to keep him around because he makes the best Christmas cookies."

Christmas cookies? Why would a grumpy old man make Christmas cookies? And share them, which apparently he did, or they wouldn't keep him, Grace mused.

"Kathy Brooks is next to him down there on the end." Kathy gave a crooked-teeth smile and even more endearing than her smile was the bashful wave that followed.

"On the end of our bench here is the fearless breakfast leader. None of us would come without the great food all prepared by our Enda here. Between Edna and myself," Marvel put a hand on a plump and what seemed to be a very tall woman, "is Rebecca. Rebecca owns the butcher shop in town, and her son, his wife, and their kids work it these days. Last but not least, next to Rebecca is Suzanne."

Poor Suzanne didn't get any additional description from Marvel. But she smiled brightly and took a sip of orange juice.

"Why don't you slide a little farther in here with me so we can make room for that handsome devil over there?"

When all were settled around the table, Luke served the remaining empty plates with pancakes, sweet caramel rolls, bacon, sausage, eggs, and biscuits with gravy, for those that felt they had the room.

"Edna, this is incredible." She stared at the mound of food on her plate, "Did you do all of this yourself?"

Edna beamed and showed a hint of pride, "I love to cook; it's always been my thing. But it's not as fun if you don't have good people to feed. So, we've served breakfast every Saturday for…well?" She thought about it. "I guess since before Cliff died. Which will be eleven years this December. He and I loved having this brunch, so we keep on having it."

Cliff. The way she said his name. It was like he was still with her. She didn't know if it made her feel sad, or if she longed to have that kind of love.

Luke reached for her under the table and took hold of her hand without breaking stride in conversation.

"Luke, it looks like you snagged an accountant like yourself?" Harold inquired.

"I know perfection when I see it," Luke said, giving her hand a squeeze.

The conversation ebbed and flowed, but lingered mostly on flow with the crew they had. Grace looked around and realized she felt just as much at home here as she did with her own family. The food, the noise, the love. She wanted to stay longer and hoped it wouldn't be too long before they made another trip to Little Falls.

CHAPTER 35

Luke closed the door to the room he'd been given for the weekend so quietly, you'd have thought he was trying to hide from the air around him. After he had it closed, he waited and listened. His head was so low to the door his ear was nearly sitting on the keyhole. When he was satisfied nobody was coming, he slipped onto the chair next to the bed and dialed Mave's number.

Mave answered before the phone had a chance to ring in his ear.

"Yellow?" Mave's greeting was muffled by whatever he had shoveled into his mouth at the time. Luke imagined Mave on the living room couch, dropping chunks of food into it as he spoke.

"Mave, are you on the couch?"

"Where else would I be?"

Luke was sure a new chunk was dropping with every word. He tipped his head back, took a breath, and tried to stay focused.

"I need your help." Luke looked to the door to ensure nobody was lurking. "How quickly can you finish your analysis?"

"A week. Maybe two. Same as what we told your pops. Everything going alright up there?" Concern replaced the sound of chewed food.

"Yeah, it's great. Just, you know, I need this to work."

"I told you," Mave said.

"Told me what?"

"Conflict of interest. It applies. You know, two parties, different interests." If Luke had been sitting next to Mave, he would have seen his friend intersect two fingers as they traveled in different directions.

"It's going to work," Luke repeated. "Needs to. Anyway, holding down the fort?"

"Sweet. Yeah. Fuck yeah. Football Sunday. Grace got any pretty friends that might want to join me? Scratch that, no women allowed."

That was enough to get Luke to crack a smile.

"If you change your mind, she has three. None that I would be willing to set up with the Mr. Relationship doomsday that you are."

"I know. I met them. They are more of a gang. And Casey, you know Casey from work? She's hot. Wait, who said anything about a relationship?"

"Yeah, yeah. Relationships, the spawn of all evil. See what you can get done by Monday. See you tomorrow."

"See ya."

Mave was the first to end the call. He sat back in his borrowed home and thought, *No problem, I didn't have any plans, I'll just work the rest of my Saturday night and most of football Sunday.*

"Love sucks," Mave muttered to himself and trudged up the stairs because he really didn't have any other plans.

Well, Luke thought after hanging up with Mave, there isn't any use in worrying about it. Yet. Then he pushed off the bed.

When Luke swung the door open he nearly tackled Edna where she stood just outside.

"Holy shi-oot!" His language corrected immediately but nothing could have fazed his grandmother. That and he supposed she wouldn't have minded the swift swat that would have found the backside of his head for his language.

"Anything you need to share, Luke Aaron?" she said pointedly. He already felt guilty. She mastered the art of forcing guilt.

"Ah, no, everything is fine. Good. Great, actually," he said, confidence building with every word.

Edna turned to go down the stairs but let her words linger behind her: "I find that in life it's better to talk about things in question, rather than find the answers before they can be asked."

Luke squinted after his grandmother. She couldn't know, there would have been no way. With a grunt, his forehead found the wall and stayed there. This wasn't going to be good. Maybe even bad.

He decided to ignore it. He needed Grace to love him and hoped that would be enough. Nothing else would do it.

CHAPTER 36

It was the best weekend she'd had in as far back as she could remember. They rounded it out with Sunday morning church, followed by brunch hosted by Harold and Sarah, her new favorite, and completely adorable, married couple. They bickered as old couples do, but it was never mean spirited. Jokes and laughter filled their tiny rambler.

The only reason Grace, Edna, and Luke could find to leave was that there wasn't any room for them to take a nap. And they needed one after all of the food they'd eaten. It was leave, or fall asleep at the table.

Grace held her stomach as she and Luke piled themselves into the car. If Edna had squeezed any tighter in her farewell hug, she would have burst.

They waved to Edna, who was sending them off from the driveway. With a quick honk and both arms waving out their windows, they were on their way.

Grace took the moment to indulge in thought. This is what her life could really be like. For the first time in forever, she envisioned a life with the man sitting next to her. Dedicated to her family, work, and friends, of course. But all of this, too.

She wanted time and experiences with Luke. She wanted dinners at the table where they'd talk about one another's day. She wanted movies on the couch with popcorn. And eventually, she wanted kids. Kids who would love to visit great-grandma's house and all of great-grandma's crazy friends.

Grandparents too; her mom would love and spoil them and, oh how she wished her dad could be here to meet Luke. He would think there wasn't anybody better on this earth for her and he would've known it from the first time they'd met. They would have been inseparable. She agreed with herself in a nod.

"Thank you for coming with me this weekend." Luke's sincere tone interrupted her thoughts.

"It was amazing," she said genuinely.

"Everybody loves you up here, so it's probably good you liked it. It's easy to love you, so I don't blame them."

His words hung in the air.

Did he mean to say that? Had he meant to say he loved her?

It couldn't be. It was just something to say when people liked meeting you. *Everybody loved you up there today.* It was an expression.

"I mean it." He looked over when they came to a stop at a four-way crossing that would take them out of town. "I'm serious. You make it easy to love everything about you."

She waited, but there were no cheesy lines or jokes, no quips to make her laugh. She sat in silence and stared at him. She was so happy she could cry, and just for the inability to hold it all the way in, she let her eyes mist over for just a moment and finally smiled.

"Me too," she agreed, "I feel everything you're feeling and more."

Their lips found each other in the middle of their two seats.

"Thank you for letting me come with you," she whispered because she feared if it were anything more, happy crackles from tears would find her words.

All she could think every second of the ride back was this is it. They've finally found each other. He's the one.

CHAPTER 37

Their hands swung back and forth before he gave a little tug to turn her toward him.

"Thank you for a great weekend. I hope you have a great Monday." Luke picked up her spare hand as he spoke.

"No, thank you for an amazing weekend. And I am going to have a great day." She proudly tilted her head and looked up to her office. Luke gave her a hard kiss and surrounded her with a hug.

Grace's eyes followed Luke until he disappeared into the next block. The tapping sound on The Bistro window startled her into a jittery jump. Aimeé's smiling face and incessant waving from the other side had her seeing that Aimeé was talking incoherently, forgetting that only the people inside of the building could hear her.

Yeah-yeah, I'm coming, her hand motioned as she breathed through the last heart palpitation and moved toward the door.

"You two could be your own romance movie." Aimeé's hand waved that away. "I'm talking full-on, love-making, Indie film. Only the truly love-starved artistic types would see it, and the rest of the world wouldn't have an idea what they missed."

Aimeé's flour-dusted hand led Grace to the front register where she placed a vanilla latte on Thomas and Jane's company tab and moved down the bar. Aimeé, an efficient one-woman assembly line, built the latte in brilliant, robotic fashion.

Grace mirrored Aimeé as she sashayed down the bar while working. Rather than set Grace's latte on the counter, Aimeé carried it to their corner table, leaving Grace no choice but to follow.

Aimeé set the latte on one side of the table and sat directly across as she motioned to the chair in a way that said sit now, and whatever you do, you better not be silent. To reinforce her expectations, Aimeé directed, "Speak."

"I am great, too, yes, thank you for asking." Grace joked out the first couple of words hoping to get a smile out of Aimeé, who was all business. Aimeé obliged but didn't take the joke and wasn't going down easy.

"I know you're doing great. I can see it in your face. That is a post-sexed face." Aimeé's finger made circles around Grace's face for display.

"I want details. All of them. Then I'm going to brag about them to our beloved friends since I'll have heard them first."

Grace sipped her coffee and eyed her beautiful, questioning friend over the rim. She tried to conceal her feelings, but her smile turned to a beam at the dizzy, unimaginable, fantastic week she'd had since meeting Luke. Aimeé scolded her with a single look. "This is why," Aimeé said with a hand displayed toward Grace's face, "I need you to talk."

"Okay, I can start by saying we didn't partake in any love-making up north. But," Grade added before Aimeé could disapprove, "this isn't my first coffee today. We were up early, two rounds," she paused for effect, "of the best, most incredible," mouthing the keyword, "sex of my life. Probably his, too." She gave herself a little pat on the back.

Aimeé threw her hands up in the excitement and wasn't nearly as worried about the crowd of businessmen and women listening in on what was heading toward inappropriate conversation.

"I need more. Tell me more. When did it start? Did he stay with you? You with him?" Aimeé reached across the table and stole a sip of latte and shrugged. "What, it's not like you need it."

There wasn't any point in trying to argue with a smooth-talking French woman. Grace reached across the table to grab her latte back, drank, and began.

"We got back to the city around five o'clock last night. I'll tell you about the weekend later, but saying it was the perfect mixture of nostalgia and enjoyment doesn't nearly do it justice. So," Grace leaned in and cupped both hands around her warm drink, "we are at the curb in front of the light post, and he leaned over and gave me this huge, stop-your-breathing kiss. I mean we had to come up for air." Her hands moved to her head and impersonated a bomb exploding. "It was mind-blowing. More mind-blowing than kitchen night and pizza night. Combined." Aimeé fanned her face, gesturing with her other hand for Grace to continue.

"On cue, and obviously better able to focus than me, Luke said, 'I'm not ready to be away from you this weekend.' And obviously," Grace pointed to herself like there was no other option than for them to stay together, "I was feeling the same exact thing."

The pitch in her voice was getting higher. The speed of her words quickened from the excitement of reliving the moment.

"Of course, I didn't want to be all *Top Gun* – 'take me to bed or lose me forever,' but I might have been a little *Top Gun* because I said, 'take me to bed or lose me forever,' and – don't give me that look, I know you know what *Top Gun* is."

Aimeé lowered her eyebrows to an acceptable height, though still perfectly arched.

"Yes, I know." She waved her hand in admission, "Just a bit of sex-envy. It will pass."

"I love that I'm getting sex-envy from you of all people. Then, the next thing I know we are in a parking spot paying the meter and practically running up my stairs trying to wrestle clothes off each other."

Grace leaned her cup toward Aimeé. "That's where I'll stop for today. The rest of the show is not appropriate for children."

"You're kidding me." Aimeé's accent was thick with disappointment. Her body slumping as if she'd been served the greatest let down of all time.

"What?"

"This *save it for later* crap doesn't work for me."

"I'll-"

"Sex!"

A string of fluent French flew through the air reaching customers on the far end of the Bistro. Curious and amused patrons sent their interest to the table and to Aimeé who laid a slap on the table.

Grace stared, watching the musical rant fly from Aimeé's red-painted lips and waited for the fire to burn out.

"It is too early in the morning for anything other than the good stuff." Aimeé calmed and continued in her second language, "So, lay it on me. And remember, I need something good to give the girls."

Amused at the feistiness that usually only displayed itself on special occasions, Grace conceded.

"Okay, Okay. The sex." She took a deep breath in and exhaled in preparation. "Holy. Shit."

Her dark eyes growing huge, Aimeé was tracking. "Oh my God, it was a holy shit."

"A holy shit. His hands knew where to be at all times. They were light but rough to the touch. His kisses, oh my, his kisses were everywhere. *Everywhere.* He might have actually been driving me to the point of craziness. I thought I was going to explode."

Aimeé shook her head in bewilderment.

"I nearly screamed Luke's name, but before I could, he was inside me, and the feeling was, oh my God, it was heavenly. But it felt like a sin. The buildup. I can't, there are no words. Then it was *hammered* in. Not fast, just heavy. Excruciatingly heavy. And so slow at first, but it was ravishing. *He* was ravishing. More, so much more than the times before."

Something happened. Grace had lost Aimeé's full attention. Then she followed her friend's voice and methodical head-turn.

"Speaking of ravishing."

Grace looked over to see Luke's smiling face standing next to her, and the quiver of morning rushed back.

"Ravishing, huh?" Luke asked, amused and feeling a bit overconfident after hearing Grace's description. Though, he couldn't deny feeling the same way about Grace – *she* was ravishing.

"Hi. How much of that did you hear?" she inquired.

Luke bent down to place a kiss on her cheek, "Enough to know we'll probably have to try it out again later on. Just to make sure it fits the description."

Grace felt her face warm with red.

"Aimeé, I hope it was entertaining enough." He winked, and moved back to Grace, "I wanted one more look at you before the day started and figured I'd still find you here."

"I'm glad you did." Her heart soared.

Luke gave her one more peck on the lips and left her eyes closed and satisfied.

"A holy shit for sure," Aimeé agreed and began her retreat to head back to work. As she made her way around the table, she bent to give Grace her own kiss on the cheek and moved across the room with a final comment. "Grace, I've never been happier to see somebody glow the way you are doing at this very moment."

Grace had never loved her life more than she did right then. The thought carried her through the last sip of her latte.

CHAPTER 38

Two weeks had gone by too fast. It's why she'd wanted the walk to the office to be slow, to savor the quiet, and let her thoughts take over.

Grace's vacation was over, but her whirlwind romance had only heated up. Since the weekend at Edna's, they hadn't spent a night apart. Luke had late nights at the office, and Grace had dinner with the girls and an evening at her mom's with her brother, William – but they'd made the time. Cherished the moments. Captured the nights. And in that time had added plenty of mind-blowing sex.

It wasn't a familiar feeling. She'd had the same yesterday – her first day back. It was the same tinge of guilt in not wanting her vacation to end. Her time and attention for Luke would now have to split time with her work.

Yesterday was overwhelming. A Monday that bombarded Grace with work she didn't even have the time to give her attention to, much less finish. She knew today wouldn't be any different. It was early so it would be quiet for a bit, and she'd be the only one there, but the work, the emails she didn't get to from the day before, were there waiting. And, she thought back to her calendar, a meeting with the board was waiting for her.

The black loafers she wore caught her attention as they clicked along the paved walk. They would have reflected the light of the street lamps if they hadn't been shaded by small leaf piles at her feet. She leaned her head back and took a deep breath.

When she stopped on the corner where she crossed to get to the Bistro, it was the first time she thought the walk wasn't long enough. She wanted more time. More time in bed with Luke, snuggled in, comforted by his love. She'd never felt that way before. Hell, she used to use work as an excuse to get *out* of a man's bed, she thought and grinned to herself. What a strange, bizarre, and happy thought.

Grace looked across the street and saw Aimeé, clear as day. She might not want to go to work, but Aimeé's fancy little shop had done its job and lured her in. She no longer wanted to be on the outside. She crossed the street and walked in and was welcomed by the familiar, sweet scents.

"You have another love note," Aimeé sang from the kitchen.

Inside she did a little dance and started toward the front. "Out in a second."

Grace slid her jacket off and snooped around the counter.

"I'm sorry to say, there is no cup. Yet." Aimeé walked in from the kitchen and began her instruction. "You are, however, supposed to order your favorite drink – even if it has too many calories. The message there was, 'You made it through Monday, and that's all the excuse you need.' I tend to agree."

She continued. "And, though there is no cup, there is this." Aimeé wafted a note in front of Grace's face, "And, seeing as you already know there is no privacy between us, yes, I read it. No, I don't think he's crazy. Yes, I think you should meet him for lunch. And finally, do you think he happens to have a brother? It would not be terrible if he were rich. I would even take him if he were slightly less attractive."

Grace heard everything and processed, but all she could do was smile down at the hand-written note. He must have done it before he left the house. He'd beaten her out of the door that morning.

"Of course, I'm going to meet him for lunch." It wasn't even a question. Even with the hoard of work that lay before her, she would make time. He was her match in every way. He made her feel incredible.

But there was no brother. "I'm sorry to say, no brother. He does have a recently broken-up best friend."

Aimeé nodded, wondering if Grace was referring to a certain dapper red-head, Travis Mavens.

"Well, it was worth a try. What will you have for lunch? I'll have it ready. If you cancel, I'll just find somebody to eat it."

"Mmm. Yes. Let's do the bisque and a Croque Monsieur. Luke can have his pick, or we can split."

"Oui, your taste is impeccable." Aimeé completed her show with a chef's kiss of her fingertips, indicating an ingenious selection.

CHAPTER 39

Prep meeting, meeting with the board, meeting after meeting with the board, and when she finally stopped running around long enough to look at the clock, it read eleven-fifteen.

Grace got up to stretch her legs and walked to the window. When she looked out, she hoped she would catch Luke as he walked by. Maybe he would be early for lunch. She imagined he would say hello to people as he passed, perhaps nodding in their direction, in his slow and confident stride.

She folded her arms and leaned against the windowpane, pleased and smiling to herself.

"Now that's a look of satisfaction if I've ever seen one."

Grace turned to see Maggie standing at the door with Seth. Usually, she wouldn't look twice, but amidst her appreciation of manly appearances, thanks to Luke, it crossed her mind. She noticed Seth was tall, just a bit too skinny, but not an unsightly looking analyst. Especially when he was holding what looked to be the reports she'd asked for. And she'd need them since the board confirmed the rumors: Wallace wanted Thomas and Jane, and due diligence was set to start tomorrow. If she thought the paperwork was a nightmare now, gathering all the requested statistics and reports to send to Wallace, at his request, was going to be worse. Oh well, she took a long breath to relax.

Grace looked at Seth again, then wondered, had he ever dated? Was he even interested in dating? Everybody out there was in the same boat, weren't they? Single or not, trying or not trying. The thought struck her that somebody like Seth could have been on the other side of her blind date.

Thinking of which, she should get that number so she could apologize and explain her standing up a complete stranger. At least reassure him that it hadn't been her getting one look and darting back out as fast as she came in. She had simply found her match and would wish him luck in finding the same. She hadn't wanted to reach out earlier but the idea of being on the other end, the stood up end, and not knowing was tugging at her conscience.

"Possibly." She agreed, knowing she was more than satisfied. "I see you pawned your paperwork off on the smart guy." She sent Seth an appreciative look, hoping he knew how much the work he did was valued.

"I will have you know I looked at the top two pages in great detail." Maggie was pointedly protecting her work and busy schedule. "These look good."

"Lucky for me – and us." Grace winked, imitating Luke the best she could. How she already loved his mannerisms. "Hey, did you happen to find a number, a phone number," she specified motioning to the folder as she held out her hand for it, "in there?"

Maggie's confused look answered her question but she offered verbal confirmation, "I didn't, but I can take another look."

"No, don't worry about it. It's from before my vacation. I should call this guy I never ended up seeing. That blind date. At the very least shoot him a text."

Curiosity filled both Maggie and Seth's faces instantaneously. Maggie's, a pleasantly surprised, you better tell me now, type of look; Seth's heated from a hint of embarrassment.

His stutter was out fast, "I-I," he waited for a beat and thought, "No. Nope. No number."

Then Seth turned on a dime and walked back across the room and out, away from both women.

"Wow, he really knows how to make an exit," Grace piped up with her eyes wide in amusement, "Interesting guy, our Seth."

"Come on now," Maggie walked into the office and leaned herself on the windowpane across from Grace, "You have to know why he acts so strangely."

Grace angled her head to think about it, and nothing came. Not even a witty idea or comment. "No, and my brain is so fried I don't even have it in me to be funny about it."

"Honey, Seth has had a crush on you since the day he started seven years ago. I'm fairly certain that is the one reason he hasn't taken his talents anywhere else. We keep him paid well, sure, but he could go somewhere else and possibly do better, or move up in the ranks."

"Does he want that?" Grace panicked at the idea they hadn't been keeping Seth appropriately engaged and utilized; in talent and position. Then thought, a crush? Had she heard that right? She had never been looking, but before Luke, she wondered, had she become blind to the flirt? Maybe her girlfriends had been right.

"Who would have thunk?" She tried for a dab of humor.

"Yeah," Maggie's tone turned humorously sarcastic, "who would have thought an eligible man would be attracted to one of the most beautiful, and successful I might add, women in Minneapolis? Outrageous."

Maggie made her way out of the room, and Grace's smile followed Maggie and her sign-off out. "I expect a dinner soon so you can fill me in on that satisfied smile, and that…" Maggie waved a hand in Grace's direction, "let's call it a glow."

Maggie was a mind-reader. It was official.

CHAPTER 40

Laughter and candlelight filled the Bistro late into Thursday night. The restaurant was empty except for the four women, as it had been since the first Thursday it opened.

Always a Thursday, because it gave all of the girls something to look forward to. That and anybody could get through a Friday, even if slightly hungover. One by one, the girls told stories of their week.

Rachel and Richard – last name not allowed – had their first kiss and subsequently, their first romp. It was, "as expected" as far as first, not overly spectacular, romps go. Though Rachel seemed willing to let it try to improve.

Casey offered to pay for the evening as she had a significant one-time consult payout for hacking into a local company on purpose to test their security. Apparently, it wasn't as secure as they thought. They extended her a contract to help consult with their team. The girls followed about fifty percent of the conversation. They understood enough to wonder just how much money Casey had stashed away.

Aimeé's week didn't really have too much to show for it except for an Officer, Christopher Finnegan, making frequent morning visits to pick up a coffee and flirt for a few minutes, which she was happy to partake in. Flirting was her specialty, second only to her baking and coffee making, which were tied for first.

The girls sped through their own updates and left little room for comment, which was unusual. They sat then, eager, and stared at Grace from each side of the table, slowly sipping their wine as they waited.

Grace started with a detailed recount of Edna's since Casey and Rachel had only heard it secondhand, then wound through lunches, dinners, frisky morning escapades, and their first slow and sensual love-making session. She paused only for their oohs and ahhs of admiration. Even Casey admitted they were a good fit and was jealous – not of the relationship, but the benefits that came along with it.

"I thought things might change when I went back to work again, but we've made it work. And dinners were the domestic kind. Like we got home, made spaghetti together, and ate it on the couch in sweats."

Rachel was fascinated, "You sweat-pant-ate."

"We sweat-pant-ate," Grace confirmed and tried to match Rachel's seriousness.

"Really?" Casey asked to be sure she was reading Rachel right.

"Really. It's a big deal."

"You're kidding." Casey couldn't see any sort of a deal.

"To not be made up," Aimeé chimed in. "Seeing the other in their natural habitat. It's very domestic. Pretty soon you won't be wearing makeup to bed and skipping a night between shaving your legs."

"Why, when you say it, does it sound like a fashion trend?" Casey asked.

The four girls laughed and sipped.

"How is everything going with work?" Rachel asked since Grace broached the subject. Casey grunted, showing her added interest – knowing she knew a little too much working for the enemy.

"I'm going to assume Ms. Hacker here," Grace pointed to Casey," already knows more than she should, but it's been busy. We are scrambling left and right trying to get data for due diligence. The teams are having to maintain their regular workload, too."

Grace took a sip to try and swallow the exhaustion that was building up just talking about it.

"We have an in-person meeting with the leaders and advisors from both companies for the first time on Monday. Maggie has been superwoman getting everything ready."

"I wonder how the meeting will go." Rachel's voice sounded overly concerned.

"Just another meeting. I have something up my sleeve so Wallace might be in for a surprise – a good surprise."

Aimeé, Casey, and Rachel nodded in agreement but shared a look that said, somebody would be surprised and it might not be Wallace.

CHAPTER 41

Grace was shocked. Just completely *shocked*, she thought again, speechless.

Grace looked up at Seth and back down at the report he'd handed her. She'd need to dive into the details of what she was looking at. The numbers were phenomenal. But she couldn't afford to not understand the where, what, and how behind each calculation, each data point.

She flipped through the first couple of pages, this was precisely what she was looking for. Praying for.

Wallace – if she handled her proposal and he handled the takeover in just the right way – might want them to continue operating as is. He'd want them to grow, sure, but the healthy and prosperous company that was Thomas and Jane could remain intact.

"Seth, this is perfect. He knew our numbers were good, but this," she trailed off, shaking her head, "he can't say no. I don't know much about Aaron Wallace, but from what I've heard through conversation, he'll be willing if it's smart and profitable. I love it."

Sincerity filled her eyes. "Thank you for taking the time to do this." Grace understood the work, the hours, the extremely long days, and the resources he would have had to tap to finish as quickly as he did.

"Of course. I would do anything for you, I mean, for the company. You know, for Thomas and Jane." He stumbled like she'd never seen. "Because you're a Thomas, so it means for you, but not you personally." Horrified, he steamrolled through in a rush. "But not that I wouldn't do it for you personally, because technically I did, because you asked, so."

"I get it, don't worry about it at all." Come on, Seth, get a hold of yourself, she thought, trying her best for a look of understanding. "I have to take this to Abbi, but I think we have a winner."

"I sent it to her." Seth's words flew out as he fumblingly straightened his shirtsleeve.

"Perfect." She got up and moved around the table to walk him out. "I mean it, Seth, thank you," She took his hand in a shake and halted at the feeling of their hands. It was strange, it wasn't a bad feeling, but she couldn't stop the slanted grin at the way their hands fit. Then she nodded, let go, and made her way out of the door, passing Maggie on the way.

Once Grace was out of earshot, Seth turned to Maggie, and all he could do was throw his head back and groan.

"Oh sweetie," Maggie attempted to reassure him as she watched him bring the hand that had just been held by Grace's closer to his body, "It didn't sound, or look, that bad from my point of view. You got a little choppy there in the middle, but overall I think you pleased Grace just fine."

Maggie lingered in the room and pretended to straighten photographs and align stacks of paper before she pried further. Grace liked her room organized anyway, so it wasn't wholly frivolous.

"Did you happen to find that number Grace was looking for the other day? I can't find it anywhere at my desk. I assumed since it wasn't in the folder, it had fallen out somewhere along the way."

She didn't make eye contact right away, she knew that would have made him nervous, so Maggie fiddled with a spare pen and highlighter on Grace's desk before placing them in her drawer.

Not hearing a response, Maggie turned toward Seth, who looked back at her like a boy who'd been caught.

"Seth," Maggie said, in a motherly tone. "If you found that number, you have to give it to Grace. It is not yours to have or to keep from her."

Resigned, Seth sighed., "I know." He moved his hand over his face in exasperation, "I just, I, what the hell, you might as well know."

"I know."

Seth's eyes shot to Maggie's, "What do you mean you know?"

"I know that you've had your eye on Grace ever since you started here. It's been almost a decade, and you've been pining. And no, before you panic, nobody else knows or has paid enough attention to know." Maggie watched relief wash over him as he backed into the guest chair across from Grace's desk. "But just because you think you have feelings for her doesn't mean you can keep that number from her. Besides, she was going to use it to call and tell whoever it was that she was sorry and she won't be able to meet him. What if that was you who'd been expecting her message?"

Maggie liked to think she'd perfected the rational scold. Her five children had turned out alright. "What could it hurt to be the guy that gives her something she thought she lost?"

"Yeah." Seth looked at least semi-pleased with that solution, even though he knew the stupid reason she had stood the man up was because she found some other jerk that swiped her up. *Luke*, he immaturely grumbled the name in his mind. He probably wasn't even a jerk if Grace liked him, and that irritated him even more.

"You never know what could happen. Be the good guy now, and who knows, if it doesn't work out with this guy, you can finally decide to make a move. Life has a funny way of working out."

Maggie wisely walked out of Grace's office, mission accomplished. Grace didn't need other people finding out more about her life than they already knew. She was finally happy, and Maggie would do whatever she could to keep it that way. Even if it meant feeding Seth a little hope. He would find his match someday. She was sure of it.

Maggie spotted Grace and Abbi huddled over Abbi's desk pointing at a document, nodding heads, and smiling with renewed energy. Grace laughed at something Abbi had said, and Maggie noted the illumination she was radiating. Yes, whatever this boy was doing for Grace was worth it.

CHAPTER 42

By the next Monday morning Grace was moving with the efficiency of a brilliant, well-trained athlete in heels. The boardroom was set up: water on the table, reports ready and stacked perfectly on the table in front of her seat. And she thought, she was looking the part.

She wore a scoop-necked, three-quarter sleeve, navy blue work dress; a thin red scarf tied neatly around her neck that matched her red heels – which weren't too over-the-top after a minute of deliberation earlier that morning – and her hair wrapped in a blonde bun that sat high on her head. Feminine, but tough.

At the end of the long conference table, Grace stood with her hands on her hips. She was ready.

Abbi walked in to get a look for herself. The women stood side by side. A force.

"We are ready for this, Grace. We will do whatever we can. We make our offer and go from there. I don't want you to forget that either way, this can be a great opportunity for everybody." Abbi motioned toward the door where all of their life-long workers sat at their desks.

"They should be here any minute. Mr. Wallace is bringing his team, and it should only be a group of four. Wallace, his-" Abbi broke off when she watched Grace amicably shake her head.

"I don't care who shows up. They all think they're important," Grace interrupted. "All I know is what we have, and it's a damn good deal. Wallace's second-hand men are irrelevant at this point. Luke!"

Grace's surprise at seeing Luke had her heart full and her nerves settling. Of course, he would come to wish her luck. That was exactly like him. She felt herself relax and, at that moment, wanted nothing more than to wrap her arms around him. Then she'd politely kick him out so she could kick butt in this acquisition meeting.

Mr. Aaron Wallace, or whom she assumed was Mr. Wallace given his age, entered the room, halting her move toward Luke. She shot Luke an apologetic smile and held up her finger, asking for a moment.

She saw Mr. Wallace nod toward Luke and brush past him with an outstretched hand, offered to her in greeting.

"Hello, you must be Grace Thomas. It is a pleasure to finally meet you." She hated that she didn't hate him.

"Mr. Wallace, it's-" she began.

"Please. Aaron. Call me Aaron. We'll be seeing a lot more of each other."

Grace corrected herself. "Aaron, nice to meet you. This is Abigail Jane. You'll recognize the name from our initial correspondence." It was a statement, not a question.

Grace attempted to move around Aaron so she could usher Luke out and thank him, but it was proving to be challenging. She felt Abbi's hand rest on her back as she shook Aaron's hand with the other.

"I have to say," Aaron Wallace started as he slowed the handshake and covered Abbi's held-hand with his spare one. His eyes traveled between the two women, "I met Raymond Thomas on a couple occasions. Mostly charity events." He nodded mostly to himself at the recall, "He was one of the greatest men I've had the pleasure to meet. I'm sorry for your loss."

"It's nice meeting you in person, Aaron. Thank you for saying that. We miss him. Very much." Abbi stole a look at Grace and asked, "Who do you have with you today?"

"This is the core team," Aaron said. "You'll be working with them for the majority. Let me introduce you all, and we can get settled in. This is Randy Flamingo, he's been with us for fifteen years and specializes in acquisitions. This is Travis Mavens, he's been with us ten years. His primary focus for our conversations together will be financial forecasting." Aaron shifted, letting Travis move in for a handshake of his own.

Grace didn't feel her heart sink immediately. With the chaos of their rush into the room she'd neglected to count the heads that filled it. When she did, Aaron cut her off by continuing his introductions. He moved just a bit, and Luke stepped forward to stand beside him. Then the dread set in.

Aaron Wallace continued, beaming with pride in a way only a father can, "And this is my son, Luke Wallace."

CHAPTER 43

The loss of breath slammed into her. Abbi's hand on her back jumped off from the startle. Luke tried to reach out to her, but all she could do was back away from his touch. She had never wanted and hated something more in her life.

He was trying to take her dad's company away from her? The only man she'd ever opened her heart for. Thirty-seconds ago she would have taken a leap of faith into marriage with him if he would have made the offer. And now?

Grace shook her head, almost imperceptibly, as she tried to clear the thoughts flooding her mind.

Then it hit her. As quickly as the sadness had come, it had turned to anger. The realization steadied her rather than shook.

Their meeting each other wasn't by chance, was it? Was it possible this whole charade of *running into her* was an attempt to make her swoon at his feet? Less in search of boundless love, and more a bottom line. Hoping for a better price on her prized possession.

How convenient it would have been for him to have the current acting President and CEO standing behind him, supporting them in their efforts. She would never have believed he'd be capable of such deceit. Not on her life.

Grace looked him in the eye, and the room turned to ice. His face shifted to concern at her sudden, unemotional front. The hurt on his face wasn't far behind, but she wasn't willing to fall for the same act twice. He could take his false care and concern and shove it nicely up his ass.

It was her turn to step forward and hold out a hand to him, "Luke, it's nice to meet you."

"Grace, we've met."

Luke's hand didn't shake hers, it grabbed and held on tight, trying not to lose her to the stony look on her face, but it didn't work. Grace tried to tug her hand away without causing too big of a scene.

Grace calmly offered for the men to take their places at the table so they could get started, although her heart thudded in her chest. Everybody did as they were told as they eyed the two of them. Nobody was willing to speak a word about Luke's obvious concern and Grace's frosty greeting.

Initial numbers – only the ones Wallace had requested – were read, agreed upon, and disagreed upon. Reports were compared, and processes were defined. Grace directed all of her questions and answers to Aaron. She didn't feel the need to include the other three at this point. It wasn't their fight yet. Yesterday, or even thirty minutes earlier, she would have involved them fully. She would have needed them. Persuaded them. They would have been pivotal in reviewing their proposal. A proposal they would all profit from. Everybody would get a piece of the successful pie.

Now, she didn't want them to have a tiny sliver.

Grace slid the friendly acquisition proposal under the rest of her papers. She was ready and willing to follow the advice Luke had given her when she'd foolishly asked his opinion. Fight. She was going to knock Wallace, and all of them, dead.

"We'll get ready for our first break here in a couple minutes," she said evenly. "As you can see, we are a very efficient and successful company. What you're offering has to make sense from a business perspective. For our customers, and especially to the people sitting outside these doors. Thomas and Jane has an unbeatable reputation – and for a good reason."

Aaron smiled, a generous smile from what she could tell, and responded, "Ms. Thomas – Grace, if I may – if we thought we knew what we were getting into before, your presentation has only impressed us further." He paused to recognize the other heads nodding in agreement. "I should confirm this is exactly the type of company we love and are willing to invest in with equal interest."

"Then I do agree with you, but I have to apologize for my honesty." Grace said, standing over the room, "Mr. Wallace, we aren't just another company with a good bottom line. Respectfully, it will not be an easy task convincing me that any amount of money is worth this company and these people." Grace looked around the table and paused when she finally looked Luke in the eye. "If I'm not satisfied with your proposal, the takeover you're planning will become hostile. And we'll fight it."

CHAPTER 44

"Grace, this is not what we had discussed. This is not what we had sent to the board. We are going to have to go back. It won't sit well with them, the sudden change in direction."

Abbi closed her office door after ensuring the words between them wouldn't be overheard.

"This isn't *at all* what we discussed," Abbi repeated, trying to navigate her disconcertion while setting her folder of documents on her desk.

"We need to be reviewing option number two and giving them every reason to *not* dissolve this company upon takeover. You know as well as I do we will not be able to stop a hostile takeover."

Abbi moved closer to Grace who hadn't moved from the window. When Abbi stood next to her, she saw Grace wasn't holding back her words to be obstinate. She wasn't able to speak through the tears that were streaming down her face. Compassion and instinct had Abbi wrapping Grace in her arms.

"Oh, honey, it will be okay. We will work this out, I promise. I know it's going to be hard, but we just have to keep our nose to the grindstone and stick with the plan. Things will work out, I just know it."

"It's not that," Grace's breathy, staggered, words were barely audible, "Luke Wallace, Luke Aaron Wallace. He's my Luke – *was* my Luke," she corrected. "I would like to believe our meeting was by chance, but this? It just feels so – I feel so dumb. How could I not have put that together? Luke Wallace." She repeated his name; her words were swallowed up by a silent sob as she shook her head.

How had she not put it together? *Luke Aaron.* She'd heard it herself.

"I was blinded by ridiculous infatuation. I'm smarter than that, but I let myself fall–" No, she wouldn't say *in love.*

Abbi's face instantly became the image of realization of all that the situation entailed, and she motioned for Grace to sit. Abbi squatted in front of her and held both of her hands.

"I might not know what Luke's intentions were throughout your courtship, but these are the things I do know. You cannot fake the kind of happy that I've seen from you over the past couple of weeks. To do that, to give you that kind of happiness – whether intentional or unintentional – he must have fallen just as hard for you. I also saw the way he was looking at you in that room, and every bit of it was shock and pain. I didn't understand why at the moment, but I would bet money he didn't realize how you'd feel. But across that table today, when he saw your hurt, it nearly killed him."

Grace heard the words, but didn't process them, she didn't want to. If Abbi could hear the questions racing through her mind, the room wouldn't have been as silent as it seemed. The pain and anger in her heart was crippling.

CHAPTER 45

Luke cornered Mave in a short hall that veered toward a hidden coffee machine. Anger and frustration filled his head to the point of exploding, and Mave was his trigger and his target. In a heated, huffing sneer, he pointed at Mave's chest and began his tirade.

"What the fuck, Mave. This," he pointed in the direction of the conference room from hell, "is why I needed you to get me the information about the company last week. So I could, I don't know," Luke spun around "show her there was another way." Luke's hands laid out in front of him, imitating the path he'd wanted.

"A way to keep her company *and* for Wallace to provide the capital to expand its business. Now I look like an asshole, and the whole thing could have gone differently. I called in a single fucking favor from you, and nothing. Over a week ago. So much for fucking deadlines." His whispered words hissed out.

Luke turned again to pace and swung back around as quickly as he walked away, "You show up at my door, and I let you live with me, no questions asked. You slowly take over every room in my condo, and I don't say a word. I shift schedules and make sure I'm there for you, and I can't get one fucking report presentation from you for this? To help the woman I love? Or," he said with sudden realization, "is that it? You can't be happy so I can't either, right? What the fuck were you even doing for the last week?"

For a minute, Mave didn't move. He just stared at his friend without saying a word.

Mave began to leave and moved his shoulder to avoid running into Luke on his way out. He avoided a run-in with another poor schmuck who was trying to get an innocent cup of coffee, then paused briefly and looked over his shoulder.

"I didn't realize I was getting in your way. I'll start packing my things and look for a place. If you need me out sooner, I can move in with my mom for a bit." Then he was gone.

Luke stood alone. He didn't realize the impact his words would have until he said them. He didn't want Mave to move out. When his hands slid over his face, a frustrated groan left his body. The coffee stranger commented.

"I'm willing to bet this isn't just a Monday thing?"

Luke looked at the man. He wasn't amused, irritated, or angry. Just looked. He wished the thoughts in his mind would stop hammering to the front of his forehead.

"Not just a Monday thing." He confirmed.

"I'm Seth."

"Luke."

The men shook hands and offered a nod.

"Can I ask what the trouble is?" Seth inquired.

Luke knew he shouldn't go here, but he had to know. "Do you know Grace Thomas?"

Seth's eyes rounded. "I do. She's been my boss, well, my boss's, boss's boss," he added, moving his empty mug up and down for every boss, "my entire working career. Nice. Smart. I don't have to tell you about her looks. It's a lethal combination. Do you know her?"

"We're dating. Were dating. Are dating." Luke was irritated that it irritated him to hear another man acknowledge Grace's beauty, even though it shouldn't have. All you had to do is glance her direction, man or woman, to know it immediately. In an attempt to ease his directness and confusion, he offered, "We just began dating. And sure as shit, I fell in love with her."

Curiously looking at Seth now and searching for answers, "Seth, have you already found the person you're supposed to be with?"

"Not yet." It was an honest answer.

"Good. Be prepared. It will fly you high and then drop you from ten thousand feet. Nice to meet you, Seth. I'm sure we'll be seeing a lot more of each other."

The men left the hall at the same time and turned to walk in different directions.

Luke made his way to the door.

Seth sauntered toward Maggie.

Ensuring nobody was around, he leaned over her computer monitor and looked her directly in the eye.

"It came."

"What came?" Maggie answered without returning the eye-contact, unconcerned until she heard his reply.

A silent fist pump appeared over her monitor.

"My   chance."

CHAPTER 46

Thursday night drinks with the girls was just what Grace needed. It had been three and a half days since the horrific meeting with Wallace and his *associates,* and it had allowed just enough time for her sadness to turn to steely resolve.

"I am turning him off. This is strictly a business deal."

Grace wheeled herself around the kitchen island to get the unopened wine bottles. She put her hair in a high ponytail and tightened, bound and determined to not give in to her friends.

In hindsight, it was probably her own fault. She had talked Luke up so much to them in such a short amount of time. Damn. She swooped up the two bottles and cradled them for transport to the living room.

The living room was positioned in the front of her home, with a view provided by huge bay window rather than a wall. It was one of the triplets – her description the beloved windows that sat one on top of the other. One just above it in her office, and another above that in her bedroom. It was one of the reasons she had to buy the brownstone, that and its old charm.

Grace carried the wine to her friends, walking past her long kitchen table that divided the living room from the kitchen. Each time she walked by, she glanced at the beautiful chandelier that hung above it. Crystals fell in tiers from rectangular black iron bars, each layer of metal and sparkle getting smaller the closer they got to the table.

Grace set the bottles next to the stemmed glasses on the wooden ottoman that was made to replicate the kitchen table.

Rachel, Aimeé, and Casey were scattered on the couch facing the fireplace and the leather chairs that bordered it. Each had their own place to cozy around the table with easy access to their drinks and a place to lean back and rest their feet.

The silence was a little too long for her liking. "Okay, seriously. It's going to be fine. It's not like we've committed our lives to each other."

Grace held any thoughts and comments inside about wanting just that when she'd woken up that morning. "It's been such a short amount of time, it should be nothing for us to go back to how things were before we met. He'll find somebody new, and I'll start defending against the takeover. Which is officially hostile."

She poured the wine into the glasses, trying to steady her shaking hand. She hadn't been able to eat all week, since the betrayal in the boardroom.

"Are you feeling anything at all when you talk like this?" The concern in Rachel's voice was evident.

"What do you mean *feeling?* That's exactly what I'm trying not to do. Then one day I'll wake up, and I won't have to try, it will just happen."

Aimeé, who was usually a fan of multiple dating partners, even voiced her opinion. Unfortunately, it was not in favor of Grace's plan to cut things off. "I don't think this is a good idea. I think you should work it out."

"How can you say that? You know what Thomas and Jane means to me. He's trying to buy and take away the one thing in my life I would do anything to keep. And, he lied to me." She said, not admitting out loud that's what hurt the most. He'd had thousands of chances he could have taken to tell her how their lives intersected.

Grace surprised herself at the quick and curt response. Rachel was a given, as a complete romantic, she would hate the idea of a lifetime of true love slipping away, or more accurately, shut out. But Aimeé?

"Well," Aimeé swung her glass around as if saying it's simple, "you were glowing. That doesn't just happen. You were walking around with all of the sex appeal a woman should have when she's in love. She gets that way, because she has, in fact, been loved. It's all we try and find in this life, is it not?"

Grace leaned back and huffed.

"I was wrong for being so willing to throw my heart around. Nobody falls in love in a couple weeks, and don't you dare say it happens all the time." She jabbed a finger at Rachel, who was the honorable hopeless romantic of the group. "Those are movies, not real life."

"It was a whirlwind romance. Not love." Grace added, looking over at Casey. "You're awfully quiet over there."

Casey's eyes moved from friend to friend, then she traced the flannel pattern on her sleeve. She was the only one that had already changed into her pajamas. Why be in anything else when she could be comfortable and drink wine at the same time? It made for walking up to bed and sleeping much more effortless at the end of the night.

"I've decided I don't get a vote on this," Casey said at last.

The three girls in unison voiced their dismay. "Oh, come on!"

"I'm serious," Casey went on. "I think it's hard for people to enter each other's lives at exactly the right time with the exact same willingness to work it out for the long haul. I think some people get lucky, but for the most part, it ends in heartbreak. Why not figure it out now rather than wait twenty years and three kids from now?"

Grace's thoughts couldn't help but flashback to Edna's house when Luke had given her the *right place, right time* speech. When she had listened to him talk, all she could think about was how she was so lucky to have found him. Now she just wanted to pretend like he wasn't breaking her heart.

It was too much to have to pay attention and be on top of her game at work. So, she would bury it. Then, in time, it would go away.

"I agree with you, Case. It just didn't work, and it's better it happened now." She tried to blink away the tears that stung her eyes and hoped the girls didn't see them. There was a time and place for that, and this wasn't it.

The two bottles went down quickly with the cheese and crackers that were eventually whittled down to crumbs on a wooden tray.

Grace loved these nights. Life was talked about and analyzed. Memories were stirred. The girls shared moments of sadness when talking about friends that had lost babies or were ill, and laughed to the point of tears when talking about embarrassing moments or reliving a funny story from their past, whether it was five days ago or five years.

Luke didn't come up again, and she was thankful for it. This was a time to escape, and all four of them knew it.

Rachel was the first to break away and move to her guest bedroom for the night. She rounded the room and gave each girl a hug and a kiss on the cheek goodnight. She was the mother-figure and the caregiver to all of them. She played a special role in their lives, and they knew it. Of the four, she would be the one to find her true love and make it last. She was too good a person not to.

The stairs made small cricket creaks as she moved up, and the girls left by the fire hunkered down under their blankets for the next round of gossip.

Not too much time passed before Aimeé excused herself and gave her own round of kisses. She attempted to get away before the girls pressed her about a particular police officer that was frequenting her restaurant, and the only response they got was: "If I fell in love with every loyal patron, or man in uniform that crossed my path, I wouldn't have enough love to go around."

Though her statement was genuine, the two girls couldn't help but feel she held something back. Only time – or their continued badgering – would tell.

When there were only empty glasses and bottles left on the ottoman, Grace and Casey began to make their way up the stairs. Not much was said, but not much had to be. Of all the nights the girls had spent together, Casey and Grace always shared the last room. Usually, due to lack of space, but now it turned into a certain kind of ritual. The last two to bed shared it.

Bed, to Grace's mind, would be the hardest place to be. Everything was dark and quiet, and allowed her mind to wander. It was almost day four of pretending like she wasn't in love with Luke. And now, being tucked into the bed they had shared, made love in, and talked late into the nights and early mornings, was proving to be terrible.

She squeezed her eyes closed, hoping to push thoughts of missing Luke out of her mind. To try and stop wondering if he was thinking of her, too. Tiny glimpses of their moments together flashed in and out of her mind like an old camera reel.

How could there be so many moments in such a short amount of time, she wondered? She was prepared for this moment, in bed, but she wasn't ready for the torment and the burning headache that came with the barrage of tears that were building up behind her eyes.

When the first tear fell, she sat up and buried her face in her hands. Grace felt Casey's body cocoon hers in comfort, and the rest of her anguish came pouring out. Her body quivered and heaved and stole her breath as she let go of her all-consuming, uncontrollable emotions.

Casey rocked her back and forth, quickly at first, then gradually slowing to help calm. The only words she spoke were to soothe.

"It's going to be okay. It's going to be okay." They were repeated like a mantra intertwined with quiet shushes as though she were rocking a baby to sleep.

Neither of them knew how long it took. It could have been a minute or an hour, but Grace thought she was finally able to speak.

"There wasn't a single bad moment or red flag until he showed up at the office. I thought he came to wish me luck." The bewilderment came again as it had in the millions of times she relived the moment, and she shook her head.

Grace inhaled deeply to ensure another round of tears wasn't ready to follow. "Every image of him in my mind, every thought, is a good one. How do I make them stop?" She asked without expecting an answer and not allowing for one. "I want to believe he didn't know who I was before we ran into each other, but it just seems too coincidental. Especially how we met – when we met. On top of that, even if it was just a crazy coincidence, then he's still trying to take Thomas and Jane away. I couldn't live with anybody who did that to me. I would resent them for the rest of our lives."

Grace stopped to wipe what was left of the tears from her cheeks and moved slightly so she and Casey could lay back down, their heads sharing the same pillow, both staring into the darkness.

"You were right," Grace admitted to Casey. She didn't have to acknowledge what she was talking about, but she went on. "It's too hard to find somebody at exactly the right time, at exactly the right moment in life."

Justifying her decision to cut Luke off, she added, "The timing is all wrong. I can't lose this company. Not now. Not like this."

Casey held her friend's hand and didn't say anything. She was afraid her own tears would fall knowing she had done this to her best friend.

Grace wondered if Casey was trying to think of the right words? She knew that holding back wasn't Casey's style, or more accurately, her personality. Whatever Casey was doing, it was on purpose, and intentional.

When Grace turned her head to look at the outline of Casey's profile in the darkness, she heard her voice.

Without looking over, Casey spoke her words to Grace in a low, selfless, vulnerable tone. "I'm not always right."

They were the last words spoken that night. The two simply lay hand in hand until each had finally drifted off to sleep sometime in the early morning. Grace felt more comfort at that moment than she had since she learned Luke was Aaron Wallace's   son.

CHAPTER 47

Luke wondered if Grace had gotten together for their regularly scheduled girls' night. His own Thursday was a lot less wine-soaked with a little more football, he thought, deciding on another beer from the fridge. And, after a couple days of stony silence in the condo, thanks to his immature outburst, Luke decided he needed to make peace.

"You're not moving out."

Luke noted he must be in for another all-night working session, but he grinned when he got the reaction he was looking for when he opened the refrigerator door so it bumped Mave as he took a sip of his freshly brewed, hot coffee.

"Fuck you. I'm staying here forever." Mave gargled his answer as he'd taken in too much of the hot drink and used his spare hand to catch the coffee that was dripping off his chin.

Luke jumped on the counter to settle in for something he'd never had an issue with. When you're wrong, you're wrong; and you should apologize. Mave seemed to know what was about to come. He turned his body to lean against the counter to face his friend.

"I'm sorry."

"I know." Mave's voice lost his sarcastic tone from the fridge-bump and grew serious, "So what's going on? What's your plan?"

Luke huffed out his irritation when he leaned his head back. He could have done about a million things differently. "I had a million chances to tell her," Luke spoke more to himself than to Mave.

He knew she was dedicated. Obviously loved her job. Missed her dad. Had the utmost respect for him; and to that point, he had respect for the man he never met just by hearing her speak about him with such high regard and love. She would have done – would do – anything for him, in life and death.

Then there was that moment at Grandma's. And the small fact that he pursued her, tried to meet her, meticulously studied her, then fell in love with her, and completely blindsided her.

"It's my fault." He admitted out loud for the first time. "We just connected on everything. Grace is fun, she doesn't get angry, she's serious when it counts, great professionally, wants the same family I do, she's beautiful..." He paused for a moment and closed his eyes.

"She's beautiful." He said it again. Inside and out. This was it. Grace was the one person for him, and no other would ever come close.

Luke knew, or maybe decided at that moment, he wasn't going to let her push him away. No matter how angry or upset she might be. Heck, there was a pretty good chance he'd make her angry or upset again throughout their lives together.

"Was there a plan in there anywhere?" Mave smirked.

Luke matched Mave's smirk with his own and answered with a simple look that said, come on dude, you know me better than that – of course, there's a plan.

Mave understood the unspoken words and watched as Luke hopped off the counter with his beer, and called after him as he walked away, "So you're starting Monday then?"

"Monday is the day." Luke put his pointer finger to the sky and declared, "Grace will be mine."

"Poker, tomorrow?" Mave called out one last casual question.

"Tomorrow."

CHAPTER 48

The leather purse and workbag smacked the chair as it was hurled down with little regard for its contents. Customers craned their necks, trying to inconspicuously spy on the commotion. Grace pouted her way back through the tables to the cash register, stomping her shiny black oxfords the entire way.

Three people back in line, Grace folded her arms with the impatience of a three-year-old. She stared directly in front of her and saw Aimeé lean her body to the left, poking her head out to get a visual around the other line-members. When their eyes met, Aimeé lifted a single black brow and moved her body back into a straight line, continuing to take orders and payments for her delectable-smelling carbohydrates.

Grace was irritated, and she was allowed to show it. So what if Aimeé found amusement in what she probably assumed were immature actions. Aimeé offered her, *we see your meltdown, but you're going to have to wait three pastries before I can help you* look. Grace exaggerated a lean in response and shoved her hip out as far as it could reach.

The quick three minutes of standing in line felt like thirty. When Grace reached the front, Aimeé's cherry-red lips smiled and asked, "How's it going, sweet?" She handed Grace their new pumpkin latte to sample before she placed the standard crappy-day lunch order. One chocolate croissant, warmed; a cup of fruit just to feel better about herself; and a hefty dose of vanilla latte with an extra shot of espresso.

When no answer came, and all Grace could muster was a frown and a self-pitying expression, Aimeé acknowledged her with a nod, sparing Grace from speaking. Grace's face looked pale and Aimeé could see the swollen plumpness the tears had left beneath her eyes. Aimeé wouldn't be the cause for another round of anguish or add to her poor friends' teary beauty blemish.

"I'll be right over once this line goes down. Get started. I'll join your crappy-day lunch."

Grace pulled her face up from the well of her hands where it hid from the world when she heard Aimeé sit down across from her. Aimeé shuffled the lattes and the food around and placed three small beignets in the middle of the table for them to share, and explained, "For emergencies."

Not able to conjure even the shadow of a smile, Grace should at least try and show her appreciation. So, she reached into the pile of beignets and took a bite.

"Now, speak to me."

The girls took a sip of their drinks, and Grace began.

"He's making it impossible for me to ignore him. He's making it impossible for me to forget that I love him. No," she corrected, "not love, but something close. It's like he refuses to remember he and his own father are trying to take away the only part of my father I have left. That he lied to me – by omission or otherwise."

Grace ripped off a warmed piece of the fried dough and continued while shoveling it in. There was too much on her mind for manners – or dignity.

"The man with the name who shall not be named is pulling out all the stops. He brought me flowers. He wrote me a note that I read once, but the way it etched itself in my mind," Grace paused to poke her frontal lobe, "I might as well have read it a million times. He checks on me to make sure 'I'm okay,' stopping in the office – once every day this week. Outside of meetings, while filling up my coffee, any and everywhere just to get us alone. He brought me coffee yesterday afternoon..." The realization hit her as she was speaking it out loud, and her jaw dropped.

"He was down here, getting me coffee. A large, vanilla latte, extra shot." An accusing finger pointed across the table at Aimeé. "My crappy-day coffee."

Aimeé put on a face of astonishment and wonder. "I have no idea what you mean. If a handsome stranger, whom I'm supposed to be angry with, came in and ordered a specific drink, two of them, I can't just turn him away, can I? It would be terrible for business."

"Three dollars and ninety-seven cents. Your bottom line might have squeaked by." Grace rolled her eyes.

Aimeé shrugged non-committedly and popped one of the French donuts in her mouth to make defending herself impossible. Grace resigned and continued as she watched Aimeé struggle with the full beignet – her cheeks puffing out like a chipmunk.

"He's not mean to me like any normal person would be after the cold way I treated him when I found out who he was. It's almost like he cares more knowing he might have hurt me."

Aimeé's sticky mouth smacked as she asked the inescapable question, "Can't you forgive him?"

"I miss him more than I ever thought I could. It's worse seeing him every day," Grace admitted. "But I don't think I could ever get over knowing he manipulated me into meeting him. Trying for some kind of an angle to the inside. I can handle a lot of things; I can't handle dishonesty."

"Then talk to him about it."

Both women turned in unison to see Casey standing next to them at the table, throwing her opinion into the mix.

"Case!" Surprise and appreciation had Grace springing from her chair. She wrapped her arms and her emotions around Casey in the suffocating embrace.

"Aimeé texted and said we might need the gang. Rachel couldn't get out of teaching this afternoon, but I can tell you what she wrote in her text if you're ready and willing?"

Grace refused to let go of the embrace and her muffled, "Sure," was barely audible.

"And I quote: 'I just have a feeling about this one.' Stop. 'Luke is a good guy.' Stop. 'Tell Grace's pretty ass.' Stop. 'To get off her high horse.' Stop."

Confused, she pulled herself away to get a good look at her techy friend and stared into her eyes to get the truth.

"Okay, fine," Casey giving in, "I added the last part. She said she's never seen you happier and she thinks you need to have a long conversation with the man you love to get the truth. Me personally, I'm not a fan of the truth."

With an exasperated sigh, Grace fell back into the chair.

"Why does everybody think I love him?"

"Because you do." Aimeé's matter of fact response didn't seem to require further explanation.

"What she said." Casey swooped around the table. She removed her layers and threw them in a heap on the empty table next to theirs. Ignoring the look of disapproval from Aimeé.

"What is the deal with the L-word flying around? You two hate love." Grace couldn't believe what she was hearing from her two free-spirited friends.

Casey didn't stand a chance at this one, so Aimeé defended their honor.

"I'm French; we love love. We love dogs, French wine, obscenely big hats, all sorts of men–"

At Aimeé's pause, the girls looked up to see what captured her attention. When they followed her eyes, they realized she was peering out the window and across the street at Christopher. He stood in his police uniform and looked as handsome as ever.

"You were saying?" Casey's sly tone brought Aimeé back from her daydream.

"Right. Well, we just love. We love everything – not Americans –" she paused for a grin, "but everything else we love. We even love love affairs."

"That's it!"

Shrieking at a tone that could have deafened, Grace had it.

"I need to find that old number! I'll have an affair." When she was met with blank stares, she elaborated. "You know? The one from the blind date. Hello? You set me up on it.

I never went because I ran into Luke. I wonder if I reached out to him he'd be willing to meet me again?"

"Yeah, I don't think that's a good idea." Casey's eyes peered toward Aimeé.

"You suddenly care about affairs?" Grace immediately regretted her choice of words.

Casey waved it away, trying to relieve the stress that hollowed her stomach. "It's not technically an affair if you're finished with Luke, right?"

"Exactly." Grace nodded and pushed away from the table. She plunged her arms through her coat and carried her work bag and purse as she would a giant load of laundry piled high in front of her face.

"Case, throw the rest of my croissant up here." Grace motioned to the uneaten puff that was brought sometime during her epiphany. "I'm going to need that to aid in my search."

"Where are you going on your hunt?"

"Home. I think that's the last place I saw it. It has to be somewhere in there. If it's not there, I'm going to scour every inch of that office."

Grace merry-go-rounded the table and gave kisses to each of the girls, then sauntered away, barely missing other customers as she weaved through tables with her armload. She was out the door before either of the two left at the table could say anything to stop her.

Casey and Aimeé finally looked up at each other.

"Should we have told her?" Aimeé asked, showing a bit more concern than she was accustomed to.

"No way. You saw how well it worked out for Luke, right? Let's wait it out. Besides, it's not like she can replace us, we are her only friends." Casey stated while pointing to the last beignet, a silent question if it could be hers.

"Yeah, maybe." Aimeé gave a slow nod, her response to both.

CHAPTER 49

Shit. Shit. *Shit!*

Where in the heck was that damn paper?

Grace looked at the tornado she left in her wake. Not like her at all, she had left drawers open, piles from drawers she emptied on the floor, tables, and desks. Folders were flat-faced and open with their paper contents scattered everywhere. Her slight obsessiveness to have things organized would kick in when she got home after work. She'd tidy up then.

If it wasn't here though, it had to be at work. She'd find a way to approach Maggie and Seth again – quietly – so the office gossip didn't get around she was on the search for a missing phone number. That would be the last thing she needed right now. And she didn't want Luke finding out she was attempting to date another man. She was angry, but not enough to punish him for it. Or, maybe she was, but she wasn't that type of person. Sure, she could be stubborn, but not mean.

And yet, Luke was still always on her mind. She was beginning to accept that's just the way it was probably going to be until she could find something that could come close to replacing him.

Come close, she thought ruefully. She knew it was impossible. She couldn't deny the great time she had with him. She also had to admit it was nice to see him, even though every time it happened, it made her just a little sadder than she'd been before.

Just come close. That's all you have to do. The words repeated in her mind like a broken record. Her new mantra.

She needed this number. It would be her saving grace.

CHAPTER 50

The view of the office was dark from the street. It was the same dimness when she walked up the stairs. When she stood inside the only light offered were reflections and shadows cast by the streetlights outside. She would be alone for a couple of hours. No noise, nobody to spy.

Now, where was that number?

She placed her bags in the office and peeled off her jacket. The tailored pantsuit fit her body and the scenario. Masculine and sexy. Perfect for sneaking – no – she corrected herself, maneuvering around the office for this damn number. Grace removed her blazer and stood in the doorway, wondering where she should start.

Maggie's desk seemed as good as any.

Then it seemed like a terrible idea.

Grace took in the massive amount of folders, paperwork, sticky notes, three-ring-binders, and yellow legal pads. It was unreal. That, and she had unearthed every single, fricking, one. No number to be found.

Grace pushed herself off the floor, brushed off her knees, and it hit her. Seth had taken the folder. He said he didn't find anything, but maybe he missed it. Was it wrong to go through an employee's cubical? Maggie wouldn't have cared about Grace going through hers and would have told her to do it herself if she wasn't there to help. Going through Seth's, though, this seemed somewhat invasive?

Well, she thought, just a glance couldn't hurt.

A glance turned into a frenzied, all-out search. The hunt took her over, and before she knew it, she was on all-fours.

"God-sakes. What are you doing on the floor?"

The accusing hiss startled her head into the bottom of the desk.

"Ouch," Grace squealed, sliding her way out as she rubbed her head. The hand that was easing the pain was the first to appear over the short cube wall. When her eyes made it over, she saw Maggie standing in front of her, hands on her hips, with a perfected mom expression. Grace knew she was about to get scolded.

"It's not what it looks like," Grace defended her hunt. Besides, she wouldn't have had to be down there if she wasn't forced to rummage through the files stacked high under Seth's desk. Why did he have so many papers?

Furrowed eyebrows told her that Maggie knew exactly what she was doing, but she waited for the explanation anyway.

"That's funny, because it looks like you're snooping through your dedicated employee's things."

"Well, that's pretty generic." Grace attempted for a bit of humor to show she expected a little more from the almighty Maggie.

"If you're looking for that phone number, why don't you just ask?"

Ah, there she was. Expectations aligned. The all-knowing Maggie came through in the end.

"I didn't want to have to ask because it's embarrassing. Maggie, come on, help me out here. I need it. I need something to get my mind off of Luke, because everything I do – and say, and smell, and see – reminds me of him. I need," she contemplated the right word because *replacement* wouldn't do; she was beginning to believe that would never happen, "a distraction."

Maggie walked over and helped her off the floor, and again, Grace found herself wiping her knees.

"Have you taken a moment to consider talking with Luke about all of this? That it might be one tiny misunderstanding?"

"Tiny? Maggie, you know as well as I do that this company is my life." She scoffed at another suggestion that she should have a discussion with Luke.

"Or," Maggie ignored Grace, "you could present the alternative proposal for a friendly acquisition you and Seth worked very hard to prepare."

"I was blinded by the idea they would go for something like that. It's not Wallace. He comes, he sees, he conquers," she responded bitterly.

When they reached Maggie's desk, Grace couldn't help but feel a little guilty that she'd already rifled through this desk before getting caught in the act. However, when Maggie reached into her top drawer and felt her way to the back, she pulled out a piece of ripped paper that had a number on it.

The shock, and admittedly mostly wonder, flashed across her face. She felt it hold there for a moment, her mouth gaping.

"How did you—" Grace was speechless.

"I know everything here, honey. I was on this mission long before you were. When Luke decided he wasn't going to let you go easily and poured on the unwanted attention, I started looking."

Maggie started to busy herself organizing her desk, something she always said led to a successful day, not paying mind to the astonishment still splattered across Grace's face. When Grace turned to walk away, she paused, hoping for questioning words to form, but nothing happened.

"I think you should speak to Luke before writing him off." Maggie let her words hang in the air, "Any man who's willing to go to that much trouble for a woman might be worth forgiving. And also, if you ever want something from my desk, all you need to do is ask. I would have told you right where to look." Maggie's tone rose with amusement.

Grace slowly shifted her body and silently snuck away without an attempt at defending herself. She walked through her office door, closed it behind her, and placed the number on the center of her desk.

Grace eyed it cautiously as she rounded to sit in her leather chair. She rested her chin on both hands as she inspected the scrap of paper. A silent inquisition. Would this mysterious number solve her problems, or at least dim the constant thought of them?

The knock on her door was light and friendly. She saw Luke when she looked up, standing on the other side of the long glass pane. She held back the urge to smile at the sight of him. It caused her to sigh and stare for a bit too long. Luke grinned and took a stored hand out of his pocket and lift it in a silent greeting.

"Come in." It was all she could muster.

"Hi." His voice echoed his wave.

Luke stepped in, and she needlessly pulled the phone number scrap off the table as his eyes didn't move from hers.

"Hi," she countered, hoping she sounded unemotional.

"I, ah, I wanted to come in and see how you were doing?"

Her eyes stung with the threat of tears. When would she stop crying? she wondered. Then vowed she would not let the drops fall if it was the last thing she did. She took a moment to compose herself and attempted a truthful answer as best she could.

"I am doing fine, I guess. Trying to not lose my dad's company. Though I feel like I'm prolonging the inevitable. Trying to forget that the man I thought I was falling for is the one who's trying to take it from me. Has Wallace," referring to the company, not the man, "ever failed at taking over a company once he started?"

"No," she stopped him before he could respond, and kept speaking. "Don't answer that. I trusted you, I opened up about this to you. The whole time – you knew. You knew. I gave, and you didn't open up to me. Now I feel like maybe we didn't meet by chance. Maybe you knew exactly who I was. And maybe you were trying to get me to open up. To show you how hard of a fight this was going to be. I feel like an idiot. Did you get the information you were looking for?" She didn't intend for it to be a question, but a part of her wanted him to explain. To have some simple, misunderstood explanation that would make perfect sense.

Her hand moved over her stomach to ease the nausea that was setting in. She wanted to place it over her heart where the physical ache felt like it was killing her.

Grace looked up, into Luke's eyes. This time a tear slid out. She quickly wiped it away, and forgetting her regard for his feelings, admitted her plans.

"I'm going to be going out with somebody else."

Luke's attention snapped to, and it looked as if he'd immediately forgotten everything she had just said to him about not trusting his intentions.

"What?" His chest caved as if he'd been hit with a cannonball. "What?"

The stun and pain carved through his already chiseled face and it nearly killed her to see.

"I would do anything for you," he finally managed in a weary and defeated tone.

"You would back off of this takeover?" Grace said, almost a dare.

"That's not fair. You know I can't do that. It's not just me that's involved." Desperation entered his voice. He knew the one thing that would save them, he simply couldn't do.

"Then I guess there's my answer," Grace said simply and coldly. "I hope you know, no matter what your objectives or methods about getting me to fall so in – well – to fall for you, worked. The past couple weeks were the happiest I'd been in a long time. So, thank you. You've shown me how I can feel if I open up to someone else."

She intended for the words to cut, but didn't realize how much they'd slice through her own heart. "I hope we can work well together for the duration of this. I'm sure from your end it will have to be hostile in nature, but that's just business, I suppose."

It was Luke's turn to feel nauseous. She watched words try to form on his lips, at the tip of his tongue. He gave in when he found none and nodded.

"Sure. Yeah, I'll try to be as cordial as possible." Luke stood a bit straighter and let his business side take over. "Please let me know if there is anything I can do for you until you hear from us."

Luke put his hands back in their pockets. His body offered a slight bow as he retreated to the door.

Grace spun her chair around to face the window as she felt the rush of tears come and snatched the phone number off the desk. She had to keep herself busy. She would send the text asking for a chance to meet. Then, work. She would work day and night until her mind had no choice but to eliminate Luke, and all the good memories with him.

CHAPTER 51

The women stared at the paper sitting in the middle of their table. They curiously eyed the crumpled number, then each other, then the paper, and back again.

"Well, you are staying true to your word." Rachel tried for a supportive tone in an attempt to find a bright side.

Grace felt the need to defend herself. "I have to. I told you everything I said to him. He didn't defend himself. Just looked shocked that I caught on. I'm not saying we didn't share feelings, but it was all built on a lie. He did seem genuinely upset that I was going to meet somebody else, but I chalk that up to male pride. When he said he would do anything for me, I told him the only thing I want is to keep my company," she shrugged, "and he said he couldn't do that."

Casey held up her hand and spoke without being called on, "I don't mean to be the man-lover here because we know that is definitely not the side I usually take, but isn't it kind of impossible for him to decide himself to let you keep the company as is?" She continued as she saw Grace start to protest. "All I'm saying is try and look at the bigger picture. Your dad's company does extremely well for its size. A company like Wallace, they could have shot for bigger potatoes, but they saw the value in what you and your dad have built. And don't forget your aunt. Abbi must see some sort of value in this, right? Maybe you should talk to her and see what she really wants the outcome to be. As unbiasedly as you can."

The last comment wasn't a jab, but it was worth saying. Grace knew she'd been stubborn about the purchase in general because of her father – probably more so because of Luke. She didn't want to look at any other option. It didn't diminish the fact that he lied to her and that the way they met wasn't as fateful as she had wanted to believe. She was a businesswoman, and a damn great one.

Grace nodded, more to herself than to Casey. She would start to dig in and do the work. That's what she was best at. Whatever happened at the end, company or no company.

"Fine. I'll talk to Abbi. See what she thinks, unbiasedly, about the whole thing. I am still going to go out with this guy next week though. I think it will be good to be back out there. If anybody can make me feel the way I felt recently, I'm willing to take the chance in finding it again. It really did change my whole outlook on life. I pictured a future, kids, a family. Even a life outside of work."

"About the number?" Aimeé's attempt to bring it up was casual enough to seem like she was simply getting back to the girl-talk. "You said you reached out already?"

"Yeah. It was simple and quick. I texted and apologized. Asked if he still wanted to get together. He wrote back he was up for it, so we planned for next week since this week is kind of busy for him."

"What's his name?" It was Rachel's turn to dig, sounding as nonchalant as she could.

"Actually, I don't know. But," Grace looked over, "Casey, you must know, you set it up."

"Nope. It was through a third party. I consult for them." Just a little white lie, Casey thought. She wondered who it was that Grace texted. It obviously wasn't the number she'd given Grace, or she would already know Luke was her intended target.

Rachel and Aimeé rolled their eyes at Casey and her inability to play it cool.

"Yeah, I guess that's okay," Grace said as she eyed the looks of concern on her friends. This needed to stop, she thought. Enough about her and this on-and-on with Luke. Time to change the subject.

"Speaking of dates, Rach, when do we get to meet," she cleared her throat in an attempt to hide her amusement, "Richard?"

A new shade of rouge blushed over Rachel's face, and the girls were intrigued.

The first plea came from Aimeé, "What is it?" Her excitement was obvious.

"Well, it's not so much *is*, it's what isn't. Richard and I stopped seeing each other."

A unanimous, "What?" filled the Bistro.

"Just listen and take it for what it is," she looked toward Grace. "We didn't have what I saw in you and Luke. You know, before." Rachel protected her logic, "I decided I don't want to waste time on something that isn't wonderful. It should be exciting. With butterflies. I should be giddy and glowing. Maybe not all of the time, but those things should be there, especially when you just meet somebody. Even when you don't know them very well the idea of seeing them again, the idea of falling in love with them, the possibilities should consume you." Rachel smiled at the thought before continuing.

"I've felt that way before. I know what it's like. I want that again."

The women smiled at their friend. At the romance of her ideals. They also knew she was referring to William, Grace's brother. He wasn't ready to commit and had broken Rachel's heart in the worst way. That's probably what allowed Rachel to move on.

Grace wondered if hate was the alternative to love. Did there have to be no road back to the man you loved to move on from him? Is that why she was so determined to make Luke such a bad guy, when really, maybe her pride was more hurt than   anything?

CHAPTER 52

"Man, she can really kick a night in the balls. I'm exhausted. How does she always stay up this late? And still, get up at five in the morning?" Casey sank low in her chair from weariness and a bit of a wine buzz to go with it.

Amused, Aimeé polished off the last drop from her own glass.

"If you want to be impressed, meet me back here at three with an apron on."

"Three!" Casey's eyes filled with disgust. Finally, appreciation fell over her, "Thank goodness my computers can run themselves overnight. I love computers. Computers love me. What more does a girl need?"

"Sex."

It was stated as fact, but Rachel laughed at Aimeé's nonchalant reply and followed up to be more precise.

"With a man. Or a woman, I suppose."

"Really?" Rachel questioned.

"Sure. Not me, but in general."

"I'm going to remain faithful to Russel," Casey said in a boozy slur as she sank even lower.

"Russel?" Rachel mused.

"Russel. My computer. He always listens, takes my commands, is always on time, talks to me, doesn't talk back to me, backs himself up so he never forgets anything...I could go on. He's truly perfect."

Aimeé and Rachel watched Casey drift off into a daydream. Silly grins plastered their faces.

"Never will I understand what, or how, you do things in your office in your tiny apartment, or your other office with all of those screens, but I'm sure it's fascinating."

Rachel turned to Aimeé, addressing her as if Casey wasn't there at all, "Our friend is in a relationship with a computer. Incredible."

"Ha. Ha."

The exaggerated monotone laugh from Casey caused a bubble of laughter from the girls.

"So I like computers. They are easy. They make sense. I can find out anything I need by hacking wherever I want. And I'm a millionaire many times over because of it."

The immediacy of the girls' facial expression changes was impressive to say the least. Both went blank, their jaws nearly hitting the table.

"I knew it," Aimeé said, the only one to remain calm.

"Don't get weird," Casey rolled her eyes.

"Unbelievable." Once again, Rachel addressing Aimeé alone, this time making light of the situation. "To think, all this time we've been paying for her drinks. And I'm poor."

"That's how you *stay* a multi-millionaire." Casey defended herself.

Rachel reached across the table and grabbed Casey's hand, "That's incredible. I am so proud of you for building something so wonderful and taking such good care of yourself."

"Another round!" Aimeé declared.

"No! Death will follow. But seriously," Casey leaned forward and gave Rachel's hand a squeeze before letting it go, "We have to tell Grace about the blind date."

"Of course," Aimeé agreed. "When will you do it?"

"Me? Why me?" Casey pouted.

They simply stared.

"Okay, I know. But they matched. They matched big time. Do you know what they scored on my assessment? Ninety-six. *Ninety-six!* That's like, Mickey and Minnie status. Or, Romeo and Juliet."

"They died." Rachel reminded her flatly.

"You know what I mean."

"Don't you find it strange," Rachel began, "that you don't believe in relationships, yet you have created the perfect dating site?"

"I had a lot of time watching with a front-row seat of how it *doesn't* work. It left little room for error on the other end. Besides, people pay lots of money to find love. It's just good business."

"Casey," Aimeé said, "you said we need to find who the number belongs to. It is Luke, is it not?"

"It *was.* But it would have shown up on Grace's phone when she entered the number. You know, when you type it in, if the number's there it will just pop up? So, it can't be Luke."

"We have to find out who it is," Aimeé went on. "Perhaps I could reach out to that red-head. Travis was his name."

"No." Casey would put that fire out before it started.

Rachel smiled suddenly. "We need Maggie. Grace found it at work, right? Maggie knows everything. Can you two get up there and grill her during lunch next week? I don't think I can get out, what with the children I enlighten all day."

"I can."

"Me too."

Aimeé and Casey nodded to each other, then to Rachel.

"Just to make sure, Luke hasn't said anything to either of you, right?" Casey inquired.

"No." Looking visibly disappointed Rachel sighed, "I've only met him once, before the Grandma weekend."

Aimeé shared the frown. "He hasn't been back here since earlier this week when he picked up a coffee to bring to Grace."

"Can I go home now?" Casey pleaded, with exaggerated exhaustion.

"You did really good." Rachel got up and stroked Casey's cheek before placing a motherly kiss on her forehead.

Casey moved the corners of her lips upward without opening her eyes.

"Thanks. Bye. Love you. Sleep is good."

With that, they were on their way late into the night.

CHAPTER 53

It was the most professional Aimeé or Casey had looked in their entire lives. Rather than an apron wrapped around her torso and flour on her face, Aimeé had on skinny black slacks with heels and a trim black crewneck sweater. The special occasion even had her black bob of hair down in light waves.

Casey wasn't far from the professional working woman herself. She flaunted a white ruffled blouse with navy blue slacks and shiny silver flats that matched her shiny silver jewelry. She worked hard to look the part but couldn't break away from the rusty bun sitting atop her head.

The two ditched their jackets and looked each other up and down in front of the office elevator. The reaction was immediate. They both started cracking up at the effort they put forth to simply fit in on the business-dressed floors of Grace's office. The laughter was followed by a high-five between them. The elevator opened to take them up, and Casey sang, "Fake it 'til you make it!" and both the girls walked in.

Pure joy filled Maggie as she saw the two walking toward her. She stood and brought her hands together in front of her heart and let a heavy breath out.

"Aren't you two beauties a sight for sore eyes?" Maggie walked around her desk and greeted the two with a bear hug that engulfed both of them at the same time. Their heads almost bumped over Maggie's as she brought them as close as possible.

"You girls need to come in here more often." She let them both breathe but didn't let them far enough away to miss her gossip. "Especially with all of the hubbub going on. Let me let you two in on a little secret."

She ushered the girls into a conference room for privacy and nearly pushed them into two chairs, then dragged over one of her own, and sat directly in front of them.

Maggie cut to the chase. "Full story, or what you're here for?"

"How do you know what we're-" Casey's confusion was cut off by Aimeé and her flat hand.

"Full story."

"I have ten minutes, then Grace will be out of her meeting so we don't have a lot of time." Maggie's feet stepped forward twice to scoot herself closer in her rolling chair, her body waddling back and forth like a penguin.

"Okay, first, the facts. Clearly, we know Grace is in love with Luke. We absolutely know that Luke is in love with Grace. Though I can't confirm that he didn't know ahead of time who Grace was."

"He did," the two women confirmed.

"Oh, yes, interesting." Maggie said, not surprised. "Anyway, he fell for her hard. Luke seems like a good man for our Grace. Sure, he has to weave in and out of large-company politics, but the word on the street is that the Wallace's are pretty straight forward, and straight-laced men. They run their company the same way." Maggie whispered her own bit of gossip, "Making a boatload of money while they're at it."

"I know," Casey agreed, "it will be nearly impossible to stop them." She added, knowing Wallace had zero intention of stopping, and there wasn't any amount of defense Thomas and Jane would be able to do.

"It's sad, but alas." Maggie slouched for just a moment to let it sink in, then was back at it. "So, it was courtesy of you two, then, I assume, Grace was supposed to meet Luke?"

Feeling no shame, Aimeé and Casey nodded without batting an eye and waited for Maggie to continue. She barreled on.

"I had a hunch, Seth – he handles our budgeting and forecasts – was up to something, but couldn't quite put my finger on it. He didn't have anything to do with Luke and Grace being at odds – they'll have to figure that one out – but that number Grace has in her fancy Burberry bag," Maggie's head nodded twice in the direction of Grace's office, "isn't the one she left in that stack of papers. It's Seth's."

Maggie thought on her words for a bit and explained at their confused head-tilts.

"I worked the file first. I saw the paper and left it in there in the off-chance it was a number Grace needed for work on the reports or presentation. Grace mentioned it in passing that she wanted it and Seth denied knowing it existed. He would have seen it front and center when he opened the file. Then, wouldn't you know it, a few days later he hands it to me."

"If he handed you the same-"

"Not the same." Maggie cut in. "I'll not let you think I memorized the number, and tell you straight away my intrigue got the best of me. I looked up the number in our global address book, the one that holds all of our employee's numbers, sure enough it's Seth's."

"What I want to know is," Maggie crossed her ankles and leaned in, "why you agreed to set them up in the first place? Luke, not Seth. We'll deal with him later." She clarified.

"They were a ninety-six," Aimeé stated as if Maggie knew what she was referring to.

The blank stare from Maggie forced Casey to explain the matchme.com algorithm and finish with a quick defense.

"I would never have agreed had I not thought they would actually hit it off. Grace deserves love, a good guy, and somebody that understands how much her work means to her. Who better than a man like Luke, who's in the same position as she is?"

Casey looked up, stating, "If, you know, you don't include the part about him taking over her company."

"I have a plan." Maggie nodded, agreeing with Casey's words. As far as she was concerned they seemed perfect for each other. She had known Grace her entire life, bright and full of love. In the past few weeks Maggie saw Grace had lost a little of that love, and it was time she got it back.

The three leaned closer together as Casey and Aimeé listened intently for the next five minutes.

"Okay," Aimeé said finally, digesting the plan.

"Okay," echoed Casey.

"We agree nobody tells Grace."

Aimeé stood and looked down, directing her French-accented words to Casey. "I won't tell, but if she finds out, I am throwing you under buses."

"Under *the* bus." Casey corrected and rolled her eyes, "Throwing you under the bus. There's only one."

CHAPTER 54

The picture of Grace and her dad wasn't different than any other a family might have taken. Honoring the start of a new school year or to mark a graduation. Theirs was the same, as it captured her first day at Thomas and Jane.

It seemed like it was yesterday when her mom snapped the picture of her dad and Grace heading off to work for the first time together. She couldn't remember being happier, with her arm wrapped around her dad and his around her. His smile was all pride.

Grace grinned at her own smile in the photo that had been framed on her desk ever since. A smile so full and white, it barely fit on her young face. She remembered her mom flashing a thumbs-up next to the camera, at the time thinking it was such a dorky thing to do. It made all three of them laugh until they cried.

Her brother had called to wish her luck, spouting something about being a nerd for the rest of her life. All she had thought was, I hope so. She knew he really wanted her to love it. All of them did. It was her self-proclaimed legacy, after all. To walk in her father's footsteps. To be just like him.

They had a magnificent family. Never had Grace felt that she or her brother were deprived of love or starved of attention. They hadn't been well-off when she was born, and her brother was only a bit older. Despite living paycheck to paycheck, her parents had given them so much.

She thought hard on it. Before the day she began at Thomas and Jane, she remembered the years getting up in the morning with her dad, knowing she was going off to school and him to work. Never thinking much beyond their simple routine: up early while the moon still hung in the black sky, they'd sit at the table, or she'd snuggle next to him on the couch, and they'd take in WCCO – his favorite local news channel – or cartoons.

It was their time. Perfect time.

Then they'd get ready for the day. She never wondered what he did all day after watching him leave every morning. She simply wanted him to get back home nearly as soon as he walked out of the kitchen door. Sure, as she grew older, her mind would fixate on new things – friends, boys, prom, picking out colleges. But the love she had for her dad, as she grew, it grew stronger, and it never wavered.

It dawned on her, though she'd never dreaded work – she enjoyed it even – her memories never lingered there long. The best part of her life, most of the memories, lived outside of the old brick walls. Family, friends, and now Luke filled her mind.

"Now that's the woman I fell in love with."

The voice startled Grace and brought her back from her recollection. She set down the photo on her desk and looked up.

Luke didn't walk into her office, choosing instead to linger in the doorway. She also noticed that he seemed calm and collected, unfazed by their recent interaction. It made her happy but brought a twinge of heartbreak she had been trying hard to avoid.

Why would that be? Did she want him to be upset? How unfair would it be for her to have broken up with him – if that's what you'd even call it – and still want him to want her? No, she decided, she would move forward from this. Let him be happy. Let both of them be happy.

And wasn't she in some kind of a mature mood today, she thought, congratulating herself. Everybody happy.

"Luke, you can come in." she offered.

Luke slipped in and presented a latte that had been hiding behind the door. Her expression must have satisfied him, she thought as she took in his boyish grin. She could have killed for a shot of caffeine, so as far as she was concerned, the grin was earned and he had saved her day.

"It's like you knew the one thing that would get me through this day. Thank you. I'm going to have to start returning the favor. Favors," she corrected, realizing he'd done more for her in the last month than she'd done for anybody in a year. What a terrible realization.

Luke sat down across from her, his elbows leaning on the desk. He reached for the photo Grace had been gazing at moments before. He wanted a glimpse of the cause for the sentimental moment he had interrupted.

Grace tried to ignore the quickening of her pulse when his hand moved closer. Why did it mean anything? she thought. She brushed off the feeling and the thought. And, that's why she'd scheduled a new date with the guy she stood up. And she was needing it more and more by the second.

"He was a good guy. I wish I could have known him." Luke had said it before, about her father, and he still meant it now.

She softened with the care in Luke's voice.

"He was incredible – but you know that from what I told you. Here though," Grace motioned to the office, "he was the best combination of personal and professional. I never felt like he was gone or working too much. Mom would bring us to visit him here whenever we wanted. We grew up in this place. He might have worked late nights, but my brother and I would never have known because he was always," Grace shrugged at a loss for the right word, "present, I guess. I suppose that's part of the reason I have such an attachment to it," Grace moved her head around the office, taking it in, "here."

Her thoughts drifted. "They were a good pair, Mom and Dad." she clarified, letting Luke come along as her mind trailed. "I know I talk about my dad and think about him constantly, maybe because he's gone. I never thought twice about how things would be or turn out." She smiled.

"He would have forced me to keep dating you even with all of this," Grace's finger swirled in the air, "going on."

"I thought I liked him already, but that seals the deal."

The honest words made Grace feel uncomfortable and had her adjusting and straightening herself in her chair.

"Luke, the thing is, I think you're wonderful, but I also feel betrayed." Grace motioned for him to stop when he started speaking. "No, it's my feeling. I can't prove or not prove that you didn't have an ulterior motive. I don't say that to make you feel bad, I say that to make sure at the end of the day I'm comfortable and not second-guessing any of my decisions. I want to make decisions for this company that are independent of you and me." She folded her hands in her lap and paused briefly before continuing. "I think we should get through this. However, this thing ends up. And see where we come out on the other end."

Grace's words surprised her. Maybe she did just need time?

The silence that followed wasn't uncomfortable, but she wished he would say something. When his eyes didn't move from hers and the corners of his lips slowly upturned into the grin she'd seen many times before, she knew he must be doing this on purpose.

Grace folded her arms and waited for him to come out with it. She added an eye-roll for effect.

"Okay," he said simply, still grinning.

"Okay?" Even more irritated than just a second before, she pressed him.

Grace watched Luke tap his latte against the one he'd brought for her. A solo-cheers and added a wink. It was infuriating and gorgeous. Which only made it more infuriating.

Luke had heard what he needed. He wanted proof, needed to see it. And he found it. She still felt it. He'd over-reacted the other day. Let a rare bout of jealousy get the best of him. But today, he saw it – her care and love for him – whether or not she admitted it to herself. And it rejuvenated him.

"Yup. Just, 'okay.' I don't intend to let you stop loving me."

"I don't recall saying that."

"You didn't have to."

Grace watched Luke do an obnoxious celebratory skip and shuffle on the way out the door, and felt his cockiness as it lingered in the office. After that performance she had to say something.

Grace leaned forward and yelled out the door, "I should remind you I'm dating other people!"

Just when she thought he might have been too far away to hear her, Luke popped his head back around the corner.

"It's okay, honey, a little healthy competition never hurt anybody. Oh," he stated like he forgot to add a simple note to his list. "And I love you, too."

Grace didn't have to turn her chair around to face the window, Luke was gone from view too quickly to have noticed her reaction. She did for the simple fact of wanting to keep her smile and his words all to herself. She might hate him right now, but   he   loved   her.

CHAPTER 55

The red jumpsuit, red lipstick, and big hair might have been a little much, but it was all she could do to make sure this night felt nothing like the night she met Luke. She felt a little embarrassed, but she wasn't willing to admit she was failing miserably. Besides, she looked good, right?

"Be sure when you get to the Bulldog you don't look too eager."

Grace eyed her appearance in her bathroom mirror and mumbled into the phone, "Too late. Hey, how did you know where we are meeting? Be honest. We talked about this. You know you aren't supposed to look at my calendar."

Grace stared at the silent phone.

"Case," she prodded.

"I cannot confirm or deny that I did such a thing," Casey continued before she could be questioned further. "I am the least of your worries. Go out, have fun, and if nothing else you'll get a free drink, maybe five. Do your best France reenactment."

"Reassuring, thank you. And we're not talking about that." The sarcasm dripped from her words.

The knock on the front door was loud enough for her to hear clear as day, three stories up. Aimeé's voice reached them from down in the kitchen, "I'll get it! Ah, Grace, it's for you."

"Did you hear that Case? Did you hear Aimeé's voice just now?"

"No, why?"

"It was her sexy voice." Grace lifted the phone close to her face and whispered, "There's a man downstairs."

"Then," Casey matched the whisper as she mocked, "you'd better go down and see who it is."

"Yeah, yeah. Okay, I'll text you later. I'm sure you'll know all the details by then though. Do not track my credit cards or hack my phone tonight. In fact, I'm turning it off."

"Come on. What if you need an emergency out?"

"Find a camera or something to peer through. But it's not coming from me! Love you, Case."

"Fine." Casey resigned, fully not intending to keep any promises, "Love you, too."

Grace slid off her heels for better tiptoeing down the stairs. She maneuvered side to side to avoid the memorized creaks. Aimeé's voice grew clearer the father down she climbed. She couldn't quite make out the words she was saying, but she heard a familiar deep, tenor, laugh.

Shit! What was Luke doing here?

Her quick, reactive smile turned to dread when she realized what she was wearing.

Grace leaned against the wall and groaned. Embarrassment shouldn't have been her first feeling, but she had to admit, all of the red was a little over the top. She closed her eyes and began a pep talk.

"Grace, pull yourself together. You look great. A little overdone, but there is nothing wrong with being the best-dressed person in the room. You told Luke you were dating so he shouldn't be surprised, and you shouldn't feel bad about it. And whatever you do, do not see your date later on and wish it was Luke."

Her voice was adamant and seemed to do the job of calming her. Or, she just moved faster than her brain could think. Before she knew it, she was on the landing. She found herself staring at Aimeé with a glass of wine sitting at the kitchen island, and Luke with a beautiful bouquet of white flowers. Not a simple bouquet, but a stunning variety of roses, daisies, baby's breath, and others she couldn't identify.

"Luke, what a pleasant surprise." She tried to keep her voice even and nonchalant.

"Isn't it, though?"

He smiled, she came undone. Then scorned herself for the feeling.

"When Maggie – who told me to tell you she was the information leak – let me know you were going on a big date tonight, I thought I should stop by and wish you some luck."

Grace moved casually to the kitchen after tossing her heels by the door.

"That's very nice of you, but I think my new date is supposed to bring me the flowers, not you."

"I know. I thought after I talked to Maggie, this guy doesn't know you yet. I happen to know you love white flowers."

Grace smiled robotically, looking from Aimeé to Luke. "I do. But that's why I'm going on a date. So we can learn these things about each other."

315

"Of course, yeah, but it also means he doesn't know how amazing you are, either. His flowers won't be good enough." Luke didn't allow space for her to respond. "So, just to make sure you get everything you deserve tonight, I thought I could bring you flowers."

He walked the flowers toward her and gently lifted her hand to place the flowers in it. Then leaned in and kissed her cheek, dangerously close to her lips. He waved a friendly goodbye to Aimeé and walked out the door.

Not turning to look at the door, Grace looked at Aimeé, more shocked than she thought she'd be after the encounter. Grace motioned with her free hand and the flowers for Aimeé to say something.

"I don't know what you want me to say." Aimeé sipped her wine, and more of her French accent filled the room. "I would let yourself love him if I were you." Gesturing to the flowers, she added, "He's reminding you he loves you. He knows you don't want to go on this date. It is your pride, Grace. Go on your date, but you won't want to keep seeing this guy when you're done. Or any other man you might date."

"What exactly do you expect me to do then?" Grace said, running out of reasons to avoid his endless pursuit of her love.

"Maybe try to just, let go?" Aimeé's hand fluttered as if she herself were demonstrating the act of letting go.

"Of the company or my pride?"

"Both." Aimeé decided.

"I'm working on my pride." Grace admitted, but, she eyed Aimeé, "What if you had to sell the Bistro?"

"Point taken." Aimeé understood *that* kind of love.

Aimeé brought her glass to the sink. She said nothing as she walked to the cupboard where she got a Waterford crystal vase and filled it with water. After she set it on the island, Aimeé picked up her purse from the stool next to her and walked to Grace. She smiled softly and kissed Grace once on each cheek and let her hand rest on Grace's arm before taking her hand.

"You know what you want. Maybe you just need a little time to come around to it. I will see you in the morning."

Before she knew it, the house was empty. The silence consumed her, and she wondered if it had always been this quiet.

She should get going, but Aimeé was right: she didn't want to. The only problem was she couldn't possibly stay here. Grace saw herself in the mirror and realized her outfit was ridiculous for the downtown bar she was going to.

What was she thinking? Grace would keep the lipstick, but everything else had to go. She would go through the motions of getting ready, regular bar clothes and all, and make herself walk out the door.

Carefully she unwrapped the flowers from their tissue paper and placed them in the vase Aimeé had filled. They really were stunning. She inhaled deeply to take in the fresh scent and closed her eyes.

She might love him, but he wasn't the only person in her life she could love, was he? People fell in and out of love every day.

CHAPTER 56

"With a love life like yours, I'd still be at work too."

Mave looked up from the conference room he'd parked himself in ten hours earlier that day. His zombie-like stare proved he'd been going through more than his share of paperwork. He wasn't too tired to go down without a fight.

"How's your date with Grace? Oh, wait, I forgot she's going out with *not you*. Welcome back to work."

"I accept your cynicism. How's it looking?" Luke's head motioned to the papers lined in stacks down the length of the table. The whiteboard contained Mave's chicken scratch, and held a scattering of numbers that so far didn't make any sense.

Mave rubbed his face after finishing a highlight and began, "Keep in mind we'll never know everything."

"Got it."

Mave looked up and down the table and pointed to the left. "This is fifteen years back. They've had an increase in profit pretty much every year. But that's when there's been a significant increase in profit, year over year. I'm talking like eight to fifteen percent. Every client they get stays with them, and every year, they add more clients. I knew they were good, but this? This is really good." Mave stood and stretched and went over his notes. "No major debt concerns, no lawsuits, and great financial statements."

"So?" Luke questioned.

"There are a lot of factors to consider, but, yeah. They are going to need more manpower."

"Would the man-power be exclusive to their existing business?" Luke asked, knowing Mave would have covered all the bases.

"Thought you might go there," Mave offered a sly, confident grin. "I think this is where we get them."

Mave walked to the right side of the whiteboard and circled the bottom number and the number just to the right. Luke's eyes widened. The number to the right was…large.

"This," Mave pointed to the first number, "would be our investment into Thomas and Jane to bring tax services into their portfolio. This," Mave led Luke to the second number, "is the potential profit even if only twenty-five percent of their existing customers used the service."

"Holy shit."

"Holy shit, indeed. This," Mave made his final move by picking up a marker on his way to circle his last detail, "is the overall potential black if we acquire."

"Dad will be sold on this."

"Yeah." It was a simple agreement. "He will."

Mave stretched his arms and legs. He moved, bent, and twisted. He rubbed his back and realized he hadn't left the room all day.

"You hungry?" Mave asked.

"Of course. My date ditched me for another dude. How much work do you have left here? Want to go pick something up? Then I'll join you in the fight against forecasting?"

"Yup."

"Pizza or Chinese?"

"That should never have to be a decision to be made. How can one possibly choose between two perfect choices? What an imperfect ques-"

Luke cut Mave off, "It's pizza. The answer is always pizza. Who are you?"

"Black Sheep?"

"Never have you spoken a more beautiful name," Luke all but sang.

Even with the impending chill of winter, they decided walking a few blocks for pizza was worth it. Without a word, they both grabbed their jackets from their temporary desks that sat with the rest of the company's cubicles. Then they were on their   way.

CHAPTER 57

Mortified didn't begin to describe what she was feeling. Grace leaned on the brick wall once she'd finished a small meltdown and made it around the building and out of sight. The hard cold of the red-shaded concrete soothed the burn she felt all over. She shouldn't be embarrassed, but how embarrassing.

Seth, of all people, had to be the one who her friends had set her up with.

"No, no, no." Grace covered her face in an exasperated whine. "They will never hear the end of this. Friends-shmends." And Luke too; if it weren't for him, she wouldn't have gone on this crazy charade in the first place.

Stomping in the direction of home, Grace muttered, "The stupid, cute, irritating, dumb man."

Only one thing would calm her down. Carbohydrates. Rather than turning toward home, she headed straight up the street. She needed to vent, yell, accuse, and eat chocolate wrapped in sugar, flour, and lots of butter.

Grace tugged on the Bistro door and was greeted with a loud clank.

"Damn." She tried her luck again to no avail. She removed her glove and pounded on the door, then added her other fist. "Come on, I know you're still here."

Aimeé made her way around the kitchen wall and smiled at the view from behind the locked door. She saw Grace's fists pound the glass as if to the beat her voice was probably making. Her lips moved, rampant during the assault. Aimeé wondered if Grace had any idea not a single word was heard.

Aimeé flipped the manual lock from inside the door and pulled. She was greeted with what she presumed was the second half of whatever Grace had been saying.

"—on the planet. Thank goodness you're here, I need coffee – no, wine – and a distraction. Chocolate. Fried."

"I can provide," Aimeé pieced together the individual word puzzle, "all of that. Though you might have to start over and attempt to slow a bit. I thought your date was this distraction you were looking for?"

Grace stared, unamused. "Wine first."

"That good?" Aimeé maneuvered through the upside-down chairs that had been propped on the tables for cleaning. Her movements were effortless and delicate. She set a wineglass on the counter and poured Grace a small glass. Then waited for her protest at the modest amount. Grace was always a fan of a heavy pour.

"I think you mean, *that bad*. It was terrible. Mortifying. I am mortified. Do you know who was waiting in that bar?" Answering her own question, "Well, of course, you don't, but I'll tell you. Seth. Like, nerdy, lanky, quiet, been working for us for about seven years, Seth. I know we are all close up there, but not *that* close. I mean sure, yeah, I've wondered if Seth dates and the typical stuff, but actually doing it, no way."

"Interesting." Aimeé stared, doing her best to look perplexed.

"So naturally it was awkward, but I tried to make it, well, not awkward." Grace sipped and trudged on.

"At first, I thought maybe I had just bumped into him, so we started with small talk. But then he asked what I was doing out and about, so I told him a date. He said he was too, and this dread, okay maybe not dread, but that feeling in the pit of your stomach when you are anticipating severe embarrassment? You just *know* that something is not going to go your way? Well, that's what I got. I just said, 'You wouldn't happen to be meeting a blind date here?' And sure enough, it was him."

Her second sip of wine emptied it.

"More." She pointed into her glass. "Of course, I had to tell him I was sorry at the circumstance, but unfortunately because of our working situation we couldn't continue with the date. I'm just, I'm just – shit. And come to think of it, he didn't seem to share even a little of the shock and embarrassment I was feeling. Unexpected balls of steel. Give him credit for that."

Grace took a swig of the new pour.

"So, what do I do when I need a clear mind? I eat beignets, and I drink coffee – and wine – or vice versa. Thank you for working nearly all day, every day. I needed you to be here."

Aimeé paused after setting the latte on the bar to accompany the wine and smiled sweetly. "Grace, I am here. And even if I hadn't been, I would have come. All you need is to ask. Me, or any of us."

Aimeé came around the counter to sit next to Grace and swiveled them both, so they were facing, and their knees touching.

"I will not give you more advice. You know what your heart wants. You are the only one that can make it be. I will always be here for you, though. That is certain."

CHAPTER 58

Grace left the Bistro in a much better mood than when she'd walked in. She felt better. Settled. But she didn't want to go home. She wandered the block outside of the office. She looked up.

It wasn't a reflection of the streetlamps that caught her eye. When she looked closer, she realized it was a shadow walking across a conference room causing the flicker. The cleaning team didn't come until tomorrow, she thought, confused.

Curiosity got the best of her. She had to know. She swung open the door of the building and took the elevator up to the office.

The elevator gave a calm ding as its doors opened. Grace tiptoed down the hall and peered around the corner for a better look.

She should have known better. Of course, it would be Luke and Travis. She couldn't suppress her grin as she watched the two men giggle like school girls. Each sitting behind huge pizza boxes. Black Sheep to be specific. She'd recognize that box anywhere.

What were they doing here? It had to be coming up on eleven at night.

Grace walked into the conference room they'd dedicated to Wallace's teams. She decided she might as well confront them and see what they were up to.

"Mind letting me know what you boys are doing here at this hour?"

Their startled jump at her entry nearly made the entire night worth it. She had to hide the smile daring to form, an effort to keep her straight face.

"Holy fu-" Luke stopped his curse. "You nearly gave us a heart attack."

"Yet, you're still here, alive and well." She crossed her arms, leaning against the door frame.

"You changed." It was Luke's turn to smirk. "I kind of liked the red pant thing."

Grace cleared her throat and did her best to brush him off. "It was a jumpsuit, and you aren't answering my question."

"Neither are you."

"Yours wasn't a question," Grace challenged.

God, he loved her. Even the banter when she was pretending to be irritated with him was fun.

Luke motioned to the room with his hand guiding the way across the table and white board. When he stood, she entered and looked around at the mess of documents, folders, highlighters, and pens that were strewn everywhere.

"We are coming up with a brilliant plan because we are brilliant. And that's what we do," Luke said cockily.

"Who is brilliant?" Mave asked pointedly, earning a chuckle from Grace.

"I am. But you did good work here, too."

Mave shoved a slice of pizza into his mouth and rolled his eyes, too hungry to fight.

"A brilliant plan," she mimicked. She didn't mean to sound snarky, but she just wanted to be irritated with him. His flowers, her crappy date, and now he was here with pizza.

She wanted pizza.

"Yes." He decided to not give her the argument she wanted, so he clapped his hands as if to wrap up their conversation and carry on as they had been before she got there. "Well, we will just get back to work then, and let you know when we're finished. Oh, would you like a slice?"

Luke motioned to the leftovers in the pizza boxes. He didn't miss Mave's look of disgust in his willingness to give away perfectly good breakfast food – tomorrow's breakfast food to be more specific.

"I'm fine, thank you." Not giving into temptation, Grace turned and attempted a nonchalant, but sexy walk back through the door. It irritated her that she didn't know what they were up to. It irritated her even more when her stomach growled in protest at her decision to turn down the delicious pizza.

CHAPTER 59

"You know it's Friday, right?"

Grace looked up feeling cross-eyed from focusing on her computer all afternoon, and noticed with a glance out her window, what appeared to be all evening as well.

"I do, and it looks like we both made it. Though I don't know how quickly I'll be finishing up. What do you have for weekend plans?"

Luke slid himself into the bourbon-colored club chair across from her desk that was now feeling familiar.

She gazed at him. He looked handsome, but for the first time, she noticed he seemed tired.

Interesting, she thought wryly, even the impenetrable, smooth-talking charmer gets tired like the rest of us mere mortals.

Grace hated to admit seeing him like this had her viewing him in a different light. He was a hard worker, she knew that, but this was something different. It was real. Something normal. It wasn't all a show, and it wasn't all a game to him. It's what she imagined he would have been like coming home after a long week of work. They would opt for takeout rather than making dinner or having a night out. They would snuggle in on the couch with their containers of Chinese, pizza, or Thai and watch the latest Netflix craze or find news to play in the background as they talked about their week.

It would be so, so lovely, she thought with a twinge of sadness. How had everything become so complicated? It was a question for herself, and she realized, the answer was unfortunate and simple – she had made it so.

Grace realized she was tired, too. Exhausted, actually. A constant barrage of work, data pulling, emails, meetings, and – hardest of all – trying to avoid Luke as much as possible. She wanted space but realized it was harder than she imagined it would be.

"Not a lot of plans here," Luke started. "This Thomas and Jane takeover doesn't leave a lot of time for the day to day Wallace tasks that seem to not go away. I'll probably do most of my day job straight through the weekend. Maybe a few drinks and a football game or two at home. You?"

Grace leaned forward and rested her elbows on her desk to think about what she'd do this weekend. The thought of coffee, walking, and lounging around her home sounded so good she wouldn't trade it for an offer to jet-set to Paris. She moved one of her hands up for her chin to rest on as she completed her daydream and smiled.

"I can't wait for the weekend. The girls and I will get together at our normal time tomorrow morning – run then coffee," she explained, "Possibly head out shopping and stop for lunch. I might make time for an extra walk or two. Mostly I want to lounge around in sweats and slippers at home. I could even get crazy and read a book or magazine – for enjoyment. Can you believe it?"

He loved her. He wanted to be inside of that weekend, living it with her. "You really do live on the edge," he said teasingly. "You had me up until 'reading for enjoyment.' Nobody does that, not really."

His smile tore through her.

"How long are you working tonight?" Luke asked, moving the easy conversation along.

"Not sure," she shrugged, "Maybe seven, eight?"

"Perfect."

Her confusion halted the words she would have bumbled out, so she just looked at him curiously.

"I mean perfect, me too," Luke said quickly. "You up for Chinese take-out? Nothing goes better with working straight through dinner than Chinese food. It's proven. A fact."

Playing along, she said, "I agree with you. But I'm wondering, who performed this study?"

"Well, me, of course. I have a solid track record of working late and making my friends and coworkers do it with me. So far, they are all still my friends. I don't think any of them have quit either, to my knowledge. So, it must be true."

"In that case, I like anything. As long as there's a side order of dumplings with extra sauce." Her mouth watered at the thought.

"I could probably make that happen. So, dinner then." He grinned.

"Dinner," she confirmed, wondering if he read her mind.

—

Half way through Chinese, they were full and laughing hysterically at stories of coworkers and friends, old and new.

They talked about family dynamics, their lives growing up, and how they thought their lives would be so different by this point in their lives. Neither was upset with where they were currently, but imagined they'd be traveling the world with somebody or settled down in the early stages of family life.

Grace wasn't overly surprised that Luke took a chance when the subject was broached.

"That could be us, you know? It almost was. The traveling, making plans, living together, visiting family together."

Luke watched her eyes mist as she followed along with his reverie.

He continued with their future, pulling her into the dream, "We could be the people who get excited at the thought of one day planning a wedding. Lying in bed at night wondering how many kids we'd end up having, wondering if they would be boys or girls. We'd be adamant about practicing tough love, inevitably giving in and spoiling them rotten. We'd argue about moving out of the city to the suburbs, and eventually, you'd win. I'd go wherever it is you'd want to be. Maybe we'd even decide to keep your place because we'd always want a place in the city. We could retire and come back here when we are too old to drive and have to walk everywhere anyway."

Grace leaned back in her chair and let her head rest. She swiveled side to side and imagined the life he described. Grace knew, deep in her heart, it really would be that simple for them. No matter how much she wanted to fight it – they worked. They fit. Everything fit, from their hands to their lifestyle, ambitions, and family.

"It really could be," she admitted. "I just can't quite get over this, here. And I've tried. I've played out scenarios. The truth is, I felt like one day it was just a rumor mentioned in passing, 'Wallace is on the prowl, and his eye is set on Thomas and Jane.' And now? We are knee-deep in due diligence, and I'm just trying to go through the motions with the truth nagging in the back of my mind: that there isn't anything we can do to stop you from taking us over. Money wins every time. I could try as I might to stop it, but you just buy shares, persuade the board to replace management, and just like that, it's yours, all yours. You slowly dismantle everything we've built here – or maybe not so slowly – to do what's best for Wallace." Grace smiled, not from happiness, but from the inevitable. "You don't see it that way, I know. But it's the truth."

When Luke didn't say anything, she went on. "So, what I'm trying to say, is that really could be us. But I'm not there yet. I was, don't get me wrong. I would have taken a leap of faith with you to the end of the world. But now, it's me. I need time. Whether we like it or not, this," Grace waved a tired finger between them, "is a conflict of interest. I'm trying to do one thing, and you're trying to do another. We are a distraction for each other."

Luke reached across the table. He rested his hand on hers, at first to comfort her, but then for him. He knew the hardest thing to do was wait for something you knew you wanted. He could tell her about what he and Mave had been working on, but tonight, he realized, it wouldn't have made a difference. She needed to find her way through this without his pushing. She needed to love him, no matter the outcome.

Luke grinned and without letting her hand go stood and walked around to her side of the desk and gently kissed her cheek. Then walked out without looking back.

CHAPTER 60

"What do you think?"

Aaron Wallace got up to get a closer look at the numbers and projections Luke and Travis had just finished presenting. He'd entertained the thought months ago, even before they explained their plan, but had dismissed it just as quickly.

"I don't think this is in line with our history or monetary plan moving forward." Randy Flamingo wasn't in favor. He had shown it by questioning every calculation, forecast, and the budget numbers they'd prepared. In the end, it only made Travis and Luke look better.

In fact, the barrage of challenge after challenge that came from Flamingo only assuaged any of Luke's lingering doubts, and he hoped, Aaron Wallace's, too. It was a solid presentation.

"What history and monetary plan are you referring to, Flamingo?" Aaron asked, always willing to let his teams state their opinions. He found it led to a better discussion, new ideas.

"We, historically, have made aggressive moves to put ourselves in a financially stable and superior position. This includes business takeover and restructure," Randy said pompously.

"We," Aaron added emphasis on we to ensure Randy understood what they represented, "have made calculated moves to ensure we are financially stable so we can provide the best service to our clients and investors. These clients need us to succeed while complying with law and regulation. By ensuring we take care of them, we, in turn, have become profitable."

Aaron Wallace lingered on his words a bit and nodded to himself. Then he directed his attention back to Luke and Travis.

"You've run this by the board? Grace, Abbi, the rest of the leaders?"

"Not yet. Looking for your input first," Luke said.

"And you think the board will like, or, be in favor of the candidates you've recommended to run Thomas and Jane?"

"I do. We," Luke corrected and nodded to Mave, "do."

"I like it. It's smart. And I like you didn't take the easy way out. Let's get on their calendar. This will be a bit of a strategy change."

Luke and Mave shook hands excitedly. Nothing beat hard work. Hard, smart-as-hell, work. Especially when it paid off. Mave slapped a friendly pat on Randy's back.

"It's alright, Flamingo. I think you'll appreciate this in the long run."

Randy stood and followed Mave out. Luke gathered his laptop and notes and started for the door.

"One second, Luke," Aaron said, motioning to his son. "Come over here for a minute."

Luke plopped his things back down and walked to the front where his dad still hovered, hands in his pockets, doing a little rock from heel to toe.

"This," Aaron pointed to a now blank screen. "It was good."

"I agree. And thanks." Luke leaned on the edge of the table and crisscrossed his ankles. "Mave did nearly all the heavy lifting. He's smart."

"It's what we hired him for, believe it or not." Aaron smiled. "Not just so you could have a play pal at work."

It was Luke's turn to smile.

"You know, I couldn't help but wonder if all this has anything to do with a one Grace Thomas?"

"The idea?" Luke began. "No, we had that in motion when we dove into their background. When this," his head motioning to the plop of papers, "was just a bullet during a strategic brainstorming session. I had the genius idea to try and go on a blind date with Grace to get her opinion and overall feel on it. As it turns out, it didn't go overly well. But the push, the drive to finish it?" Luke nodded and folded his arms. "Absolutely. She's good, dad. Great, actually. She's intelligent, works harder than many I've seen and gets her people to work harder for it. But she treats them well. She's amazing at it all."

"We're still talking about the business here?"

Luke grinned as he replied. "Mostly."

"She knows you love her?"

Luke looked up.

"Don't be so surprised," Aaron said. "I saw you stumbling around that office. Bringing coffees, lunches, dinners. Pining away."

"I was not pining."

"Own it, son."

"It was that bad, huh?"

Aaron Wallace smiled. "Or that good. Matter of perspective. You planning on doing anything about that?"

"Yes. I'm actively waiting."

"Actively waiting?" Aaron was amused.

"It's torture."

"You want to know torture? Meeting your grandma Edna for lunch this week and having to explain how you got to be 'actively waiting' in the first place."

"Shit. What day?"

"Language. Tuesday."

"Sorry. Women are hard." Luke's hands found his face.

"No, son. They are right." Aaron walked to the table and put a knowing arm around Luke's shoulders. "If they think we messed up, we probably did."

CHAPTER 61

Grace walked in to see Maggie – a vision in peacock blue – happily waddling in and out of offices, dropping off files, bringing papers to desks, and smiling from ear to ear. Grace wanted to try, but she was too tired to match Maggie's enthusiasm.

"Maggie." She couldn't help her bland tone.

Maggie either didn't care or didn't catch the monotone as she nearly sang her responding, "Hello!"

"What has gotten into you?"

Maggie continued to move a mile a minute. Grace joined her in stride after she plopped her own bags next to Maggie's desk. They weaved, paused, continued, and rounded Maggie's desk three more times making deliveries as she went on and on.

"This is the best time of the year. It felt cold this morning. Not just chilly, but cold. A new year is on the horizon," Maggie trilled.

"It's October. In Minnesota. It's either freezing or beautiful. It could snow tomorrow. Did you say New Year? Are we skipping over the holidays this year?"

"Yes." Maggie paused for a moment. "No. Don't you just get that happy feeling this time of year? Everybody is lighter. Excited. Genuinely friendly. They are looking forward to Thanksgiving, football, hunting. Then that snow you mentioned will fall, and Christmas will be right around the corner. We'll celebrate and start talking about resolutions we are going to make for the new year."

Maggie looked sideways at Grace as she added, "Of course we won't keep any of them."

"We are Minnesotans, we just act like we like all of those things," Grace said exhaustedly.

Maggie laughed. "Did you know your dad loved this time of year?"

Maggie walked up to stand next to Grace, dropped the pile of folders on the desk, and leaned on them. "He said there was something about the cold that allowed people to think. The constant running around during summer and fall stops. The winter gives people time to reflect and plan for the new. It always stuck with me. And gives me a little pep in my step."

Grace just listened and smiled. She couldn't be irritated at that. Even in her exhaustion.

"Your father was a special man who understood life. Living. It was more than just work. And you can feel that here." Maggie sighed. "This is a great place. But when you walk outside into the fresh air, you see there are a lot more possibilities out there than in here. Just food for thought. I must have food on my mind. I'm meeting your mom for our weekly lunch today."

Grace tilted her head. "What if you don't know for sure if what's out there is great – or even good?"

"Sometimes you just have to take that chance."

"I've been hearing that a lot lately."

"Must be something to it then," Maggie said, sweeping past her to deliver more documents.

CHAPTER 62

"Mom?" Grace called into her childhood home and tossed her bags on the chair as she'd done throughout grade school and college when she'd come home. William simply dropped his things on the floor, usually in the middle of the doorway, and nearly drove their mom mad.

"Are you here?" She yelled a bit louder after no response.

A loud crash echoed down the hall, and Grace took off. Panic filled her body as she ran from the guest room to the office, not sure where the sound originated.

When she reached the master bedroom, she saw her mom on the floor with a pile of boxes surrounding her, and heard, "Well, shit," mumbled from her mom's direction.

"What are you doing in here?" Grace asked. Not able to help the giggle that trickled out, she covered her mouth to hide it. You never knew what kind of mood your mom was in when all the contents of a closet were nearly crushing her. You had to tread lightly.

Lydia jumped nearly lifting her butt entirely off the floor and screamed. "My goodness gracious, Grace, you nearly killed me."

"That's funny. It seems to me you're trying to do that all by yourself."

Her mom laughed as Grace found an open space on the floor to leverage herself so she could help her mom to her feet.

"What are you doing in here?"

"Well, I had to look for something your dad gave me years ago and, for Heaven's sake, I forgot where I'd stashed it away. I assumed it would be in your things, but haven't been able to track it down. Then I remembered it was in a Thomas and Jane envelope and figured I tucked it away in a box full of that old paperwork. Here," Lydia heaved a box into Grace's arms, and it nearly made her collapse, "let's take this one to the kitchen table. I have a good feeling about this one."

"How in the world were you carrying this? It's so heavy. Hey," Grace said, as she struggled, "did you know dad liked this time of year?"

"Probably that kickboxing class I've been taking. And oh, yeah." She waved her hand like it was old news. "Absolutely loved it."

"You're kickboxing? How did I not know that?" Or, she thought, all of these things?

"I didn't tell you. And I guess I figured you already knew."

Grace was shocked there would be anything her mom wouldn't tell her. Especially after her dad passed away. They, William included, had been inseparable.

"Why wouldn't you tell me about kickboxing? That seems silly."

Lydia ignored her. "I want you to read something. Which is what got me on this whole kick. Well that, and Maggie, who told me at lunch about everything that's been going on at the office. Something about a plan?" Lydia looked up and flicked her hand as if it was above her knowledge, "Anyway, it got me thinking."

"Sure, I'll read anything. Is it a legal document? Are you worried about investments? Maybe William would be a better person to help."

"No, no. None of that. Here," Lydia handed her a delicate card that looked like it had been opened millions of times. "Take this to the living room. I'll be in the bedroom and office trying to clean up some of the disasters I've made."

How strange is this? Grace thought as she eyed the worn Hallmark seal that long ago might have held the edges together.

Grace sat in a blue fabric rocking chair that must have been thirty years old and curled into it. She opened the envelope and pulled out the card. Tears welled in her eyes when she realized what she was looking at.

A card to her mom from her dad. He must have written it before, but when he had known he wouldn't have long.

It was a picture of two figures walking hand-in-hand into the sunset. The text on the front was worn as if a thumb or finger had grazed it every night since it had been given.

"To walk beside you has been life's greatest adventure."

Grace covered her mouth to hold back the sobs. After sitting for a moment to regain her composure, she wiped her eyes with the sleeves of the sweatshirt she'd changed into after work, took a heavy breath, then opened the card.

My Lydia Grace,

I love you more than you'll ever know. More than I'll be able to tell you. I'll tell you every day from where I am. You'll know because you'll feel it. That's how strong my love is for you.

You think about life a lot when you're nearing the end of it. The same thought keeps running through my mind, and it's how much I'll be missing you and how much it will seem like I'm not there to help you through this. Sweetie, it's going to be hard, but you can do it – and I will be there. You're so strong. The strongest woman I've ever known. The most beautiful, but the strongest, too.

William and Gracie are going to need you, but that's nothing new. You've been their rock their whole lives. I always knew I had the easy job of coming home and being the fun dad. You made them into the wonderful people they are. I'm giving you all the credit for that, and I'm so proud to do so.

Sweetie, I could write on and on telling you of my love, but I know you know how special we are. Best friends in life. We were pulled together by chance, and it changed our lives forever. I remember how you disliked me at first. But I couldn't live without you.

I was asked the other day if I would give anything to have a couple more days. The fact is, I wouldn't change a thing. I wouldn't risk the love we have, the life we've built, the family we've made. Not for a few million dollars, not for an extra day, or an extra lifetime. Being loved by you was my whole life.

You're not going to want to read this next part, but I have to get it down because one day you'll be ready. You'll be ready to not be alone. The thing is I'll always love you, and you'll always love me. And allowing yourself to love and care for another person doesn't change that. It's simply allowing yourself to be loved by another. Not more, not less, just loved.

We have our love now and forever. I love you so much.

Yours always,

Raymond

The rush of love and longing for her dad caught in her throat, her emotions uncontrollable. She watched her mom come into the room; felt the nurturing swaddle as her mom's arms wrapped her in warmth, trading places with her in the chair to hold her and rock her as if she was just a baby.

"Shh now, Gracie. It's okay. It's okay. Your father, what an amazing man we had. We have. You know, I feel him all around me all the time. I must have read this card every day, a hundred times a day. He gave us such a wonderful life. And look at you and William, my beautiful babies. I see so much of him in the two of you."

Grace knew she was talking to console, her words to soothe, but knew every word was true to her mom.

"I still miss him so much, mom."

"I know, honey. Me too. You know, this letter, he knew I would need it. More than that, he knew long after I needed it, I would cherish it. He was so wise. So loving. So kind. He worked tirelessly to provide for this family. If I hadn't known he

349

was doing it out of love, I would have told him to hang it up years before he passed to just spend time with me, with us.

"We talked about it a lot. Just pack up and take off. Maybe fly to Europe, load up the car for a road trip across the States, or maybe one of those cruises that takes you to those European castles. I wish we would have done that."

Grace felt her mom shift beneath her and realized she was probably squishing her to death. When she tried to get up, she felt her mom tighten her arms and not let her go. She simply turned so they were facing.

"Do you want to know what my favorite thing to do with your dad was?"

Grace found it surprising they'd never talked about it. That she didn't know. She nodded.

"You and your brother were off at college. You know your dad. He was such an early riser, just like you. He would tip-toe around for only so long before he would start clanking around in the kitchen."

Grace smiled.

Lydia went on, "I would hear it and try my darnedest to fall back asleep to get a few extra precious moments – you know when bed feels just right in the mornings? Sure enough, I wouldn't be able to get back to sleep, so I'd stumble down and he would be in the kitchen dressed and ready for us to walk out the door. Some days I'd be so irritated at his rushing me, but you know, once I was up it was nice having more of the day. He always understood the importance of not wasting the time we had.

"Then we would hop in the car and just be together. We'd go to the corner gas station, get a coffee for me, and your dad would get whatever he felt like that day. Donuts, pop, coffee with more flavored creamer than was probably good for him. We would go grocery shopping, or to a store to pick up something you or William needed. Or we would go to one of those hardware stores to think about ideas for the next house project. But we would just be. And we would talk, or not. But that time together, it was so simple, but it was everything."

Grace couldn't help but relive the weekend at Edna's she shared with Luke. He'd done exactly the same. Up early to adventure around the town. It was silly, but it was time together. She wanted that. She wanted it to be with Luke.

"Gracie, I need to give you something."

Grace felt a pat on her backside.

"I've had this since the funeral."

Her mom held out an envelope with their company logo on it.

"William and I watched you leave the funeral that day seeing you so heartbroken, we both agreed that any company business could wait. The time and grieving were more important. But now, with all of the talk about, well, you know. Don't look at me that way. Abbi, Maggie, and I talk regularly. I was worried you might need it. It could be important."

She took the envelope and opened the seal. Nostalgia welled in her heart, knowing it had been sealed by her dad.

In an instant, he was with her, like no time had passed. The document was a financial statement from the month she had taken over as CFO. They'd had their best month ever. Now she was the acting CEO, and that came with its own challenges. But, with every change, things became better. That was an interesting thought.

Grace paused when she saw a shadow of ink seeping through the paper. She turned the statement over and found her dad's writing.

We've accomplished something great here! <u>You</u> have accomplished something great here. Keep up the good work, Gracie. But never forget why we do it. If this is where your heart and ambition stay, I'll be so proud. But should your heart take a chance on a new adventure, take mine with you.

Love, Dad

The laugh came as a surprise. She looked up at her mom, and more giggles bubbled up with fresh tears. Her shoulders lifted and fell. Her sigh of relief was audible.

Grace jumped up and smacked her mom on the cheek with a kiss. She flung her bags over her shoulder and nearly leveled William as she rushed out the door.

"Love you! Bye!"

———

William walked in and eyed his mom. Lydia just lifted her hands and said, "The girl knows what she wants."

CHAPTER 63

A weight was lifted. Promises made long ago had lost their significance. A burden had lost its hold. And though she would have gotten there eventually, her love for Luke encouraged her. Her father's words assured her. She knew what she wanted. And it wasn't a building. It was a man.

Grace nearly floated into Aimeé's Bistro and found her friend resting a hip against the bar, in casual conversation with Christopher. He tried hard to seem as relaxed, but when it came to Aimeé, he had a nervous tell. His left foot casually scraped the floor with the toe of his boot. Grace smiled at the sight and waved as she navigated to their corner table.

"You're looking slightly less miserable than you were a bottle of wine ago," Casey said, a knowing tone filling her voice. She screeched a chair next to Grace and winced at the piercing shrill.

"It's because she's realized she is, in fact, in love. Don't you agree?" Aimeé said while setting two coffees in front of the girls.

"My heaven." Casey picked up the steaming cup and held it to her face as if she was holding a cup of gold. She could probably afford it if it had been. "So, let's hear it."

"I had a Maggie and Mom double-header."

"Ah, yes," Casey simply agreed. "That'll do it." Not willing to share she knew more than she let on. But she was happy Maggie hadn't deviated from the plan and that it seemed to run its intended course.

Aimeé gave a knowing nod as Rachel rushed in apologizing for being late.

"What did I miss?"

"A Maggie-Mom combo," Casey recapped.

"Ohh." Rachel drew out the sound.

Grace felt the anticipation as her friends stared at her expectantly. She took a moment to appreciate their three beautiful faces.

"We meet on Wednesday with the board. And," she gripped her cup, "Whatever happens, happens."

"Whoa." Rachel and Casey verbalized their surprise.

"Whoa is right. And, I'm going to go to Luke. I want to be with him. I was just with Mom, and we read a letter from dad, and we cried; then there was another letter, and we hugged. And now I know what I want. I know what I need. And I know I want to go through this life with Luke. The good, the bad. Loving him, probably being so angry with him. But I'm so excited for that, too. Love is what matters. And it needs to be him."

Rachel screamed. A piercing octave only dogs could hear.

Casey confirmed her comprehension in the only way she knew how, repeating, "I heard something about a letter, then another letter – both from your dad – then you cried, then you hugged, then you realized that you loved Luke. Pretty much cover it?"

"Exactly." Grace nodded. "What do you think?"

"Now you *have* to tell her." Aimeé looked at Casey, setting her latte down and letting the hard gaze force guilt. A move that meant do it now.

"Tell me what?" Grace said, crossing her legs under the table and leaning forward.

"It's about your date," Casey began.

"My blind date? From like, months ago? Or recently?"

"One and the same."

Grace sat back and lamented. "What about it? It was awful. I wish I would have never reached out again. Poor Seth. It was not my best moment."

"That's the thing. That wasn't supposed to be your moment," Casey hedged.

"Now I'm just confused." Grace looked to the other girls for help.

Aimeé rolled her eyes. "You are exhausting," she told Casey. She turned to Grace. "Seth was not your blind date. You were set up with Luke because he asked. Casey did some freelance consulting for Wallace. Travis Mavens reached out, Casey put you and Luke through her dating assessment just to see if it was a good idea. You were a *ninety-six* percent compatibility. That's good," Aimeé explained. "Then she had a decision to make. Don't go through with the set-up, just because maybe there'd be a tiny, teensy, conflict of interest, or–"

"Or maybe you hit it off with an awesome guy," Rachel interjected.

"I did a full background check. Checked finances, Luke's phone records. He is – as far as men go – not a bad guy. Pretty good, in fact," Casey added in a rare moment of male-appreciation.

"She means great," Rachel corrected.

Grace sat for a moment. She tried to follow and process the chain of events. "So I was on my way to meet Luke when I ran into Luke?" she repeated slowly.

"Yes." Casey agreed.

"Exactly." Rachel was getting excited.

Their voices mingled together.

"And he knew that?" Grace continued.

"I'm going to say yes." Casey was cautious. "But only if you promise to take it well."

"Interesting," was all Grace could manage.

"You're not mad?" Rachel asked.

"No. No, I don't think I am."

"Why?" Aimeé wondered, mostly out of curiosity.

Grace smiled. "Because every moment I can think of that makes me happy, all of my thoughts and memories – and I mean the big ones – not a single one of them has to do with work. If he intended to do anything other than make me fall in love with him, he failed miserably."

"I love that he failed miserably!" Rachel cheered.

The women laughed, and in their laughter, the last bit of her hurt and sadness for the company fell away.

CHAPTER 64

Grace hadn't seen Luke all day. She'd avoided Seth like the plague. She didn't want him to feel bad, but she had a job to do. She needed to focus and couldn't have any distractions.

When Grace looked up she caught a glimpse of a perfectly positioned gray bun and sprang out of her chair and bolted for the door.

"Edna! Hi, what are you doing here? It's so good to see you!" Grace intercepted Edna at Maggie's desk and wrapped her in a hug and Edna squeezed her like only a grandmother could. She loved Edna, too. Seems when you decide you love one person, you end up loving a whole slew of them.

Edna pulled her away to get a better look at her, just as she had done the first time they'd met.

"I thought you were beautiful the first time I met you, but look at you. You are a vision of sophistication today, my dear. Look at those shoes. Hold on," Edna wasn't finished admiring. "Do a little turn for me."

Grace laughed and obeyed. As she circled, the shimmery flow of the gray skirt caught the air and floated with her as she turned. Her cropped, matching gray sweater, was just the tailored yin to the skirts' yang.

"I bet Luke can barely keep his eyes off you when he's strolling around here." Edna knowingly smirked out the words when she was once again facing Grace.

"I haven't seen him stroll, or do anything like it, around here today. Seems he's avoiding me. It's my fault."

Grace received a tender pat on the cheek. "It's nobody's fault. Though it won't stop me from giving that young man a good talking to. I'll do it at lunch. He bribed me here so I could bring him something from the house. If he's not here yet, I'd love to catch up and hear what's going on in your world until he decides to show his handsome face."

Edna enthusiastically said, "Nice to meet you," to Maggie, and the two shared the perfect little hand squeeze as they parted.

"I'll tell you, this view isn't anything to shake a stick at." Edna walked to the window, and Grace joined her.

"I was so proud of this office."

"Was?"

"I am," Grace admitted. "I am very proud. It was my dad's office. I kept most of his things in place. Couldn't get myself to move them out. I was named CFO while he was still alive and I know it's because I was good at the job, not because he was my dad. He actually kept the company reports for that first month I was in charge of our bottom line. I found out last night."

"That's sweet. I would have loved to know Raymond." Edna continued at Grace's surprise at knowing his name, "Luke told me about him. How do you feel about it today?"

Grace softened at the thought of Luke sharing intimate details of their relationship with Edna. That he'd take the time to tell her about her dad. Luke was a good guy. Great. The best, actually.

"I'm happy my mom waited so long to give the report to me. Had she given it to me when he passed, I wouldn't have understood its significance. He wrote me a note on the back where he circled our profit. Silly, I know, but we always circled the profit when we could genuinely agree that the number was a result of the people who worked here loving their job, not because we'd charged more for our time or added an extra hour here and there when we billed a client. We would never do that, but it was a big deal for us to believe in our team's happiness and protect our company vision. I know that's a long way to explain it, but ultimately, he said we'd done it, so now I can move on."

"He was a wise man," Edna said warmly. "Somehow, these men get us to do crazy things. Like, move us to middle-of-nowhere Minnesota. All in the name of love."

Grace hadn't forgotten, but she hadn't paid enough attention to all of the people that had risked what they'd known – what was comfortable – for love. Not knowing what they would do next, but willing to figure it out.

She was good at this work. She loved it. And she could do it somewhere else if that's what it came down to.

"It seems to me when two people are meant to be together, little else matters. I shouldn't share our private conversations, because Luke should be telling you this himself. But Luke told me he was so taken with you when he first met you. He knew he was taking a risk by trying to start a relationship. Yet he couldn't quite help himself. And if you know Luke, he doesn't take risks easily, not with that stubborn old man of his. He also doesn't take lightly to giving up an opportunity. I know he wants to find love. He must have had some kind of feeling about you." Edna smiled sweetly at Grace, "I have found some love stories are short, but when people really work at them they can be long and beautiful. I think yours might be the latter. Not always easy, but that, too, can be a wonderful thing. Did I mention my husband moving me to the middle of nowhere? I could have killed him. But we made it and oh how we loved." Edna chuckled fondly.

Grace's smile turned flat as Seth walked into the room. Oh no, he had that look in his eyes. Embarrassment was already burning her cheeks.

"Edna, this is-"

Seth cut her off. It seemed more out of nervousness than rudeness, but it caught her off guard.

"I'd like to date you," Seth practically shouted, firm and resounding. More like he was demanding it rather than suggesting. The boom of his voice caught him by surprise as much as his audience.

Oh God, she thought. And from the looks of it, he wasn't stopping.

"I realize the other night was not what you expected," he forged ahead.

Okay, this was getting out of hand. Grace moved toward Seth and hugged him. To comfort? Maybe. But more to try and hold his words inside and spare him – and her – the embarrassment.

"Seth," Grace started as she pulled back slightly catching a glimpse of Luke as he looked on from the doorway.

He nodded curtly and turned. "I'll be waiting by the door when you're ready, Grandma." Then Luke walked away without another word.

"Oh, come on!" Grace said, laughing out her exasperation at the chain of events.

"Seth, no, stop." She released Seth but held off his next proclamation with a finger that nearly poked him in the nose.

"Edna, this is Seth. Seth, this is Edna. Edna is the grandmother of the man I'm in love with – who now probably thinks that I am actually dating somebody else."

Grace didn't give him time to register the rejection. "You are very sweet, Seth. You're very smart. But I am not your person. You have a person somewhere." She motioned to indicate wherever in the world that someone might be with an exhausted wave of her hand.

She should stop while she was ahead.

"Very nice to meet you, Seth," Edna said, trying her best to be polite and not wanting to make this poor man feel more embarrassed than he needed to be. "Seth, would you mind walking me to the door, as I don't quite remember where I turned off?"

Edna gathered Seth's elbow in hers and let him guide her through the door. She made one final turn and shot Grace a wink on her way out.

Grace let the full laugh huff out and plopped back into her   chair.   Unbelievable.

CHAPTER 65

Maggie hummed as she made her way around the office the next morning and drifted over to Seth's cube when she saw his desk light on earlier than usual. A little consoling and grandmothering never hurt anybody. She set a pile of files on the corner of his desk but didn't speak.

"I definitely don't want to talk about it." Seth didn't look up from his computer.

Maggie wondered how to help poor Seth. She'd seen him down before, but this was worse. She could see humiliation weaved into the lines sagging below his eyes. He was far too young for the likes of those.

She inhaled to speak, but her words were cut off.

"I mean, I had to, right? What if she would have said yes, you know? I'm totally smart." Seth said sheepishly looking forward as if he were having the conversation with himself. His arms reaching out as he spoke only to find their way back to his face.

Maggie smiled and let him go on 'not wanting to talk about it.'

"She's the prettiest girl – woman – I've ever seen. Funny. She's funny, too. She's genuinely nice. Girls just are not that way anymore. They want to know how much money you make and if you're clean and do yoga. I don't do yoga, I'm a man. *Of course* I would do something more manly than yoga."

She waited patiently for more words to come.

"I don't know exactly what that is right now, but not yoga." Seth looked up at Maggie for the first time. "I really messed this up, didn't I? Things are going to be weird forever. I don't want to leave this job. I love this job."

The thud from Seth's head hitting the desk reverberated and was felt by Maggie, who was now leaning on the edge to ride it out. Then he offered a theatrical sigh.

"Seth?" Maggie's eye caught the corner of his desk where a crumpled piece of paper was slightly hidden by his pencil holder. "Hand me that paper."

If Maggie thought she saw humiliation earlier, the fear that replaced it was worse. If she hadn't felt so badly for the poor guy, she probably would have grinned and given him friendly grief.

"Seth, what were you thinking?" Maggie scolded, but gently.

"I thought it was my chance. It was in her files, so I kind of put my number on a different sheet of paper and let her find that one. You know, instead of, the real one."

"It could have been a client. Or her doctor. Or–"

"I know! It's awful. But that day, she told us what it was for, remember?" Seth pleaded. "And now she knows I switched the numbers and it's even more awful," he muttered miserably.

"Okay. Okay, now. Just calm down and stop worrying. You need to buck up. It's nearly straightened itself out, but you need to pull yourself together. You're making me nervous, and I don't get nervous. When you pull yourself together enough, you just find time to get in there and apologize. She's not going to think one thing about it, so you've just got to clear the air. Got it?" Maggie stood with her hands on her hips, looking at Seth expectantly.

Seth's head hit the desk for a second time as he muttered, "I'm the worst," on the way down.

"There, there. I've seen worse. Don't beat yourself up about it." Maggie patted his head on the way by. "This doesn't even make the top five."

Maggie smiled as Seth's groan followed her toward Grace's office. She'd be in by now, and Maggie had a delivery to make. Grace needed to know to go easy on Seth, not that she would have been hard, but just in case. And, though she probably had memorized the numbers, Grace deserved the original crumpled piece of paper from the man that held her heart.

CHAPTER 66

Luke stared at the light shining from Grace's office, willing it to turn off. If it turned off, he'd be able to fight the urge to walk in and tell her she's being childish. Insane and foolish and childish.

He froze when he saw her shadow pause, then move back and forth across the room. He realized he wasn't breathing as he stalked, and it only irked him more.

Now who's being childish? he thought as his foot kicked, skimming the sidewalk.

"You probably won't get her attention from down here."

The slamming of his heart against his chest dulled, letting the embarrassment of being caught take over. He didn't know if it was worse or better knowing it was Aimeé, Bistro owner and best friend to the woman he was staring at.

Well, shit.

"Yeah, I think she's not interested in my attention at the moment."

"You're talking about Seth, then?" Aimeé said, amused.

"What?" He'd heard her, but he needed to hear it again. He wanted Aimeé to confirm it was true, to fuel the anger building inside of him.

"Seth, you must know him? He works with Grace." Aimeé said casually, confirming his suspicion. Hoping she was pushing all the right buttons.

When Luke shook his fists in frustration, he realized he probably looked ridiculous, but not enough to try and control himself. When he swung around, he saw Aimeé standing patiently, not reacting to his tantrum. Simply stood, waiting for him to finish. He calmed and walked toward her.

"She loves me," Luke said. It wasn't a question, but it wasn't the confident statement he was shooting for either. When did he get so damn wishy-washy?

That's it, he determined. He knew he was right. They belonged together, and he'd be damned if he wasn't going to give Grace a piece of his mind.

Date *Seth?* He scoffed, too irritated to remember he'd liked the poor guy who was now the brunt of his outburst.

"She loves me." Luke said, this time with conviction and a finger pointing at Aimeé.

"Okay."

He heard Aimeé agree before he skipped off into a run toward the building. His adrenaline was high. He took the stairs two at a time.

When he reached the third floor his breath and legs felt heavy, but continued, he'd made a commitment after all.

On the fifth floor, he swore and walked to the elevator to ride the rest of the way up. Adrenaline could only take you so far.

The quiet of night allowed the faint sound of Grace's voice to travel down the halls of the office. He loved the sound of her voice. It was feminine and confident. She always spoke as if she knew what she wanted. The way his name had exclaimed from her mouth...No, he shook his head. He didn't want to think about those memories or he'd get some unwanted desire pumping through his veins. He'd never be the same from those nights spent together. She'd ruined him.

"I will always love it here, nothing will change that."

His heart sank as the words she spoke become more audible the closer he got. When he was at her door, he saw her on the phone, looking outside, saying she had to get going because there was a call she had to make. She was fiddling with a small piece of paper that looked like the one he'd seen on her desk – the day she told him she was going to start dating other people.

He saw the signs, they were there. He just hadn't wanted to accept they were true. Grace was dating Seth. She really had moved on. That was just nauseating, he thought, as the sickness crept through him.

He watched her hang up and turn toward him. She must have heard his groan of disgust. He was miserable, and her eyes were smiling like all the weight in the world was lifted from her. She was happy. That was even worse. She was beautiful. But it was still the worst.

"Luke," she said, her energetic tone bringing on a frustration he'd never felt before.

"Just no." He held up a hand motioning for her to stop and followed it with a finger silently asking for a moment to gather himself.

He couldn't. When he began to walk away, he heard feet behind him, and he whirled to see her take his place at the door. He spun back around, suddenly energized by his disbelief.

"I just – I'd like to – no. Is this really about Seth? Do you really like him? I mean, I guess he's tall. Taller than me, if you're into that sort of," his finger made a line straight up and down, "thing."

Grace's smile wasn't overly smug, but it was enough to allow him to make a fool of himself. So, he was going to go for it.

"You know what your problem is? You don't know what you want. You think you want this company so badly. You think you want Seth," he hissed, his tone bitter with irritation and dripping with a callow whine.

"You know what I think? I think you have no idea what you want. I think the entire time we spent together, starting this," moving his finger back and forth between them, "this romance, you didn't bring up the work once, except to tell me your company was being sought after. Do you want to know what you *did* talk about? Growing up with your dad and how great your parents were. You talked about your girlfriends like you were born to be in one another's lives."

The way Luke described her, and them – the girls – filled her with more love than she'd had before he started his rant. She'd let him finish. Besides, it was the most precious thing she'd ever seen and heard.

Luke continued, "You get all girl-looking at the idea of kids and a family that you want to have one day. You looked at me like I was the only man in the world that mattered, and if you weren't losing your mind, I think you'd've realized I was looking at you in the same damn way. I still do. I bet you don't tell *Seth* those things or look at *him* that way."

Now he really was being childish. But it was the truth as far as he was concerned. He forged on.

"I'm going to go ahead and leave him out of this for now, even though I'm aware of what's going on here." Luke motioned to the piece of paper she was still holding, now under one of her crossed arms as she leaned in the door frame, her lips pursed in a smile, allowing him to get on with it.

"None of those things are about this company," he continued, his voice cracking with the impassioned words. "None of them. All of what you love is out there, in life, while you're living it. Do you honestly think your dad would tell you 'No, don't you dare be with a man who loves you so much he'd give up anything to be with you; you be sure to keep this pile of bricks running?' Sorry." He put up his hands in defense after the pile of bricks comment knowing she loved them. "The bricks are nice, you know, for bricks."

Grace hid her grin with her fingers.

"You have all of these amazing things but haven't taken two minutes to think about how damn lucky we are to have such – fucking – *shit,*" he felt exhausted. "I'm not swearing at you. But shit!"

Luke's hands were in his hair as he paced away. Regaining what was left of his composure, he concluded, "We found each other. Can't you see that? People live lifetimes looking for the feeling we have when we are together. I want that. I want you to want that. I can't make you want it, but I want you to. I want you to want me."

Luke finally shoved his hands in his pockets where he felt the small box he'd asked Edna to bring him when they'd met for lunch. It should have felt exhilarating. He should have been nauseous for a different reason. Instead, he was enervated and sick at the thought of a life without Grace in it.

"Jesus, Grace. I think I loved you from the first second I saw you."

He was done. He'd said all he needed to say. Feeling the faintest sense of relief, his head fell back, and he sighed.

"I'll leave you to your business tonight." He said simply, pointing to the paper once more, then started toward the exit.

CHAPTER 67

"You know, it's funny," Grace said, taking a step to follow Luke. "This."

She held up the now antique-looking paper, motioning to it.

"It was given to me by the girls, a blind date they set me up on. I would never have gone, but I know them, and they would never set me up with somebody they didn't think I'd hit it off with. Or," she laughed, "they would have badgered me until I gave in. But they would have made sure it was worth it."

She watched her desired effect play across his face, just a touch of dread, but hopefully it wouldn't last long.

"It's funny how things work out, though, isn't it?" She went on, slowly making her way to him. "I never went on this date because I ran into you. Then I lost it – well, forgot about it really – because I had been so smitten. You were perfect. Everything I thought I could have ever asked for in a man. So much more, actually." She paused wistfully and knew they were both replaying memories in their minds of those first few weeks together.

"But you being all of that – wonderful, charming, devilishly handsome – it would never have worked. Because at that time, no matter how perfect you were, you were disrupting the only thing I'd cared about, and I wasn't ready. I needed my dad, and he was here. In these walls, in my walls." Grace walked out and ran her fingers along the old, exposed, stone walls her dad had insisted on keeping.

"So, no matter how much you tried, or gave me space, it only confused me more. I couldn't focus on you because I need to focus on this, here.

"A couple people saw me struggling. You were one, but I couldn't listen to you because in my mind you were causing my struggle. That, and you're a man, and sometimes that's enough. But they helped. My friends, my mom," she gave a somber smile as she added, "and even my dad, in his own way. All of their advice was a little different, but it all came down to the same solution. I needed to start over."

She flicked the paper in her hands.

"With this. I am going to start over with the man I was supposed to meet that night. Give him a call and see if he wants to buy me a drink."

Grace nodded and began entering the number into her phone.

When his phone lit up, he stared at it. Luke turned and looked up. He waited to see if there was anger, resentment.

Grace smiled and shrugged. When the phone rolled to voicemail, Luke looked down once more and watched the screen dim and listened to Grace's voice leave him a message.

"Hi, I was given your number by one of my girlfriends. I know we were supposed to meet quite a while ago now. I'm sorry I couldn't make it. This cute guy distracted me, and my senses went right out the window. That's not like me, by the way, I'm usually very sensible. So, if you're up for it, I'd love to meet for a drink, maybe start over? I think you have my number."

The click to end the call was audible, and a second later, Luke's phone lit up again.

One New Voicemail.

Grace watched Luke process the information. He knew the date, the first date was meant for him, but he couldn't quite believe what had just happened.

When Luke heard it, he didn't slow and he didn't hesitate. In one simple message, he was given all the answers he needed.

Grace felt the exhilarating rush of excitement and anticipation as she watched Luke close the gap between them. Joy exploded from every part of her as he wrapped her up and spun her around. The only thing she could do was circle her arms around him and hold on tight.

Luke set her down but held her close, not wanting to let her go. So he simply held on, unmoving, until he finally found words. "I feel like I should apologize for standing you up, and I assure you it will never happen again, for the rest of our lives."

"The rest of our lives," Grace repeated. Loving the sound of those words. Loving him. "I could get used to that."

"What are you going to do with this space?" Luke asked. His eyes moved around the building.

"No way. I'm not touching this old pile of bricks." Grace's eyes slanted.

"You're going to need to expand," Luke said, deep in thought. "Well, unless you want to keep fighting. But I think being president of our newly acquired company, Thomas and Jane, sounds a lot more pleasant."

"Did you just – what? President?"

"Apparently Abbi thought you'd be best suited for the new role if Thomas and Jane continues to operate independently. We think the board will agree tomorrow." Luke said with a wide smile.

Grace tried her best to hide her excitement as she registered the news.

"The space, you ask?" She tried to play it cool. "I don't know, I haven't had much time to think about it. And seeing as I'll be swamped the next couple of months..." Grace said, taking in Luke's response of a curious tilted head. "I'm going to have a lot going on. I'll need to start planning for a move, and I'm going to need to go dress shopping." Humor sparked in her eyes.

"Dress shopping? Actually, that reminds me."

When Luke let her go, she worried she might have gotten a tad carried away. But hey, he was going to have to get used to the idea. She watched him as he struggled to pull his hand back out of his pocket then fumble the small box to the ground. Though she couldn't see what it was, she realized he wasn't getting back up. Her mouth dropped open.

Luke remained on one knee and took Grace's hand in his.

"Grace Lydia Thomas, please don't cry."

Grace's free hand flew to her face, and she felt joyful tears well in her eyes, dangerously close to falling. But she couldn't help it.

"It hasn't been a long time. But the time we've spent has been filled with more meaning than some people have in a lifetime. You have made me *feel*. Your compassion, your love, your humor. Everything about you, I've fallen in love with. I've fallen in love with you. What I'm trying to say is, I'd like to spend a lot more time with you – every single day – for the rest of our lives. If you'd like to marry me?"

Luke opened the small navy blue box with an intricate gold design along the edges. And on the inside, the perfectly round diamond sat simply on a gold band.

"Oh, my God. Oh, my God, yes! Yes, I'd like to marry you. I'd love to marry you. Luke Wallace, you are the best man. And you're mine."

Luke slid the ring around her finger, and she surrounded him.

Kneeling in front of him, she held his face in her hands. She felt happier than she'd ever been. She loved this man.

"I love you so much."

"I love you so much."

LET'S REVIEW...

Did you love it?

I'd be so grateful for your honest review of
Conflict of Interest.

Then, continue reading...

Continue to the next page for a special excerpt of
In the Business of Love,
Book Two in the *Taking Chances* series.

IN THE

BUSINESS

OF LOVE

Book Two in the Taking Chances series

PROLOGUE

How was it possible that the sound of her mom and dad arguing from the kitchen made it all the way up the stairs, through her closed door on the opposite end of the house, and over the sound of Tom Petty blaring on her radio?

Casey slid off the side of her bed and wedged herself between its sturdy white wooden frame and the blue paisley-patterned wallpaper, then covered her head with a pillow to drown out the screaming voices. The muffled tantrums barely made their way through the feathers, but somehow they crept in.

Ian and Linette Saunders were having one of their bad nights, filled with endless yelling and blaming. Average nights were filled with silence at the dinner table, followed by the nightly news or one of the two shows they actually agreed upon (*Law and Order* or *Survivor*–it didn't escape Casey both shows usually displayed some form of torture).

Good nights were a rare occurrence, but when her mom had a work event or dinner out with friends, there was a sense of normalcy–happiness even. She would talk to her dad about her day over a box of steaming pizza and she'd get to pick the TV show or game they played.

Casey lowered the pillow and let her eyelids close as she leaned her head against the wall. She could sit there for hours trying to block out the strained voices of her parents. Or, she thought, she could escape.

She pushed herself up using the side of her bed and the window frame, then crawled across the bed to the cordless phone on her nightstand and dialed. With every ring she sent up a silent prayer, *please be home, please pick up.*

"Hello?"

Casey felt herself relax when she heard the calming sound of Raymond Thomas' voice answer her call.

"Hi, Mr. Thomas, it's Casey."

Casey cringed as her mom's screech reached through the phone, only to be outmatched seconds later by the booming sound of her father's retort.

"Hi Case, are you looking for Grace?"

"I am."

Casey could hear the smile in Raymond's tone as he said, "Let me run and grab her, she's just finished with her homework. I'm sure she's ready for a friend."

"Thanks, Mr. Thomas."

The sound of footsteps and Grace mocking her brother–that she had a phone call and William hadn't received a call from Rachel yet–had Casey grinning in spite of her parents' anger echoing throughout the house. They both knew their friend Rachel was more in love with William then she imagined Romeo and Juliet had been with each other, but that didn't stop them from giving Grace's brother crap every chance they got.

"Case!" Grace happily sang into the phone, but the happy left as soon as she heard the background. "Oh no. They're at it again."

Grace didn't have to question what was going on anymore. She knew from years of experience her friend's parents would fight for hours. Their seemingly unlimited ammunition had the ability to take them straight through the night.

"At it again," Casey confirmed, and looked at her door. Over the years her feelings during her parents' epic fights had changed from sadness to irritation. Irritation was easier, but she also felt it changing her. With the sadness, she held onto hope. With irritation, she became closed off and distant. Her guard was constantly up, and she slowly let the idea that she would be alone for the rest of her life harden in her mind. She would keep her friends close, but love and life with a man, a partner with whom she was supposed to commit her life to, would never happen for her. She wouldn't let it.

Not if this is what happened when you did, she thought to herself grimly as she listened to her mother's voice rise in a crescendo of bitterness.

"Do you want to come over? Dad already said it would be okay. Just stay the night and we can get a ride to school with William tomorrow." Grace's words caused Casey's mind to start calculating.

Casey looked at her computer and thought about the work she was going to try and get done tonight. She had finished her homework too, but had plans to hack into her English teacher's computer to change her grades again. She did *not* do well on their latest *Scarlet Letter* paper and had to change that. Subjectivity was hard, facts were more her style.

Anyway, if she thought her parents were mad now, she didn't want to see them when they found out she got a B. Perfection was a rare topic her parents tended to agree on–when it came to her, that is.

Her thoughts paused as she felt the angry dagger of her mom's voice pierce her heart as she screamed, "When Casey graduates, I am done!"

"Good riddance," her father spat, sounding dejected.

The finality in her dad's response twisted the dagger.

Casey breathed deeply and tried to hold the tears that had welled in her eyes from falling.

"Yes," she said, a whisper into the phone, "*please* get me out of here."

Without a moment of hesitation, Grace replied, "We are on our way. Ten minutes."

"Thanks, Grace."

"Anything for you. See you in a few."

When Casey heard a click and a dial tone she placed the cordless phone back on its base, packed books and binders into her school bag, then shoved in pajamas and an outfit and struggled to close zipper. She took one last look at her computer and decided her grades could wait–or she could sneak onto Grace's computer when everybody was sleeping.

Casey scrawled a note telling her parents she'd gone to school early knowing they wouldn't check on her until morning, then looped her book bag around her shoulders, hopped back over her bed, opened the window, and climbed out.

The trellis on the side of the house served the Tuscan-style home her parents had built years earlier well, and it served as an escape for Casey to climb down. Hopping the last two feet onto the front walk, Casey made her way to the end of the driveway to sit on the curb and wait.

The neighborhood was quiet. And though she'd had the thought many times before, she was certain *this time* the silence had never sounded so good.

Casey knew if she looked back she would see the glow of the kitchen lights and the silhouettes of her parents deep in their argument. So she looked out instead.

The houses were all different. Some craftsman style, some modern, some that looked as if they should be on a New England coastline, or the Italian countryside. Though, most of those had direct access to the lake.

One day, she thought, she was going to own one of those houses. So she could hear nothing but the peaceful sound of water rippling against a lazy beach.

Casey closed her eyes to see if she could hear the lake tonight, but the only sound she heard was an old Jeep engine rumbling closer. She didn't open her eyes, but it was enough to make her smile.

She was saved.

Before William's jeep could slow to a stop, Grace jumped out of the passenger side door and ran toward Casey.

Casey felt Grace's arms wrap around her and couldn't remember anything that had ever made her feel so safe. William climbed out once he put the Jeep in park and walked around to the embrace, cocooning them both, squeezing so tightly both of the girls laughed and let out squeals as they tried to wriggle free.

Gradually their arms all fell and one by one they filed into the Jeep so William could drive them home.

—

Casey walked into Grace's room and threw her bag onto the top bunkbed–*her* bunk. Years ago, Lydia and Raymond Thomas had agreed to put bunkbeds in their house so she and Rachel would have a warm bed to sleep in whenever they stayed the night. If her computer hadn't been at her parents' house, she would have moved in with Grace a long time ago. It was more of a home than her parents had even given her.

"I called Rachel," Grace said as she walked in and closed the door behind. "She's coming, too."

Casey eyed Grace and tipped the edge of her mouth up in a grin, not saying a word.

"I know," Grace responded with a smirk of her own, reading Casey's mind. "She just wants to see William. But I made her promise no boy time, until after girl time."

"You're a real hard-ass, Thomas."

"Don't I know it," Grace said, as she tied her hair into a blonde knot on the top of her head. "So, I'm not going to ask you to start until Rachel gets here, but I am going to ask how you're doing?"

Casey crawled onto the pink, teal, and purple geometric shapes of Grace's comforter, and stared at the ceiling. It was a simple question with so many not simple answers. So the easiest answer was, "Fine." Casey turned her head. "I'm doing fine."

The doorbell saved Casey from Grace's narrowed eyes and further explanation–for the time being.

A quick three knocks and a flowery voice sang from the other side of the door. "Hello sexy ladies, anybody in there?"

Casey and Grace stole amused glances at each other before Grace replied, "In here, and ready for you so we can get started."

Rachel bounded in with flushed pink cheeks and daydream eyes.

"You couldn't go ten seconds, you're mush," Casey said, disgusted. "So much for no boys until after girl-time."

Rachel floated over to the bed and fell in a spin next to Casey, an act that had Grace laughing.

"How am I supposed to say no when the *cutest* guy in the world traps me outside for a *holy shit* make-out session before I can even set one foot in the door?"

Casey ignored Rachel and looked toward Grace. "We've lost her. There's no hope. And, she's pathetic."

"*She* is right here," Rachel said while bumping her hip into Casey. "And you haven't lost her, she just happens to be in love." Rachel turned and her face grew serious, "Now, tell us how you're doing."

"I-"

"How you're *really* doing," Rachel added, cutting Casey off from her standard '*I'm fine.*'

Casey stared at the ceiling and felt Grace sandwich her next to Rachel, then linked their arms together. She thought about it as the three of them lay in a row.

She was, of all things, confused. Why would two people agree to a life together only to fight all of their time away? How could two people who had at one point in their lives been in love enough to make a vow, dedicating their lives to one another, hate each other so much? When would they see the way they acted toward each other was making their own child feel so unloved?

Casey sighed. "I feel...thankful." She looked from Grace to Rachel. "Thankful that I have you. Because I know no matter what happens, here, I'm loved. And I'm learning from my parents' mistakes. I'm never going to get married, no matter how much I think I love somebody, I won't do that to them or myself."

Grace stole a sad look at Rachel. They didn't say anything else, just laid with their arms intertwined, and snuggled in a little closer.

Casey relished the feeling of warmth between the friends she knew she could always count on, and thought, with friends like this, she'd never need a man to marry anyway—she had all the love she needed right here.

CHAPTER 1

Casey swung into the Thomas and Jane LLC building a little after eight and sauntered into her new office. The unexpected perks of the Wallace Corporation joining forces with her best friends' company lent wonderfully to her schedule. She could enjoy an early cup of coffee with Grace at the Bistro, work on her own ventures while cozied up at their corner table, then climb the stairs to her consulting assignment–integrating the two companies' different technologies.

Who would have thought all these years later Grace would be running her own company and Casey would be in the perfect position to help her out?

The project was massive, but so was the paycheck. And after some great negotiating, she had the authority to build her own teams to handle the workload. Casey only had to plead her case once when she wanted to hire a *former* hacker to handle security. In the end, she won out with the expectation that she keep a watchful eye on the frightfully brilliant teenager.

Casey stood outside her glass-paneled door and stared at her reflection.

Well, she thought, *there was* one *downfall.*

Her tailored dress pants and crisp oxford shirt were a little too preppy and a little too far away from her usual jeans or sweatpants. But, she had to admit, her butt looked good in the fitted forest green trousers. And the velvet chunky heels did give her a nice lift. Her red hair was twisted securely in its signature bun–some things weren't worth the effort. She nodded once in approval, figuring she looked professional enough.

Pulling the door open, she walked into the office filled with screens, cords, boxes of routers, laptops, and empty diet Mountain Dew bottles overflowing from her recycling bin.

Hmm. Either she was going to have to cut back on her intake or talk Maggie into scheduling an extra pick up.

"Some people eat real food for their meals, but I suppose, to each their own."

Casey didn't have to turn around; she was able to match the smooth voice to the tall, well-dressed man.

"Travis, good morning. I didn't realize you were so interested in my eating habits." Casey turned as she responded and presented a sweet, forced smile that matched the sound of her words.

Travis smiled and welcomed the sarcasm he knew he'd find, and took in the firecracker of a woman he'd been unable to resist since she first walked into Wallace Corporation for her interview. She hadn't given an inch when asked to compromise on the technology they should use to upgrade all of their systems, and she had given even less when Travis eluded to the two of them sharing dinner, a coffee, or even small talk in the break room.

The former made her perfect for the job. The latter was what sealed the deal with his buddy, Luke Wallace, who gave final approval when it came time to hire for the position. Travis was certain Luke made the decision to approve not only based on Casey's skills, but also in knowing she would drive Travis crazy while she was there.

"I'm interested in a lot of your habits." Travis paused only for a second, but long enough for Casey to scowl. "The main one being the integration. How are you managing?"

Casey dropped her green canvas satchel on the corner of her desk–the only free space she could find–and looked up, irritated at Travis' response. She didn't want him to be interested in her habits–work or otherwise. She was doing her job and doing it pretty damn well. As for her personal life, things were easier at a distance.

Besides, with some space between them, she wouldn't have to smell his spiced cologne, see the smile lines crease at the edges of his lips and eyes, or listen to his voice as it coolly delivered compliments or witty remarks. And he was smart. Smart enough to keep up with her.

He was, Casey realized, *herself*–but in an extremely handsome and manly package. *That* was even more irritating.

"Everything is going according to schedule," Casey clipped. "Andy and his team have the new environment secure and it's been tested. It can handle more load than we would ever need from it. Theresa and her team are ready to make the switch to the new platform. All of the backups have been done, we have a final backup scheduled for Friday evening. All of the announcements have gone out letting everybody know they won't be able to log in beginning at nine Friday night. They will be able to get in again Monday morning beginning at six. We'll send out additional daily reminders, and a final right before cutover."

"That's actually ahead of schedule." Travis' tone was serious.

"Is that a bad thing?"

This time, Travis grinned at her irritation. "No, just pleasantly surprised at your efficiency."

Casey began to speak to defend her work, but he went on, catching her off guard.

"I knew you were the best, but I'm beginning to think you're priceless."

Casey's mouth hung open at the compliment and forced herself to close it.

Really? she thought, what was she supposed to say to that?

"Thank you." Casey let the stale words fall out. She intended them to be a little more combative, but Travis left her no choice but to be nice. The ass.

"You're welcome. Have a good day, Casey."

Travis knocked twice on her door frame and smiled on his way out.

"For the love of sanity," Casey whispered angrily as she threw an empty green bottle toward the door.

"Yikes!" Grace squealed, stopping in time to let the bottle fly in front of her face and into the hall.

"Shit! Sorry." Casey plopped in her chair and sank.

"Rough morning?" Graced asked as she slid into a chair across from Casey after placing the stack of boxes that were using it carefully on the floor.

"Travis was just here."

Casey watched Grace's eyes grow wide with amusement. "Ah yes, Travis. He's just so terrible, isn't he?"

Casey scowled her response.

Grace gave a teasing smile. "You do realize you have to work with him for another three years?"

"Yes." Casey rolled her eyes and went on looking for something solid to build her case on. "He's just so...nice."

"I like to think that's a description that fits nearly everybody that works here. You don't seem to have a problem with the rest of them."

Grace was leading her on and she knew it.

"Yes, but not all of them look like him. The stupid model-looking, good-smelling, nice-shoed jerk."

Grace pinched her lips together trying to hide her smile. She had accomplished what she set out to do this morning so she figured she could move on.

"Want to grab lunch today?" Grace asked, changing the subject.

"I like lunch," Casey admitted begrudgingly, not wanting to leave her anger behind so quickly.

"Great, what time?"

"Ten minutes?" Casey responded, wanting that precious distance from Travis and his allure as soon as possible.

"I tend to eat later than eight-thirty in the morning, but if I could I would make an exception for you. Unfortunately, I have meetings until noon. Want me to swing by when they're over?"

Casey sighed and accepted. She should probably do some work and earn the generous paycheck she was receiving for the job.

"Yes."

"Perfect! See you in a few." Grace chirped her reply, not thinking twice about the one-word, bland answer she received from Casey. They'd been friends too long to read into the delivery.

Casey huffed out a breath then pulled her laptop out of her bag, clicked it into its stand, powered it on, and smiled.

Now *this* she could do.

She could tune out the world around her and build an infrastructure that would make even the geniuses in the Silicon Valley jealous. She slid her earpieces in, selected her favorite Zeppelin playlist, and got to work.

CHAPTER 2

Casey trudged through the March blizzard cursing Minnesota, the weather gods, and the meteorologist. The gods for making it snow, and the meteorologist for telling her she wouldn't see a day without snow for another three days.

When she swung the Bistro door open she was greeted with an empty room and a blazing fire.

"I love you," Casey said in a sigh as she moved toward the warm flames with outstretched arms.

"I love you, too." Aimeé stated her response in a low French purr.

Casey shook her head and pointed to the fire, then said, "But I do love you, even more than this fire."

"For that, you will receive the first choice of wine. Second bottle goes to Grace since she's prepping for wedded bliss."

"Seems acceptable. I would like a crisp Pinot Grigio so I can pretend it's warm and sunny outside. I'll let you pick the poison."

Feeling the warmth from the blaze moving through her, Casey peeled off her black jacket, houndstooth scarf, and wool mittens before meandering to their table.

It might have been freezing and snowing outside, but Aimeé had already transformed the Bistro into a picturesque spring scene. Little white vases held happy, white and yellow flowers with leafy green stems as a garnish.

Casey settled in and pulled out her laptop. She might as well work and check her schedule before the rest of the girls got there. She opened her Matchme.com calendar, and the feeling of dread was immediate.

Has it already been a year?

"No, no, no," Casey whined as her head found the top of the table.

"Ah, how I remember fondly the agony of a man. Lucky for me it worked out in the end." Grace came up to the table and set herself in the chair across from Casey. She went on, "What did Travis do to you now?"

Aimeé joined them at the table with the wine and poured as she and Grace exchanged amused looks.

"It's not Travis," Casey said flatly, "It's fifteen million men and women across the United States. And the team of leaders that help me run the most successful dating site in the world."

Casey couldn't help the pride that seeped into her words, but she was still crabby. The worst part was she'd have to keep up the lie she had told the executives and the board.

"I don't feel bad for you one bit," Rachel said as she swooped in, snagging a glass of the liquid gold Aimeé had just poured and placed on the table. "You're a multi-millionaire with two houses, and you get to work with Grace.

I work with child terrors who forget the last day of school is three months away, not three days."

"Aww, Rach." Grace stroked the arm of her pretty, petite friend. "Money doesn't make you happy either, just look at Casey."

The laughs were quick but Rachel wasn't done with her pity party. "Really? Casey makes more in two weeks than I do in a year. Let that sink in."

The three women stared at each other and tried to do the quick math in their heads, then moved their looks from one to the other before slowly nodding.

Without taking the time for compassion Aimeé agreed, "Yes, I think you're right. Okay, you don't have to pay for drinks tonight."

Rachel thought about the offer, then nodded. "Done. I'm no longer upset. What's going on with Match Me that has you so grumpy?" she said, turning her concern to Casey.

"Our spring and summer events are starting. This Friday we are having our annual kick off meeting. So I'll be sitting in front of a screen full of people who think that *love* is the best thing in the world."

"Love *is* the best thing in the world," Aimeé said simply, while pulling up her own chair, joining her friends as she did every Thursday evening.

"You know, I agree," Grace said holding up her nicely diamonded ring finger, the gem sparkling in the warm light.

"Why do it if you don't like it?" Rachel asked Casey, knowing that loving what you do was more important than the paycheck you received. Though at the moment, Rachel was only half on board with that logic.

"For some reason love is a great business to be in. People will do just about anything to fall in love–the lunatics." Casey shook her head, then paused, knowing that wasn't the real reason, and her face paled.

"And..." Casey continued slowly.

"Spill it out," Aimeé encouraged.

"It's 'spit it out.'" Casey assisted Aimeé with the English slang, then hid behind her hands and let her muffled words escape through her fingers. "They think I have a boyfriend. A *serious* boyfriend."

Laughter filled the room as the girls' heads fell back, holding their glasses of wine high ensuring they wouldn't spill. Their free hands holding their stomachs and wiping tears from their eyes.

"They think you *what?*" Rachel exclaimed as she tried her best to compose herself.

"See this," Casey pointed to her friends, "this is not what friends are supposed to do. You're supposed to be supportive and understand that I think love is a sham. And completely realize why it's so hard for me to have to pretend to have a boyfriend."

"Why are you pretending to have a boyfriend at all?" Grace couldn't help but wonder why Casey would even consider it. She liked the thought of a man in her life even less than actually having one.

"Three years ago board *kindly* suggested I use Matchme.com to find myself a significant other." Casey's mocking tone held an edge. "I was," she searched for the word they had used, "unsuitable representation of the company I created."

Casey scoffed and took a sip of her wine as she recalled the conversation with the team, led by Carrie Bolden,

the blonde that seemed to be overly invested in the staff–
getting along particularly well with the men. Why was it she
always seemed to flock to them rather than the women?

"They can't really expect that from you, right?"
Rachel looked around, then back and forth between Grace
and Casey, the two that would know more about business
expectations than she ever would.

"Technically, no," Casey began, but her eyes fell
after looking to Grace who was reading her mind, a mirror of
her own expression.

"But the board can, for the sustainability of the
company, choose the leadership." Grace said it as if she was
reading from a manual.

"That cannot be true. It's Casey's company, is it
not?" Aimeé's concern was apparent.

"We're a publicly traded company. When we made
that transition–when I agreed to that transition–I put most of
my fate into the hands of others. I needed to, so I could start
other ventures and work on other things."

At the time, Casey knew going public was the best
decision for herself, the staff that had worked by her side day
and night, and ultimately the customers. But now? After three
years of keeping up the charade of having a boyfriend, it
seemed terrible.

At one point, they were going to want to meet him.
And unfortunately, she felt her excuses were reaching their
expiry, and the team was getting restless.

"What will you do?" Grace asked the question for
everybody at the table.

"Head to the lake, have the meeting, and pretend for
as long as I can." Casey shrugged. "Then, I'll have to come
up with something."

'The lake' was the affectionate term used for Casey's home on Lake Minnetonka. And it didn't slip past the girls, as each of them loved the house, *and* loved visiting the house.

"Um," Rachel began, "I have all the faith in the world in you, Case, and I don't mean to shift the conversation, but…"

Casey sighed, knowing where the conversation was headed. If she didn't know her friends truly loved her, she'd be hard-pressed to believe they were friends with her because of that love, but rather *the lake*.

"Did you say you were headed to *the lake?*" Rachel smiled, knowing she had Casey.

"I might have."

"When?" Grace pressed.

"Early tomorrow morning."

"I'm coming!" Rachel cheered, and threw her hands in the air.

"Me, too!" Grace agreed, not caring that they hadn't received an invitation from Casey, and knowing Luke was slated to help Travis pack up his room since they were selling his loft.

Then they looked to Aimeé.

"We've been having some…" Aimeé decided not to dive into The Bistro's financial issues quite yet, so she opted for a sliver of the story, "employee issues. But I can ask Christopher to come in during his shift to check on things. So yes, I am in as well."

Casey did have to agree it was like a mini vacation when the four of them got together at the lake over a weekend.

She thought through her schedule and glanced at her laptop that still sat open on the table. Closing it in a single motion she held her straight face.

"My last meeting ends at two." Casey let the corner of her mouth turn up, then watched her three best friends cheer and lift their glasses.

It was hard to be so damn cynical when you were surrounded by the best women in the world. And, at the end of the day it wasn't hard to admit it would be a really great weekend.

CHAPTER 3

Casey groaned when her alarm clock blared and startled her out of a wine-induced sleep.

"Why?" Casey moaned, covering her eyes, and pressing on her head where the ache was building.

The Thursday night ritual was a beloved event. Never missed, never a plan broken. Though many times they vowed to leave the second bottle of wine corked, it never quite worked out that way.

Casey rolled out of bed, slid on her decade-old slippers, and shuffled sleepily to the kitchen. She opened her medicine cabinet, then the fridge, and washed the aspirin down with a cold swig of her cherished Dew. The sweet burn of carbonation tickled her throat and watered her eyes. She wondered if there was a better feeling in the world–aside from sex, adding the criteria to her thought.

Thinking on the topic, today was the day. She would face her company and their expected pressure on her love life.

'When will we meet your boyfriend?' 'Has he hinted at popping the question?' 'It's been three *years.'*

People were nauseating.

Sure, she created a massive, successful dating website, but that didn't mean *she* had to partake in the business of love.

Casey's head fell forward and her wavy copper curls fell over her face. She sighed then inhaled the sweet scent of orange blossom that lingered in her hair from its wash the night before, and felt resigned. She'd have to tell them the truth. She prided herself on being honest, and it was time she stopped pretending to be something she wasn't.

What she was, was great at her job. Great at pairing qualities in people that nearly promised relationship success. And she could put it into writing, then into an algorithm, then into code.

Maybe her team at Match Me wouldn't approve of her love life–or lack thereof–but they couldn't deny her ability to provide one for their customers in a perfect match.

Yes, she would tell them the truth. They needed her. And that was that.

Casey lifted her head, turned, reached back for the green bottle, then marched to her city loft bedroom to get ready for the day's work and the weekend to follow.

—

The drive out of the city always felt like she was heading on a road trip across the country. The sun coming up behind her glistened off freshly fallen snow, giving the open road ahead a sparkle. The farther she drove, the more frosted trees she saw. And in just a couple of weeks the snow would be melted and she would be surrounded by green grass and budding trees.

When Casey's phone rang she saw *Ian Saunders* appear on the dashboard of her Range Rover. She couldn't close her eyes to make it go away, so she simply groaned, then accepted the call from her dad and tried not to sound like it was the last thing she wanted to do to start her day.

"Good morning, Ian."

A long time ago Casey had started calling her dad by his first name. It was around the time she'd learned he was dating somebody who wasn't her mother. She was younger then and didn't understand the intricacies of the relationship, but it had hurt nonetheless.

Her mom had moved out by then and had moved on to her own boyfriend. But her parents were still married. That's what she didn't understand. And she couldn't quite explain why she was only mad at her dad.

Perhaps it was because she had still respected him. When her mom had left, she left everybody behind, including Casey. Her dad always made sure to care, to call. But as the years passed, she never returned to the affectionate title her father used to own. So when he responded, she heard a bit of the hurt in his voice at being called by his name.

"Hi, Casey. How are you? How was your week?" Ian asked, as he did every Friday, his voice filling the vehicle over the Bluetooth speaker.

At the very least, her dad made an effort, even if the blueprint was the same every time.

"Doing good. Heading to the lake now. I have some Match Me meetings today that require my attention. How are you?"

Somewhere over the years their conversations had become cordial, and their interest in each other's lives had become normal.

Those first couple of calls she took after years without speaking had been harder than she ever imagined they would be. She'd be forever grateful those times had passed.

"Yeah, we are doing good here. Pamela and I will try and make it to a play downtown this weekend. She likes those." Ian continued without hesitation, as the conversations about his long-time girlfriend now came naturally, "You could, well, you could join us if you wanted?"

The invitation didn't surprise her, as he'd been offering for her to join them for the better part of two years. What did surprise Casey, was that for a moment, she considered it.

"I–thanks for the invitation–but I'm having the girls at the lake this weekend." Casey didn't usually explain, but something inside her wanted her dad to know this time it wasn't because she didn't want to, it was because she couldn't.

"Oh sure, no problem. How are the girls doing? I haven't seen them since..."

The pause was her dad trying to navigate the terrible years and probably hoping he didn't just navigate himself into an awful memory both of them would rather leave behind.

"Since graduation." Casey helped out, offering a lifeline. It had been her college graduation when they had all been together last.

The girls were invited. Her father showed up knowing she was in the 2008 graduating class. There weren't student lists, no valedictorian announcements–since MIT didn't have them–just faith that Casey would be there. It marked the first time her dad made an effort to reconnect with her. His pride in her was stronger than whatever discomfort reuniting after four years of not speaking would cause.

"Graduation," Ian confirmed, and cleared his throat uncomfortably, wondering how far he could carry the conversation, "I'm still proud of you. A 5.0 from MIT. My brilliant girl."

"Yeah." Casey still wasn't good at accepting his praise. "Thanks. Well, I should probably get inside." Casey eyed the stretch of highway before her and immediately felt the guilt of the lie.

"Right, of course. Ah," Ian held her on the line and struggled to get the next words out, "have you heard from your mother?"

"No." The answer was sharp and finite. "Goodbye, Ian."

Worry and sadness breathed audibly through the phone and her dad relented. "Goodbye, Casey. I love you."

Casey tapped her finger on the steering wheel to end the call without a response, and forced her breath come and go in heavy waves as she tried to keep calm.

Why would she hear from Linette Saunders? *Whitley.* Linette Whitley, Casey reminded herself. Her mother wasn't quite as delicate as her dad when it came to moving on. And why would *he* care?

Linette had married the man that had made her unfaithful and started a happy family of her own. One filled with new children that apparently deserved Linette's time, attention, and love. A new family that was so wonderful Linette could forget she had Casey at all.

Casey didn't have to be an IT whiz to learn about Linette's new family either. She simply had to log into every social media platform out there and see the obnoxious, happy pictures everywhere.

Images strewn all over social media of her mom laughing as she hugged her three young daughters, looking at them as though they were the light of her life. Or, when the daughters weren't present, the photos were of Linette and her husband jet-setting around the world, holding champagne glasses high in France and rare bottles of wine in Italy and Spain.

The funny thing was, the happy pictures her mom was flaunting online for the world to see, looked eerily similar to the ones in photo albums she'd looked at as a child. She went through them endlessly as a young girl and could almost feel the laughter of her mom and dad when they were dating, the happiness during their fairytale wedding, and the ecstasy of their honeymoon shortly after. Images of building their house close to–but not on–the lake, then standing proudly on the doorstep when it was move-in day.

The happy pictures continued through their first pregnancy. Casey would stare at herself as a sleeping baby in her mom and dad's arms with their hospital gowns still tied around them. Their smiles tired, but so full of joy.

Then the pictures stopped.

Casey pulled into her long drive, parked, then allowed herself to press her hands to her eyes as the memory recall was forcing a new ache in her head.

The pictures had stopped when she was born. They had been happy–until she had happened.

Casey opened her eyes and shook her head slowly. Well, maybe she wasn't a good baby, had been a troublesome child, and a teen who was more interested in computers than sports or boyfriends, but she was great at being a friend. And at her job.

The looming craftsman-style home that sat before her was proof of that. She was a genius when it came to computers and coding, great at working hard, and good at juggling multiple ventures. So maybe she wasn't good at being a daughter, but she was damn good at working and she would enjoy the enormous fruits of that labor.

The tiny loft in downtown Minneapolis was efficient and necessary. This? Casey looked up at a house that was probably more suited for a Colorado mountainside or a Lake Tahoe retreat, and grinned. This was excessive and *utterly* over-the-top *un*necessary.

Creamy white, gray, and brown rocks stood as sturdy pillar bases and accents surrounding the home. Deep espresso brown siding wrapped every inch of the four-story house except where large windows were strategically placed to ensure every angle offered a luxurious view.

Casey could have gone through the garage but she climbed the steps to the wrap-around porch and walked along the wooden panels until she reached the back of the house.

The view of the lake was breathtaking. A low line of steam formed over the frozen water as the morning sun from the east lightly kissed the far side of the lake.

Turning to move inside, Casey reached for her keys in the side pouch of her laptop bag, then unlocked the wide French door that sat in a wall of floor-to-ceiling windows looking out to the lake.

It had only been a week since she'd last been home but it didn't make the welcome any less warm. She flicked the switch to the rock-framed fireplace that centered the room and rose to the two-story paneled ceiling.

As she turned she took in the kitchen that was remodeled with Aimeé in mind. If she had to stop working at the Bistro, Aimeé could pack up her entire operation and move it here. Casey moved through the sitting room that was Grace's favorite place to lounge and read the stacks of books lining the walls. And as she moved, she saw the little breakfast nook that led out to a small framed porch, where she would be sure to find Rachel sipping coffee and looking out, romanticizing the view.

Other parts of the home were remodeled for comfort, for parties, or to ensure whomever stayed the night had a nice place to lay their heads. And Casey agreed, the bedrooms were exquisite. Hers especially. But it wasn't her favorite place in the house.

Casey turned the corner and stood looking through the paneled glass doors that led to her office.

This, she thought, was for her. She pushed the doors open and immediately relaxed.

Two rugged, chocolate-colored couches paralleled each other, and she smiled as she walked between them to the front of her desk. The desk was an expansive six-foot executive desk that provided the perfect base to three sleek monitors. When she was sitting at her desk, she had all she needed right in front of her. And when that wasn't enough, the wall to her right had six screens mounted in two rows of three.

Typically, she used the screens on the wall for monitoring the businesses she wasn't dedicating her time to that particular day. So today, while she worked on Match Me, she would be monitoring her Thomas and Jane, LLC dashboard and email. And of course, she would put the bottom three monitors on local and world news channels. Just in case she wanted to do a little digging into world markets.

On that topic, Casey thought, "I wonder." Mumbling to herself as a curious look came over her face. She slowly maneuvered to the other side of her desk, flipped on the fireplace that sat directly behind her, then sat in her chair, and made a smooth turn to face forward.

She knew she shouldn't, but...

Casey connected her laptop to the monitors and slowly lifted the top, debating her next move.

Technically she wasn't supposed to look into her friends' lives without their permission, but in this case, she wondered if one of them might be in trouble.

Aimeé had never been very open about her finances, and when they had been in France for Grace's birthday last May, they learned there was more to Aimeé's grandmothers' death than she was willing to share. Casey's concern had started then.

But she respected that boundary. Family was delicate. She knew all too well. But if Aimeé was in trouble, and asking Christopher–a childhood friend and local police officer that had taken a liking to Aimeé–to look into it, maybe she could lend a hand.

Casey logged in and authenticated herself three times before she hopped from one IP address to the next, ensuring if anybody happened to be watching, they couldn't trace the hack back to her. She found Aimeé's bank records, then dug into the data. Her fingers flew over the keys quickly and surely.

Eyeing the time, Casey determined she had exactly ten minutes of digging before she'd have to get ready for her call. So she scanned, filtered, searched account balances and discrepancies, and filed the information away so she could come back to anything that piqued her interest later on.

Casey sighed when she catalogued at least five numbers on Aimeé's bank statements that looked to be suspicious from one month to the next and backed out of the account without anybody, or anything, knowing she'd been there at all. Reaching blindly into her bag, she stared at the scenic mountain view her laptop background and found the unopened bottle of diet Mountain Dew, and evaluated what she saw as she sipped.

The cash flow fluctuation from month-to-month for the Bistro had always been consistent, peaking where it should in the winter and summer months. But the expenses, payments made, coming from Aimeé's business account looked off. She could look at personal bank accounts, but when it came to her friends, those were off-limits–that was her own rule.

Casey entered a couple commands on her keyboard and within seconds Match Me calendars, folders, and applications sprang to life on her monitors. She clicked open her video monitor to get a look at herself before she joined the call and decided the view was good enough. The makeup and collared shirt she threw on that morning would suffice. She looked down and arched a brow. Her ragged jeans were comfortable, but that's about where their appeal ended. So she would stay seated.

Within minutes everything she would need for the call was at her fingertips. Monthly customer reports, financial reports, company employment satisfaction surveys, and details for their upcoming spring and summer events. And, scanning the *Magical Match* emails, she couldn't help her exaggerated eye roll at the ridiculously excessive success stories of people who had found love using her site.

She was happy for them, sure, but let's face it, not everybody got engaged on a beach in Hawaii to a man that looked like Ryan Gosling as he presented a five-carat princess cut diamond ring. It would attract more desperate-for-love members, but it would also be setting them up for unrealistic and improbable expectations. She supposed that's what the marketing team was shooting for.

Casey dialed into the team call and turned her video on. When she did, faces from around the state and across the country sprang to life. She smiled at the group of men and women sitting before her and greeted them.

"Good morning, everybody. How are you all doing today?" Casey didn't have to force herself to be nice, since she genuinely liked most of the crew.

"Good morning." The team echoed their responses, then sat and stared as they waited for the remaining seats to be filled.

Casey noted Carrie Bolden hadn't joined the call yet and didn't feel the least bit guilty when she hoped she'd be absent.

It wasn't that she didn't like Carrie, she just found her completely obnoxious. Maybe it was the fact that Carrie seemed effortlessly put together and conversation came easy to her. Maybe it was because if Casey hadn't found Carrie so…whatever she was, she might actually think she was nice, funny, or even *like* her.

Just as the thought entered her mind it fell away. She scowled when she saw Carrie's video feed brighten the screen.

"Good morning!" Carrie's voice practically sang out the words. "It's so good to see all of your beautiful faces today!"

Oh for shit's sake, Casey thought, *really?* 'Beautiful faces?' Yeah, there was no way they would ever be friends.

"Casey, it's so good to see you. How are you?" Carrie directed her attention to Casey alone.

"Carrie," Casey's labored response came out with the appropriate level of enthusiasm, "I am great. How are you?" The smile she plastered on almost hurt to maintain.

"I am doing just so well. We are all so lucky in this life, aren't we? Great family, great friends, great jobs."

The 'great jobs' comment got the room to chuckle.

"I do want to get down to business, Casey. I think I see your calendar is booked completely today so we'll only have you for a few more minutes."

"Unfortunately, yes. I have to meet with our technology leadership for the remainder of the day."

"Okay, we'll take what we can get then," Carrie continued, not wasting any precious time. "As you all know, we have three major events coming up. One, we'll have our April Escape at Casey's house to go over all of the final details for the Spring Fling Conference, and ensure everything is in place for the Love Gala in June. Casey, is everything set for April? Do you need anything from us?"

"Everything for April Escape is scheduled."

"Great! Then there is just one more topic."

Here we go, Casey thought. It's now or never.

"We've discussed image and branding with our marketing executives and we really think it's important for the company, and our customers, to see their creator as a living example of what we represent. We would like to meet your significant other and would be *over-the-moon* pleased if he could join all of our events this year. Because…"

The pause made Casey nervous.

"We'll be featuring *you* in a series of articles and promotional materials!"

Casey blinked, unable to speak.

They what?

Carrie took this as her cue to continue as the cheers and mumbling from the rest of the team subsided. "You have the right skills, the right drive, and quite frankly the right look. You're exactly the type of person we would choose for an advertisement, so we are going to use the best representative for it.

"A powerful, successful woman balancing life, work, and a relationship! Isn't it wonderful? Now if we could just get your boyfriend to pop the question! Wouldn't that be perfect for timing!" Carrie giggled like a school-girl.

Casey slid her eyes to the email still open on one of her screens, then stared at the couple on the beach. She wasn't those people, nor did she want to be, but it sounded like the decision had already been made. *Shit.* So much for putting an end to her lie.

"So," Carrie nudged, "will we meet him in April?"

"Ah," the word dragged on as she tried to quickly think of something else she could say, "sure."

Sure! Casey yelled inside of her head. *That was the best you could come up with?*

"Great! We are all so looking forward to meeting him."

Then Casey saw it. Something that had been missing from Carrie's left hand before today. The thin gold band almost went unnoticed, but when Carrie had moved a strand of her blond hair away from her face, she saw it.

"Carrie, why didn't you tell us you were engaged?"

The color drained from Carrie's face. Casey almost felt badly for asking the question. *Almost.*

"It's nothing at all." Carrie brushed it off. "Just a decorative band, nothing more."

Casey watched Carrie look down and move on to the next subject without reverting her attention back. She wondered how Carrie could be so outgoing, but so secretive. That wasn't her style. So, Casey danced her finger in circles over her mouse and thought, maybe she'd look.

After excusing herself from the meeting Casey popped open the Match Me database and searched all of Carrie's details–and noted not once had she clicked on a profile.

Interesting.

Carrie had mentioned long ago she loved the site and was an avid user. Casey looked through a few more databases and turned up empty handed.

Unless…Casey clicked a few more keys, changed her search criteria. She stole a look at the time and scowled when her schedule forced her to pause her search.

"I'll be back," Casey said to herself. Then clicked into her next meeting and left Carrie's and Aimeé's secrets behind.

Want to keep reading
In the Business of Love?
Head to Amazon.com for your copy
today!

Books by Katie Bachand

Taking Chances Series:
Becoming Us (Prequel)
Conflict of Interest (#1)
In the Business of Love (#2)
A Business Affair (#3)
Betting on Us (#4)

Standalones:

Christmas Novels:
Postmark Christmas
Waiting on Christmas
A Borrowed Christmas Love Story (coming Nov 2022)
The Worst Christmas Wife (coming Dec 2022)

ABOUT THE AUTHOR

KATIE BACHAND is the author of contemporary romance and sweet holiday romance.

KATIE lives with her husband, son, and golden retriever in beautiful Minneapolis, Minnesota. She hopes in her novels, and in life, you find great friendships, great love, and great appreciation for the wonderful world and people around us.

Visit Katie on her website
https://katiebachandauthor.com

Visit Katie on any of your favorite social media outlets by following the link below, or searching **KATIE BACHAND** on Facebook, Instagram, Pinterest, and Twitter.

https://linktr.ee/katiebachand